An Aesthetic of Obscenity:

Five Novels by

Jeff Nuttall

VP Festschrift Series:

Volume 1: Christine Brooke-Rose
Volume 2: Gilbert Adair
Volume 3: The Syllabus
Volume 4: Rikki Ducornet
Volume 5: Raymond Federman
(Edited by G.N. Forester and M.J. Nicholls)

Reprint Titles:

The Languages of Love
The Sycamore Tree
The Dear Deceit
The Middlemen
Go When You See the Green Man Walking
Next
Xorandor/Verbivore
by Christine Brooke-Rose

Three Novels — Rosalyn Drexler
Knut — Tom Mallin
Erowina — Tom Mallin
The Greater Infortune/The Connecting Door — Rayner Heppenstall
The Penelope Shuttle Omnibus — Penelope Shuttle
Conversations with Critics — Nicolas Tredell
The Utopian — Michael Westlake
Image for Investigation: About my Father — Christoph Meckel
Meritocrats — Stuart Evans
Bartleby — Chris Scott
How to Outthink a Wall: An Anthology — Marvin Cohen

New fiction:

Mirrors on which dust has fallen — Jeff Bursey

other Verbivoracious titles @
www.verbivoraciouspress.org

An Aesthetic of Obscenity:

Five Novels

JEFF NUTTALL

Edited by Douglas Field & Jay Jeff Jones

Verbivoracious Press

Glentrees, 13 Mt Sinai Lane, Singapore

This edition published in Great Britain & Singapore

by Verbivoracious Press

www.verbivoraciouspress.org

Cover drawing first published in *The San Francisco Earthquake No.5* (1969)
Author photo on p.426 courtesy of the Roger Birch Collection.

ISBN: 978-981-11-0119-9

Printed and bound in Great Britain & Singapore

First published: *Snipe's Spinster*, 1975, Calder & Boyars; *The House Party*, 1975, Basilike; *The Gold Hole*, 1978, Quartet; *The Patriarchs*, 1980, The Beau & Aloes Arc Association; *Teeth*, 1994, in *The World One Day Novel Cup Winner 1994*, Images Publishing.

CONTENTS

INTRODUCTION

Douglas Field & Jay Jeff Jones

During the early 1960s, although employed as a school teacher, Jeff Nuttall was in a steady and self-assured sashay across a number of creative disciplines: painting, sculpting, blowing jazz, making happenings, illustrating and cartooning. He had also been trying his hand at writing and later claimed that 1963 was when he became a poet, the year that he produced a first collection *The Limbless Virtuoso* (with Keith Musgrave). It was also the year he launched his self-published *My Own Mag* (*MOM*), intended as a confrontational exhibition in magazine form, which usefully helped him engage with other writers. Of most significance was William Burroughs, who came with a provocative agenda to take literature in an abstruse new direction. Nuttall's own writing impulses mutated into illustrated short comic strips; fiction-like tales, although poetically abstracted and catalysed by obscenity, one of his lifelong creative themes.

This was also the point where Nuttall decided to purge his earlier literary and artistic efforts. He claimed in an interview, "I burned over a hundred paintings and three novels on the lawn of my London house around 1964, or was it '63?"[1] It wasn't till 1966 that he published the first of his longer, illustrated short fictions — *Come Back Sweet Prince* — and began to circulate the new manuscript of a novel titled *Boy with Face of Sour Apples*. Across the Atlantic, Lawrence Ferlinghetti and Mary Beach were sufficiently impressed that each of them included extracts in their magazines; *City Lights Journal* #3 (1966) and *Bulletin from Nothing* (1965).

Nuttall's first UK publication of a full-length novella was *The Case of Isobel and the Bleeding Foetus*; from Bernard Stone's Turret Press (1967), which was also published in the USA with a Beach Books Texts & Documents edition.

During these years, what purported to be a new fiction movement had developed in London, formed by a small group of mutually supportive writers determined to move beyond the genres of novels that dominated the era's literary publishing lists. These mostly included kitchen sink anti-romances, cynical, university-set picaresque works or straight-faced novels of London intellectual life, seamed with adultery and existential angst and often hyped as insights into the emergent "permissive society". Instead, the new fiction group favoured the "antinovel", chiefly associated with France's nouveau roman movement.

Bob Cobbing's Group H had provided Nuttall with an appreciative community for his poetry, a place to find his voice and get published. His new efforts at fiction took him into London's experimental prose group where he became a member of *Writers Reading . . .* "a co-operative of prose writers concerned with new forms, styles and language. By giving public readings throughout the country we intend to create a new audience for our work and start a dialogue through audience participation and/or protest."[2] The other members were Paul Ableman, Alan Burns, Carol Burns, Barry Cole, Eva Figes, B. S. Johnson, Ann Quin, Alan Sillitoe and Stefan Themerson. Johnson regarded himself, not only as the *de facto* leader of the group, but its authority on what new fiction should be. It might well have been Johnson that drew Nuttall to *Writers Reading*, but it is little surprise that neither Nuttall's membership, nor the co-operative itself seems to have lasted for long.

Despite sharing the same age, teaching occupation, formidable talent, corpulent body frame and dislike of social realism, the legacies of Johnson and Nuttall have diverged since they both appeared in one another's publications: Johnson in Nuttall's mimeographed *MOM*, and Nuttall in Johnson's 1973 anthology, *All Bull: The National Servicemen*. Since his suicide in 1973, aged forty, Johnson's significance in British avant-garde fiction has been rediscovered, thanks in part to Jonathan Coe's biography, *Like A Fiery Elephant: The Story of B.S. Johnson*, as well as a clutch of academic books published in England and France. While much of Johnson's relatively Lilliputian output has been regularly reprinted, all of Nuttall's Brobdingnagian's oeuvre, apart from this anthology, is scandalously out of print.

When Johnson railed against the state of British fiction in *Aren't You Rather Young to be Writing Your Memoirs*, demanding that "Novelists must evolve (by inventing, borrowing, stealing or cobbling from other media) forms which will more or less satisfactorily contain an ever-changing reality," Nuttall was busy capturing this ever-changing post-war reality across the width of his creative activities.[3] Whereas Johnson declared that "I choose to write truth in the form of a novel," Nuttall chose to write truth by inventing, borrowing or cobbling from every media available.[4] In this he found more in common with another experimentalist of the time, who would become one of Britain's most admired writers, J. G. Ballard, who embraced ". . . the use of newspaper clips, political clichés, and other fragments to show how erotic energy is mobilised for war, for industrial production and for consumerism."[5] Ballard and Nuttall were entirely in accord in their regard for obscenity as a subject.

Nuttall's disavowal of "a seemly literature which *contained* its emotions" is also telling.[6] Significantly his work spills over from one genre to the other, refusing to be contained: Nuttall's fiction has a charged poetic intensity, which he frequently illustrates with drawings, just as his poetry bleeds from verse to prose. "I paint poems, sing sculptures, draw novels," Nuttall described his work in the *International Times* (*IT*).[7]

Of course, for much of this time Nuttall remained firmly under the influence of Alexander Trocchi, who had set "a liberating if nightmarish standard for a generation of artists and writers who enacted a retreat from the word as much as from the object . . ."[8] Apart from Trocchi, Nuttall's creative sources included the blood and shit extremes of European performance art cross-referenced with the Dada-inspired cut-up practices of Burroughs and Brion Gysin. Claude Pélieu, one of his frequent correspondents, inspired him further in the same direction. To Nuttall, the experimental tropes of the Parisians (Alain Robbe-Grillet, Nathalie Sarraute, Michel Butor, Samuel Beckett) that appealed to others in *Writers Reading*, must have appeared rather tame.

Examples of Nuttall's fiction display an impatience with the constraints of words and language; the predictable course of a line carrying a thought across a page. The conventional order of such stuff and narrative traditions were beneath his initial ambition. Nuttall wasn't preoccupied with well-wrought description and dialogue that attempted to simulate real events. His objective was far more provocative: to lure readers into original experiences, from the carnal to the cerebral, from high art to low down and dirty humour. His strategy included the prospecting of biological intimacy, through conduits and chambers, tactile immersions in flesh, fluids, viscose matter; resurfacing where instincts manifest through swelling, dilation, tumescence; changes in hue, temperature, scent and flavour. He was a shameless chronicler of the body, as labyrinth and topography. His commitment to his material was intense and sustained.

To suit his subjects, his style had free licence; shifting from psychedelic Gothic to a malicious burlesque to Grand Guignol. He was Rabelaisian. He parodied classic crime writing, investing it with the inner rampages of psychopaths. There are fragmented pastiches of lurid plots, lustful dames and dodgy coppers and often the destruction of the innocent. His former partner Mandy Porter said she remembered him reading many crime novels, " . . . what springs to mind is Elmore Leonard and Raymond Chandler . . . Derek Marlowe is someone else . . . I recall Jeff giving me a copy of *Echoes of Celandine* after he'd read it and loved it."

He produced three early novellas with cross-over themes of obsession, murder and abortion. Real life serial killers cast shadows over the contents of *Isobel, Pig, The House Party, The Gold Hole* and *What Happened to Jackson.* Nuttall's protagonists may be motivated by love or lust, but are also compelled to keep things unbalanced, duplicitous and primal. There's emotional or actual blood on their hands. He sets them to provoke, tease and disturb each other: to lean self-destructively towards conditions of danger as well as hungrily liquescing into each other's flesh.

While several works of fiction (*The Gold Hole* [1978] and *Snipe's Spinster* [1975]) were published as conventional novellas by established publishers, most of Nuttall's fictional works were small press publications, often displaying the author's cover artwork and disregard for proofreading. Even though he signed with Curtis Brown, a powerful London authors' agency, we could suspect that Nuttall skillfully thwarted any opportunity of literary success. Refusing such temptation would have been stiffened by Trocchi's warning: " . . . anti-literature is rendered innocuous by granting it place in conventional histories of literature."[9]

Besides that, he was emphatically self-contradictory. It made him, to hear him tell it, always ready to move on, dissatisfied at last with the work itself and he was either underappreciated or misunderstood in any case. But perhaps the artefactual finality of publication didn't much concern him. More than that, for him there was " . . . the condition towards which all art aspires, to rid itself of meaning, achieve the purely aesthetic, to create a structure completely outside the material structures of the world . . . to sew immortality into the very fabric of life . . . the purpose of increasing obscurity — what the Sunday-comic critics call 'difficulty' . . ."[10]

Despite the range of his fiction, many of the novels and novellas are peppered with dialect and dialogue, here from *Teeth*: " 'e was well regarded, sir. Pop'lar chap, sir." Nutttall's fictional works, even the most violent or erotic, are underpinned by humour, which is sometime filthy and sometimes droll, like the beginning of *Snipe's Spinster*: "I got my haircut in 1971. I was in Edinburgh and I used an Edinburgh barber." There are moments of surrealism, sometimes involving a foetus, a recurring theme, along with pigs, in Nuttall's work. His frank descriptions of sex and references to murder are juxtaposed with lyrical passages which explore the possibility of transcendence from the mess and horror of H-bomb life. Or as Nuttall put it, his work is characterised by "a determination to find beauty and transcendence (not to mention art, and form, a new language and humour) in the areas of experience from which one most readily recoils — particularly those of bodily nausea and sexual pain . . ."[11]

Snipe's Spinster

The cultural temper of the 1960s and early 70s was famously revolutionary, the default setting for a youth-themed society where hormones and drugs were racing through the bodies of its writers and artists as much as its delinquents and revolutionaries and many writers were determined that they would be all these at the same time. After Nuttall thought he had separated himself from the counterculture with *Bomb Culture* (1968), he then needed to define himself as more than the author of that "bestseller". He somehow expected *Snipe* to do this, with its tale of subversive, cack-handed plotters too busy drinking, drugging and shagging to get their conspiracy together, bound more by audacity than revolutionary accord. The erotic diversions include Snipe's Lolita-like girlfriend and golden showers in the cab of a derelict HGV.

In first person, Snipe relates their assassination conspiracy to eliminate the "Man", probably thinking of Richard Nixon, but more than that; to eliminate the symbolic power as well as the actual person. In *Bomb Culture* Nuttall wrote: "The American Anarchist movement . . . and New York Black Mask group has, for some time, been drumming the hard and hip fact that liberal idealism and beat mysticism will not save the sinking boat in time, that violence is the only realistic measure in political protest, politics being a power structure and force being the pivot on which power rests."[12] Black Mask was one of the most uncompromising of the outlaw artist collectives, producing *The Screw* mimeo magazine and eventually developing into the radical group, "Up Against the Wall Motherfucker" or "Motherfuckers," to their friends.

One figure in the London underground, that Nuttall took a dislike to, was Mick Farren, the pop journalist and lead singer of the Social Deviants (which had modelled itself somewhat on MC5, the Detroit band busted by the FBI). Farren worked briefly at *IT*, then attempted to establish British branches of the Yippies and the White Panthers. He published several underground insider books, such as *Watch Out Kids* in 1972. Nuttall describes Farren's revolutionary cynicism in *Bomb Culture* and in *Snipe* lays into him twice, although not linking the two characters. Firstly, as the anonymous pop music editor of *IT*, and later as the character Mojo Tippet, who muscles in on the plot to hit the Man, even though he is distrusted by the key conspirators.

At various times in the narrative Snipe drops his disguise and speaks as Nuttall, analysing the failure of the previous decade's radical ambitions, blaming its digressions into mystical whimsy, such as flying saucers and arcane secrets; its indulgent, even romanticised, violence and its enslaving cults; particularly the Manson Family. Nuttall quotes generously from writers who influence his thinking, Hunter S. Thompson, Norman Mailer and Ed Sanders among them. *Snipe* owes some of its attitude to Thompson's *Fear and Loathing in Las Vegas* and Sanders' *Shards of God*, but is utterly original.

The House Party

In the introduction to *The House Party*, Nuttall wrote that the novella arose "after my determination to arrive at some point of literary structure as multi-levelled and self-perpetuating as *Finnegans Wake* . . ." and his wish to create "a literary adventure-labyrinth as dense and interpentrative (sic) as a Pollock or a Shepp ensemble."[13] Nuttall's drive to innovate is evident in this short, self-illustrated work, which thwarts linear reading with cartoons, sections from newspapers and cryptic marginalia. While it may be a parody of the country house novel, *The House Party* has more in common with an abstract expressionist painting. Nuttall's use of newspaper headlines and columns, along with the lack of plot, suggest that Burroughs haunts the text.

The four main characters — Sir John, Henry, George and Isabel — are not plotted, but fleshed out through set pieces, which are frequently sexual, comic and absurd. As if seen through a constantly shifting kaleidoscope the characters interact in repeated events and dialogue, with slight, irrational variations. As Nuttall explains in the introduction, *The House Party* is not concerned with "the mere pursuit of happiness," rather it is about "the worshipful adherence to a painful situation," which will be "illuminatory and fulfilling."

The novella is truly Daedalian, an insistent, modernist enigma and reminds us that Nuttall had also celebrated *Finnegans Wake* elsewhere as being, "The bible of the subconscious . . . a book written not only about dream, in the language of dream, adopting the voice of a dreaming man. . ."[14] But Nuttall was also an admirer of Dylan Thomas and *The House Party* has parallels with *Under Milk Wood*, a sensational experimental work of its time, including its opening montage of villagers adrift in night dreams with their wished for or recollected erotic encounters. *The House Party* is never so cosy or whimsical and specifically addresses itself to "the visionary potential of sexual hysteria".

The Gold Hole

In *The Gold Hole*, Nuttall continues to explore painful psychosexual landscapes with a disturbing novel set against a backdrop of the Moors Murderers, Ian Brady and Myra Hindley. The novel begins with a newspaper article which details the murder of a ten-year-old girl whose body is found with a poem composed by Sam, a troubled and methedrine-fueled poet, who is trying to work through his fractured relationship with Jaz.

During letters that the couple writes to each other — but which are never sent — Sam gives an account of their impetuous escape to the countryside and the erotic intensity when Jaz conceives. Jaz's letter reveals the horror of her subsequent abortion to Sam, who is also sleeping with Terry and Susan. In a surreal and disturbing section, "Arrival," the aborted foetus speaks and describes his or her awareness of being alive, and then dead.

Throughout the novel, Nuttall refuses to allow the reader resolution or the comfort of certainty. Sam's lyrical poems to his mother, who abandoned him as a child, hint at the root of his destructive nature. Sam, who does not have an alibi, may in fact be guilty of the child murders, although the presence of the mysterious man with dyed red hair, possibly an alter-ego, compounds the uncertainty of the murderer's identity.

The Patriarchs

At the beginning of the novella, the narrator observes how the "poet Jack Roberts has dominated the narrow world of English letters for at least fifteen years," adding that: "As it happens this is little credit to him. English letters during these fifteen years have been in the hands of a talentless and unadventurous group of poets who see to it that most good writing doesn't get published. The lyric force which Roberts possesses is sufficient to procure for him a certain distinction amongst these carping utterers. The academic orthodoxy of his early work has ensured its publication."

Like his narrator, Nuttall had little truck with the post Second World War literary establishment which he believed was controlled by "dictatorial criticism" that championed "a seemly literature which contained its emotions and subjugated itself to the more trustworthy principles of philosophy and ethics."[15]

"Jack Roberts", in fact Ted Hughes, appeared at the Ilkley Literary Festival in 1975 promoting the publication of his collection, *Cave Birds.* Regardless of whether or not one liked Leonard Baskin's accompanying illustrations, a certain poetic snobbery developed regarding the coffee table book that resulted. It was a time when literary festivals were becoming the "done thing" in gentrified, rural outposts, a long way from their origins as bacchanals and brawls in Edinburgh, London and Cardiff. Nuttall had a "love-hate" relationship with Hughes' work; " . . . admiring its erudition and economy but loathing his acceptance and apparent enjoyment of the establishment's admiration, sophistry and honours."[16] The portrayal of Hughes reading in the Pump Rooms, with Nuttall's Hughesian pastiche is entwined with a complex, sometimes nightmarish account based on Nuttall's own medical procedure and stay in hospital the previous year. According to Mandy Porter, Nuttall had a hernia operation and a rib removed. He was discharged with strict orders to cut out the ale, but Porter said he "replaced it with vast quantities of dry white wine and the much hated salad."

Drawing the two accounts together, Nuttall fictionalises his actual engagement as a guest reader at the Arvon Centre in Heptonstall (once Hughes' home but transferred to use as a writing course retreat), where the course tutors included "Ambleman" (Paul Ableman), who cuts Nuttall's reading session off with a plea of "For fuck's sake, how long is this going on?" and describes Nuttall as a "pornographer left over from the late sixties."

Like other Nuttall fictions, there is a background tragedy in the dark, history-laden Colden Valley where Arvon is based, concerning the unwanted or deformed babies thrown over the waterfall in the valley's deeps, and later for disposing of the bodies of children worked to death in the Victorian mills.

Prior to *The Patriarchs* Nuttall wrote a review of Hughes' book-length poem *Gaudete* (1977). This features a Reverend Lumb and his descent into a pagan underworld. The setting and the protagonist's name is drawn from that of Hughes' former house, "a place so charged with what Lorca called 'duende' that facetiousness dies an early death in an atmosphere dense with some primal violence." What he remarks positively about *Gaudete* is its final section, poems within the poem by the resurrected Lumb. " . . . certainly Hughes' best, spacious, bewildered, wonder-struck . . . they seem to me to be light at the end of the tunnel whose walls are formed of *Crow* and *Cave Birds*."[17]

Teeth

This is a novella that was almost lost, unmentioned in any of the bibliographies; as if Nuttall had disowned it. The occasion of its writing and publication could partially be the reason for this; it was the result of a Soho boozeratti escapade, a writing competition restricted to novels written within 24 hours. Moreover, the novels were written under the organisers' scrutiny during a lock-in at The Groucho Club.

Since the aim of the competition included preparing and producing printed copies within the following 48 hours, the four judges—Kathy Lette, John Clute, Denise Danks and Maxim Jakubowski—were each given a quarter of the completed entries to read. There were 28 contestants and Jakubowski recalled, " . . . because of the sheer number of entrants on the day and time limitations for the judging, each judge was only given a dozen or so of the texts and the final results were calculated on the basis of our individual notations and markings . . . But the whole process was terribly chaotic."[18] The winning and second place novels are of modest interest. Since Nuttall's much more convincing entry was only awarded third place that might account for him treating it as one of his less deserving creations. He did regard it with enough fondness, however, to keep a copy among his personal book collection.

He explained the plot by saying, "Emotions are like the weather. People are blown about by them. We have no control over nature or the elements, which why men become frightened and women ride on the wind."[19] *Teeth* is easily Nuttall's most conventional work of prose although the fictive nuance and erotic dynamics are unmistakeably his. The principle characters, Hugh and Fenella Finch, are struggling in a marriage that has been deeply wounded by infidelity and corrupted by a life of cosmopolitan privilege. During a holiday in the South Hams of Devon, they discover and decide to buy a large, moody house. It overlooks the sea and has been left undisturbed since the death of its former owner, Major Robinson.

They hope that its remoteness and the surrounding pastoral vitality will help heal their marriage and reignite Hugh's aggrieved libido. However, the property comes with sitting tenants, the lusty Voisigna Devauden and her mad daughter, Ursula. Brooding and somewhat feral, Voisigna might have been the tall presence who invaded the house after dark, silently watching the Finches in their bed and leaving shit behind on the staircase. Nuttall and his family spent a number of vacations in Salcombe, close to the setting of the story, and perhaps his holiday reading list included Agatha Christie or Daphne du Maurier.

With instinctive, rustic cunning Voisigna perceives the Finch's dissatisfaction and neediness; Hugh's urge to settle the score and Fenella's frustration. As Fenella paces and rants through her "fucking haunted shit house" she recalls her indiscretions and refutes the blame, "Because he thinks, I, me, it, us, the human female marriage tackle is sacred. Poor darling. Poor old crazy erectile dumb bum. More wine. No. Gin."

Teeth, along with other novellas in this collection, displays Nuttall's ability to create female characters who are vital, sharp witted and self-assured. Sometimes they appear as a muse with attitude or the avid counterpart of a fugitive satyr, but they provide his work with the human emotional charge that balances his full-on innovations with language.

ENDNOTES

1 Steve Hanson, *A Tiny Book about Jeff and others: Nuttall and the Yorkshire Counterculture* (Todmorden: Nowt Press, 2013), 6.
2 Promotional leaflet, London, undated.
3 B. S. Johnson, "Introduction," *Aren't You Rather Young to be Writing Your Memoirs* (1973) http://bsjohnson.co.uk/2015/02/introduction-from-arent-you-rather-young-to-be-writing-your-memoirs-1973/
4 *ibid.*
5 Charles Sugnet, *The Imagination on Trial: British and American Writers Discuss Their Working Methods,* ed. Alan Burns and Charles Sugnet (London and New York: Allison and Busby, 1981), 8.
6 Jeff Nuttall, *Bomb Culture* (London: Paladin, 1968), 54.
7 Jeff Nuttall, "The People," *International Times* 9 (London: February 27 — March 12, 1967), 10.
8 Anthony Wilson, "A poetics of dissent: notes on a developing counterculture in London in the early sixties", *Art & The 60s, This Was Tomorrow*, ed. Chris Stephens and Katherine Stout, (London: Tate, 2004), 98.
9 Alexander Trocchi, *Cain's Book* (London: John Calder, 1963), 59-60.
10 Jeff Nuttall, *Performance Art: Memoirs* (London: John Calder, 1979), 18.
11 Jeff Nuttall, "Introduction," *The House Party* (Toronto: Basilike, 1975), no pagination.
12 Nuttall, *Bomb Culture*, 63.

13 Jeff Nuttall, "Introduction," *The House Party* (Toronto: Basilike, 1975), no pagination.

14 Nuttall, *Bomb Culture*, 97.

15 *ibid.*, 54.

16 Tony Ward, *Jeff Nuttall: A Celebration* (Todmorden: Arc Publications, 2004), 24.

17 Jeff Nuttall, "Jeff Nuttall reviews GAUDETE" *New Yorkshire Writing* 3 (Bradford: Yorkshire Arts Association, 1978), 4.

18 Maxim Jakubowski. Correspondence with Jay Jeff Jones, 2016.

19 Rowland Morgan, Ed. *The World One Day Novel Cup* (Upton-upon-Severn: Images Publishing, 1994), 8.

SNIPE'S SPINSTER

In the light of universal protest, the prisoners on Dartmoor decided to have a sit-in.

MARCEL MARIËN

Chapter One

I got my haircut in 1971. I was in Edinburgh and I used an Edinburgh barber. I had been in Edinburgh a year. From '65 to '67 I was in London. Happenings, lightshows, electronic music. '68 and '69 busking and talking to local anarchist youth groups up and down the land. Edinburgh in '70 for the Festival. The formation of the band. The closure of the Arts Lab. The moving of the Traverse and the subsequent subtle changes in its policy. The haircut.

It was easy. The morning sun slanted industriously across George Street. I walked across that shaft of sun that penetrated the big window of the largest room in my large apartment. I picked out a succession of five chords on the piano. Then I went into the bathroom to talk to my reflection in the mirror. My reflection was repeating itself. It was coming out with old, old contentions, striking old camp attitudes. A little to the right for the alienated intellectual. Head back, look down your nose for the ecstatic jazzman. Head down, up under wreathed brow for the street soldier with his back against the wall. Beam for the Irish bar-room raconteur. Closed eyelashes for the visionary lover. Haircut for a new start. The sunlight in the next room looked cleaner, more useful than it had ten minutes earlier.

So I bought five white shirts with plain collars, three ties of the kind that my Uncle George wears, a sports jacket and two pairs of black needlecord levis. Then I took from my cupboard and dressing-table two peasant smocks, three pairs of luridly patched denim levis, two pairs of white canvas bell-bottoms, three headbands and a handful of neck beads made of wood, seeds, acorns, sea shells and pebbles, many of them presents from friends. Petronella, whom I met at the Stones concert in Hyde Park. Jo, who used to work at Indica.

After lunch I took them all down to the Lane and sold them for a pound. On the way down I got my haircut. Not too short, but short enough for me to have to quell memories of the humiliation at Catterick in '55, of the mad woman from Barnet who agreed to give me a trim and then, salivating foully, couldn't or wouldn't stop.

In the late afternoon I climbed King Arthur's Seat and took a four-hour measure of LSD. I looked at my haircut from some way off and saw the piles of exercise books, the old leather football boots, summoned to my side there on the short grass. Janet walked across the netball court at the foot of the mountain, waving. She shouted to me that she'd passed six subjects in School Cert but failed French. I didn't reply because whilst she told me all this I had fucked her all three times again; the time in her own front room with the afternoon light coming through the green curtains, the time when we broke into the empty warehouse on Edgar Street, and the time in the shrubbery behind the County Hotel, wet earth, drunk. It was appropriate that the Scottish sun should gild our celebrations like music. My penis, growing in my new needlecord trousers, demanded first the bottom of a desk against which to test its rigidity, then a bedroom mirror in which to stand amongst its new-grown bed of hair, then the sun, at the realisation of its full development. I masturbated shortly before dark, adoring myself slowly and carefully. My ejaculation was like a bullet being drawn from a wound in my own flesh, delicately, caringly, and with boundless subsequent happiness.

The acid wore off about half past eight and I went home, clip-clop down the mountain, down the steep streets, over Princess Street, lights of Leith winking like dropped glass. Lindylights. I had a pint of heavy in a bar on Thistle Street. My body, after all the rich bright light that had shot across the magic city into my time-warps, swam in browns: brown beer, brown varnish, warm, earth night-wood; swam with gratitude. I went to bed after a light supper of Ryvita, cheese and milk. It had been a decisive day.

And here I am, still in Edinburgh, waiting for Crane. I have moved but slowly since my haircut three years ago. My hair is still short. The lovely Sandy left for North Africa last summer and hasn't written. Two attempts at homosexuality have, as before, been mere embarrassments born of loneliness and frustration. It's a lousy trick to use friends like that. I should have known, should have remembered the fathersmells of every male body, the rasp of male lips, the quivering otherness of other men. Then came Lindy of the harbour lights, and the band that plays the Pees. My starting again with short hair was based on a will to care, to tie all the knots again, a desire to use moral knowledge. Maybe Crane and our mutual decision will be something different again. The decision is just now as abstract as anything in the human consciousness can possibly be. The actuality of what we intend sets up a woollen numbness that immediately thrusts the mind back into the painless area of mere surmise.

I can see Crane now. He is coming across the road where the station taxis stand, towards the Refreshment Room. He is lunging towards me, dragging with him a little chain of memories. He is lunging the way he used to lunge across the Drury Lane Arts Lab theatre, eager to please me with the sound network he had set up, eager to share a new stash of special dope with me, eager to show me something he had just read in a book newly stolen from Better Books. And I am standing drinking, maybe clinging a little to my Guinness. Guinness, destined to be the last remaining treasure of British civilisation, is something to savour and something to identify with. Even the bottle looks and feels a certain way. With its brown glass over its black contents, its label the colour of the stout's dense froth overlain with fine classic lettering, its body and its clear round neck, it is a bottle which is not pretending to be a wine bottle, or a perfume bottle, or, in the manner of recent lager sixpacks, a hot water bottle. It is a beer bottle. It clinks on my glass. I like that about Scotland. It will be the last place to fall to the era of the plastic schooner and the paper cup. Guinness in a glass with a fine amber head. It is a shame Crane is lunging across Waverley Station to interrupt my solitude, my integrity, my identity, my pleasure, my glass of porter.

Crane has the road manager's lope. He is, in fact, wearing custom-built high-heel boots and loons, but he walks across the buffet as though he were barefoot. In the sixties he was always barefoot. It seemed important then. The attitude of mind persists. Corso: "It's just that I see love as odd as wearing shoes."[1]

Crane's hair is tied up behind and his beard has gone. "Hey man," he says and kisses me wetly on the mouth, unaware of the prickling Presbyterian maidens on all sides.

"Hello Crane, you old motherfucker," I say embracing him. It is some time since I greeted anyone so openly. We stand grinning. I am a little bashful.

"Now what we gonna do?" asks Crane. "Talk now an' get drunk later or the other way around?"

"You eaten?" I ask.

"Yeah, I ate on the train. Cardboard pie man. Wild."

"Well let's drink and talk at the same time. Okay?"

"Someplace we can take a little grass?" I look round trying not to show my spinsterish irritation. Nothing louder than a loud American.

"Yes," I say, "Castle Gardens." I don't like my spinster. She is a bore and a virgin. She never learns not to goad me into ambitious moral decisions. She is the best person I have in that tribe my skull contains and I hate her for it.

We climb the ramp and walk into the gardens. We find a reasonably isolated spot, away, even, from the admonitory stone eyes of Sir Walter Scott, and Crane lights a joint. He offers me a drag and I take one. October bonfires. Hayseeds. After that I refuse.

"He's definitely comin' next month man, an' his wife an' daughter's comin' too."

"In the same party?"

"Nope. He goes ahead with the brass band and the Secret Service. An' they stay, under a false name, back home in London—or Paris or wherever."

"Who got this information?"

"Goofball, man. He bin ballin' the governess."

"Sounds a bit far-fetched."

"Far-fetched nothin'. Goofball comes outta jail, right? Hasta get a job ta buy them awful downers he eats, right? Naturally it's spikin' the autumn leaves in the park. Every day along comes this very cute but oldish chick on her way over the lawn to the White House. One day she happens along just as Goofball is takin' a leak against one of the presidential trees. She smiles. He smiles. They both laugh. Next day she gives him a ride home in her Volkswagen. An' the next day she takes him to her home. Asks him if he wants to take a leak in her salmon pink bathroom. An' there it is."

"Did you see Stuart in London?"

"Yes man. He don't wanna know. He says you're a bourgeois motherfucker an' you fuck with a mess of middle class intellectuals, an' you is a fake an' a phony an' he don't want nuthin' ta do with ya."

"Cunt. And what's the route?"

"Well man, he wanna see the cultural bit. He comin' here for the Festival. He goin' to Ireland to kiss the old homestead. He goin' to some kinda big folk bash, eisteddfod or somethin', over in Wales. He get his own private train. He reckon to sleep in it sometimes. Here, he gonna stay at the Waverley Hotel."

"Sounds too good to be true."

"Well, can't all be gold man. We gotta see. Wanna toke?"

"No thanks."

"We gonna use a bomb?"

"Dunno," my stomach turning inside out, leaping with alarm at the realisation of the practical things to be done.

"Pretty thorough. A good ole bomb. WHOOSH, man."

"Whoosh." I spit. I feel immersed in nausea, part fear part self-disgust, mostly that huge moral loneliness that happens when you take a step entirely alone, contravening the moral responses of the whole world including yourself.

"It's him I'm after. Not anybody else."

"Kinduv uncool, Snipe. You wanna get the daughter. It's a ransome job."

"An' if they don't pay?"

"Well man, we turn her out."

"For whom?"

"For *whom*," mimics Crane. "Why man, for the man in the fuckin' moon. We chop her man. Gotta happen. Look at them Arab and Jap cats. They don't fuck around."

I giggle, a little giddy with this returning psychopathy. It always brings wings, great wide dark wings. Phrases of Bataille rattle through my memory like tickertape, phrases to read which, ten years ago, were to be immediately drunk: ". . . the sacred and the forbidden are one . . . the sacred can be reached through the violence of a broken taboo . . . an enormous possibility opened up towards profane liberty: the possibility of profanation . . ."[2] and Bataille quoting de Sade: "The soul passes into a kind of apathy that is metamorphosed into pleasures a thousand times more wonderful than those that their weaknesses have procured them."[3] Bataille defining poetry: "Poetry leads us to the same place as all forms of eroticism—the blending and fusion of separate objects. It leads us to death, and through death to continuity. Poetry is eternity; the sun matched with the sea."[4] I am giddy with psychopathy because I am melting into history. Access to that "kind of apathy" has suddenly flooded my self with poetry. I melt into the ocean, I float into the sun. I redefine myself with rocks of morality and caring. I change the fucking subject. We make for the Sporran Club with its coy tartans and its awful bagpipe-blowing dolls.

Gertie serves us two pints of club Youngers, which is just that shade more gassy than pub Youngers and Crane, mildly stoned, is delighted with the beer. He dips his fingers in it and smooths his mustache. He belches playfully.

"Now then, you old mother, what in the fuck you been doin'?"

I grin. "Blowing," I say.

"Blowing what? Glass? Sax? Your lid?"

"Piano mostly."

"Yeah? A group? Everybody says you bin off the scene."

I walk over to Gertie's piano. She keeps it remarkably well-tuned considering the shit that gets tipped into it on a Sunday night. I play the piece I call "Pilp". It is all corners with the spaces between the corners left clear and silent. Out of "Le Marteau Sans Maitre". By Thelonius Monk.

"That's 'Pilp'", I say when it's finished (on an indigestible flattened ninth).

"Fuckin' right it's pilp. Pilp pulp. What is this man? You puttin' me on?"

"No," I say levelly.

"Huh?" says Crane. "Man, what's been goin' on in Britain? Las' time I was here, the Cream, the Hendrix Experience, the Floyd, *Sergeant Pepper*—oh man."

"That was all shit," I say and hope that I haven't spoiled the warmth of our reunion or marred that hand-in-glove co-operation that is going to be necessary if we are to bend history or even slightly dent it.

Chapter Two

When the Chicago blues singers, Muddy Waters, Howlin' Wolf, Buddy Guy, enjoyed their sudden popularity in the early sixties, the degree of amplification they used throbbed straight to the wide open proletarian nerve centres of the South Side. It lent their style grace, power and far greater range, but it was an impediment between them and the young white middle-class audience they had previously attracted in their acoustic, ethnic guise. The white audience, with its subdivisions of students and political dissidents, had treasured their Alan Lomax field recordings of Mississippi blues and wagged them defiantly in the levelled countenance of rock and roll, as clear proof of the superiority of truth unadorned, performed by man at his most humble and lowly. But when the diamond rings and grease-conked hair and 100 watt amps blitzed out in all their muscular brash vulgarity the character of urban blues in the middle of the century was undeniably different from the account of anthropologists and sociological music writers. A reorientation of liberal values was demanded and began to be articulated.

The concert at St. Pancras Town Hall bore this out. When the audience applauded the polished harmonics of Robin Hall and Jimmy McGregor and rejected Champion Jack Dupree for his flash, his dirty lyrics, his vaudeville and circus showmanship, his grinds and bumps, his backside on the keyboard, it became clear how deeply immersed we were in the essentially bourgeois concept of good taste and how little we understood the wayward and magical formations described by real proletarian culture.

Bob Dylan, who knew at that time just exactly what was "blowing in the wind", was quick to reorient his values, developing very quickly from a passable imitation of Woody Guthrie's unvarnished country noises, to the high poetic stylist he was at his peak. The old purist folk fans who adored the way Ewan MacColl hugged his ear as though struck with a sudden mastoid, who thought there was no more profound evidence of honesty and political integrity than the way Peggy Seeger slid around looking for her notes, recoiled from Dylan's appearance at the Newport Folk Festival in cowboy drag with enamelled guitars and rock-and-roll amplifiers. Their purism, with its heavy rural nostalgia, its distrust of the city as a creative form, and its hard left-wing distrust of all media, seeing journalists as the subtlest and strongest thread in the capitalist cobweb, had to go by the board. There were points to be made and ground to be gained. Cultural opportunism could not wait on naïve principle.

The preciosity of the purist persuasion, with its wastage of that special energy called urban vulgarity, had to be corrected. The masses of the pop-mesmerised delinquent young, the teds, the mods, and the motorcycle cowboys, had to be reached by the chief evangelist of an idealistic and desperate dissident culture. Whatever he may say now to cushion his premature old age from the painful and thought-provoking questions of fans and journalists, Dylan, like his idol Guthrie, was an evangelist. And Ginsberg, the courageous old queer who had set himself no smaller task than that of saving the world, had seen in Dylan not merely a poet who was his equal in imagery and metrical skill, but a mouthpiece for that evaluation of the historic situation whereby the anguish of despair became the vision of possibility. He had appointed Dylan to a certain tactical post, and the peaceniks, in turn, came to accept pop electronics as a piece of cultural strategy.

Peaceniks, in those days, wanted to know. It is no accident that the rendezvous of the Underground were not pubs, clubs or discotheques, but bookshops. Better Books in London. Peace Eye in New York. Giat Froget's in Paris. City Lights in San Francisco. The Paperback in Edinburgh. They read continuously, not just the journals of folk and jazz, not just one another's poetry. They read Marx and Engels and Russell and Fromm and Thoreau. They read Hegel and Sartre and Heidegger and Shaw and Nietzsche. They read Kerouac and Ginsberg and Corso and Ferlinghetti. They read Steinbeck and Dos Passos and Thomas Wolfe and Nathaniel West. They read Osborne and Lessing and Colin Wilson and Adrian Mitchell and Christopher Logue. They read Teilhard de Chardin and Thomas Aquinas and the *I Ching*. They read *The Guardian, The New Statesman, The Observer, The Sunday Times, The Times, Time and Life, The Daily Worker, The Daily Mirror* and *Mad Magazine*. They read Blake and Burroughs and Beckett and Rimbaud and Joyce. And they saw about them a vast drift of people so ignorant and consequently so bored with their empty lives they walked willingly and eagerly towards the big bang and the big numbness, lubricating their slippery progress with the usual rationalisations about the facts of international power and the spirit of Dunkirk. And they wanted to spread a certain amount of knowledge that the qualifying flavour of life might be improved and the Gadarene stampede be halted. They were, then, educators, and it was as educators that they accepted the media.

The peaceniks were good educators, skilful and crafty. They were McLuhanites before McLuhan threw the whole of history into the ebbing and flowing of a plastic evolutionary fungus. They knew that a climate of mind is the prerequisite of a process of learning. To take over the electric empire would be to inoculate knowledge into the fizzy pop of the media con. Dylan, first despised at Newport, was held, within three years or so, to be right.

The media, electronics, Tin Pan Alley, broadcasting, comics and tatty mags, were not only the back door into the heads of the people, they were, perversely, the people's own cultural province, the Catholicism of the final century. They became the righteous arena for cultural crusaders where, oh joy of joys, middle-class idealists could rub up yet more closely and so more pleasurably to the envied, romanticised and clumsily-aped working class.

"We had a lot of faith," I say to Crane.

Crane is lying on my divan smoking his seventh joint. When he exhales he makes a little whinnying noise in his throat that strikes a note somewhere between a guinea pig in orgasm and a septuagenarian at stool. Between drags, or tokes as we call them in the subculture, he draws on a bottle of red wine as though it were the nipple of Bessie Smith. After each draught he grins ferociously and breathes out through his lower teeth. Little droplets of plonk make their way down his newly shaven jaw, pink like the thin blood of the anaemic.

"Spirits of Faith, Sprites of God, Voices of Victory. What the fuck ya talkin' about man. Gospel singers?"

"Wading into the floods of the aether ducts with a black and white flag and a cerebral hardon."

"Satellite screwsman, daddy. Orgone rockets. Oh yes."

"Such faith that *we* had the power in a bellyfull of words. Only a few of us. Like General fuckin' Custer surrounded by the whooping hollering scalp-hungry music of the spheres. Never dreaming for a minute that *they* had the power. They had it wired. Switch on the fuckin' power."

I grab the wine from Crane before it's all gone. I feel it gather in my midriff like a handful of iron filings going rusty.

"Remember the Isle of Wight?" I ask.

"The Isle of Wight, man? Why fuck with these garden parties. I remember Woodstock."

"The Isle of Wight was before Woodstock. Dylan was at the Isle of Wight. It was the first shock Crane. All those people. Never since Aldermaston."

Crane's face wreathed with disbelief. "Aldermaston? Crawl outta the ark, baby. How about Gettysburg?"

I do not kick Crane. I have kicked people who have talked about Aldermaston as they talk about the bomb, as they talk about Parker (Charlie that is), as they talk about jazz, dismissively, as though all true value lay with the trend, as though the fashion were the touch of the Gods, as invention is in art. I have punched such people and even tried to stab one. But I do not kick Crane. It is the third time since his arrival that I have not kicked him. I am slightly worried by the fact that I do not want to kill the Man when he comes but I must, and three times I have wanted to kill Crane and I must not.

"Anyway, the Isle of Wight; there was this tall guy running it, Tommy Farr's son."

"Who's Tommy Farr?"

"Fought Joe Louis."

"Who's Joe Louis?"

"Father of Cassius Clay."

"Ya mean Mo—"

"This guy was running it. The cables for the speakers ran round the arena and the speakers were there like castle walls on either side of the stand. The stand looked like a city gate. And sound came out of those speakers, mate, like arrows from the wall of a medieval fortress. Sound bristled out of those speakers, me old mate."

"Yeah," gasped Crane, and closed his eyes, "the power!"

"The sound hit the sea all round, penetrated the prison walls, extended clear to Ryde, six miles, an area six-by-six, thirty-fuckin'-six square miles of power man."

"Oh don't," moaned Crane, his hand rammed down the front of his loons.

"Filled the village of kids outside the arena like crows in the sea-slanted trees, kids in blankets with their heads full of hay and bellies full of chewed glass phials, the village of tents and coats and twinkling fires and free cocks in the milky channel water, in the soft light that fell like flute music."

"Blowin' baby. Go!"

"And the second day the kids started to climb into the arena. To sit on the fence, on the cables."

"Yes."

"And Tommy Farr's son—"

"Who's Tommy Farr?"

"Tommy Farr's son said 'Will people sitting on the fence around the arena please get off. We're losing power.'"

"Did they get off?"

"Oh Crane. Fly away."

"What?"

"Piss off. Go and have a wank."

"I don't dig you man. What is this trip you're puttin' on me? Hang loose you mother. Don't be so uptight."

"I'm just saying we thought the power lay with knowledge but it didn't. It lay with them."

"Listen you mother. The power is the power. Forever and ever, amen. Take a toke on this joint—Do I *invent* the motherfuckin' power? Do you give it to me? Does Nixon give it to me? Or Schnixon, or Donald Duck or Ho Chi Minh? Outta the air man. Outta the aether. I breathe it in. Outta the cosmos, baby. Ya dig electronics? Electronics is a great scene, man. It *connects* with the power. It *strikes* power."

"Like striking oil."

"Gold, man."

"A discovery."

"On tap. Turn on the light. Tune into the power, baby. It don't *belong* to no fucker. It's *free* baby."

"Do you Yanks always have to find things?"

"What?"

"Can't you ever *make* anything? Do you always have to find it ready made? What do you do when the land of plenty is used up?"

"Move on, naturally."

Mimicking, "Move on, naturally."

"Well right," says Crane. "It ain't gonna be where it's gone from so it must be someplace else."

"What?"

"The *power* Snipey, the *motherfuckin' power*. Oh you turn me on. You really turn me on."

"The power is with the man who owns the tap, or the plug, or the cable, or the loudspeakers. The power is with the guy who's selling that other power that you're talking about. The power I'm talking about is with the guy who controls the supply. He controls you. He has power over you."

"Ah shit. He only thinks he has. He don't realise—he don't *realise* what he's sellin', man. Like he thinks he's got you there in his hand, but what he don't know is he sold you wings, man. Weeeeeee. You gone. You ain't in the palm of his hand. You ain't no-where. You is with the real power baby. The cosmos. The light."

"And you leave the earth to him. To gang-bang just how he likes. You're off in the cosmos while here in this little local piece of cosmic phenomena he can shit on history."

"Ah Snipe. What inna fuck's happened to you? You got the menopause or somethin'? Listen, I'll rap to you about *history* man. Why am I here?"

"We're going to hit the Man."

"Right. Why we gonna hit the Man?"

"Because of Vietnam and the South American mines and the Chicago trial and the bomb and napalm and poison gas and the smog and the money and the pigs."

"And why else we gonna hit the Man?"

"Why else Crane?"

"Because we know that history ain't nothin'. That Vietnam ain't nothin'. That the world is but a glass bubble man. That the Man is no more than a tick of the second hand of a cheap clock baby. That it don't *matter* baby, so we gonna do it for *kicks*. An' we can do that man, because we connected. *We* got the motherfuckin' power."

And Crane lies back pleased with himself. I take the wine and I go into the kitchen. I shall not kick Crane. Neither shall I cry. Have another little drink. There's a fine fat moon over the Castle.

"Hey," shouts Crane from the other room. "Tomorrow we gotta *score*."

Chapter Three

It didn't take long after Dylan's Newport appearance for the media to take over the peaceniks. The confusion between somebody singing over the aether and the idea that the singing was disembodied, coming from the aether itself, soon gave so-called progressive pop a counterfeit authority. It was a desperate need for the incorruptible voice, the dehumanised voice free from all fallibility and compromise that made' people look so hard for the voices of the Gods that they were prepared to recognise such voices in the messages of cut-up writing, jumbled into accidental phrases, into the playback when the Pink Floyd left their guitars propped against the amps and disappeared.

Cage's rediscovery of the *I Ching* gave a source of material that could be read like language unimpaired by the mortality of some other bloke. If ecstasy was streaming straight from the Gods through the transmitters, those old dull artifacts that bore the thumbprints of mortality, paintings and sculptures in which you could see the fallibility of the human hand, acoustic music in which you could hear the breath and clumsy effort of the musicians, writing that aroused the old straight difficulties of hard thought and hard talk, these were clearly a waste of time. Knowledge could be junked. Art could be junked. Invention was just the pathetic fumbling of some ego-tripper trying to be God. It came from no true genius. It came from some other bloke, as prone as oneself to use his gifts for purposes of domination, trying to "put his scene on you". God kissed few people and always came uninvited. God was delivered best depersonalised through sound mixers, the wrinkles of the chosen oracles ironed out by technicians. That way it really sounded like God. Anonymous. De-individualised. The everything voice from everywhere. The Absolute. The only true reality. Hunter Thompson: "The room was very quiet. I walked over to the TV set and turned it onto a dead channel —white noise at maximum decibels, a fine sound for sleeping, a powerful continuous hiss to drive out anything strange."[5]

So the peaceniks became flower children and the flower children became hippies and the hippies scorned all book knowledge and all individual invention. I recall the empty-faced man who told me that all people getting up alone to perform in public were fascists. Was Buster Keaton a fascist? Yes, Buster Keaton was a fascist. Was Lennie Bruce a fascist? Yes, Lennie Bruce was a fascist. Was Basil Brush a fascist. Yes, Basil Brush . . . .

Energy was handed over to the electronic suppliers, to the government authorities, to the impresarios and the studio technicians. Power was lost. The original bid to take over the media was reversed. It completely back-fired on its precipitators. Dylan, the prime mover, became a showbiz hack, peddling cheap deals of nostalgia. In '68 I was drinking with the music editor of *International Times*. "What revolution?" he asked, pityingly.

"You're rare," I whisper to Lindy. "Nothing is fresh without rarity. Familiarity goes stale. That's why you have to have art."

"Oh shut up about your art and do something about this," says Lindy, seizing my preoccupied prick as though catching trout and sliding it wet through her thin hand, her hand dancing with its tenderness, fingers fluttering to a standstill as the fish lashes out rigid along her wrist.

She is a hard-headed young Scot, all savagery and dry irony. She rests me immensely after Crane. Crane, short-measured on his morning deal, is combing the city for his vendor. I have told him he'll have to go to Glasgow. Maybe he's gone. I did not tell him the contingencies of a trip to Glasgow. Maybe he'll never return. Maybe I don't have to go through with it. All there is is action. All action is decision. All there is in the world is yourself kicking the maybes around as hard as you can.

"Even Hendrix is stale and he was the best," I say.

"Hendrix was marvellous. If he was around I wouldn't be lyin' here with you."

"Endless arpeggios and inversions of the blues scale, wringing out the diminished fifths and sevenths. Parker had done it. Dolphy had done it. Muddy Waters had done it. And the wa-wa pedal, an electronic version of the old wa-wa mute that King Oliver invented, that Ellington orchestrated to perfection. Throw all this old gear together in Hendrix and in five minutes the whole world sounds like the Led Zeppelin. Non-stop."

"I havena heard of any of those fellas. It's pro-bably because they weren't sae pretty."

"They didn't have to be pretty."

"Mebbe they didn't havetae be but if you can be pretty—why not? If you can sound nice you might as well look nice as well."

"Elvis had done that. Even that. It had all been done Lindy Lu."

"How about you doin' it?" says Lindy. She slides along the seat of the cab until she can breathe and mouth and salivate along my prick. Quickly she reaches under her pleated skirt with both hands and whips off her knickers. The hair at her crotch is a whisp of vapour in a clean sad sky of rose and amber. Her cunt is a raw, wet, tiny shrimp of a thing that grips like a baby's mouth at the nipple. She bends to me, her cunt close to me.

"Even the bloody poets were doing a rehash of symbolism. Rimbaud's image chains, vowel colours, Verlaine's fatalistic masochism, Baudelaire's souped-up transgressions, obligatory homosexuality all round, the legions of the fleet-footed beautiful boys who never grow old: Neal Cassady, Kerouac, Corso, O'Hara, Lamantia, McClure, all of them getting on a bit now, all them getting . . . ."

She had me into her. The great fluid colours came down like dark and she drowned me to death for the second time that dinner hour.

Afterwards she sat on the petrol tank between the seats, her bare brown legs crossed and a smirk on her face. "What were you talking about back then?"

"I was regretting the failure of invention in the arts."

"You mean nothing's happening?"

"Nothing really. People stopped it happening."

"Why?"

"Absolutism."

"Absolutely." She smacked a piece of bubble-gum out in a little shock of sarcasm.

"People think what always was will be, in all important respects. They address themselves to eternity which is eternal because it doesn't change. An artist is naturally going to mess them up. Anybody with ideas is lying. Scientists pretend they aren't. They really want not to be lying. But artists are inventing unashamedly. A scientist is like a Yank. He says 'I have discovered this.' An artist says 'I have thought this up.' An artist, then, is untrammelled. He's irresponsible. Without any reason or any faith in anything but the health of continuous change and the fun of precipitating it. He tells powerful fibs and history acts them out. So that won't do you see, because we are searching for Where It's At, and the Light, the Tee Ar Yoo Tee Aitch, aren't we, that's what we're after isn't it. Artists? Liars and ego-trippers. Elitists. Fascists. Let us all of one accord consider Life and let us forget imagination."

Lindy laughs: "You're a big-headed bastard Snipe."

"Big enough to love you right."

She becomes serious. Clear black brows level. Bright hard black eyes. The shade of hair at the corners of her level mouth. Her mouth a delicate sculpture of sandalwood.

"Let me tell you something my love."

"You tell me something Snipe."

"All the truth there is is the lies that get told well enough to stick. God, my little love, is not the silence that's left after the world has gone. God is some bugger's poem, to which many more poems have been added. God is a piece of language."

"Snipe," she says, laying a fucksmelling finger on my lower lip and tracing the lip's outline with her fingernail. "You'd better be right about lies because you're lying now. I've got to go."

She struggles into her knickers, pops a kiss on my nose, bangs open the cab door and jumps to the ground. I throw her satchel down to her.

"See you at home time?" she asks.

"Don't know my love, see me when you see me."

"Okay." She laughs brashly and runs down the alley like a foal. Her limbs are a gangling celebration of grace. They are not the systematically formalised professional grace of the ballet dancer. They have an authentic grace precisely because they know no system. All language that is poetry must tap the unsystemised, the illiterate, the eternal. I mutter a prayer: "But it's the way we have to live for you, you fucker. It's our nature to have no nature."

Chapter Four

The Man walks out of the lift and I ask him for a light and a Secret Service man hits me and I go down. Cancel dream. Start again.

The Man walks out of the bathroom to find his bedroom occupied by myself, Crane, Allen Ginsberg, Hugh Scanlon, my mother, Lindy and the Pink Panther. All of us carry guns except Scanlon. Silly. Cancel. Start again.

The Man struggles out of the crashed car. Jerry Rubin, Charles Manson, Lindy and Mickey Mouse signal to me from the trees at the edge of the motorway. Crane sits bolt upright in bed and shrieks "Messages! Mothafuggen messages."

I switch on the table lamp and regard Crane's green, sleep-grained face as it hangs, turned ecstatically to the cracked ceiling, lips moving. His legs are fully extended under the blankets. I reach for a cigarette, find half a licorice paper joint and say "Shut up Crane. You're spaced."

"Oh man," rubbing one of those straight knees against the other like a child suppressing urine, "that interstellar, transpersonal telstar come a-beamin' in on me now." Nothing in the dark dour wastes of Scotland was less luminous than the low ceiling towards which Crane was turned to receive the tappings of the Gods. "He ain't comin' at the same time as his family. That's a front—he lands a week later at Dundee."

"*Dundee*!"

"Yeah, an' we gotta, like the problem, no problem, gotta get him from there down to Stonehenge."

Swift circling aerial shots of the turning British midriff, down the Western coastline from Silvery Tay to ancient Salisbury Plain. The Aquarian sacrifice, of course: "*Stonehenge*!!? Oh Crane, go to fuckin' sleep."

"Doncha see man? He gonna be there for Lammastide."

"Yes yes."

"*That's why he's a week later*. He's the last and ever King. Flick-knives and mistletoe baby. Wait til that mornin' sun hits that good good good ole stone."

"Really fine grass, Crane. New knowledge indeed. How could we have failed to see that the Secret Service was a Druidic organisation? I mean it's so obvious. Those Masonic handshakes, those mystic unions with the Brotherhood, those magical, telepathic tapes, the double meaning of the word Watergate."

"Oh man, now you talkin'. Like it ain't—"

Crane pauses, swallows, belches noisily and continues. He is talking breathily through his lower teeth again, the way some people used to play tenor, so that you could hear the spittle. "Ain't no organisation. There is only one organisation and that is No Organisation. There is only one thing an' that is No Thing, no body but Mr Nobody. Welcome man to Nosville the only town in the Cosmos. You is an honorary citizen of fuck-in' Nosville. An' the Druids didn't run nothin' no more than the fuckin' pigs run anything because they is all programmed, man, to carry out Nothin', exactly and particularly and perfectly nothin' but Nothin'. An' that is why we is here and Dundee is there and the old Nowhere sun shines down exactly on that nothin' nothin' nothin' stickin' stone at *exactly* dawn, baby, because we carry out the book man, and the book is"—Crane does a radiating arc with his fingertips like a stage conjuror demonstrating nothing up his sleeves— "Void, man, void."

"Oh thank you for the Grade Ten enlightenment routine, O Zen master. Now have a wank and get some sleep."

Crane obeys my instruction noisily, giggling a little before sleep, and wakes at ten.

We were glad to entertain the Gods in 1964. They seemed a stake in possibility. To name and to assume a God was to establish camp, as it were, a few short steps into the wilderness, and to note the position on the map of psychic enquiry, so we weren't too particular about which Gods. Any old God would do. We welcomed the lot, duly enrolling in any church we stumbled upon. We wanted bivouacs in the wilderness because in civilisation we had just suffered a colossal defeat. We had believed in a freedom and had cried out against the evils. Our beliefs and cries had proved ineffectual so we had to do two things. We had to reinforce our beliefs by granting them divine authority. Our arguments in the terms of materialism and hard economic politics had been ignored. They had to be expanded so that they included concepts that remained unsealed at one end, concepts that were merely initial perception. We had to provide our polemic with power and information that was beyond that of our defeaters. Secondly we had to move on away from the place of humiliation, which was society as we knew it. By doing so we would expand and change society as we knew it. The tactic was to stop wasting our inadequate energies confronting the establishment on its own terms. The tactic was to achieve, translate and present a quite new, and workable alternative. We addressed ourselves to exercises of perception that would carry us beyond the fringes of society. In these exercises Gods are useful. Landmarks, you might say.

Bob Dylan, at that time croaking his way onto the international bardic chair as no other man had, by singing the right thing at the right time; providing our predicament with the first ingredient of transcendence, poetry; chronicling the times with a rare participatory insight; sang exactly what was going on.

Alan Watts and Gary Snyder and Jack Kerouac introduced us to Buddha, and Herman Hesse, discovered rather late, consolidated that outpost. It was a good outpost because it was one at which Dylan's words "it doesn't matter" were underlined with scholarly authority. Allen Ginsberg introduced us to Krishna and the Church of Hari Krishna began to drone its boring three note nursery chant up and down the chilly halls of the alternative society. Ed Sanders had long laced his racy East Side hep talk with the expletive names of Thoth and Ra. "Rapid the ooze in the clotted nothing," he chants. "No voidal tampax holds this dripping/ when the machine-lines harden/the flesh becomes ooze/ and the poem is ooze,/ /O/Zeus/Osiris/Zagreus/ downriver from the Crotch Lake . . . ."[6]

We raked the dead ashes of Madame Blavatsky and Aleister Crowley for a kiss or two from the Pharaohs. Robert De Grimston announced his "Process Church of the Final Judgement" and proclaimed himself to be Jesus Christ. This identity he shared with Charles Manson, Michael De Freitas and at least three other Black Power leaders, also with several of anyone's best friends. The name of Christ had also been bestowed by hosts of adulators on Lennie Bruce, James Dean, Charlie Parker, Jimi Hendrix, Jim Morrison and Jean Genet. All religions are an attempt to give substance to the void beyond death, but death is, seemingly, a closer characteristic of card-carrying Christs. Those called Christ are probably about to die and those calling themselves Christ are probably about to kill somebody. The Sermon on the Mount seems to have been left out of the script.

De Grimston ran a close third to L. Ron Hubbard in the race to start one's own church. Scientologists proliferated and even, for a while, engaged the acute intelligence of William Burroughs. L. Ron Hubbard ran a close second to Timothy Leary whose League For Spiritual Discovery was never completely cleared of the suspicion that it was formed as a means of taking acid legally. Established churches are permitted hallucinogens by US law as a special concession to the Peyote Indians. Leary even published a pamphlet, *Start Your Own Religion*. With all that acid around it was inevitable that many people were going to.

Acid is a mathematical thing. From the welter of normal experience we choose to recognise only those experiences we can use. We filter experience through a selection process automatically all the time, picking out a few salient items and losing the rest. We do this with non-empirical information as well. We "remember" a few items of what we know, we "forget" the rest. We impose a grid on experience. All our grids are different.

Acid changes the grid from the one we have chosen, and precipitates a selection process whereby the remembered or registered items are not selected according to their usefulness, but according to mathematical patterns.

One can, for instance, look over a landscape and all that the eye will record will be the landmarks measuring off regular distances of, say, two hundred yards as far as the horizon, sometimes beyond. The mathematical grid, being as abstract as it is strong, can continue without perception to provide its vocabulary. It will merely repeat images, ad infinitum, like a kaleidoscope operating in any of the three dimensions.

Or one's eye picks out only those buildings constructed in, say, the late 18th Century. The 19th Century being "forgotten", whole cities become transparent.

A mind trying to find its way through a city will see the city in two dimensions, as a map, and so become incapable of movement; no one can walk onto a wall.

Metaphorical characteristics can create rigid categories. A person with slightly round, dot-like eyes, being held to be snake-like, will appear scaled. A person heavy and lugubrious, being held to be elephant-like, will grow a trunk.

When first encountered these re-shufflings of memory and experience are believed, according to the Freudian yardstick that the hidden is more authentic than the customary and obvious, to be the "real" nature of things. People seeing these irrelevant patterns are apt to feel that now they understand after a long period of confusion and falsehood. They seldom realise, until sometime later, that, true or false, their new understanding is unusable.

Instrumentality being thus removed, as it ultimately always is by mathematics, one is comparatively powerless. The oceanic, non-utilitarian qualities in experience swamp the senses which become senselessly ecstatic. A senseless ecstasy is a loveless ecstasy. Love, normally the guiding power of ecstasy, is itself guided by bilious dreams of colour and is therefore ludicrously applied to stones and teacups.

One's power gone, one is apt to panic. The metaphorical categories feed the alarms. Old coats turn into pterodactyls. All the hallucinatory bestiary of panic dances on the walls.

Some dope users get so adjusted to the passive situation that they become acutely sceptical of anything but the passive role, feminising themselves to the point of feebleness and seeing all demonstrative energy as fascist, all individuality as vaulting ego. The dying fall creeps into the forms of the culture: the gesture that loses impetus before it reaches completion, the sketched-in semiquavers at the end of a Charlie Parker phrase, the apologetic mumble in the Lee Strasbourg school of acting, and in Robert Creeley's syntax.

Being adjusted to the passive role one sees patterns. Symmetry, of all human structures, needs least invention and therefore least thought. Patterns are what is left in the passive mind when perverse and asymmetrical invention are asleep. This is where acid is close to schizophrenia. Schizophrenic drawing, far from being the expressionist ejaculation which befits the popular concept of madness, is, above all things, systematic. All Louis Wain did to his famous pussy cat as he went madder and madder was geometricise it. It did not dissolve in rivers of emotion. It did not transform into images of the gods transmitted from the other side of time. It crystallised into patterns of perfect symmetry. The unhappiness of schizophrenics surely largely derives from their painful realisation that the universe is systemless. In the face of this pain they "forget" the universe and live according to their system, which, in terms of their daily "senseless" rituals, the absolute precision of their pictures, the frequent punctuality of their repeated acts, the airtight anti-empirical consistency of their myths, is mathematical.

So we all took the wonder drug, went mad, lost our technique of pragmatically using the world, panicked, or "freaked out" as we used to say, at the senselessness of pattern and the patternlessness of sober experience, eventually experienced the universe as perfect pattern and went all gaga at the beatific harmony of it all.

"Time ceases to exist," proclaimed McClure. "In moments of great tension or stress the mystics know it; the elaborate and artificial structure of time dissolves and they make contact. Space becomes a *hall of glory* containing casually and invisibly what was once the monumental reality of Time. You stand on the snowy summit or the warm steppes of a vision. You have the view of a colossus or a tiny creature of love."[7]

"The LSD rocket has just been launched" sang George Andrews. "Brain waves travel at the speed of light/shot through by all the stars/fierce liquid movements turn me inside out/ I am in all the worlds at once . . ."[8]

'Freewheelin' Frank Reynolds of the Oakland Chapter of Hell's Angels reports, "The Hell's Angel mind has rapidly expanded within the past year since we came into contact with LSD. It has held us tighter together. We know that we can never be broken up. As Bob Dylan sings, 'There are no kings inside the Gates of Eden . . .' —we the members, the majority, see this thing clear. This is why we'll never be crushed or broken up. Furthermore this is why there will always be Angels Forever Lasting . . . I would debate with an atheist now."[9]

The Angels' own historian, Hunter S. Thompson, recalls, "There was madness in any direction, at any hour. If not across the Bay, then up the Golden Gate or down 101 to Los Altos or La Honda . . . You could strike sparks anywhere. There was a fantastical universal sense that whatever we were doing was *right*, that we were winning. . . And that, I think, was the handle—that sense of inevitable victory over the forces of Old and Evil. Not in any mean or military sense; we didn't need that. Our energy would simply *prevail*. There was no point in fighting—on our side or theirs. We had all the momentum; we were riding the crest of a high and beautiful wave . . ."[10]

We were so stirred by patterns we formed churches. John Michel looked at the English landscape, a landscape so kicked about by history it forms a veritable rubbish tip of systems and patterns, agricultural, industrial, military, legal or aesthetic—a chunk of the Earth's crust so richly inscribed with ideas it takes on the depth and complexity of a well-carved shithouse door. John Michel saw leys, the old pilgrim Druid paths. He was a keen science fiction buff so he registered points where flying saucers had been spotted. Where the saucer paths crossed the leys he got all excited. With a headful of Joanna Southcott and William Blake, a witty perception of the connection between the English hippie and the Shoreham Ancients, and a breastful of everyone's hunger for the Gods, he registered Glastonbury and "those feet in ancient time". Putting the registered pattern together he made a convincing enough religious proposition to send hordes of the faithful down to Stonehenge and Glastonbury Tor every summer, to provoke Harry Fainlight to write an excellent poem which he read "between two lions" on the Trafalgar Square plinth at the end of a Vietnam demonstration, to inspire a magazine, *Albion*, and a pop group, the Third Ear Band. I remember lying utterly drunk and utterly tripped out in a Notting Hill Gate basement in 1967 whilst the minds and spirits to become the Third Ear talked across my floating perceptions. "We gorra group already man, but like we don't do gigs, we don't play. Like the sounds are already there man . . . ."

Constant throughout a kaleidoscope of similar superstitions was the idea that history as it was written, having reached the point of bloodshed and human disaster called the Twentieth Century, was a small aberration, that the kindly and fanciful beings who had long ago inhabited the earth were only hiding, either under the ground (Tolkein, Manson) or on another planet (Michel, Bolan), that the arrival of the Aquarian Age would see true history restored and the economy of steel and plastic would be relegated to the earth ("Where it belongs": Leary), not as a result of any political action in the pathetic old existential manner, but as an evolutionary inevitability. With such historic jingoism on our side it scarcely seemed necessary to actually arm or organise ourselves when we finally did make feeble attempt at revolution in 1968.

So we registered the ancient conical mounds and hummocks that punctuate England between the motorways and we took Tolkein seriously. Marc Bolan, a poet of strong if whimsical gifts, fronting Tyrannosaurus Rex, and recently lapsed into glitter-camp and post-Yippie cynicism, proclaimed that his "people were fair". One of the first to inject these beliefs into popular music, which became increasingly tantric, he was the makeup on the eyelids of a ritual head. Jim Morrison was the brain in the skull of that head: "We're getting tired of waiting around, with our heads to the ground. I hear a very gentle sound. What have they done to the Earth? What have they done to our fair sister? Ravaged and plundered and ripped her and bit her, stuck her with knives in the side of the dawn, and tied her with fences and dragged her down. I hear a very gentle sound, with your ear to the ground. WE WANT THE WORLD AND WE WANT IT NOW."[11] The heroic relevance of this demand, of course, being betrayed by its proximity to the sandal-stamping demands of a child in a tantrum.

So along they came, the religious pop groups. The Beatles cast Lucy in the sky into a tomorrow which never knows. The Pink Floyd flirted with the Piper at the Gates of Dawn, giving the entombed remains of Kenneth Graham a hefty kick before flagging down their saucerful of secrets. The Incredible String Band talked about peeling the layers off their gnomic onion and the San Francisco Dead were Grateful. The musical devices of the time, wild pedal work, the electronic vibrato extending to feedback, and the thunder of electricity destroying itself as the Who smashed up their gear, were the musical expression of a desire for sexuality relieved of mortality, for erection following its implication beyond the confines of the fallible penis. They were the sound equivalent of a winged penis, a spacecraft, a Cadillac freed of gravity. They were the musical equivalents of what the Gothic architects tried to do with stone. Snatches of Monteverdi crept into the collage. The transcendental spirituality of sex was creamed off with a ladle provided by Wilhelm Reich. The loyalties, the contracts, the sweat, smegma and sperm and, banish the very thought, the babies, were momentarily forgotten. In the first issue of their magazine the Process carried an article exposing what a nasty and undesirable business birth had always been (an interesting reversal of a very beautiful article by David Melzer in *Journal for The Protection of All Beings* six years earlier). George Harrison transformed impotence to abstinence and squatted down with the Maharishi.

And Charlie Manson registered the network of waterways running beneath the Nevada Desert, tied that up with a creepy crawly brand of Hobbitry and registered extraordinary inner patterns in the Beatles' song lyrics.

"Manson began to listen to the song 'Helter Skelter' off the new Beatles album with earphones and somehow, as of a miracle, he began to hear the Beatles whispering to him and urging him to call them in London. It is unfortunate that Manson evidently did not know that a helter skelter is a slide in an English amusement park.

"The girls say that at one point Manson placed a long-distance phone call to London to talk to the Beatles. There is no doubt that the song 'Helter Skelter' on the white Beatles double album is a masterful, insistent rock and roll number—and it is very weird sounding, especially the long final section which fades out twice at the end, sounding like a universal march of wrecked maniacs.

"'Charlie, Charlie, send us a telegram' was what he thought lay beneath the noise plexus of the composition 'Revolution No. 9'. It was felt that if one listened on headphones, one could hear the Beatles softly whispering just that. As it is, so be it. 'Rise! Rise! Rise!' Charlie would scream during the playing of 'Revolution No. 9' (which Manson associated with *Revelation*, Chapter 9). Later they wrote 'Rise' in blood on the La Biancas' wall.

"It is necessary to listen to the white Beatles double album to understand what Manson was hearing and seeking to hear. The album, as a whole, is of confusing quality. It has flashes of the usual Beatle brilliance, but it was produced at a time when the Beatles were locked in bitter quarrels and this is reflected in the album.

"The album has the song 'Piggies' of course, and, more creepily, a song called 'Happiness Is A Warm Gun'. Other songs like 'Blackbird', 'Rocky Racoon', etc., were interpreted strictly as racist doom songs".[12]

The Beatles, then, having whistled swiftly through acid, meditation, Zen, Hinduism and pop-Maoism, were bound, in their collective subconscious, to contain some of the messages Manson was getting from them, the climate of which "Maxwell's Silver Hammer" was the overt expression. Despite his association with the lunatic mesh of California blood cults like the Solar Lodge of the Ordo Templi Orientis, and the Kirké Order of Dog Blood, Manson's basic tenet that he, and indeed all enlightened people, were both Christ and Satan, that the artificial dichotomy between Good and Evil should be challenged by acts which fused them both, had rather more than respectable ancestry in Zen Buddhism, tantric ritual, the writing of de Sade, Nietzsche and William Blake. No fool, he was, as he claimed, "a very positive force" who collected "negatives". The revolutionary bloodbaths of France and Russia, the blood-mysticism of Russian Nihilism and African Mau-Mau, are not irrelevant by comparison. The old trick of dismissing the Devil as a fool can hardly be used on the man who said, "You people think with your mind. I do it differently. I've spent my life in gaol. I've stayed a child while you have grown up. I don't judge anyone. I judge only myself and I am content with myself. You want to put me in a penitentiary, but that is nothing. You kicked me out of the last one. I didn't want to go. I liked it there. And then children come at you with knives. You told them what to do. I didn't tell them. They're the children that you didn't want and I took them on my garbage dump."

Hunter Thompson's wild and hilarious chronicle of his current way of life is, from start to finish, an ironic, savagely self-deprecatory examination of the moral cul-de-sac in which we, left over from a revolution that went off at half-cock, flounder, with our casual hallucinations, our cynically contrived schizophrenia, our habitual sado-masochism, our inability to expect anything but violence, betrayal, and yet more violence; but this story, together with other fragments drifting over from the Coast, indicates a nightmare more fantastic than the Apocalypse could ever have been, a nightmare in which we lie and wait:

"I slumped on the bed. His performance had given me a bad jolt. For a moment I thought his mind had snapped that he actually believed he was being attacked by invisible enemies.

"But the room was quiet again. He was back in his chair watching 'Mission Impossible' and fumbling idly with the hash pipe. It was empty. 'Where's the opium?' he asked.

"I tossed him the kit bag. 'Be careful,' I muttered. 'There's not much left.'

"He chuckled. 'As your attorney,' he said, 'I advise you not to worry.' He nodded towards the bathroom. 'Take a hit out of that light brown bottle in my shaving kit.'

"'What is it?'

"'Adrenochrome,' he said. 'You won't need much. Just a *tiny* taste.'

"I got the bottle and dipped the head of a paper match into it.

"'That's about right,' he said. 'That stuff makes pure mescaline seem like ginger beer. You'll go completely crazy if you take too much.'

"I licked the end of the match. 'Where'd you get *this*?' I asked. 'You can't buy it.'

"'Never mind,' he said. 'It's absolutely pure.'

"I shook my head sadly. 'Jesus! What kind of monster client have you picked up this time? There's only one source for this stuff. . . '

"He nodded.

"'The adrenalin glands from a *living* human body,' I said. 'It's no good if you get it out of a corpse.' "[13]

"So now, less than five years later," says Thompson elsewhere, "You can go up on a steep hill in Las Vegas and look West, and with the right kind of eyes you can almost *see* the high water mark—that place where the wave finally broke and rolled back."[14]

"You are definitely menopausal," says Crane over his bowl of muesli. "Bacon an' fuckin' eggs. You gonna go on foulin' up ya system?"

"My father ate bacon and eggs, my grandfather ate bacon and eggs and so do I," I say and I mean it.

"Oh wow," says Crane.

"My father also bet on the gee-gees, drank ten pints of watery mild every day from a straight glass. My grandfather bred whippets and racing pigeons and my great grandfather won the bare knuckle contest at Pontefract Gala in 1896."

"Look homeward angel," says Crane, and belches.

"I eat bacon because I dig the taste. Good and salty. And I'd hate to get so fuckin' healthy I never got the sense of the saltiness of the world again —"

"Salt of the earth," says Crane and belches again.

"—So full of the harmony of things I never heard any of them good old funky sounds again—"

"Oh Snipe! Musical bacon already?"

And I, I don't reply. Because again I am curiously near tears.

"You know," says Crane. "You *are* a *motherfuckin'* sentimentalist. You are huggin' the earth like a character out of—out of—*Hemingway*. We got off the ground a coupla years back. We got *away*. We learned how to *fly*. Butcha can't fly if ya don't believe in flying."

"You can only properly fly when everybody gets off the ground with you. Solo flights are out. It's got to be the revolution."

"Yeah," says Crane, angry at last. "And you start the revolution by starting the flight. You show everybody *how*."

"Standing at their side."

"*No*. You, you, you fuckin' *square*."

"Yes."

"For Christ's sake why?"

"It's kinder."

Crane reels to the other side of the kitchen clutching his crutch as though in pain and the phone goes. Lindy.

"I quite fancy a bit o' comfort for once. Anyway, the cab needs cleaning."

"Twelve o' clock then. Watch the neighbours."

"Hoho! Child rapist. See ya."

Chapter Five

Lindy found the cab. Actually a massive Scammell with flat tyres and the engine missing, parked and forgotten in an almost inaccessible alley in Dean Village.

I was drunk after a gig. Those indigestible ninths and fourths, those deeply embattled discordant keys which turn the Pees as sour as last week's milk, were themselves embattled with twelve pints of Newcastle Brown somewhat to the northeast of the world as seen from my umbilicus. The consequent acts, indigestion being translated into misbehaviour, were likely to precipitate my speedy arrest. After instructing about three passers-by to go and dip their noses in shit I approached a matron at a bus stop, caressed her buttocks, told her she was the earth mother first, and then that she was a stupid fucking cow for not recognising a compliment when she received one. Lindy, at the head of the queue, on her way home from evening class, led me into an alley that the Leith Police might not visiteth us. We sat in the abandoned lorry until her combination of cool child's grace and hard-headed humour had sobered me. And then, at her verbal suggestion, I fucked her. She was twelve then. As wise as a rose.

After that the cab became a love nest. She papered it out with corny floral wallpaper samples and got little conical vases with plastic flowers which attached to the wall by suckers. She got cushions for the seats, a coloured rug for the petrol tank and painted faces on the dashboard dials. I got a padlock and bolted it to the driving door. There we managed to be something more than cosy.

But today Lindy wants to stretch out and so stretch out Lindy shall, all six-and-a-half stone of her; and the down that makes a continuous sheen across her belly on down the inside of her thigh shall celebrate the line of her repose.

I get rid of Crane at 11:30. At 11:37 Tom McGregor calls.

"Get yer fucken coat. We're goin' out," he says.

"I can't," I say.

"Ye can't afford to argu," says McGregor. "Shift!"

He sounds as though he's right and I wonder what he knows. I leave the door on the latch for Lindy and we go to the nearest pub.

McGregor is an Anarchist, a real one. He comes from Glasgow infrequently and he always goes back there. He claims to have been a childhood friend of Stuart Christie and who am I to argue. When I first met him in 1961 he was a Y.C.L. organiser. In '69 he was very busy with the Working People's Party of Scotland. Since then he has managed to fuse some of his many contradictory passions in the Solidarity movement. His biggest claim to distinction is, however, that he discovered the military explosives that were to be stolen for the activities of the Angry Brigade. The Angry Brigade remind me now of those many jazz combos called the All-Stars. Drawn from wildly varying persuasions and directions, All-Stars took name and status that seemed to indicate some permanence and common purpose. Having done that and laid down a few performances that were marred only by warring virtuosity they then dispersed back to the fertile ground from whence they came.

"Dundee," says McGregor, the beer dripping down his chin.

I have that swift feeling of panic you get when all the possibilities open up.

"Coincidence," I tell myself quickly.

"Coincidental with what?" says McGregor, hitting his consonants in fine old Glaswegian style. I envy McGregor his PPU badge. Surely as old as Aldermaston, the broken rifle is worn smooth and bright like a blazer button.

"Oh nothing," I say. "My mate Crane had a dream about Dundee."

"Well I bet a quid he didn't dream that the Man was due to disembark there next week."

"Next week?" I echo while my brain says "Coincidence. Coincidence" over and over to itself.

"Next fucken week, man."

"So?"

"So we've got to organise a demo fast."

"A demo? What for?" Why not have a circus? I really need to be floodlit when I do the deed. "Feel like a demo at Stonehenge?" I ask hysterically.

"Are ye stoned or something? Thes es serious."

"Look Mac, I've got to get back to the pad. You know, there's a bird coming round and—"

"Ah've come over frae Glasga tae talk to yu, cunt, and ye'll stay here an' talk. Ye can fuck yersel' to death after that."

"What's to talk about? I haven't been into demos for some time."

"Ah've been to listen to yer band a wee bit lately."

"I noticed."

"I like it. I'm pleased tae see ye've dropped all the middleclass hippie stuff. Nothing guid can come from America now."

"Yips and Weathermen?"

"Creations of the media. Ye don't mean to tell me . . ."

"Black Mask?"

"Ye'll be quotin' Marzalek next."

"Root of the Panthers —"

"Don't make me —"

"Anyway my music is more American than rock and roll. I play jazz."

"Ah well, the blacks can't properly be called—"

I don't really respond to these well-trodden paths of ethnic surmise. I interrupt: "Back to the demos."

"Well, I wis hopin' yer style o' music segnified a return to proper political activity instead of all this fuckin' aboot wi' drugs."

"You mean demos?"

"I mean participatory support as opposed to bourgeois individualism."

"Strange words for an anarchist. You'll not be short of support for fuck's sake. You know that, Mac. The middle class is ever ready to join impregnable hordes for the good of its conscience, never mind drugs and gobble-guitars. Get over to the University Union. The May 1st Group can't have moved onto double summertime just yet. There's the good old W.P.P. of Scotland and the International Marxist Group, or has the Blackburn halo tarnished?"

McGregor buries his big pale face in his hands and blows tiny bubbles between his enormous lips with a noise like an uneasy soda-syphon.

"And should an ex-member of the W.P.P.S. be able to bring himself to approach the heretics of the Maoist movement there may even be a tendril of the Communist Party of Great Britain Maoist League. Or failing that, the student flinch from greatness being what it is, the Communist Party of *Britain* Maoist League might be nurturing a fledgling plant."

"Fine irony Snipe. Yu've got an awfu' short memory. We nearly won, ye know."

"That 'nearly' might have been a damn sight nearer 'definitely' if you were a bit more certain of who you meant by we."

"We, Snipe, is always the working class."

"Oh right. Fine. Let us take ourselves down the docks then. Over to Grangemouth. Out to Cumbernauld. If the bickerings of the Socialist Labour League and the International Socialists drives you out of Trotsky's cooling shade you can try and warm up the remains of Keir Hardy with the Federation of Great Britain Marxist-Leninists or the Revolutionary Socialist League, or, fuckitall, why not? The Chartists."

"They'll be there. Don't yu worry yer heed."

"Oh great. And Trotsky revitalised by the Workers' Fight, maybe. And we haven't thought about the old grandaddy left, the C.P., Glasgow Y.C.L., Young Socialists, Young Liberals, Woodcraft Folk . . ."

"Snipe. Let me answer all this torrent of sheeite with one fact. This is first and foremost an anarchist demonstration."

"Oh, well now. International maybe. Black Cross? Black September?

No, never. Too messy. The Organisation of Revolutionary Anarchists though, I dare say, and maybe a contingent hot foot up the motorway from the League of London Anarchists. How do they get on with Solidarity? There must be some familiar faces on all sides."

"Don't throw sheeite at Auld friends."

"Indeed no, Mac. Now I wouldn't do that."

"It's an anarchist demo—"

"You mean all those others won't come? How unsporting—"

"And yu should be there."

"Why?"

"To show yer solidarity."

"With whom?"

"With the fucken anarchist movement."

"A wide field, Mac, very wide. But my solidarity is even wider than that. I identify with everybody and the only opposition to me finally, is God and Death."

"What the fuck does that mean?"

"Let me tell you a story." I glance at the clock behind the bar. I hope she waits, but not on the stair where the neighbours can see her slender pubescent figure and report me to the Welfare. "Do you remember the last of the big Grosvenor Square demos organised by Tariq Ali?"

"Bourgeois revisionist."

"W.P.P. S. jargon."

"Get on wi' yer tale."

"The I.M.G. split the march into two, the nonviolent going to Hyde Park for speeches and buns, and the violent going to the Square for a punch up that actually literally ended with the bloody but glorious demonstrators, calling themselves, for some reason, Maoists, and the bloody but glorious pigs, joining hands for Auld Lang fuckin' Syne, if you please—Remember?"

"Aye. I remember. Ye ken I remember. We wis together."

"After the demo we were together for the usual bevvy. When the march gathered on the Charing Cross embankment I was on my tod. Very much so. However I joined the so-called Maoists. Polemic has never really been my game. Tariq could go talk to the trees. I wanted blood. But I always wanted effect, so when the march reached the Aldwych it occurred to me that things would become nicely unmanageable if half the march turned up Kingsway and eventually entered the Square from the Park Lane side. Thus the police strategy might have been confused."

"Aye," says McGregor, Scottish disgust leaking from beneath his kilt, "Bourgeois individualism strikes again."

"Strategy," I say. "Common fuckin' sense. Like, is the point to get into the Embassy and wreck it? Do we attack the police cordon in order to get to the other side of it, or do we attack it because we like attacking police cordons—something to do til the rugby season starts? What was needed was an unplanned, unannounced, unexpected tactical march. But we don't want to do that, us demonstrators, do we? We've never wanted to do it, have we? I wonder fuckin'-well why."

"Es that yer story finished?"

"No, it's not finished. In order to achieve my strategy I ran back down the march, past the I.M.G., and the C.P.G.B.M.L. and the C.P.B. M.L. and the I.S. and the O.R.A. and the F.G. B.M.L. and the C.P. of Waltham Cross, Surbiton and Palmer's Green, until I arrived at the Socialist Labour League of the London School of Economics Banner—"

"Whit rhetoric. Half those organisations didn't exist in '69."

"They were there Mac, they were there. Familiar faces. Anyway, I, there, at that point, made my suggestion. 'Who are you?' says the tall blonde god with the flagpole. 'And what political organisation do you represent?'"

"And you said yu were an anarchist?"

"No, I said I was a human being."

"Meaningless slop."

"Wobbly slop."

"The Wobblies—oh Christ. They were Yanks. Antediluvian Yippies. They had no fucken notion of workin' class culture and how the movement must be rooted there."

"Historically, McGregor, the movement has its roots in the individualism of a few, not bourgeois, aristocrats. A Marquis and a Prince, no less."

"The roots of anarchism were planted by them in the garden of the working class. Workers' control."

"Ask Jimmy Reid about anarchism."

"Ask Stuart Christie about Jimmy Reid."

"Or better still ask Stuart Christie about Albert Melzer."

"I can tell you whit he'd say."

"Oh that's no fuckin' news. The point is, we're a bunch of theorists. Even on the march and in the battlefield we stop all operations to argue polemic."

"Politics has to start with polemic. That's why it's superior to capitalist pragmatism. Have the obvious faults in your own reasoning never occurred to you? You align yersel' wi' humanity one minute but I notice you live alone and follow yer own eccentric path. You preach solidarity on the left but you can't even work alongside yer auld mates. The polemical search for the right programme is something that has to be done thoroughly. People born into homes with few words win their words hard and they like to make sure they use 'em to say exactly what they mean. Bourgeois ambiguity and bourgeois hypocrisy, called, I believe, tact, isn't a thing a working man can 'hide behind—or even fucken want to."

"Politics has to start with root moral convictions. It's the superficial moral questions we bicker about, and so become divided and ineffectual. In '68 it was pretty good. Pretty marvellous. The high point of the whole thing. Hunter Thompson says he can see the crest of the wave from Las Vegas. The crest of the wave was at Nanterre. Hippies, communists, anarchists, and the French working class, not asking any questions but getting on with the job. They had a revolution there beyond Lenin's wildest dreams. They scrawled no cant about bread and potatoes on the walls of Paris. They scrawled poetry; Breton, Lautreamont, Eluard. It was, briefly, a revolution about vision. Not about making the best of what we've got, but about the invention of the impossible by imagination and art and wild love. Now I am such a miserable old bastard these days that I might be called something of an authority about why that revolution failed. Through dope and idleness and false concepts of history and freedom, but my spinster within is always ready to shut up when one and all are prepared to acknowledge that we are all about the achievement of perpetual orgasm on earth and the sharing of the materials that the earth provides to that end."

"Ye're fucken sex mad."

"What buggered the revolution of '68 then? They started talking and they started to bicker and they finished up playing that old Trots and Commies game whereby you waste so much venom on your nearest cousins you've got none left for the pigs."

"Yu still havena done yer readin' have ya. Party programmes and revolutionary theory will only weaken by association with deviationist elements."

"And it's always the other poor sods who are deviating. Revolution will only happen through concentration on the main issues, strategy for those issues, and ultimate numerical power. Now if your demo—Oh piss off."

And I suddenly see that I've been conned back into that endless Wednesday night front-parlour harangue of the British left and hunger even for Crane and his dope-shrouded lunacy. And I relish briefly, for the first time, how the gun is going to feel, nice and heavy in my pocket like a bag of gold. And I need to get to Lindy quickly to touch the thread of quicksilver that forgives my fallibilities.

I mumble my excuses and go. I carry the image of McGregor still stamped on my mind. Black donkey jacket. Patched levis. Khaki fatigue cap. Woolly beard and one ear-ring. Filthy striped football shirt. Blue eyes. His head shaking pityingly.

Chapter Six

Crane is standing in the kitchen. He has returned from the Post Office where he has collected a cheque. He has cashed his cheque and bought a bottle of Glenfiddich. He has drunk a quarter of the bottle, which he holds in one hand. He has taken the elastic band out of the bun into which he knots his hair, so that it falls in Bohemian splendour over his shoulders. He is wearing a grubby tee shirt with a picture of Mr. Natural on the chest. He is wearing a pair of green sailor-front loons crumpled around his ankles. His massive penis is erect and it is filling the gentle palm of Lindy. His free hand is inserted into the front of Lindy's dark blue school knickers.

"Hey man, you didn't tell me about this," Crane chortles.

I am not immediately able to reply. I am dealing with the fact that the walls suddenly breathed and shifted, glittering with scales, as though we were trapped between the bellies of four standing, breathing reptiles. And I am dealing with the fact that half a pint of McEwan's bitter has suddenly flooded back into my mouth in a convulsion of total rejection whereby one not only refuses the evidence of one's senses but regurgitates the contents of one's stomach as well. This I spill out onto the kitchen floor quickly and gladly. Further, I am meeting the sad grave eyes of Lindy and assessing the fact that, sad and grave though they may be, there is not a shade of apology in them.

"I'll be in the other room," I say. I go into the other room and play the first phrase of "Sweet Lorraine" over and over to myself on the piano.

After a while Crane comes in and sits on the divan. "Man," he says. "You should see your fuckin' face." He screams. Laughing.

"Man," he goes on, "I think this maybe hasta be a duel. Yep. I think this really hasta be flick-knives at dawn. I mean, man, I don't know what came over me. Like you are my best friend Snipey, and fuck, the last thing a man can ever do is—" Crane's voice breaks in giggles "—stick a coupla fingers up the cunt of his best friend's girl. Like fuckit man. It was the giddiness that came over me man, and when my head cleared there was this smegma all over my—"

There is an aluminium box on the piano containing cocaine. It has been on the piano ever since I last sniffed cocaine about eighteen months ago. I throw the box at Crane's head. Crane yelps and holds his face in his hands. There is blood running over one eye.

"Giddy spell Number Two," I say.

"Okay," says Crane. "Okay. Now that's how it happens. Some mother claims something. Some other guy uses it. The guy that has to own things finds that the suction pump he uses for a heart is wounded within. He that bleeds within hasta make the other fucker bleed without. It's still the same old story—" Crane sings. "*But*," says Crane. "We wrote finish to it five or six years ago and *you have forgotten*."

"Touch Lindy again," I say, "and I'll kill you."

"Oh yeah, I know you will. I know. It ain't one another we supposeta be killin', softhead."

Lindy comes in. She laughs a little at Crane's blood. "Serves ya right, ya dirty old bugger," she says. Then to me: "But you don't own me Snipe, nobody owns me. And you don't own sex. It's not that wee a thing."

"You gave yourself to me," I say.

"We loaned ourselves to it," she says. "Together, of course."

"No," I say. "It has to be rarer. It has to be more than phenomenon. You can't live like that. There's more."

"I've fuckin' well got to live like that," she says.

She has a whiff of the Doubleyoo El. The middle-class women have got to her. Those whose husbands are truly idle, who therefore believe that the entire male population is realising itself and getting its rocks off on the shop floor at the expense of the poor raddled wives, have whispered in Lindy's downy mouse's ear. And it must be another time, away from Crane with his hands smelling of young cunt and his breath smelling of Henry Miller, some other place where I tell Lindy that in the beginning was the sky and the earth, and the sky god was called Tiw and had a high soaring prick, and the earth god was called Freya, who had a dark loamish cunt, and Tiw was all risk and pomp and pathetic gambles. Tiw was always attempting to fly. And Freya was always preparing the ground, on which she knew he must fall, with soft herbs and ferns and roses. And Tiw was all mouth and trousers and piss and vinegar. And Freya was solid as the very rock and warm as the mud.

Tiw resented the seasons. They made him cold when he reached high altitudes. They made him hot when he cut down jungles. The seasons drew the flesh and blood out of the pit of Freya every month as the moon dragged the brine across the mountains of the seabeds. She was friendly to the seasons. She was the seasons.

So from these fundamental divisions, earth from sky, sea from land, man from woman, there came the myths and the morals to celebrate these fundamentals. Tenderness, with its poetry of flowers and subtlety, with its smiles and silences and soft, moist places, became a necessary aspect of any human activity, and it was women who did it best. Dynamism and will, with its poetry of form, of wood and metal, of energy fractures and invincible muscle, became another necessary aspect of human activity, and it was men who did that best.

And men learned how to tend sick children and women how to kick like stallions at their tenth orgasm, but the qualities, the central climate of these opposite feelings remained in the opposite genitalia.

The human activity that took most fully of these opposite qualities was love, because love was the roof under which the opposites met in ecstasy and fusion. And because love was how the subsequent young had to be treated.

Thus men like Titian and Rembrandt and Shakespeare and Beethoven, and Rubens and Blake and Picasso and Louis Armstrong knew that a *fullness* had been achieved that matched the quality of ripe corn and summer orchards. This, love, was the technique of positivity.

And I shall tell Lindy how, in a threatening time in a threatening society, the earth and the sky are seen to be threatening. So the behaviour that takes place on earth, under the sky, is seen as a mere role, an imposition. All conditions cease to be opportunities and become cruel limitations. One's flesh is not a palace but a prison. The earth is an anvil and the sky a hammer. One's children are parasites, warble flies, tape worms. One's parent is one's overseer, one's torturer. One's interrogator-lover seeks to be one's father. Intercourse, unless done purely for one's own crude pleasure, is oneself being used. Love is possession and oppression.

Everyone in such a time is after freedom from love, from lover, from family, from parents, from birth, from menstruation, from flesh, from the earth, the sky, from life.

And Women's Lib, poor bourgeois virgins that they are, have convinced themselves that Nigel, with his car, his secretary, his expense account, and his mysterious afternoons at the golf club, rigged the whole damn show. Lindy, who lives in a council flat in Leith, should know better.

"Like, why don't she move in?" says Crane. "Your bed'll take three. We could start a fuckin' commune man."

Chapter Seven

The only light in the cab is from Adelaide. Lindy left the apartment and I spent twelve hours sinking heavy and imagining myself in a confrontation with William Bloom. Bloom has been around the scene for years. Lately he's taken to writing soft porn in which his detestable narcissism is given full rein to trample across his political and creative pretensions. His heroes are opportunist little shits shagging their way into situations of petty dominion, self-congratulatory cartoons from the world Jenny Fabian described to Johnny Byrne in *Groupie*, the hordes of handsome and despicable bisexuals who crawled across the scene like larvae as soon as the media made it a paying proposition. I have hammered Bloom into the ground in seven different bars, tortured Crane to death twice, slept six uneasy hours, and here I am, sober but shaky, drinking in the light from Adelaide.

Adelaide is one of the handful of gas streetlights remaining in Edinburgh. She throbs and splutters on her bracket down at the end of the alley. Her light is green as the fronds of riverweeds under troutwater. Her light is a dim church, a place defined by the sphere she casts that is coloured by bad gas as church light is coloured by bad glass.

And Lindy's body is a shoal of Christian fish swimming in ovals of luminous and moving muscle. Through the Adelaidian shallows, motes of fish-light flashed shyly from Aladdin lanterns in a night dim with smoke of a dying sexual carnival.

Her moist and whimpering rodent having lapped the white from me is shooting coils and lines of red musk down the green stream, moisture glistening quartz on thighs like saplings rising from the shadowed shores and sinking in the midstream catching stars to drown them.

"Lind," I am saying, "O my love . . ."

And "Snipe" she says, her hand, in love, afraid of the wild space of love it's called on to define.

And so I tell her then about the sky and the earth and William Bloom and she says "Yes. But what about Lindy and Snipe. It's you I love Snipe, better than the fuckin' sky."

"Because of the sky."

"And then, in love, I think it may well be I am the earth. But I'm something I must use Snipe. When I drive down on your cock it's the movement of the earth and all that stuff, but it's my decision. Aren't you just a wee bit talking about the Life you call so fake and forgetting the Imagination you rate so high? Now if I'm to remember Imagination, Snipe, I'm going to be a fucken teapot."

"This isn't a teapot sort of time."

"I just changed it. Have a cup of tea," she says and, crouching suddenly, pisses all over my chest.

"It's a teapot," she says. "I've been a teapot all along."

"It's a church," I say. "A ladychapel."

"Now Snipey, it's a poor wee place that has but one use. It's a drag of a person that has but one mood. Tomorrow I'll be a fucken tornado and you'd better learn how to fly and swim. And if you're such an inventive artist isn't it a bit more inventive to pray in a teapot than in a church?"

"I don't care what you call it. I revere it. Anybody who doesn't can't see it properly."

"Properly?" she smiles.

Adelaide likes the pisstide. With cheap glass jewels she likes it. Lindy smiles on.

"Now," she says, "our commune wi' Crane."

She's wiped my chest with a dozen Kleenexes and is crosslegged now on the petrol tank, smoking a cigarette.

"Your ma's going to really dig it," I say. "And you really fancy Crane?"

"I don't love Crane, Snipe. Crane is Pepsi-Cola and you're guid wine, but there's fuck-all wrong wi' Pepsi when a lass's a bit thirsty maybe."

"And that's why you like communes. What about ma?"

"Ma mither's nae business likin' or no likin' communes. Ma mither's thirty six an' she's seven bairns and varicose veins and a nasty cough. The peak of her life is Bingo, and a black eye, roughly twice a year, is the peak of passion she draws from me father. An' she's a lively woman still, fine bones and fond of a fuck."

"In a commune she'd be sackcloth and ashes in a year, I've seen 'em. High breasted neosquaws withered in their kaftans with dope, birth pills, abortion and lovelessness."

"Ma mither—"

"Your mother, my archangel of the twilight, is worn down by seven kids and no money. The back of your father's hand doesn't help. But she is sustained by the depth of her relationships—intertwining psychic roots. Your mother might be pathetic but she's dignified with it. She's decent."

"Decent? She'd sleep with anybody."

"But one man she shags continuously."

"The man that pays the bills and breaks her nose."

"Your father. The father. The man isn't the pivot finally. The pivot is you and your siblings."

"What in the fuck's a sibling?"

"But in communes, my star of the impermissible, the great thing, the really great thing is that there ain't no pivot, no anchor, no constant."

"*Right.*"

"Kids are denied this function. Consequently they become little banshees screaming for identity."

"What kid wants it?"

"Every kid needs it."

"I need me mither and father scrattin' each ither's souls oot because o' me? Like a pain in the arse I need it."

"Pains in the arse are sometimes informative. Yes."

"Yes whit?"

"Yes, you need it. If the commune thing had really ever got off the ground, which it didn't—like it's old hat already—*Scandinavian* old hat—the earth would be full of kids, well maybe not abandoned kids, but kids whose relationship range was shallow in the extreme."

"Who wants a deep relationship?"

"Nobody chooses one. Everybody, being in total control, wants things cool. But while things are kept cool by the moment they get fucking hot by the year."

"Oh Snipe, what are you saying now?"

"If you refuse the extremity of the moment, keeping your cool, the extremities gather, pile up unspent, and you find yourself maintaining an inappropriate *sangfroid* on top of a stockpile of unresolved emotions. Cool assumes that everything's okay. If things over a period of time haven't been kept right they are very wrong and then cool is a silly thing to be."

"And what's this to do wi' communes?"

"Well a rota of duties on the kitchen wall is no real compensation for those deep-seated identities granted by the job that has to be done by you and you alone when there's nobody else who can, who *cares*, to do it. In a commune you can pass the buck when the rota moves round. But *in love* with your others the buck won't pass. Your guts aren't quiet until you and only you have done the job that only you can do. And because your mother has always satisfied her dictatorial vitals in this respect she is, triumphantly, a woman with fine bones still fond of a fuck. I've seen commune princesses sewing up their labia. Literally."

Lindy laughs. Well there are some bizarre images around and the sewn-up cunt is one.

"They'd get some awfu' drastic obstructions," she says.

Laughing we finish the rest of Crane's Glenfiddich until it's time to send Lindy back to the lady with fine bones.

Walking whistling out of the Adelaidian streetlight. The Man steps out of an entry and opens his overcoat. She kicks him in the crotch and walks on. The Man is asleep in the other seat, a purple hole in the middle of his forehead. Border patrols are shining a torch into the cab.

We are driving down the motorway, Lindy and I, the plastic flowers nodding in their conical vases. The Man is standing by a petrol station, thumbing. I stop to pick him up and the sten guns blast from the high shoulder and the bridge. The Man is calling to me across a busy road in Birmingham. "Fascist!" he screams. "God damn Fascist!"

Chapter Eight

If you play the changes of "Basin Street Blues" (or "Gimme A Pigfoot" or a dozen and more of those old TOAB Vaudeville Circuit numbers from the boozy adolescence of jazz) you can take the tonic third as a pedal note and play the whole song around it. That is, in fact, the rich structure of "Basin Street Blues", the reason why it bounced Armstrong and Teagarden into such tautly related arpeggios, the reason why it is a standard still yielding something, even unto me and my clutch of manic depressives. We started using songs almost as soon as we formed. All of us had been playing what Benny Green calls rubbish, which is to say free, or, more precisely, in the chromatic style of Ornette Coleman and Archie Shepp. All that public orgasm had cleared the air the overused corners of Tin Pan Alley, so that, as the fumes of the orgy cleared, actual tunes and songs and ditties, remaining in the dawn, appeared with a combination of freshness and familiarity that restored their usefulness.

So "Pilp", the first of the Pees, starts with the Basin Street chord sequence and uses a structure which meanders as far from the tonic third as possible without losing it.

My band is called the Queen Victoria Jazz Band because the pub where we play is a tiled floor with four brown-panelled walls and a glass ceiling called the Queen Victoria. The merest noise we make rings round this mausoleum with apocalyptic splendour. I have a bassplayer, a saxophonist who plays alto most of the time, a clarinettist, and I play the piano.

The bass player has a broken finger on his left hand and is called Sam. The alto player has a wart on his upper lip and is called Eddie. The clarinettist has watery eyes and is called Tristram. Tristram is of noble birth.

When we play "Pilp" I play the note, over and over again. Sam plays the chords, the good old corny chords with a bow. Eddie plays on the scale of the key note which is B Flat and Tristram plays on the scale of the note I'm playing, the tonic third which is D. The effect is one of two melodic lines which are mathematically connected but aesthetically discordant. There are no solos when we play "Pilp."

Eddie plays lyrically, even sentimentally. He can make a sax sound like a Jerome Kern melody played by Paganini. Tristram plays with a sound like the squeak of rubber on glass. His great inspiration is the near-forgotten Chicago clarinettist, Frank Teschemacher, and he listens to the intonations of "Pierrot Lunaire" ceaselessly. He is about as melodic as the meths drinkers giving song in the Grassmarket on a Saturday afternoon.

We usually clear the saloon bar in about fifteen minutes but we have been known to do it in five.

After about three weeks in a pub it is usual for the landlord to ask us not to come back. In the past we have been known as the Crown Jazz Band, Fairley's Jazz Band, the Black Diamond Jazz Band, the White Feather Jazz Band and the McCallum's, Campbell's and Bob's Bar Jazz Band. The landlord of the Queen Victoria has a vast collection of bagpipe records, an adjustable hearing-aid and a photograph behind the bar of himself standing with an arm round Sandy Brown, the distinguished Scottish clarinettist. As a consequence of all these possessions he has allowed us to stay at the Queen Victoria an extraordinarily long time, sometimes applauding us with whoops and a stamping of the left foot that would be more appropriate at the Highland Games.

We think we sound okay. Crane does not.

"So we'd better cruise over to Dundee tomorrow, case the scene, yeah?" He fidgets, looking around the empty bar.

"Dundee's a front," I say. "Your midnight ESP was in fact a Glasgow rumour picked up when you were enjoying the fruits of your shopping over there the other day. It must be a front."

"Listen Aunt Jemima, my voices are right voices. When do we get the roscoes?"

"Oh," I say. "You can catch 'em anywhere. Some of the nicest girls—"

"Yeah yeah. Dig this Grimaldi." Crane is getting shirty again. He has suffered a lot. The scar over his left eye, "Pilp", and now revolutionary frivolity. "I wanna just ask you this. All this shit about the eternal original polarity of the sexes, the nuclear family, the straightsville in which your heterosexual pedals paddle, does it not extend to *nice noises*?"

"Well man, I've *heard* of cunts that could sing—"

"I mean on one hand, man, you are *refusing* to fly with the gods because everything is human invention, you say, and there ain't no gods and there ain't no eternity. On the other hand somebody gets a little inventive with their gender or their sex life and you call down the big Nordic fertility gods, all them dark hairy old motherfuckers from Germany and Scandinavia who were already fucked up with icebergs up their assholes before the world began. Now where is it now, you mother? Make that work like you say your goddam awful music works. No. Correction. Make it work better than that, man, *much* better than that."

"Birth, love and death have been around longest," I say. "Artaud and Burroughs have attacked them by *refusing* them. They will probably go. There's no reason why they shouldn't. It's certainly possible. But I—I shall kiss them goodbye. You know what we just played?"

"Shit."

"No. Basin Street Blues."

"Oh wow. Why not play a little something really wild like—say 'Land of Hope and Glory'?"

When the Queen Victoria Jazz Band reassembles I announce that we are going to play "Pleep", another original composition. It is a romping number in 6/8 time with a music hall piano part. The alto and clarinet play the theme in unison for fifteen measured minutes. The theme is "Mr Tambourine Man". Crane throws beer mats.

I thought up "Pleep". I thought up "Pilp". Eddie thought up "Plup" and Sam wrote "Ploop". Tristram is still struggling with an idea called "The Discovery Of Victoria Falls After A Particularly Heavy Downfall of Rain". Inspired, he claims, by McGonigall, Satie and Dick. Bentley. He can call it what he likes in his own festering mind but when it is complete I shall announce it as "Plop". Each of us did each idea alone and each of us does what the composer wants. The composer gives us lots of space, as I've described. Each composer compels us to take more liberties than most jazzers do when left to themselves. But that muddy, comfy, mean average of the collectively improvising collective subconscious is something we avoid, having, as jazz musicians, narrowly escaped with our lives.

Not that collective or communal art is discard-able in our opinion. Village fetes, ceremonies, customs, national costumes and New Orleans jazz all have their special karma, as Crane would put it, just like Lindy's Pepsi pokes, but the mean average is not so much an occasional merit as an absolute necessity, defining the exercise. He who fucks around with his national folk costume destroys the tradition, and, like he who departs from any custom or ritual, betrays the community. In the strict critique applied to New Orleans jazz Louis Armstrong and Sydney Bechet were proven to be downright bad blowers.

So the merits of the communal in art are bought dear at the price of conformity, self-effacement, and a carefully contrived mediocrity. Equality, mutual construction, trust and communal love are coins each with a negative flip side called creative cowardice, overdependence and that thick democratic glue that blunts the sharper knives of romantic love.

Selfless souls with humble eyes and patient hands there may well be in the well-dressing and the Maypole dancing of the ages, but there are also refugees who hide in the community from the demanding searchlight of their own imaginations, soothing their creative consciences with the self-congratulation attendant on this aesthetic do-gooding. Thus a deeper betrayal occurs. Men deliberately refuse their possibilities.

"And" I say to Crane, "as cowardly artists hide in communal art, so cowards hide in communes."

"Weak people come to communes, man, for succour. Wounded people. People fucked up by the straights. They come to be helped to revive."

"Cowards," I bawl, a little pissed. "You wanna help 'em? Chuck the fuckers out."

Chapter Nine

I don't always play the Pees. That curious rigour we apply in the Queen Victoria Jazz Band, of absolute individual sovereignty, of absolute discipline, of exact non-sense (non-sense being what you do to language forms to make them geometric) I sometimes come away from, backpedalling into one tradition or another to rest where the standards are established and the methods safe. It is weak but pleasant to do this, to play a little swing or a little New Orleans jazz, or perhaps even a little Schubert or Mozart. There's a coming home feeling. One can hear applause, even deep affection. Someone always says "Why don't you do this all the time instead of messing about with all that shit down at the Queen Victoria?"

And the people most likely to do this are those younger people who have given the spearhead of the avant-garde back to international Marxism, believing themselves to be carving out the spirit of the seventies when all they manage is a caricature of the late fifties, young people who therefore look to art for pleasure.

"Hedonists," I say thickly into Lindy's pixie-sized tit.

"What's a hedonist?"

"People who live for their own pleasure. Contrast David Bowie with Bob Dylan. Or Bob Dylan with Allen Ginsberg. Or Allen Ginsberg with William Burroughs."

"I only ever heard o' the first two."

"You only want to know the first two. It's a slow fall from a man with such an acute moral sense his only pleasure is relief, to a man so bereft of any moral sense his only belief is pleasure."

"That's Bowie?"

"Hedonists, him and Lou Reed. Arch hedonists."

"It's a sad kind of hedonism," and, her Scottish dockland tongue rather hilariously attempting the adored subtopian whine, Lindy sings one of Bowie's songs about dreams and breakthroughs, about lovers left drained by love, about lovers alone in landscapes from which all colour has faded, about lovers smiling in the dark, wan children too wise for terror, weary of world-weariness, succoured by love so sterile it offers nothing better than guilt and apology for guilt. She sings a song with a ruthless insight into emotional bankruptcy.

"*Don't believe in yourself,*" I quote back. "*Don't deceive with belief. Knowledge comes with death's release. 0 Heavenly Father I have sinned but look where I've bin. It's making me lazy . . .*"[15]

"*Oh my and what shall we wear, oh my and who really cares,*"[16] sings Lindy.

"*I do what I want and I want what I see. It only happens to me,*"[17] I sing.

Lindy switches back to Bowie. This time she sings of cold refusals, of consolations no wise child can accept, of immunity to the fond, corrective parental gesture on the part of those who understand exactly the nature of what is being undergone.

"Set it against this," I say.

"*The motorcycle black madonna two wheeled gypsy queen*
And her silver studded phantom caused the grey flannel
dwarf to scream
As he weeps to wicked birds of prey who pick up on
his bread crumb sins
And there are no sins inside the gates of Eden."[18]

But Lindy is as pert as her mouse tit. Bowie has an admonitory song for Robert Zimmerman, one for a general who quit his troops, a seer and a bard who has allowed his inspiration to run so dry the children are left voiceless, trying to fill the gap where Dylan once croaked revolutionary facts, with slogans and graffiti. Even handicapped by her harsh Scottish vowel sounds Lindy imitates the voice well enough to show the longing, the nostalgia for a lost optimism that flared too brightly and too briefly.

I wince. "Hedonist?" asks Lindy. "Open yer fucken ears."

"Okay. So Bowie's permitted to say something. The kids will take art from Bowie. Why?"

"Well—It's mebbe because he's sae pretty while he's at it."

I bite Lindy on the nipple, hard. "Do you think I should play pop, or c. and w., or r. and b., or Cow and Gate or—"

"I think you should be happy," says Lindy, a dark dream against the green waters of Adelaide. "About that I'm *very* serious."

So with the Man's shade scarcely faded from the seat where we sprawl, and the bag of gold in my pocket becoming, once again, a gun, I love Lindy, who dwells where happiness still exists. I love Lindy and I seldom play with Hamish Menzies.

Hamish is a clarinettist with whom I played in my very first jazz band fifteen years ago. At that time we were both students at London University. Hamish has a mustache, a centre parting, a pipe, a Fair Isle pullover, sleeveless, and a shiny tie. As I went wailing into the subculture, so Hamish went where his father had always been, into Courier House, Dundee, the home of D.C. Thompson Publications, where he works as a reporter on *The Sunday Post*. I cannot hate a man who works on *The Sunday Post*. Nor can I hate a man who plays clarinet *exactly* like Johnny Dodds. Nor can I hate a man whose weighty Toryism dissolves in the face of personal loyalty, even to the point of supplying me with information that will lead to the assassination of the Man.

So, having despatched Crane on his morning shopping expedition, an increasingly difficult one, as the Glaswegian merchants, displaying that tacit code of the Underground, use blackmail underlined with a blow or two of the open hand in order to raise the price by 50% on every deal, thus necessitating that Crane should find a different merchant on every foray, I am seated on the shuttle train to Dundee.

I am cancelling the growing moral panic that besets my guts as the moment draws nearer, by submerging my mind in the beauty of the coast, when I see Jack Howell. He is puffing up the central aisle through the carriages, his eyes and hair wild and his cruelly twisted mouth just as near his right ear as it ever was

Nobody ever asked Jack about his mouth but it's clear that the muscles on one side ceased working at some early stage in his young career, leaving the muscles of the other side free to pull it as far round to the right as stretched skin would allow. And Jack has developed the personality to go with the wolfish anguished grimace thus achieved.

Isolated from any lasting affair not so much by ugliness as by the desperation he brings to love through his horror at his own appearance, detesting himself to a point where self-destruction is his only perverse way of loving himself, and somehow, in all this, harbouring the irony that his ruthless intelligence casts over his own miserable situation, he sees the world properly, through a vast panoramic window of pain; and thus he approaches his politics properly by throwing everything he can at the window in an attempt to break it.

I love Jack. The last thing I want to do is involve him in the plot. He sits down opposite me.

"In this together Snipey," he says.

"Who told you?"

"I went to see Ian in Notting Hill Gate. He told me Crane had come up here for some mysterious purpose that doesn't take much guessing at. I'd just got off the London train at Waverley Station when I saw you."

"Oh shit," is the best that I can find to say.

Jack laughs that wild mirthless bray. "Crane's a cunt, man. You can't do it with Crane. Now listen. Here's how we do it. I hang around the hotel lobby. Act nervous, dig? Focus attention on me. Build it up. Finally I take the lift to the nth floor where the Man's room is. I am carrying a brown paper parcel. It contains a home made bomb. They arrest me and question me while you go and do the deed."

"You just want to get your mouth knocked straight."

Jack's pale wild eyes glaze over with tears and then blink angrily clear. "Right?"

I don't reply. I merely wish to Christ I could stop this internal weeping and wish that instead of killing the Man I could kill that grim old spinster marshalling me on through my days, with her dead-eyed pessimism and her contractual decisions.

As the train rattles merrily across Scotland, Howell talks merrily of despair. Since he was a very young fan of a band I used to run in Coventry Jack has gradually grown paternalistic towards me. Besides two years of heroin addiction he has something like six suicide attempts behind him. Far from being the usual pity-gambits, Jack's suicides were private and secret and unsuccessful. After the fourth I noticed the badly healed scars on his wrist one night while he was fixing. "Oh I'm sorry Snipey," he said. "It's alright. Don't be upset."

I still have a letter from him which he wrote in '69: "You're such a fucking kid Snipe. All you older faces are kids. Kidcats. Oh never mind. I mean you still think, *you still think*, you're going to make people into that shining ideal that never was. I mean it's a joke and young people can see it's a joke and they're right.

"'Wanna hear a good one?'

"'Yes.'

"'Well there was this ideal, right? He used to be kind to everybody and only screw women he wanted kids by, and he used to believe that he would get better all the time if he tried hard enough and that he was gonna save the world'.

"'So?'

"'So he was right and everything came out right in the end.'

"'Oh no !' Big fall about. I actually got a laugh with that one at a party the other night. I'll defend you to the end Snipe because you're so damn sad and sadness is always worth defending. But you can't lay it on us Snipe. I live by the flash of the pain in my guts. All. I hope for is that the last moment, which is every moment for me, will be *complete*; that is, *completely* destructive *completely* final. We live in the strength that comes from perpetually confronting our own suicide. We have a kind of sick pride because we don't cling to any love of life on a wrong basis, or visions of Jesus Normal coming into his millennium. The only millennium is the white flash and the red pain that comes from knocking your head against the gate of oblivion non-stop—and the complete black velvet of oblivion on the other side: WE ARE THE OUTLAWS: WE DEFY LAW AND ORDER WITH OUR BRICKS BOTTLES GARBAGE LONG HAIR FILTH OBSCENITY DRUGS GAMES GUNS MIKES FIRE FUN AND FUCKING: WE ARE THE FORCES OF CHAOS AND ANARCHY: WE ARE EVERYTHING THAT WE SAY WE ARE AND WE ARE PROUD OF IT. WE ARE OBSCENE LAW LESS HIDEOUS DANGEROUS DIRTY VIOLENT AND YOUNG.'[19]

" 'Or Ginsberg. Remember Ginsberg: They saw it all! the wild eyes! the holy yells! They bade farewell! They jumped off the roof! to solitude! waving! carrying flowers! Down to the river! into the streets!'[20]

" 'Or Dylan, always Dylan: 'Darkness at the break of noon shadows even the silver spoon. The hand made blade, the child's balloon, eclipses both the sun and moon. To understand you know too soon there's no sense in tryin' . . .[21]

" 'All our singers are priests who scream with bitter joy in the faces of those, even you, who can't face death, who seek to immortalise themselves in absolute principle . . .' "

The letter rambled on into a dream of maternal cannibalism.

He talks now: "—this chick. Like shit and blood all round the room and we made it. Born again into complete ineptitude. Crawling about in wild times, babytimes at the other side of arsehole repressions, pre-identity, pre-ego. Smiled at me, that long off-to-one-side knowing smile of grace that she smiled through all shit and stench and wreckage of that room, and the hotel manager comes busting in, his feet crunching on the chick's spike. Animals, worse than dogs, the dogs in the street and so on and so on. And then no food for three days. Rain. Ouch. What a fuckin' giggle . . ."

Oh I love you Howell. How the hell did it fail with wisdom and energy like yours? How did all you pained kids leap over the edge of experience and not come back with the magic powers you thought you had, you should have had? Why is even Howell now superceded by a generation who can take the risks and the leaps with such dulled spirits that they convert even those landscapes of hell into a grey and cloistered room, kids to whom the most savage sunset is, like all else, a dull wet Sunday afternoon, really? Why don't you go away Howell? You fan sparks in fires from which the broth pot has been shifted.

We steam across the silvery Tay and I explain to Jack that I am going to see Hamish and get the knowledge and that I will report back to him. We arrange a date and a time as we get off the train and who should be there to meet us?

Chapter Ten

"What kinda game are you playin', motherfucker?" asks Crane. "And who is this soul brother here? Major Hoople?"

"Hi Snipe," says Tippet. Mojo Tippet I have slowly grown to know and detest. Swarthy in the best underground tradition of negro-semitic good looks, his hair as short as a skinhead's, cropped down from the Angela Davis Afro cut he wore the last time I saw him, he cuts an impressive figure on this dour provincial railway station. As clearly as his style and demeanour once proclaimed, "I am wild and visionary and delinquent and can hardly stop myself from playing the bongoes," it now proclaims, "After a decade of orgy and debauch I have reached that high cold plain of enlightenment from which a purposeful revolution must be wisely and coolly conducted." In fact he wears the insignia to which Jack is entitled, but in which Jack would have no interest at all, very much as an officer's mess fop of a hundred years ago might have worn the red and gold of his uniform. Peacock feathers for the impotent.

"Mojo showed just afta you left. We came along on his wheels. He gonna tie up the Salisbury end."

"The what?"

"Well, we gotta have music at Stonehenge. Mojo and his band—the Juvenile Delinquents—a real groove, yeah?"

Mojo drags on a hand-rolled licorice paper cigarette as though it were a joint. "Deal me in," he says from his chest without exhaling. His voice sounds like Ginger Baker's. One of those smoky respiration-economy croaks.

"Looks like you're dealt in," I say, aiming it straight between Crane's eyes. Jack is laughing silently behind my left shoulder.

Mojo smiles one of those indulgent beams that he intends to be shot through and through with endearing urchin charm and mischief. "Right, baby," he says. "Right."

We go and drink beer in the nearest pub, all of us that is but Tippet who drinks coffee and then coke, sneering at the tea lady when she registers her disbelief at a non-drinking man.

"Yes Co-ca-Co-lah," he mouths. "Like they 'ave in England." And then "Man, where are these peasants *at*?" as he sits down.

I don't know why Tippet is here unless he's going to sell the inside story to *Rolling Stone* under a fake name. Tippet has always been a great man for standing next to the most active man on the scene until the cameras come along. Then Tippet stands *in front* of the most active man on the scene. His first self-appointed job was playing guitar in the office of the *International Times*. He showed considerable perspicacity here. *IT*, dope, and electronic pop were not at that time fashionable but they were shortly to be very fashionable indeed and, as vultures herald death, so Mojo's presence heralded that Underground death that comes with fashion.

Apologetic at that time about his abysmal ignorance in the fields of literature, jazz and politics, he was, as the newshounds profiled him and as the cameras snapped him, anxious to ignore these areas as irrelevant, dragging into the limes with him the meretricious panoply of clothes and pop and pot.

Since then, his nose ever to the wind, he has donned and discarded terms like hippie, Yippie, White Panther, and social deviant as fast as the changing hang of his jeans. He is, in fact, straight out of William Bloom's tales of love and opportunism. His most recent project has been the writing and publishing, about a year too late, of a British *Do It*, the pics and revolutionary fervour somewhat clouded by the in-group sour grapes creeping into the British version of anything.

And I, I am by no means free of the sourest fruits of the harvest as I sit in a dark, cold Scottish boozer regarding Tippet in the jungle apparel that befits his present stance of modish militancy.

One thing I have determined upon. Tippet, however well it should serve our purpose, is not going to jail for this plot, from whence to howl his howls of self-important self-pity.

I explain about my "source of information" without mentioning Hamish's name, and I arrange to see them later. As I depart Jack's eyes follow me, open, frightened and defiant. Mojo's eyes are looking at Jack, supercilious, pitying and stupid.

Jack is the hope and Mojo is the failure. They mutually threaten one another.

Chapter Eleven

I buy a present for Hamish. An LP of Freddie Keppard. He says he is delighted, that he hasn't got it in his collection, and thereby lets me know that he has.

He knows everything about the Man and tells me. We drink two pints of heavy each, swap a couple of jokes, recall a couple of good sessions and make our separate ways.

The other three are waiting in Johnson's Bar at opening time. I escort them to the most private table.

Tippet stands up and talks loudly, for the benefit, largely, of the fat little blonde behind the bar whose watery obsessive stare indicates the terrible mess she must be making of her drawers. "Really Snipe. All this fuckin' secrecy. It's alright man, you don't have to tell us a thing."

"I thought you wanted dealing in."

"Well, like we have to keep you happy, Snipey man. We have to make you feel as though you still count. Because while you're playing in your—what is it?—*dance orchestra*?—we gotta get on with things, right?"

"Is that bloke on the level?" asks Howell, his eyes as wet as oysters.

"Listen baby," says Tippet, "when we want to talk about like, levels, y'know? Well you ask me about levels man, because it's like levels that are my special scene, sound levels, spirit levels, level schmevels, you fuckin' name it man."

"Terrible jokes," says Howell.

"I don't joke baby," says Tippet, flicking open a flick knife and cleaning his nails like somebody out of "High Chaparral".

"Okay, what's your plan?" I ask Tippet.

"He—" Crane digests a mouthful of beer. "He—pretty good like. All the information."

"Take it easy," says Tippet. "Take it easy. Drink your horrible grandad beer."

"Tippet, I've got to get back to Edinburgh."

"What for?"

"Get the gun."

"We got nearly a week, man, a whole five days. Keep your cool."

"Has he told you the plan?" I ask Crane.

"Simple," says Crane. Tippet purrs and- smiles a little smile of self-congratulation.

"The man comes by boat and goes by private car to stay at Falkland Castle. He arrives at five p.m. next Wednesday, right? He don't wanna attract no attention, right? So it's a minimal bodyguard, right? Like Secret Service back and front. Three bombs man, in the Celtic pastoral twilight."

"Yeah," I say. "Right. What about Stonehenge?"

"Maybe one o' the daughters, hey?"

"Yes, yes," I say. "Much better. Okay, you stay here. Drive over the route to Falkland a couple of times. Stay in, or someplace near, Falkland. I'll go to Edinburgh and get the gun."

"Bombs man. Say, what was the story your pigeon had to tell?"

"Same as yours," I say. "Look at the route before we decide on guns or bombs."

"Let him play," says Tippet. "Let Snipey play. Give him his skipping around time. See yer tomorrow Snipe. Fuck off."

"Shall I come with you?" asks Howell.

"No," I say. Outside the pub I stumble up an alley and vomit. I hurry to the train, narrowly avoiding the hurrying figure of Tom McGregor.

The night plane to London leaves in three hours. The Man is booked into the Inn On The Park from five o'clock tomorrow. He arrives at a private airport near Romford two hours previously. He has his wife and his children with him and Hamish Menzies has two copies of the collected performances of the primitive New Orleans trumpeter, Freddie Keppard.

Chapter Twelve

It has to be alcohol and nausea all the way to London Town. First in alternate waves, the fear arising and the whiskey quelling, jangles of alarm and hysteria drowning on slow steady waves of drunkenness. Then the merging of the two, the whorls and scummy tides of dissolved mind given added distortion by the motor energies of revulsion. Remembering the practice of ten years since, I fish in the energies for the fuel to animate me beyond the claws of my superego. So finally I come to that near forgotten but familiar state of mind, the crystallisation of the dark licence I felt in Princess St. Gardens when Crane first arrived and the size of the leap we contemplated first presented itself; finally that drunkenness beyond relative argument, that soaring on the absolute; finally, in fact, sadism.

But even then, with the tight-arsed hostess glaring more and more pityingly at my flask of Bell's, and Bowie howling waspishly out of the cassette recorder on the knees of the languid American Ivy League puff across the aisle; even then, with the automatic images of razor lacerations across the strained material on the hostess's rippling haunch and the bother boot crashing into the crutch of the American queer, there is still the knowledge and the decision, my spinster with eyes the colour of a washingday sky telling me: "The Man is somebody's father, uncle, son, husband. He is two arms and legs, balls and fallible brain like you, Snipe. Like you. All he ever did in Vietnam was what *his* spinster told him to do. He is going to look at you as he dies. He is going to suffer pain. The political chaos following his death may be worse than the dictatorship he maintains and the butchery he precipitates. But we, we have decided haven't we? I have my stern carbolic finger right up your arse."

And Bowie carps on with his song about children who are spat upon as they try to change the planet that they're set upon, remote from all comfort and succour, knowing what and why and how long they must suffer, knowing, as they feed the monkey and the rat, just who they are and where the hell they're at. The cassette shivers to the end of the reel and I laugh weakly. The Man walks out of the toilet where I shall presently go to vomit, sits opposite and buries his face in his hands. So even after the hostess has said, "Excuse me, sir, I don't think you should drink any more," and I reply, not to her but to the Man, hunched sobbing, "It's okay, luv. Don't upset yourself. We all do our bit in the happening. It's all the same in the end," even then from my cockerel's roost of sadism I see the historic panoply of sadism spread out like a diagram. The cheap ex-army pistol that doesn't work beyond ten yards range is tucked in my belt under my shirt, warm and firm as its Freudian equivalent. The dark mass of Yorkshire swings beneath me like shadows on a compass face. I know even in the midst of its thrill that the tingling in my skin is the shrill crescendo of a tintinnabula that started to stir for young Britishers sometime in the beginning sixties. It was part daring and it was part violence. Violence, first presenting itself as the necessary means to transgression, then proving itself to be the sugar of transgression, the sweetening, the very wine. Doing new things in the world, to one another, was part of a perverse revenge for that inadequacy and impotence bequeathed us by our ineffectual peaceful protests. The impotence visited on us by the State; the State's castration-by-indifference principle had granted a licence that sewed a thread of angry gold into the colourless canvas of our puritanism. My spinster, who makes sure that all my decisions are carried out with all available knowledge, has it all laid out for me on my diagram.

Besides de Sade, Genet looms there: "I give the name violence to a boldness lying idle and hankering for danger. It can be seen in a look, a walk, a smile, and it is in you that it creates an eddying. It unnerves you. This violence is a calm that disturbs you."[22] His words are so appropriate, so exactly the ones I need. My lips move in actual gratitude for the leavening poetry as a Crusader's lips might have moved in prayer as he rifled the treasure troves of Islam. Poetry for the movement, for the generation even. Poets toying exhilaratingly with the special country of double standard, violence singing the same wild songs as it faced two ways. The tone of Ginsberg's "Howl" sounded out again for good reason. The poem that achieved immediate effect, more immediately than any broadsheet or tract; and its beginning tone, accusatory, recriminatory. But the famous "best minds" of his generation, "destroyed by madness, starving hysterical naked,"[23] wronged, misplaced, wasted by the evil or plain banality of the age, relegated to the slum and to suicide, are carried, by the poem, into a lyric celebration of the wild times to be had. The "best minds" who

" . . . fell on their knees in hopeless cathedrals praying for each other's salvation and light and breasts, until the soul illuminated its hair for a second,

who crashed through their minds in jail waiting for impossible criminals with golden heads and the charm of reality in their hearts who sang sweet blues to Alcatraz,

who retired to Mexico to cultivate a habit, or Rocky Mount to tender Buddha or Tangiers to boys or Southern Pacific to the black locomotive or Harvard to Narcissus to Woodlawn to the daisychain or grave"[24]

And that ultimate suicide by which point the celebration has reached such a pitch that mind destruction, of which society stood accused, has become transcendence. The disinherited young have been bestowed by right of their sore wrongs with nothing less than sainthood, purity arising directly out of alienation:

"the madman bum and angel beat in Time, unknown, yet putting down here what might be left to say in time come after death,

and rose reincarnate in the ghostly clothes of jazz in the goldhorn shadow of the band and blew the suffering of America's naked mind for love into an eli eli lamma lamma sabacthani saxophone cry that shivered the cities down to the last radio

with the absolute heart of the poem of life butchered out of their own bodies good to eat a thousand years".[25]

And over there speaks Lennie Bruce, about his wife's death: "I saw the back wheels go over Honey's soft young body. I heard her hips crack like the sound of a Chinese fortune cookie. The next moment the truck, coming behind the Packard, also ran over her.

"I raced to her and threw myself upon her. I felt something warm and wet and looked down. It was her intestines. Oh, my sweet wonderful baby, my wife, every combination of everything, my mistress, my high priestess, I love her so much, please God let this only be a nightmare.

"Her face was grey and there were puddles of blood around her. I yelled 'Oh God, why are you punishing her for her sins, why?' "[26]

Even now I can't, from my lofty perch, see the exact point where the Keystone violence creeps into this true confession. I still have to force back a titter as I recognise the truck as a familiar comedy prop, as I hear echoes of Lennie's endless jokes about Jewish masochism and Jewish guilt. Even now I'm not quite sure if that really is necrophilia showing its fangs there. But I do recognise the ambiguity and my drunken soul relishes it.

The *Naked Lunch* now. The real mindbender of that failed decade. Puritanism in tatters with a puritan licence. John Wesley with his cock out. A. J.'s annual party, the Great Slashtubitch: "When he is angered the charge of it will blow his monocle across the room"[27]—the cartoon panoply of Bur-rough's much-argued Swiftian satire, and then the slow encroachment of erotic detail, the sex super-ceding the humour. "He close his eyes and squirm. She lick up the perennial divide . . . . A great pearl stands out on the tip of his circumcised cock. Her mouth closes over the crown."[28] Those deliriously epicene present-tense-plural verbs. The vision of hell is showing its other face as the Devil's paradise. A little more scouring humour, Steely Dan III, the dildo, then the murder—"She bites away Johnny's lips and nose and sucks out his eyes with a pop . . . . She tears off great hunks of cheek. . . . Now she lunches on his prick . . . . Mark walks over to her and she looks up from Johnny's half-eaten genitals, her face covered with blood, eyes phosphorescent . . . . 'No, Mark!! No! No! No!' she screams, shitting and pissing in terror as he drags her to the platform. He leaves her tied on the platform in a pile of old used condoms while he adjusts the rope across the room . . . and comes back carrying the noose on a silver tray . . ."[29] Those musical intervals, four clear periods to allow each erotic impulse to fade in its own time before the next begins. The timing of a virtuoso performer. And finally, what else beyond murder? The vision: "Her neck snaps. A great fluid wave undulates through her body. Johnny drops to the floor and stands poised and alert like a young animal.

"He leaps about the room. With a scream of longing that shatters the glass wall he leaps out into space. Masturbating end-over-end, three thousand feet down, his sperm floating beside him, he screams all the way against the shattering blue of the sky, the rising sun burning over his body like gasoline, down past great oaks and persimmons, swamp cypress and mahogany . . . ."[30]

The ambiguity. Evil revealed or Faustian man come into his millennium. The motivation was muddy. Were we to clamour at society's gates for our birthright? Was society to make itself tolerable to us so that we could enjoy some constructive participation and be relieved of our awful fates; or were we, who were too insensitive or timid to have registered our despair quite as wildly as the poets, were we to hurl ourselves into the doping, the dissipation whereby we might also *become*?

Corso, Ginsberg's soulmate of that time, killed his "fat pontiffs of kindness". Bremser howled his need for crime as a means of separation. Norman Mailer, having extolled the virtues of psychopathy in "The White Negro", described the landscape of escape and further revolution more clearly than any. When Lennie Bruce describes his wife's death, there is ambiguity. When Mailer describes the death of Rojack's wife the issue is clear:

"For ten or twenty seconds she strained in balance, and then her strength began to pass, it passed over to me, and I felt my arm tightening about her neck. My eyes were closed. I had the mental image I was pushing with my shoulder against an enormous door which would give inch by inch to the effort.

"One of her hands fluttered up to my shoulder and tapped it gently. Like a gladiator admitting defeat. I released the pressure on her throat, and the door I had been opening began to close. But I had had a view of what was on the other side of the door and heaven was there, some quiver of jewelled cities shining in the glow of a tropical dusk, and I thrust against the door once more and hardly felt her hand leave my shoulder, I was driving now with force against that door: spasms began to open in me, and my mind cried out then, 'Hold back! you're going too far, hold back!' I could feel a series of orders whip like tracers of light from my head to my arm. I was ready to obey. I was trying to stop, but pulse packed behind pulse in a pressure up to thunderhead; some blackbiled lust, some desire to go ahead not unlike the instant one comes in a woman against her cry that she is without protection came bursting with rage out of me and my mind exploded in a fireworks of rockets, stars, and hurtling embers, the arm about her neck leaped against the whisper I could still feel murmuring in her throat, and *crack* I choked her harder, and *crack* I choked her again, and *crack* I gave her payment—never halt now—and *crack* the door flew open and the wire tore in her throat, and I was through the door, hatred passing from me wave after wave, illness as well, rot and pestilence, nausea, a bleak string of salts. I was floating. I was as far into myself as I had ever been and universes wheeled in a dream. To my closed eyes Deborah's face seemed to float off from her body and stare at me in darkness. She gave me one malevolent look which said: 'There are dimensions to evil which reach beyond the light,' and then she smiled like a milkmaid and floated away and was gone. And in the midst of that

Oriental splendour of landscape, I felt the lost touch of her finger on my shoulder, radiating some faint but ineradicable pulse of detestation into the new grace. I opened my eyes. I was weary with a most honourable fatigue, and my flesh seemed new. I had not felt so nice since I was twelve . . . ."[31]

The digestion of the sadistic into our day-to-day thinking had several aspects then and I can see them all. As peaceful protest failed, and McGregor continued with his self-indulgent marching, the handful of us who were desperate enough could see quite clearly that the middle-class revulsion that led us to recoil from H-bombs and napalm was the same token that made us ineffectual before the ruthlessness of those people whose ruthlessness we detested. Mailer was the crucible of this preoccupation, groping towards impossible negritide as he addressed the Pentagon demonstrators, trying drunkenly but magically to say that flower-power was poor medicine. The world was structured in such a way as to make it necessary to be more swinish than the pigs in order to displace their power and make compassion a possible and workable spirit in the world. Angel Bengochea, the Argentinian guerrilla, sitting on the stockpile of armaments that was eventually to blow up him and his followers, surrounded by "death squad" police, many of whom were chosen for their limited or perverted mentalities, said "I know that we cannot achieve a just society unless we achieve what is human by inhuman ways. That means battle. It is a battle in which we must dehumanise ourselves so that, by being inhuman, we can achieve what is human."

The Gurdjieffian test of this was to bathe ourselves in those sensations the revulsion towards which rendered us politically ineffectual. We espoused the sensations of nausea and violence that would make efficient guerrilla fighters of us all. The Baader-Meinhoff group of West Germany, leaping from the springboard of the '68 revolution as John Brown and Quantrell leapt from the springboard of the slavery controversy a hundred years before, embarked on a career of headlong car theft and bank robbery. Ingrid Siepman, her beauty, her gun, her white silk scarf. Professor Witter, bombed as he prepared to operate on the brain of Ulrike Meinhoff. Dr Humer with his Laingian "socialist patients' collective", connected to Baader-Meihoff, convinced, with all of us, that mental sickness was due to the "inherent mental sickness" of capitalism. That other member of the international Red Army, Hiroko Negata, the "sokatsu doctrine, the bringing together of isolated facts to form one coherent principle" (Dada? collage? cut-up?)—her interpretation: "Once the process of sokatsu starts only death awaits" — the shaved heads of her four female victims who died tied down in the snow under the hideout, her destruction of their "bourgeois tendencies" like make-up and sexuality. And thence to the bloodbath at Lod airport, also work of the international Red Army, Black September, Rome airport, the shaven-headed scapegoats of Derry and Belfast, the postal workers with their hands blown off. The residue of that vast revolutionary force of '68, their wild ideology, based on poetry and vision, having dried up on them, continue the violence, as dope takers continue the smoking and the tripping long after the apocalyptic light has died, by relating to groups like Arab guerrillas and the IRA whose connections with socialism are tenuous, whose connections with the vaulting revolutionary poetry of '68 are nil. Merely because the CP indicates some tactical and opportunist sympathy for such causes. Merely because violence has, by now, become a way of life, like the mere structures of scoring and selling have become a way of life for the doper. To join the Arabs or the IRA is a way of continuing.

And the other point I can see is that we were / are living in perpetual terror. A factual cognisance of the world confrontation, the present holocaust in Vietnam, and the coming world nuclear holocaust, made it necessary to use and redefine our terror as part of our sensibility. Behind this was the belief that fear begat self-destruction and the way to positive living was to lose our areas of trauma by familiarisation.

Thus the Institute of Direct Art, floundering doggedly through their programmes in bombed-out Vienna, bathed themselves in blood and shit, in a series of happenings taking place through ten years. Herman Nitsch cut up animals and strewed their innards over naked people, making the presentation of naked human flesh and violated animal flesh into a series of graphic visual metaphors and equivalents. A live human penis hanging through a sheep's brain leaves the assaulted senses uncertain whether dead flesh is alive, live dead, or whether, and here is the message, there is any difference.

Gunter Brus devoured shit publicly, after drawing on his body with a razor blade. All artists pissed in one another's mouths. Otto Muehl made his own body and that of his wife into an internal and external creative playground using the alimentary and sexual functions as a sort of painting machine, devouring and excreting and redevouring colours and textures, substances and qualities, wholesale, as thoroughly demystifying the body aesthetically as it is demystified medically in hospitals. His aim was / is to redefine life as a kind of joyous midden wherein *the whole* of experience can be taken, enjoyed, accepted, digested. "The elements of art to come are: eating, drinking, shitting, and pissing, fucking and killing people. These are the hot irons of our time, always pushed aside and not mastered until today. Murder as art. In earlier times animals and men had been ritually slaughtered in masses to feed milliards of witchel-stomachs. Masses of witchels have themselves slaughtered senselessly for political aims. Medicine makes deadly experiments with witchels and animals. Only art shall look at this inactively? No! Direct art also asks for its bloody tribute."[32] His most elaborate event, interrupted by Heathcote Williams, was surely his decapitation of a chicken, strapping a dildo to the neck stump and having the twitching bird thus fuck his wife.

The fusion of the most hideous with the most beautiful was by no means new. It was part and parcel of the function of the Hindu dervishes, it extended back to the Bacchae. It was a fundamental contention of Zen Buddhism. It is behind Blake's "Marriage of Heaven and Hell" and the thinking de Sade. The Process were on to it.

All those self-appointed Christs who also claimed the powers of Satan looked up at me from my diagram. "Know them," said the spinster.

"Alpha and Omega redefined not as polarisation necessitating choice, but as the completion of experience conceived of fear and panic, as a necessary exercise in metaphysical enlightenment." Sanders again, talking about Manson: "One of Manson's summer 1969 raps was about how groovy fear was, is. 'Getting the Fear', as he called it, was an exquisite physical experience. It's actually an old LSD phenomenon—conquering a period of intense fear. But Manson decided that the entire substance of expanded consciousness was fear—the 'infinite plain of fear into infinity.' "[33]

And the fuel of these processes was always there, not so much acid as the Vietnam war and heroin, the incredibly vicious facts of life in the American heroin market. Veterans returning to Mom and Apple Pie after countless Mai Lai atrocities had accustomed themselves to butchery as a day-to-day commonplace to such an extent that murder was an easy thing to have recourse to on Main Street. In any case, most of them had cushioned their shock and terror by experiencing it through the oceanic tides of pot and heroin, the way I was using alcohol now, thus confusing the atrocity with hallucinatory nightmares and relegating both to a distanced category of insignificance. To live with monsters is to develop a technique whereby the monsters can be either ignored or tolerated with that impregnable supercilious smile of the doper (or perhaps, more simply, the dope).

The media reflected violence then, in the early seventies, not as protest and satire as in the fifties, not as diabolism and transgression as in the sixties, but as simply part of the ordinary vocabulary of experience. Not just the twisted humour of a revolutionary minority is sick now. All humour is sick. It is now as easy to talk and joke about kicking in a baby's head as about the football score or the price of beer. Hender Hayman, an artist who committed himself to a sequence of events wherein he mutilated himself to the point of death ("By the time I actually was able to attend one of Hender's things he was already short several digits on both hands, one eye, both testicles and several random patches of flesh."[34]) is reported with facile irony in the Underground press. Bowie chants blithely about a metropolitan midden in which reality is only recognised through pain. The whips crack against the PVC. The competitive whimpering gobble-queens wallow at the death-trough. Robert Crumb's cartoon characters bounce their way through the dope clouds, sticking one another's limbs in their own cunts, crawling in and out of one another's arse holes, joyously reducing one another to pieces of jaunty lecherous plasticine in the best tradition of Don Martin. S. Clay Wilson's pirates and bikers and dikes hack one another to fragments, slurping merrily on the blood, the sperm and the smegma. It seems from my perch a matter of months before Peckinpah's movies are recirculated as comedies.

Burgess's *A Clockwork Orange*, intended-as a grim warning in 1963 about the way things were around 1972, is a microcosm of the whole development. An allegory about affectlessness arising out of a depersonalised society, it was seized by Kubrick, the master of Cinematic camp, as a platform on which to show his paces. His "Singing In The Rain" sequence, however, wryly retreading the warm old Gene Kelly sequence, with the young psychopaths kicking a man's face in with the formality of a Busby Berkeley spectacular, was exactly the complete division between cruelty and serious involvement that the skinheads, already nurtured on Bond and Steed, wanted the media to provide them with. One might suppose that to kick someone's head in didn't hurt or kill, or if it did either or both one might wish it didn't matter, or one might wish one didn't get kicked back by someone ever; or one might wish not to feel revulsion or guilt at the sight of one's own brutality; or one might wish immunity to the law, or, at any rate, one might wish that complete omnipotence, that broad advantage that has ever been the blessing of the comic book super-heroes; or, and here lay the important chance, one might wish immunity to the morality, one might, now that brutality had been rendered so broadly stylish and commonplace, might, quite accurately, expect to be forgiven.

If public statements embody the public attitude, as I believe they do, Kubrick's "Singing In The Rain" sequence was a public formalisation, even aestheticisation, of cruelty, that said, loud and clear, behind the thinnest of moral pretences, "Kicking people is okay."

The reversion on the part of British working class youth from pop-hip as laid down by the Beatles and the Stones, whose sympathy for the Devil had spread along with a number of diseased rumours about the death of Brian Jones, to working class uniform, speech-forms and behaviour structures, was first a move into the safety and brute power of bigger hunting packs, bigger, even, than those of the Hell's Angels, the adulation of whom by all leading pop gurus preceded this reversion; and secondly into working-class Powellite attitudes of racial hatred for Pakistanis, mob hatred for students and queers, that gave licence to kill and maim with the warm approval of one's parents.

Manson's girls hunted the LA bourgeoisie, the skinheads hunted Paks and queers. The young guerrillas fired off their sten guns and exploded their bombs, seemingly deciding the target by a turn of the card or a throw of the dice. Who was hunted and why, is, it appears, deep down, irrelevant, as long as young people who have to act out the *normalisation* of brutality have someone to hunt and some flimsy moral umbrella under which to track and kill them.

"Fitzgerald," claims Burroughs, "wrote the Jazz Age just as surely as Kerouac and Ginsberg wrote the Beat Generation." The panorama of burlesque and horror called *The Naked Lunch* was written in the mid-fifties and published widely in the mid-sixties. It has taken ten years for the creation to be completed.

And the gun is warm against my liquor-live belly. "Heathrow," says the spinster. "Move."

Chapter Thirteen

The man behind the bar at the airport only has full bottles and miniatures. It is a special occasion. I feel like malt. He has no malt.

I settle my arse into a chair in the passengers' lounge and wait for the dawn.

I feel better. On terms with my own particular cage of horrors and distanced from the tormented zoo of the generation. I feel as I felt the only time I had delirium tremens. The spiders kept coming so I just kept watching 'em.

Across the lounge is a beautiful German woman with her two children. The daughter must be about eleven. She reminds me of Lindy. I have no paper to write to Lindy. I have, in fact, no address. Neither am I sure I can spell her surname. I buy a box of paper handkerchiefs, fall over a chair on the way back to my seat, and settle down to write.

"My Lovely Beautiful Wild Angelic Girl," I write. Then I bite my lip savagely, determined not to weep, just yet, take a long pull on the bottle, and carry on. "Somebody has to have a go. I'm going to have a go. I have to make myself into some kind of reptile to do it. I. have to quell my tenderness but I've got a fucking great gutful of tenderness and perhaps the best way to be rid of it is to spend it on you. It's important not to be sloppy in this letter. It might be the last fucking letter I write. But there are some important things to be said and I've got to try and say them without sentimentality. I feel like weeping all over this desolate fucking place but I shall not, I shall not. Another little drink.

"If you can come to the outside of yourself and look in you'll be able to see something very important. Your fabulous little body is a cat's cradle of muscle and energies. Your mind and soul are another very very delicate network of ideas and impulses. All these strands cross and re-cross one another within the system which is you. You have the great talent to allow them to do this without them once getting knotted. This is called grace and you have it, located somewhere where the strands are best oiled at their point of greatest complexity.

"Not everybody's got it. I haven't. Jesus Christ, here I am, Raskolnikov II and I look (and feel) like a pile of mammoth shit.

"But you, you have it.

"It's the quintessence of energy, you see, energy's highest form, more marvellous than the lightning or the sun because it's actually useful and it's wondrously absurd. You couldn't laugh at, or even with, the sun, could you now? The sun can't dance to its own pattern.

"I'm doing the dire deed because I think that you can see now that energy is threatened, mostly by corruption and abuse, which deadens. Corruption isn't bad because it angers Gods, or Nobodaddy in any of his forms. It's not bad because it's wrong or evil. It's bad because it deadens. It fatigues.

"I used to think that the depreciation of energy was an evolutionary thing—second law of thermodynamics and so on. Then I thought it was a cultural fault rising out of dislocation with nature. And now, while I haven't junked the first two possibilities, it does look to me, from where I'm sitting with a gutful of whiskey besides the tenderness, and with a heartful of you besides Woodbine smoke, as though energy is threatened by a few, a very few men. It's the old wet-blanket-at-the-party-thing. 'I'm so mean and miserly I can't enjoy myself so I'm going to set it up so that nobody else can'.

"There's a very few of them. They've got it rigged so that their special failings are the shortest way to the top. Acquisitiveness and fear. The old dark tight-lipped repressions of the conditioned arsehole. Having got to the top they're so impoverished all they can think to do is impoverish the world. There's very few of the bastards, but none so powerful as the one I'm after. I've seen the set-up very simply and I'm going to do a very simple thing.

"You are the most beautiful emanation of what I'm trying to defend. Don't pine or weep. You won't anyway. Just be. As hard as you can.

All my love,
Snipe."

And I post it c/o Crane, to my address on George St. There doesn't seem much hope that it will be delivered.

I go out into the warm damp Autumn night and weep for an hour. Then I go back and drink myself to sleep.

The airfield in Essex has the air of a tennis club. I buy an Ordnance Survey Map in Ilford, take a bus to the next village, then approach it across the field, jumping ditches and climbing hedges, the gun, in my pocket now, knocking against my hip.

There is a club-house where a caretaker, wearing an old RAF uniform jacket and a huge moustache, potters about. And there are two Secret Service men looking like Secret Service men stalking the runway. Essex Constabulary are busy too. At least five cars are circling the field, each stopping for a fag and a natter with one of the Secret Service men every time round.

The road, a very narrow one with high hedges, runs behind the club-house. There is a gate onto the road to the right of the club-house from where I am situated. The road continues along the side of a cropped hayfield which lies next to the airfield. In the hayfield is a rick made up of heavy rectangular bales of hay and in the rick is me. From here I can see everything thank you very much. About two o'clock one of the constables wanders across to the rick but I hide under two bales at the top. He tips a couple of bales over at the foot of the rick with some difficulty, then goes back to his car.

About four a group of club members fall out of the club-house. One wanders over to the hangar, immediately opposite my rick. The others pile into an old Humber and sweep off after a noisy farewell to the Secret Service man on the gate.

I feel fine. Unreal. Still a little drunk although steady and clear from the adrenalin that courses through me.

And there it is. A small bright plane. With the sun winking on its wing.

I take the gun from my pocket, empty it and throw it from me. I descend from the haystack and walk along the hedge. I feel suddenly terribly tired, but the winking sun on the wingtip has determined me not to shut myself off from the jewels of living for whatever time I have left.

"You have shut yourself off from the jewels of living," says the spinster. "The sun will never shine again for you." And the cow is right. The sun glinting on the landing plane excites me now not at all. Nor does the Secret Service man walking towards me across the airfield.

What does excite me is the Man's face as he alights, complete with family group, for all the world like my parents arriving at Scarborough in 1948, with my brother and I in our Sunday best. There it is, even at a hundred yards distance clearly that familiar crumpled edifice of disappointment and total spiritual bankruptcy. That foreskin of a face. And there, I can see, are the teeth, clicking up that toothpaste smile behind which he hides from the people of the world. Those who lie in sickness of spirit like me and my companions of the failed revolution. Those who lie in sickness of body like the people of South America, like the people of Vietnam.

So I become angry as the Secret Service man draws near, very angry. I can see that there is no health in a plagued house and I can see that the head of the house is the source of the infection. And as the Secret Service man draws near my anger puts the sparkle back in the sunshine. I race back along the hedge to the hayrick to get the gun, ducked double, out of the Secret Service man's sight. I can hear his feet on the airstrip tarmac as he breaks into a run. I can hear a police car by the club-house rev its engine feverishly.

The gun is where I dropped it. I blow chaff from it and slide a couple of bullets into it. Then I mount halfway up the irregular side of the rick to see over the hedge. The Secret Service man is immediately below me as I prepare to shoot and jump the hedge at the same moment. I can see him clearly. He looks like my Uncle George. I aim at him as a taxi pulls up in the lane.

"Snipe," yells Jack Howell, running towards me. "Snipe you shithouse. Wait for me!"

Endnotes

1. Corso, *The New American Poetry*, Ed. Allen, Grove Press.
2. Bataille, *Eroticism*, Calder & Boyars.
3. *Ibid.*
4. *Ibid.*
5. Thompson, *Fear and Loathing in Las Vegas*, Paladin.
6. Sanders, *Peace Eye*, Frontier Press.
7. McClure, *Meat Science Essays*, City Lights.
8. Andrews, *Burning joy*, Trigram.
9. Reynolds, McClure, *Freewheelin' Frank*, Grove Press.
10. Thompson, op. cit.
11. The Doors, *Strange Days*, Elektra.
12. Sanders, *The Family*, Rupert Hart-Davis.
13. Thompson, *op. cit.*
14. *Ibid.*
15. Reed, *Transformer*, RCA Victor.
16. *Ibid.*
17. *Ibid.*
18. Dylan, *Bringing It All Back Home*, CBS.
19. King Mob Echo.
20. Ginsberg, *Howl*, City Lights.
21 . Dylan, *op. cit.*
22. Genet, *Thief's Journal*, Penguin.
23. Ginsberg, *op. cit.*

24. *Ibid.*
25. *Ibid.*
26. Bruce, *How to Talk Dirty and Influence People*, Peter Owen.
27. Burroughs, *The Naked Lunch*, Calder & Boyars.
28. *Ibid.*
29. *Ibid.*
30. *Ibid.*
31. Mailer, *An American Dream*, Andre Deutsch.
32. Muehl, *Mama and Papa*, Kohlkunstuerlag (Frankfurt).
33. Sanders, *The Family*, Rupert Hart-Davis.
34. From *The Drummer*, 29 May, 1973 issue.

THE HOUSE PARTY

Introduction

The early seventies saw a wind-down of a period of incredibly dense change and development in art. If things are at a halt it's because the way of mounting complexity leads to the meditative vacuum. Kaprow leads to Beuys. Pollock leads to Reinhardt or back to Malevitch. Parker leads to the long simple notes of Rollins. White on white. Black on black, white sound, the world falling away to reveal Laing's No Thing. I'm a naive optimist. Rather than sit in meditative prayer with my mind blown as clear as Leary's I attempt to continue to build. In this building, myself and my comparatively unremarkable sexual predicaments are not so much a field of study or a point of argument, more bricks and mortar, construction materials, fuel. *The House Party* follows,

after my enormous determination to arrive at some point of literary structure as multi-levelled and self-perpetuating as *Finnegans Wake* — which, as I wrote ten years ago, stands with Picasso's *Guernica* and Schoenberg's *Moses and Aaron* as a monument past which subsequent innovators have failed to go;

after my preoccupation with the interplay between auto-suggestive images and formal accident;

after my wish to create a literary adventure-labyrinth as dense and interpentrative as a Pollock or a Shepp ensemble.

My work has always been preoccupied with the visionary potential of sexual hysteria. Certain poems in "Songs Sacred and Secular" are clear statements of a determination to find beauty and trancendence (not to mention art, and form, a new language, and humour) in the areas of experience from which one most readily recoils — particularity those of bodily nausea and sexual pain (not the sadistic kind — the moral kind).

The burden of *The House Party* is stated fairly clearly in the final paragraphs. It is, I suppose, a perverse and aggresive form of pantheism, the worshipful adherance to a painful situation in the belief that such a situation is likely to be more illuminatory, and fulfilling, than the mere pursuit of happiness.

J.N.

The House Party

by Jeff Nuttall

RSVP

They bought a whole beast's length.

Stretch it on a slab to the boldest bidder. Cut it up in slices for the maiden's tongue.

Susan knew the velvet of his connection (my club is really a translucent animal, sleeping in clover after the murder). Susan screwed him into her valve, locked onto his ten stroke pump, she stroked his pink plush with appreciative fingernails. An extraordinary crowd of lovelorn birds are dressing up in colours for a round of spikes and spades. "Susan's gone," Isabel said, crying, "really gone. She doesn't know the score, she hasn't been around," and while she spoke the acid spilled about his system by her own betrayals on a Cornish holiday — "proper yobbos — caravan goin' up and dahn like a fuckin' boat in the water" — weren't yet dried, the grazed erosions and the tenth degree burns not yet healed.

Susan in a Windsor pad. All the West Indian names and the endless methedrine.

They took it where it lay. Found themselves on the bar-room floor, Lord have mercy on a poor old whore.

Up to the first floor like a whorehouse relic in a sacred smoking, the fires of inquisition licking under the door of Room 504, that seventh grade heaven on the old fifth floor . . .

Downstairs door clapping against the night banishing the frost and moonglow with the boom of its broken lock.

"Ironic man with bare genitals, get your leering head out of my window, a bad cook that draws and

ISOBEL'S SISTER SUSAN
FAVOURS SPADES.

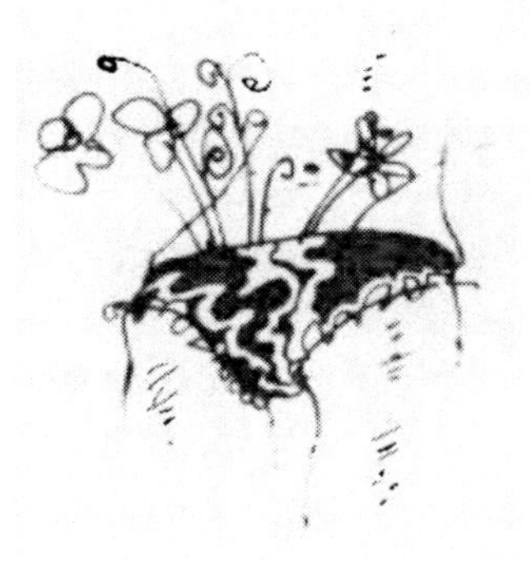

FANTASIES OF FORTIES
SPUN IN SIXTIES
AND SEVENSIES.

stuffs the carcass of a cock that's overlong dead. Don't waste time with cookery. Leave the cuisine and attempt a curettage. Every cock-cook's a surgeon to resuscitate the brats whose early death hacked the plumes from my peacock tail.

Peeled lips so wetly to light. Look first, leave the whisper soft with old darlin' sleep. Knowing smile, cocaine, leave rest and morphine. What? Leave you?

I leave the crumb of a cured habit (don't mean a fuckin' thing to me, I tell you, hasn't since her little scene with a bisexual car thief in Cornwall) and I hang my dreams to air and dry in the linen cupboard next to the immersion heater."

I don't want to hurt you, Henry . . .

"Not exactly the quiver he left me. A whole bundle of arrows of desire."

"Spasm of light is the sweetest song, make no mistakes my old love, my bud, my blossom. I'm Adam and Oratorio from the brink of the rose. I'm generation, the after-hours saxophone. Too much blows around the lovers, too many crooked blues. When Fats Waller died he said, about the howling Kansas wind, "Ol' Hawkins is surely out there, blowin' up a storm." Leap scattered petals. Settle the prophet. Plant a new child in the front garden of the crematorium. Confound the prophet's worst threat."

YOU'RE GETTING TO BE A HABIT WITH ME . . .

Hurt me hurt me?
Scrape me up.

MY DARLING, ALL THE WORLD IS WAITING FOR THE SUNRISE...

A couple clapped the dyed actors as they bowed in their rainbow and trucked out into the rain.

"Young, red we are. Evening went first. Now follows our bridal night. Young as Susan we are, with her gutbucket bargains. We see methedrine tops and a whip to spin 'em.

Mountain map tunnel where we met first, found later by a small boy on a winter walk through the dank Yorkshire woodland."

LULU THE RAG

DOLL GETS AN ATTACK OF B.O.

She took readily to the near bald skin. Rat's back. Shaved model's crutch. Crucial mother's armpit.

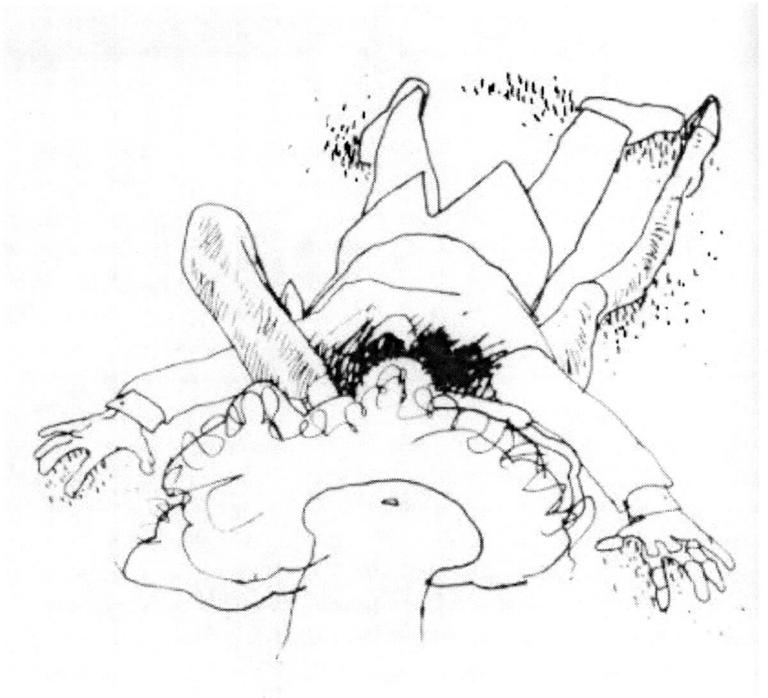

HENRY THE HIPPO IS DYING TO MEET YOU.

HAVE YOU AN APPETITE FOR HIPPO PUDDING?

Closed his eyes, she yawned her legs, hippo gargling, uvula red in the mouth, and moving to the scrape of stubble against those pendulous inner lips (like, your cunt's got piles, got pudding, got some intimate bags of wrinkles down there, couched in the babyhair like prunes in meadowgrass) —Yawned her legs for the club of his head "Brighton Combination completely overrun by skinheads. They just came and took over, she said," said Jasper.

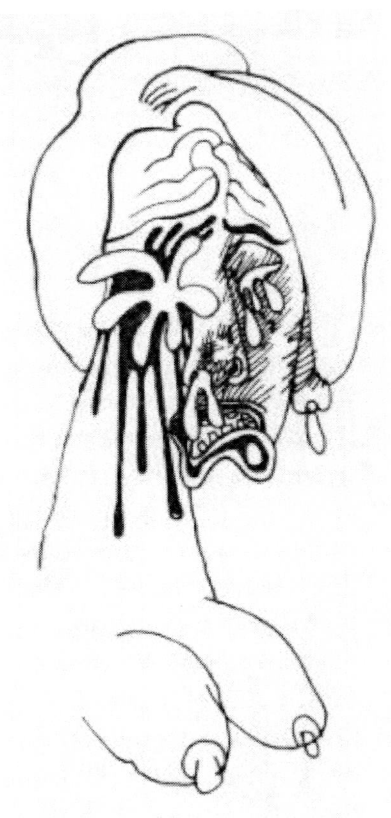

HENRY HIPPO AND
CHICKEN LICKEN
HAD A SUPER FUCK.

HENRY HIPPO MEETS
A STICKY END.

Sometimes he saw her on the floor of the discotheque with her vast calves, dear calves, loved thighs, with her almond eyes dead as stone to the tinfoil ceiling (that's the wrapping for your limbs when they've shrunk from massive meat to spitted chicken).

Sometimes it was wet Saturday rain up the alley and a piece of torn wrapping paper blew to her leg like a soiled butterfly and clung there and clung there and fluttered.

With a shaved skull, like that, he thought, a prick is hardly a necessity, becomes an iron mini-model of the whole man. Can they make their skulls throb? Do they spurt curses up from whale holes in their heads, sperm whales battering through the tides of class oppression and welfare emasculation? Do their heads pulse and go purple as she sucks them into her lack-hole? Pete Yardley's drawings of the cadaverous nympho looking down in boorish satisfaction at the pair of comic Charlie Chaplin boots, jutting out of her mange, all remaining of her assimilated lover.

His daughter was in the bathroom without her eyes on yet, in her pink cream and flannelette child's pyjamas. Frousty as a baby animal. He waited (better be sure) til she'd washed and the adjacent bathroom door closed just outside the patterned glass of the lavatory door. Nursing his hideous winkle, recalling her praise of it (peeled down the blue pants he wore so as not to show too much of the khaki of the weekend's nerve-and-Guinness farts — so, released, it sprang back against his belly — said "That's nice" knowing its need of dignity) listening to the internal colours of grief dispelled by sheer blood speeding up his penal (yazyaz) tributaries.

Kick of her arse in its lime-green bikini tart's drawers. Peel of the knickerleg wide of the hanging lips. Other man's prick. Shaven club. Red braces dropped from white-shirt shoulders so the loose jeans fell to the Brighton pebbles, lips stretched like a rubberband over it . . . Risk a look. Yes that's better. Half an erection. The flush handle bites your shoulder if you lean back. Close your eyes. What if Billy or one of the boys, my little boys, comes and ola; peers through the glass. No clarity, just a sense of fever and movement "Dad, what are you doing?" "Why are you jiggling about in the bog?" Pea in a pod. Stone in a rattle. Creak and knock of the plastic seat. There. Now maybe I can keep my temper through most of a family Sunday.

"Good morning 'eadmaster. My name is Mr. Bates, and my son Master Bates."
"Well he can't come in here."

Jiggle and jum
Pedal and pum

Floor of the discotheque. Alley at the side. Stones of the beach. The grass of the cliffs at Peace-haven (that week-end a couple of lifetimes and three clear murders since) Shut up man. Don't think. Breakfast.

Egg was a day and the day was a field and the field was an answer.

Egg answered day and
the field answered the
day.
"How fat for a fumble?"
"Eggwhite as yellow for
thin."
"How white for thimble?"
"Fat tumble and pink
as a shell."
"How seashore the
shingle shell shrapnel?"
"White shell and thin
pink yellow."
Mr. Henry had a pink
egg. Run round the
whites of Mr. Henry.
Mr. Henry talks to Edna terribly.
The terrible egg in the
Henry day is talking to
Edna.
"Suck yellow. Suck
yellow."
"Yellow away with a
wog's wing."
"Fuck yolk. Fuck yolk."
"Cream away off with
an arab's armpit."

CLARION CALL
THE HERALDS OF
THE STICKY FINGERS
"Pass the toast," said
Billy.
"Say please," said Edna.
"Keep the paper out of
the marmalade," said
Henry.
"Fried or boiled?"
asked Edna.
"Don't like eggs," said
Willikin.
"Soppy," said Sam.
"Don't argue at the
table," said Ruth.
"I wasn't arguing," said
Willikin.
"Trying to put the blame
on me," said Sam.
"My eggs got something
funny in it," said Billy.

Yorkshire granite (green) topped by Yorkshire clay (ochre) topped by slag — a compound of shale and coal and slate that reared up on the other side of the stream, bearing the verticals of ash, the ashen royalty, silver, and violent mauve against the slag. Sir John stood at the edge of the stream, his head sunk in his muffler and then sunk between the collars of his finely tailored greatcoat like the hulk of a toad in mud.

"Beech is a dirty tree," he said to George and George's shade shimmered in the crisp cold of the air. Sir John ignored them both. Sir John stood like Ruskin on a Cumberland crag and looked at the stream. "All over cow's arseholes, look at the holes in the bark," and the yellow wince at the memory of her animal hanging lips died slowly away like pain fading from a tiny wound. He let his finger drag around a wooden replica of her cunt. Frozen it was, in wood, frozen before history, in the times of the giants, a fossilised monument to the days of frank animality, of great horse-collar vulvas visible on the women who crawled. Her great thighs. The great swinging bones of her thighs. Another yellow cloud of pain dispersed through his /elephant dying/ gut. George and Sir John were gone.

DA WOID:
And God in his infinite wisdom wrought woman out of ash, and he spake thus: "Ash thou art and to ash shalt thou return. Ashes to ashes and all that banana. Henceforth shalt thy practise be known as 'Getting thine ashes hauled.'

Billy scrambled down the mountain map tunnel after Edna. Edna disappeared into the arch of the tunnel. She had wellingtons on, so she could wade under the hill of slag, through the pale orange continents of dead leaves accumulated to turn black and scummy at the stream's edge. "The model of energy's progress," Sir John had said.

All that caring, all that aching love going sour in a snivelling murder impulse that turned a golden snake somewhere just below his throat. Starting all that again, should her horse collar sprout the fresh flowers of her grovelling desire. When she said, "I want a baby Henry," it sounded like some grim confession. "I've got cancer" "I had it with your best friend" "I want a baby, Henry."

Billy got to the bottom of the valley, looked up the tunnel after his mother, shouted "The green nose people will get you."

Shouldn't be surprised he thought. Shouldn't be at all surprised. The bastards get everybody.

"What's the matter, Mr. Puggy-wuggy?" asked Ruth.

Do not respond to this patronising whimsy. I don't have to be every fucker's fat clown, least of all yours, you incestuous little prick teaser.

"Well said, old man," muttered George and vanished again, leaving a dull after-image of his white tie and shirt front. "Ruth has great need of you," Edna had said.

Five pints of Guinness in the evening.

"Them wor all mines ower theer," said Tom Barret, looking like a puff from the coal-dust in his eyelashes. "Fuckin' cowboy-oiles all owert' 'illside." Drunk enough for numbness . . .

HENRY JUMBO IS CAPTURED BY THE GREEN NOSE PEOPLE. HOW CAN HE ESCAPE? KIND WIDOW PUGGY-WUGGY WILL DRAG HIM OUT BY THE KNACKERS.

HOUSEWIFE Jean Adams sniffed suspiciously at her daughter's new toy, Lulu the golden-haired rag doll.

Summer's a season that lies across the years like a lazy woman. Walking down Suffolk Street towards Norwich castle, he felt like a clammy underarm still smelling of the afternoon, felt the hairs and underflesh of gone summers heavy in the seven o'clock sky.

The way she lay across the Hereford buttercups the way Edna lay across the June-bug birth bed, way Isabel lay across the London park, the scummy successions of thundery female summers, weather throbbing threat of period blood across their shaded bellies.

Buttercup bug
and thundrey
throb.

Buttercup tells trumpet.

Wye sings dead Celts.

Willow hangs soft fronds of faded knacker-hair.

The London park was girdled in metal like a whore in a corset ad. The London park spoke police metal and it wasn't buttercup brass.

The birthbed stank of its rotting clangorous copper-handled pennies clink, odour of cunt-blood to a schoolboy nose.

Time for dinner
Time for dew
Time for me and
Time for you
Time for the garden
Time for tea
Time for you and
Time for me

Nose blood sticking on your lip like London park. Copper residue like vegetable faeces in your summer stubble smoke...

His voice on late-night hysterically pissed phone-calls surely sounded like a form of diarrhoea. He talked in the evening like he shat in the morning, peppering the receiver with black drops. "No need to use a hogbrush for my distress. Haven't passed anything solid for a year or more."

Summer sends a bodydown of garden fires through the shrubs — pale evening flesh flattering the cedars like her body (summer's) shaped the

Welsh ferns.

Who is the woman crossing the lawn like smoke?

"George . . ."

"Yes?'

"Can you see her?"

"I'm busy."

"I think she called."

"You can see. I'm reading."

"Called your name . . ."

"Shut up."

"Do you like the smell of lawn clippings?"

"I like the smell of fresh-cut pages in an old uncut book."

"Does it say anything about her in your book?"

"It just says words. Shut up."

"Read me the words while I watch."

"George read: "Hysteria goosecries at the end of his arm.

Alarmed by the concierge
Drew up her drawers, mopped drops . . .

Peter Brook once
said I was a man of
passionate
common sense.

The density of eagle feathers
Metal hooks above the pianola . . .

Cock an occasional doodle-do.

Eagle squeaks at the end of his right arm.
Her cunt got raw with sweat from the Mediterranean heat.
Goose cries gobble the Roman day.
Paid for it! Paid for it!
At the end of his arm he displayed a worm that crawled into the curtained corner of the room where I go to remember . . ."

"She has no feet. If there was wind I'd say the wind blew her . . .
. . . In Brighton wind round the corner kicked me over, lumbering slippery sole to slippery sole on the rainy pavement of the promenade. Isabel was blown ahead, beyond, back down past the closed arcade — a leaf, brown with ancient veins like the claws of a tiny bird on the back of her hands. Leaf caught, spun, slowed at the edge of the whirlpools of farther gusts, then turned to a trajectory beyond, sped down the course of a glass-green sea wind like autumn shards in a swollen river watched by the false philosophy of Sir John. Weight of her? Nothing. Volume? Enough for the kind of brat my squat cock might fart into her membranes? Never. Tossed back, both of us, past the lover's faces, laughing through window breath-mist from the safety of the corner snack bar. There's no wind here though, yet she moves as though blown . . ."

Cackling mothergull shattered her glass teeth.

Catch her
Snatch her
Save her swift

"Draw the curtains."

"But if I draw the curtains the light crackles along the carpet like goosefires."

"I can only hear the pages rustle as I turn over."
"I can hear the skirts rustle, unless its the evening stirring the hollyhocks."
"You're really a bore."
"Her muslin drags across the dew."
"Your voice rakes across my mind."
"I swear it's your name she calls."
"My name is etched in summer snailtracks across your fly."

Smell summer smoke

"Dragonfly."
"Calling . . ."

George closed the book and stood up. He liked the set of George's head yet. He liked the colour of George's head. George had black eyes. George wore a grey Burton suit and a woollen tie. He said he was going to drink some coffee.

Smell the shades of stocking tops.

When George met the woman she had worn grey serge. A two piece costume. Pale stockings.

STARS OUT IN

SHANKLY SHAKER

Light enough to be carried without effort.

When Dad and Jack picked her up she sagged. "Could you straighten up? asked Jasper. "You should be straight."

The easy jacking of her horned hips into horizontal gear. Straight as a lath, as a reed, as a young felled pine. The light of the four candles on her childsflesh face. Always, always a child asleep when her eyes closed — tiny parings of black in the olive smoothness of her complexion. Candle-light on olive smooth skin. Don't touch.

"You're to be envied, of course," George whispered.

Frightened savages gathered round a princess washed up on their island beach. Their shaven heads displayed their bristles like the points of gleaming needles.

The party was greeted on the shores of the island by Big Chief Skinback and his daughters Winkle and Trip.

"In the name of the Father, Son, and Holy Harry Roberts," said Jasper. He wore his clerical beret, muffler, shades, morning coat and football shorts. He stood on the table surrounded by the eddies of incense of chips from the Combination kitchen behind him. Dod gave the tapers out. Circle of flames. They felled her bridegroom of death like a callow bullock. Laid him on the bier beside her unmoving body. "Give us a kiss, luv." "Yes, give us a kiss . . . . . ." around the circle of flames.

The princess didn't move on the cold marble, in the myriad light of black Christmas. Skinheads sprouted claws, reaching up her bridal shroud to her cunt which he knew was, by now, shedding its first menstrual petals.

In the name of the flounder

"In the name of the original amphibean, the thalidomide veteran and the one-eyed squib" — Jasper announcing the hymn from his rickety folding pulpit.

The youngest and most serious started to burn her. Hot taper fat fell on her melting drapes. His flames ran rapidly over her bare feet, calves. Wince of sleeping irritation, pain, twisted her black arcs of brow exquisitely. "Give us a fuckin' kiss then love."

And of the slump

They asked her gently, groped her spattered gusset gently, tortured her with a quiet purposefulness. The corpse must be made to live, the candle-lit dream made real. Young mother be made to talk to our bleeding lonely skulls.

And of the wholesome roast

"Flocked behind as we carried her out, George."

"Goslings, Henry. Twitterers."

"Packed around as she flooded my mouth with saliva of pain."

"Slavering at the wellspring, one might assume."

Of the sacrificial outlet

"Hooked claws, anxious and grabbing around my hand that shielded her crutch."

"Powers competing for the decisive fundamental delta."

Of the wasted antirrhinum

" 'Get me in that corner' she said. Her twisted willow against me, her love wetness feeding at my tongue and the hands, dry sticks and hooks, dry male anxiety and urgency, obtrusive hunger, pressed, prising, plunging (snapped a thumb back wince at my shoulder). till they died off, went out of the dressing room. The youngest stayed at the window to watch her dress, her bra-cups as black and minute as her eyelashes in sleep or her eyebrows in pain. Oh fuck, I love you in the cold green sea light. Oh fuck, let's find a taxicab quick. Let's fuck quick. I love you."

The man at the taxi rank who had to be helped ("Arse first mate") into the back of a black-and-cream cab wasn't drunk. The dried blood on his hands wasn't from punching walls or gravel.

Kiss me again on the backside. What an alternative. Off we go!

" 'E'd been stabbed," said the little scrubber with the black satin bell-bottoms. "Dahn the Kalahari, 'e said."

"Why didn't he phone for an ambulance?"

"Fucked if I know."

"Please let's get home Henry. I love you. I want your baby."

UP AND AWAY GO

THE FLYING PIGS

There she met an old man

Sad goose under the piano quacks about grey days and the mothergoose glasses of old women crawling enuretic from the folds and hummocks of broken shoes. "So many children she didn't know what to quack."

("Fuck me, Russians are in," said Isabel, looking down at her decorated knickers.)

—But lay on her back in the evening and watched western lovelight turn to black, the stain on the crumpled linen, stiffening under her scabbed back, and saw the generations dragged on schoolboys bent pins through the treacle of the sunset, waving to them, waving to them.

Who wouldn't answer prayers.

(Later: "How about putting your coat down? Gary's a nice guy. I don't want to mess up his blankets . . .")

Grey kissed the grey goose under the piano. A man in a dinner jacket stood in the shadows by the Venezuelan fern.

She took him by the knackers

"Why John," his brother said, "Have you a glass of sherry?"

(Later: "Take it aht then." Tampon thread meandering amongst inner lips and hair — primaeval maggot suffering a blind nativity out of the palping earth. The delicacy of pink stains on the softness of cottonwool hanging from the pale blue string gave them the idea for the washing

And threw him in the fire.

line of tampons stained with coffee the following night.)

"I've a cup of tears, old chap," said Sir John affably. He stepped out of the shadows. His white front was splashed and marked. His jaw hung loosely away from his upper lip in an expression of inane cynicism.

(Root of a fat prick streaked with blood scum. Blood running into mystery along the contours of the floating veins. Blood glazing the brute purple of the helmet to a deeper sunset sweetness. Blood like tiny shards of silken twist in the drops of sperm she left on the coat — Invaded eggs, bad pearls, the sweet whisp of ache in tears.)

Column of blood?

Scarcely a satisfactory architectural device

"Cup of tears," winced his brother. "Everyone is very lachrymose at this party, either by inclination or morality. Cup of tears be blowed, Sir John. Come, take something a trifle more cheering."

The woman entered, sidling past the door with a scandal of silk hissing and gossiping all round her hasty thighs. She sank to a mountain of colour and gloss on the divan beside Sir John. Sir John turned away with a wince.

"John," she spoke softly, her voice the echo of her soft throat. "John," she put a hand like a timid animal at his sleeve. When he turned back his face was bathed in the lines and colours of complete contempt.

Column of blood as a corkscrew or a pig's tail. That's better.

The modern pig is a strange sort of animal. It can fly like a bird.

"Dress, blue/white gingham (Adrian) — Judy Garland — 'Wizard of Oz'?" How indeed is it possible to conceive a market in which the most precious and poignant relic of all can be sold, the Ruby Shoes (by Adrian) which Little Dorothy put on in 'The Wizard of Oz' to dance down her yellow brick road? Once they sold shadows; and now they are selling the rags of shadows.

"Something will conic to lift me out of fatigue." He sank with brute amiability into swamps of Guinness and she strode across the Windsor, a wild and beautiful antelope who should have been arrogant but who enjoyed a different kind of pride. Who should have been regal but who enjoyed the supreme sovreignty of the gutter. Who sang, full-throated with love when the Irishman stood swaying perilously above the tables, in front of the accordionist, and quivered his young throat perfectly up to the top notes of "Danny Boy" —"But I'll be there in sunshine or in shahadow. Oh Danny boy, oh Danny boy, I love, you, so" big brown eyes, big sweet throat, big moist cunt, all eager in her tremulous little body.

COCK ON A COIN

His brother awoke with the sun on his pyjama sleeve. One blackbird shrilled urgently in the garden as though alarmed by the sun.

(Writing on paper damp with sperm —a more or less circular patch at the intersection of the golden mean on this notebook blank.)

CHICK ON A JAG

He walked to the window and noted with considerable amusement the clarity of June sunshine hot as breakfast butter on the wreckage of the previous night.

(Wet of her on the bus, unbuckled the belt of her jeans, his hand under and between those big-boned spaced buttocks.)

Julia and Sir John lay sprawled like war corpses on the lawn. Sir John's head was sunk into Julia's clothing like a fist in a midriff. Julia's black gown was thrown up to half conceal her face, to half reveal the subtle grey of her buttocks where her tights were clawed down. One side of the trestle table was collapsed. Cloth and contents had spilled onto the lawn like milk.

JUMP ON A BUMP

(—Long smoky pastures of Worcestershire "Fuck me please fuck me." What here on the back seat of the X91 Red & White with the plum faced conductor coming near to collect more fares and the dowager four rows forward looking back puzzled through her spectacles?)

The woman sat on the seat by the rockery. She looked gauche and awkward. Her eye make-up made holes in her head, cigarette burns.

TIT ON A ROCK

"Good morning," called his brother cheerfully.

She turned slightly away. A white butterfly fell to Sir John's humped shoulder like a falling leaf.

He leaned out of the window so that the sun struck the shoulders of his pyjamas and his shoulders looked, with their pyjama stripes, like a carnival awning.

(Wet of her like tears and sweat and dew and cloudburst of loveslime over his hand running back to the wrist, oiling the tight pure arsehole. "Get it out then. Please get it out.")

COCK ON A TIT

But the woman rose, retrieved her enormous hat from where it rested on the shrubberies, and walked across the lawn with her loose-shanked stride. He and George carried Sir John and Julia indoors. They undressed them with difficulty. Julia was extremely beautiful, the night of her striking up from her thighs across her shallow abdomen, the dew of the previous night in swathes bathing her laving her salvation slave.

COCKATITCHICK

Straight through rock with an axe

(— Tugged at his zip like a famished child, seized his prick under his sweater and pulled as though to wrench it off and eat it. Snowdrops through the wool of his sweater. Her laughing moan of gratitude as the bus churned, an inexorable tank, through the Wych Cutting and Herefordshire lay back like Sarah Bernhardt drunk among her jewels — thinking of her wet as he leaned through the window of the goodbye train — dry grit, grit metal tight nip of her warm mouth like the pull of her vagina on his middle finger goodbye kiss — wet of the tears of her huge almond eyes . . .)

Straight through the cutting with a rutting

"Pick up the stuff on the lawn, Henry."

"Indeed yes. Scrape through the debris."

The drift and the ebb and the flow of it, scraps, the scrabble of crumpled up paper and playbills, champaign bottles half under turf, and the moss underfoot. They carried armfuls of the calligraphy of orgy and wrote with it across the trees.

FLOWER IN A BOWER

(— So he ran for the lavatory as soon as her waving pinpoint figure was lost down the diminishing goodbye platform and shot a second bunch of snowdrops into a piece of thin British Railways toilet paper, set it in his notebook for safe keeping to freshen the pages and give to her and help her through till springtime.)

Sir John got up at eight o'clock. His hump and his ague and his tremble at the edge of the lawn.

His lip, his uncertain hand, his pallor under the mellowed evening light. He was beckoning.

HELLO

W-101 One Hat — Greta Garbo
W-102 One Leotard — Ann Miller
W-103 One Shawl — Claire Bloom
W-104 One Witch's Hat — Margaret Hamilton — 'The Wizard of Oz'
W-105 One pair boots — Jeanette MacDonald
W-106 One Brassiere and panties, black lace — Kim Novak
W-107 One bedjacket — Mary Astor

The same cataloguer's hand, you feel, also juxtaposed lots 115 and 116 — "Pair panties — Gina Lollabrigida (sic). 1 Apron and Cap — Greer Garson.

Dear Isabel,

She always liked pork chops.

Your hatred for food is your hatred sometimes for me. I could see little but your knees in their dark nylon skins where I lay on the floorboards of the cafeteria. The store was closing. Salesgirls were ushering down to the ground floor while you squashed curried stew against my tight lips and then danced around. me. They deserted the long silent counters as you smeared steak-and-kidney pie over my lips and nostrils.

I was angry. "She has to have her catagorical rebellions," I said to two dead customers by the tea counter. "She's occasionally reasonably intelligent" — collecting myself, clearing myself, letting my irritation die down and then finding you'd gone.

But she couldn't stand mutton whiskers.

Mutton who?

You were two floors down (or twenty floors down?) Your man was stocky with crisp blonde hair.

"Time to go," I said.

"Let me have one more ride," you said.
The butterfly roundabout spun violently at the swing I gave it. Your man fell away, but you, spurting flash of hatred from your eyes in my direction, were suddenly naked, standing at the perifery of the roundabout, and you flew above it, your hair long and soft like it was when you were young, your limbs flashing like paperknives of sandalwood. You took the man up with you into the spin and lay there, cradled in an embrace that was in turn cradled on butterfly

Dog and Jasper.

They went to Ostend, then they went to Baden, then they went to Le Touquet, then they went to Torquay.

steel and vaulted by the ceiling of the darkening store become night — The closed shop submitting its glitter to eternity and that eternity now a cauldron for your spinning flight.

Afterwards you wore the multi-coloured woollen hat that he'd bought you. I resolved to destroy it.

"Time to go," I said.

Much love,

HENRY

"You can't possibly send that," said George. He had come in from the garden. He wore an old leather motoring coat that had belonged to their mother. A dead leaf was caught in his hair. "Summer's gone anyway," he said. "Seen Julia? "

"No."

He turned to Henry and leaned closer. "Come on sunshine. What's on your mind? "

"Three boxing rings without ropes and the big black tower in the middle of the hall."

"Column of death, eh. Weighty symbolism, I'd say."

"Alternate overhead beams on the boxing rings." Jasper crawls. He reads out loud from the evening paper while he crawls.

A leg through the black wrapping of the tower half- way up. An arm through. A prick through. Then a finger. Jasper crawls

Isabel struts around the ring and Jasper watches from below. Her long legs and corded muscles. Her new peach-ghost g-string. 'Right up me crack! Ooh!'

'What's that scar?' asks Jasper.

'When I was small' — appealing little London wail — 'When I was small' — 'Small' — evacuee perhaps — 'I had an operation. My twin inside me. Me 'airy growf.'

'Hairy growth? ' asks Jasper.

'Yeh-h-h.'

I chats 'em up
I drags 'em dahn
I votes left
I feels just right
I lays me dahn
I 'as 'em up
'Ello sweet'eart
'Urry up.

Kiss on a tiny tit — the growing density of square undergraduate embarrassment in the crowd.

Two of my fingers took me up the accompanying honky-tonk keyboard in dischords.

"Scarcely the ladder they should have been climbing. Julia will die when I tell her." The leaf stirred in George's hair.

"If she's not already dead."

"Silly boy. Do go on."

"She walked the aisles between the rings. Jack punctuated everything with shouts, with claps. I played plangent barrelhouse.

The boy she chose from the front row had blue pants when she got the jeans off him — staggered away to the shadows with an erection as vulnerable and humbling as a child's."

"Over-exposure, I'd say."

"Dogged barrelhouse. St. Louis woman with yo' diamon' ring, as she followed him judge, lawdy Mr. Judge, sen' me to the 'lectric chair, followed him and his stalk-on, hand on his knackers. In randiness she becomes a simpering and sweetened snake. The insinuation of one thigh — gauzed — against the other.

THE BLEEDIN'S THE BEST WHEN THE WIND'S IN THE WEST

Mutton who?

Bitch and whiskey

That's a funny
flower.
Then pick it.
Why did you
laugh
when I picked it?
Really, you're a
scream.

"Because
God made thee
mine"
I cherish thee-
ee,"
speaking as one
silkworm to
another.

Football whistle, then darkness. Light up on the Canadian bird's bedroom. Bert says, showing us in, 'Don't mess up the sheets. You wouldn't like it if anybody messed up yours.'

Light up slowly from the electric wall fire. Nonetheless, too cold; the Leeds fog seeping through the window chinks and the mad woman across the hall, who knocked on her floor to keep Bert and Janet awake in their basement flat — 'When we moved in the walls was all splashed and smeared with blood from the junkies that 'ad been in 'ere before.'

Too drunk to tolerate cold or seek out the elusive heat from the wall fire — warm air on my bare thighs and prick — cold eiderdown beneath me. Too drunk to see the scoops and scallops of dim red smouldering light moving over her naked muscle like shoals of horning whales?

Too drunk to do anything but concentrate on my own erection (remembering the naked magic of the boy's and the white mushroom, grown overnight, luminous white, sudden among the brown leaves and sage grey of the winter woods). Spilling up into her, according to promise, 'If you pull out tonight I'll never speak to you again.' "

"Interesting reversal. Queen Victoria doing a bloody handstand," said George, rubbing the bridge of his nose.

"Her resplendence. Her small royal animal. 'You came to me at last.'

'Came to me' meant like that, like 'Sang to me' or 'Clove unto me' — when I'd thought that before, when she'd lay sobbing and raw under my cruder insistent body in another cold bedroom, I'd thought she meant 'Come to me' like 'Be mine, give in to me' — when she'd lay there a month previously, sobbing 'You won't come to me.'

We got up in a green fog. The mad woman across the hall opened her door as we left, and followed us out onto the step, not shouting, nor muttering, nor striking, but staring, staring us down the road to the fog-beaded, rusted metal bus-shelter."

"Come on," said his brother, "let's go and find Julia.
All her little gossiping silks will drive that crap right
out of your so-called memory."

Other rubbish is more immediately evocative. 131 pairs of Roman sandals, 13 gladiator nets, two boxes of arrows, model German planes from 'Mrs Miniver,' miniature Roman galleys from both 'Ben Hurs' (the 1926 ones made of genuine copper and three times the size of those used in the modern version). What can a Whipper's Uniform and a Stinger's Uniform look like?

He didn't see his brother through four years until that summer. He knew about the woman from the first brush, from the earliest anticipatory imaginings.

He found his brother one day in the wash-house behind the house. He went down the yard, knowing he'd find something,

Rub-a-bub-bub.

found George bent over her like the imprisoning summer wind embracing the bow, the grace and pathos of a cut sapling.

Woodchopper's Ball
Woody Herman.
Parlophone
Blue Label.
Super
Rhythm Style.

Knot-hole knees with the knee-cap an underbark bulging through skin of suntan like the head of a baby emerging. So with the elbows, the shoulders, the knuckles. The round of the eminence extruded its nakedness and the slack of the familiar skin spread back around the bone, the bone under the skin, concentric circles of it; growing emergence, erection, the knobs and the joints of her ambling raw-boned system.

"I can't imagine them," he whispered to his brother one evening. "Her diddies, her titties, her little flappers, her danglers."

"Lovelust watery slid down. Right down the bottom of the greasy grass," said George.

Splash at the top
Tinkle down the drop
Slap on the slab on the lowermost rock.

"I could nudge you and smirk. I could snatch at your cobblers, old sport, old man, old cripple, down there by the Beggar's Gate, ass's ears nailed on your bone head ossified with passion."

"Grass that I greased with a blood of squashed suns," said George.

"I could nudge you their nature, the lillyblow daffodils set in reverse, the childslace cupcakes turned in their cream, the swell and the suck-swell."

"Lay in the wet, in the swim, in the fishes and kippers that float up her fuck-tunnell," said George.

"— The shake and the tremble, the fear and the pride."

"Red hill. Red meadow," said George.

"Give us a kiss mate, you with the streaks and slashes of short grass all down your cheeky prick. I could nudge you the mothersquash and the proud erection."

"Set sail in the sunset," sang Mother Kelly mildly.

"Screwed in the front of her were her tits," said my brother. "Plugged on the facade like a double

accessory twinkling fairytree headlamps. Door-knockers, drawer knobs, lover's warts, radio dials, tender for tongueing, the spread of the brown of the pink of the muscle, the gland and the throb and knot and the love knot, the flower . . ."

She came first through the French windows with a parasol and naked breasts, painted lilac and pale blood with summer shade. Her head, tilted, received the rose reflection from the parlour carpet.

I saw her in the light

"I could kiss taffeta," giggled George. "Oh how we danced on the night of the purple moon. 'June is a detestable month for may bugs,' Sir John said, letting his venom into the laurel shrubbery. Oh how we danced up a long steel ladder. A lady doesn't reel in a schottish or a flatfish slashed from the pit of the aristocracy. And isn't that Dulcie Evensong? And isn't she looking for you, dear boy? And isn't that a parcel wrapped in linen she's hiding at the root of the Venezuelan fern?"

and I loved her

I saw her in the cool vegetation

It was two years later that his brother sent on Sir John's first letters.

My dear George,

I must say that it was more than a pleasure to encounter your hospitality for the second time last night, and now you must forgive me if I presume too much in tendering my congratulations to you on your splendid choice of a mistress.

and I loved her

It is not frequently that a man of my years is moved to such a pitch of excitement by a young acquaintance. May I say again how fortunate I consider you to be, and how I wish you the very best happiness, which I'm sure you both deserve.

I saw her in coloured water softly.

Yours sincerely,

John Applegate

My dear George,

I cannot move for gratitude and regret. I am cramped with it, bent with it, bedridden, ratnibbled, weeping on the tip of my pen, my brain all viscoid with the odour of ash of roses and excretia rising from the grooves at the sides of my fingernails.

Emotional generosity is rare. Sexual generosity is virtually extinct. That the nobilities remain in an acquaintance of mine enthralls me, that it exists to my advantage mortifies me. I can only adore her flesh with the same pure impulse that turns my moral adulation in your direction.

and I loved her hard.

Always indebted,

John Applegate

A BIG HAND FOR JUMBO

Gown, white crepe, heavily, beaded shoulders — (Adrian) — Katherine Hepburn 'Philadelphia Story'.

Here are Norma Shearer's gowns for 'Marie Antoinette'.

We're gonna hang out our frontal lobes

They became wartime dolls. It was all about wartime anyway — Birmingham Temple Meads, the late train, the squaddies banging their kit bags up into the corridors from the platform below. Pork pies and crisps. Soldiers at the opposite table, a Pioneer and a cook.

They all sang war songs, Bless 'Em All, Comin' Round the Mountain, We're Gonna Hang out the Washing on the Seigfried Line. The holes where the noises were bought with gulps of McEwan's were round, were carved in wood. Adelaide wept about leaving Jasper. She wrote messages in brown pen on a paper plate. Jasper ran up and down the corridor, yelling and dancing. "Showing off," said Yvonne.

Goodnight sweetheart

He thought about Ted and the mountains of jammy objects. From behind a blindfold, Ted, known only by sound, had sounded like an awful beast, a cannibal pig. Ted had sounded like a beast at the lintel, the mad ox in the thicket.

Run rabbit up the smoking hole

He looked at Jasper's round mouth. "The long and the short and the tall," sang Jasper.

"Bless all the sergeants and W.O.I.'s." sang the cook.

I'll see you tonight in screamland

He enjoyed himself very much. "How did you get on in Edinburgh, you dirty old bugger ?" he asked Jasper. Jasper threw beer over him. "I still stink today," he told George later. Yvonne and he walked up the road from Euston to King's Cross, pissed as arseholes. Yvonne got the tickets.

We'll meet again, in the blood, in the rain

Keep smilin' through

They sat in a compartment with an ornate old woman.

"When I was living at the Abbey I was most closely, most intensely, myself," he told Yvonne. "Even though I was dead miserable and always pissed." Yvonne laughed gravely. She could remember his early morning shivering tears as clearly as he could remember the closeness of those dawn skies through the bare December trees and his conviction that his child, the second in six months, was rotting in the kitchen wastebasket under the Nescafe tins, the Woodbine packets, the Guinness bottles, wrapped in pink paper tissue, just as she's taken it from her weeping knickers in the icy winter night.

There'll always be an in

It's time to say goodnight

Yvonne remembered the rivers of liquor he sunk after the phone call.

"Gin and quinine."

"Whose was it?"

"Yours of course."

"Gin and quinine? You didn't tell me? You little bastard."

"When is a child not a child?"

"When he's — er — bought it." (aborted — get it?)

Later: "I came on in the bath. Lost a lot . . ." — Him, ironically: "Lost a lot.." "Drunk. Had to be walked round the grounds. Then just lay and cried for days saying I'm sorry, Henry. I'm sorry. Sorry . . ."

Yvonne remembered him fresh as an onion from the pub and the phone box, slinging his blistered wit around her midnight hash party until everybody froze into sharp discomfort despite the hash.

"Intensely yourself ," Yvonne echoed.

"When is a conception not a conception."

"Yes."

In bed the war had gone. The English Second World War is the property of the railways where its zeitgeist inexorably remains.

"When it's — er — mark you! — late (immaculate — dig? dig?

In bed Isabel took him into her rocking warm quim and nursed him to sleep. Jennifer, in the next room, was puzzled about the baby, didn't understand.

Isabel said: "It'll be a bloody messiah, mate. A superb child."

An inch away from his wet jaw, beneath the bread-white thighs of the girl he was sucking, was the Guardian, crumpled. An inch away from the parsimonious crack of her arse was a photograph of Michael Moorcock looking like a messiah himself. The girl had comforted him earlier. "She's come on? No messiah this trip. Poor love."

He'd got the kids off to bed. Billy cried for his mother. The girl sat and watched.

"When is a kiss not a kiss."

After the kids were in bed she watched the tears slowly come to him. She took them onto her shoulder, then onto her hardening breast, then turned slowly under him, quickening to a series of elusive climaxes.

And a cold untouchable voice said "What does it mean now, then?" and Michael Moorcock glowered up through the fat portal of her crutch like an insane familiar come to prod his sense of his own ineffectual

"When it's a cunt."

"That's not funny."

stupidity.

"I've come on," she'd said over the phone.

"Never mind. We'll try again."

"Yes."

Now blethering self-pity into the wrong hole at the bathos of it all. Messiah-building, a task requiring stamina and patience.

"Mind like a sewer."

The world ran in and out of all the apertures in his head.

Stars reflected
in a brain drain.

Kiss the stars goodbye, friends.

"Jumpsuit, greige crepe, white strip trim. Made for Ginger Rogers, 'Weekend at the Waldorf'; worm by Marilyn Monroe, 'Asphalt Jungle'.

The Teachers' Seaside Inquests

Time for a tinkle

He feared mostly the hours alter sweat-and-piss time. Sweat-and-piss time occured, with reasonable regularity, at a quarter past two ack emma. He woke in a sweat, a cold malodorous sweat. He scored and tunnelled his way through all the unfinished corners of the previous day's more thorny conversations. He revolved his bad conscience under the baleful drunken glare of his rationalisation kit. He got up. He pissed. He went back to sleep.

The sleep he went back to was a no-man's-land of mangled identity. A teddy-bear paw to his magical cunt, he would walk naked down Hereford High Street persuading Sally Oxlade not to take the aspirins with all the charm and wit of a Wilde. "Suicide, my dear Isabel, is a refuge of the potential schizophrenic. One personality requires a French retreat wherein to Hyde. The other merely does without tears like a laughing Jeckyl."

Time for a joke

It was the frequent emergence of the word Bella or Isabel that he feared most, in these transpersonal excursions. Not only did he address it to Sally Oxlade, but also to the girl spreadeagled on the newspaper with Moorcock hammering his face and the schoolboy howl of his unfortunate name up through her triumphal arch; and also, finally, he addressed it to Edna. Poor uncomplicated Anne Hathaway Edna, who hathn't hath it away for thome yearth despite her daisy face and her buttercup eyes.

Difficult wrinkle

He could never, for example, forget the occasion when he placed a delicate though half-sleeping index finger on the throat of his wife, drew it down in arabesques worthy of Scheile or Belmer, curving round a nipple, implying an umbelicus and hooking gently into the terminal point of her clitoral crevice, then breathing into the bedroom air, through a fog of Guinness and halitosis "Ah-h-h you're a lovely girl, Isabel."

When the buttercup broke

He feared walking with Sally out of Hereford High Street, through the cathedral Close and onto the lawn of the Bishop's Palace where he had introduced Sally to the woman. The woman had been reading "Howards End" and his brother George had been barely visible in the huge bay window of the music room.

Elegant flutter

"Sally," repeated the woman abstractly. He wondered if she was drunk. "Sally. A name I always find remarkably suggestive. I mean one never actually threw a petrol bomb at one's Aunt Grace and Gracie Fields was never up my alley."

He could hear George's mephistopholean laughter. George's exacerbating sense of bawdy ever cut across the grace of his surroundings. He imagined her regrets fluttering around her thighs and trembled to see Sally's reaction when they escaped the hem of her petticoats.

"Perhaps if you come inside you can find a servant and perhaps the servant could find us drinks," the woman said.

Blue blooded bibbing

He feared drinking the wrong sherry from the wrong cunt and he feared more cock crowing under the velvet drapes of the mahogany table.

There was a steel engraving depicting a sloe-eyed wine harvester. It hung opposite the window.

Somebody's coming

"If this bloody bottle doesn't provide me with one more' glass I shall have to help Julia with the flowerbeds around the north lawn," the woman murmured. There was the sound of someone breathing in orgasm in the next room. "I like pictures like that," said Sally, looking at the engraving.

He was, in fact, only two rows away from Isabel. Her tattered lace shawl clung to her stained and shallow breasts. Her five lovers, with autumn in their curling bodyhair, loaded grapes onto the ox-carts a mile away towards the horizontal hills.

"I can't get to you," he said.

"The Messiah will be a noble vintage," she said, tossing her hair back, squelching grapes against her bruised left nipple.

He feared what he was anxious for. The colour of the early morning hours was metallic green. His evil breath turned to the taste of metal and the flavor of his saliva seeped into his blood and he walked in his blood down the grey loneliness of Sir John's study.

And somebody's fibbing

"Ah Henry," said Sir John. Why was it that his voice sounded so young in the half-dark? "You won't," he said "Think too ill of me. It might seem an extraordinary thing to assert but nonetheless I must, I want to, I will. The original difficulty was a coincidence. It occurred at Torquay. She and I were drinking in the hotel lounge. George was on the verandah.

A shade of discolouring mood is the best phrase I find for it. It entered all of us at a twenty past eleven, like a cloud passing over the sun. As it occurred she caught George's eye through the French windows and I saw what passed between them. I tasted, I felt, its pure evil.

When the shade passed it left us stained and different. It was the night that she left my room. Ostensibly to the bathroom, probably intended to. I'm quite in control. What I tell you is exactly true. I'd like you to leave me now, old boy, if you don't mind."

I spent my life avoiding miserable old farts with half the Bible rewritten in Irdu
across their bib and tuckers. I spend my life keeping out of debt, jail, and dark brown studies, where the leather reeks of protestant errors and classical crimes.

The woman sat, oddly, in the hall at the foot of the stairs. Oddly because the hall was unheated and the night was none too warm. There was a deep furrow between her eyebrows like an incision. She looked much older. "Where's your brother?" she wailed.

"He'll be down in a minute," called back Ruth. "Billy! Breakfast is ready."

He was used to a narrative of waking punctuated by battering feet on the stairs.

The warmth of the bed presented itself to his conscious body as a variation on the soup shade darkness of his dream. Edna had got up some time since. The hollow she'd left behind was symbolically empty and cold. "Allegory," he thought, "is the final falsification of symbolism, and symbolism," he smiled "is a falsification of truth. My wife Edna is a hot little pie, and it's I who have no appetite."

After breakfast he entertained Sir John in his lounge. They played a handful of old 78 records — Jessie Matthews, Gertrude Lawrence.

He was only talking to Sir John because he wanted to flatter the impulse of pity he had rescued from the soup drain.

"It's difficult to recognise the otherness of someone you love to the point of your own dissolution," Sir John rambled on, garrulously. "You bathe, d'you see, in the honey of a lovely day and the flowers haven't noticed you. Their growth is indifferent and the weather will betray you.

I've pictured them many times. Nothing more than your brother reclaiming his own, I tell myself continuously. But if she was his and not mine throughout the dream, then the purity of those nights with her on which I'd staked my new self was a delusion, and a delusion, and a delusion and a dream, dear boy, are not the same thing at all . . .

I've pictured them often but I won't bore you. I know you can run your own little pornographic shadow shows. No, I'll not bore you.

The problem, however, that I would tax you with is that with which I'm now faced. What, my dear Henry, do you do with the dross, this detritus," his quaking hand attempted a rhetorical gesture towards his body "Now that it's existence is disproven? The society provides for the dead and it disposes of rubbish in its more accustomed forms, but what does man or society do with a human machine deprived of the human individual to run it?"

He looked towards Sir John and was impressed by the authenticity of the void in his oyster eyes. "Would it be impertinent to suggest that you succour your sensibility on the colours of your own regret?"

"Regret?" Sir John arched his pendulous white brows. "Regret? My regret is buried, dear boy, buried under rock. What remains of regret among the prehistoric strata I cannot suppose."

"Dig. Drill. Penetrate."

"With whom?"

"By yourself."

"My dear boy, the self is a lie. How can
nobody regret their own absense?"

"WHAT'S
HE SAY?"

"HE'S VANISHED
AWAY."

TO THE MEMORY OF
ONE WHO DIED
YOUNG

"W-932, 1 Gown, black lace, Jean Harlow." This was worn in 'Saratoga', made when the saddest of the cinema's Golden Lasses was dying, and finished with a double playing in her long shots. There is the burberry that Clark Gable, Harlow's co-star, wore for luck in every modern role he played after 'Comrade X' in 1939; and the clothes worn by Judy Garland and Mickey Rooney in 1938, still the world's ideal children, in 'Babes on Broadway'.

Gnomes on the March

AND IT'S CHRISTMAS DAY

At Christmas time little Edna commenced her turd rolling. He had always thought it remarkable that a woman so adorably small so round and compact, should pass stools of the same endearing quality.

ZUNK!

At Christmas time she rolled them into four separate piles, apportioning off her various droppings to the children with some objective thought and then an adroit twist of her finger and thumb. She was a healthy woman, by and large, so her movements were hard and odourless, leaving little deposit on the fingers that sorted them.

THUNK!

"Willikin's already had thirty shillings spent on him," she would say "so this should go to Sam. If you buy anything more than her share of what Aunt Joyce sent."

DRUNK!

On Christmas morning the stockings acted as a magical talisman. The very spirit of Christmas lit in the children's faces as they flocked around one another's stockings, check and eye alight with a flush of the most indecent lust. As Christmas morning wore on the lust burned brighter and brighter, eyes thickening with tears of venom as unequal gifts were carefully measured and bitter reprises written up in their festering little minds.

By tea time, nerves and bellies raw with food and jealousy, the boil would burst "Gerroff my science set."

"Well it was promised to me. Anyway, you took my Beano Annual."

Til finally Mummykins was moved to tears at the poor spirit in which her widow's mite had been received, sagely asserting

BUNK!

that if her arsehole had a reverse gear she'd take all the glittering toys and ram them back up again.

"When I found out she had her first bout of – you know, first became ill . . ." Firelight played across Sir John's face. The shadows of his scowl were a sooty black. "I tried to stop them taking her away. Hid her in a room for weeks. She played with her faeces like a child with mud. When they broke in, the red velvet on the upholstery was caked. She wore her wedding dress and the white satin was streaked. She said nursery rhymes."

He could hear her cry from the hall. Hunk of Humpty
"Humpty Dumpty had a great fall.
All the king's horses and all the king's men
Couldn't put Humpty together again."

Slowly he crushed the eggs in his pocket.

"You mustn't fuck and you mustn't wank for two days before. That way we'll be sure," Isabel said. The white ran from his fingers. It tasted of metal. It reminded him of his ejaculation showering like rain down the thin black fabric of her bell-bottoms. The painted ceiling of the converted church, with its stone bosses and groins, was only a foot

White of egg

above them. The dressing room loft was over the bar. One surviving perpendicular window ventilated both. He wondered if the handful of drinkers in the pub below could hear his gasp of release. The nearness of the ceiling reminded him of treading the catwalks on the scaffolding when they painted the bosses at Hereford.

On a lady's leg

Her saw her cunt like a rondel and four piggish faces emerged together, fringed with oak leaves. A mad boar ran through the theatre in the chancel, knocking over one of the floods.

"We still have trouble from reactionary clergy," said Dickey Drain. "You know, drinking, experimental drama, nudes on consecrated ground."

The swell of a blister pearly.

He pressed the banks of the blister and the snowdrops splattered all down the back of a hog. Sir John told him how the woman counted while the man who garrotted his pigs with a black nylon stocking pearls in the custard coloured ward snickered under the washbasin.

This little
pig ran
wee-wee-wee
All round the
body of
Sharon T.

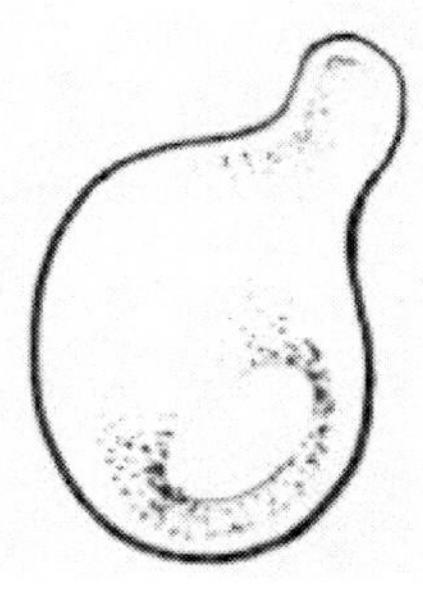

The blister pearl 2.

"You can take the bristles off his white thigh like shaving a pig." He found the blister pearl in Barnet Market one distant summer Saturday.

"Ever see a stone like that? " asked the stall holder, under the Garden of Flora on her wicker hat.

She wore the pearl on her little finger. It was mounted on an antique ring from which the cut glass had been prised to make room. Purity of pearl with a festered form. Bad marriage. Dropped from a deseased divinity. Ovoid like ejaculations welled into new forms as they slid down Isabel's seventeen-year-old throat. The purity of her young wet eyes, then, there among the Saturday celandines with the thick salt lingering on the back of her tongue — "No, it was beautiful. I'll do it again if you want . . ."

"How much d'you want for that ring? "

"Oh it's not for sale dear. Oh deary me no. Wouldn't part with that."

"Ever buy a funeral dome?"

And sometimes, walking with George, he would lead George into the shop down the hill by New Barnet station, turn over an antique or so. Peer into a musky jug or two. And if she was there he would ask to buy the ring again. "No," she would say. "It's a blister pearl. They're very rare. I've got another one somewhere. I'll see if I can make it up for you." But she never did and as the winters passed and Isabel shed her ragged broken children, as the woman walked repeatedly down the front path of Shenley Hospital and caught the Green Line bus back to Sir John, the woman in the shop got colder, angrier as if the spunky blister on her pinky held some surviving germ of a bent virginity that he was trying to have away.

"No, but Edna's got a vast collection of witch stones."

Between the miscarriages and the mismarriages Isabel mismanaged with a handful of mischosen lovers (a nose in a Volkswagon on a steep hill is unlikely to stem any skeleton's screaming lack) he rang her up. Usually from rank phone boxes, with a gallon or two of beer in him

"Ever purchase a Staffordshire dog?"

promising the ring as a stamp on their ultimate permanent coupling, as a halo over their sun sinking slowly behind Paradisical palms, as a crock of gold for the end of their rainbow. The more the promises intensified, the further away went the garden. The further from the garden they travelled by his own drooling indecisiveness, the more the woman in the antique shop defended her talisman.

"No, but Isabel's got a stuffed terrier on wheels."

Her husband was a faded little man. He offered Henry a snuff box once — "Do for yer purple 'earts," he said.

Isabel dressed quickly. He lay on her caved-in bed nursing his prick absent-mindedly and watching the lines of elastic describe the ridges and subtle vales of her emaciated body. "Come on," she said. "If you want to catch that half-past eleven train into town."

"Ever put a deposit on a paperweight?"

The day was spitting brightly, cold showers out of a lit sky. It's a day like that today. It whips a kind of bland benevolence over the ridge of Wyke and pins it in the sky like a Victorian religious banner. The day flaps in the sky. The day says "Health is awake."

"No, but I've worked a bit on a wet sheet."

They struggled through the buffeting brightness to New Barnet Station.

"Do you collect relics?"

"When I took the Yorkshire Woollen bus to Halifax the little hills to the right of the road that drops and swings down from Norwood Green were swollen with a subtle gladness, were beginning to anticipate a choir of starlings in the sooty twilight."

Their visit to the shop was hurried. She was obsessed with objects in glass or Perspex spheres or domes. A shrimp of hope of the wanted child swam sleeping in clear love liquids in her scooped out belly. The praying twist of magic swam in its womb in her narrow skull. Her eyes wept clear birth slime.

The domed funeral doves were not for sale. There was a glass paperweight full of butterfly wings. There was a test tube full of coloured sands.

"And the dirty drawers of St. Theresa."

"How much does your wife want for her blister pearl ring?" he asked the man resignedly.

"Not for sale mate," said the man, then smiled. "You've been very patient."

He went to a Dickensian cupboard in the back room. He found an envelope in one of the pigeon holes. He shook a blister pearl into his palm. "There mate. You've been very patient." The edge was chipped. Their unbegotten child swam in the wet core of the stone.

"And the afflicted singer of St. Saturday."

"How much?"

"That's a present from me mate, for your

patience."

Ed O'Donnel, the jeweller to set the pearl on the dawning ring, blew a crude trombone out over the waking hills of Halifax.

"Premature triumph, friend," said his, brother, and turned away from the view. The sky banner flapped madly against the rocks of spring over his head. The railway viaduct dropped its columns into valleys of light.

"It was, it really was."

"Do you take the spring lightly?" asked George, picking his way carefully along the cobbled path that led back to the road.

"I'm weighed down by the spring light," he replied.

Sun
Rock
Dropped
Down
Gobs
& Drops
of Oil
& Mineral
To cool
And Standing
Dark

"Sir John, of course, is virtually blind," said George. "Lies in that idiotic bamboo chair on the terrace looking into the sun for hours without the flicker of an eyelid."

"Actually," he said, forcing his tongue into difficult regions, "What I'm preoccupied with at the moment is finding the resourses in a famished soul to acknowledge the sudden sense of benevolence around me. As soon as I begin to see the world in terms of pearly tits I begin to get hardening of the arteries. The lovely lithe thing about Isabel is her titlessness. No more than robin's eggs. That, on the other hand, precipitates a hardening of the prick. The other, fulsome, thing makes me freeze. Yet it's all there, milkiness, a gentleness. Why refuse it?"

George stopped. The light in the sky was so bright his head, in silhouette, was hard black. Nevertheless he could see the familiar lines of supressed ridicule form around George's mouth.

"You're going to have to drive yourself onto the jolly old spikes of ice again, I suppose," he said. "Really, you and your gestationary difficulties. You flee the full maternal element in everything, break your heart when your titless mistress aborts and miscarries, then, as though carrying the highest banner yet for free will and independance, you try to turn her into a mother despite her boyish appeal. And where in hell's name will you go then, Lord Randall? Up Shit Creek without a paddle?"

Shit Creek without a paddle was in flood in the crown. The Co-Op mechanic with ponderous gut was sounding out about Pakistanis.

— "Bate 'em owert' 'eyad wi' yer fuckin' prick. 'Umiliate the bastards."

Guinness turns the bedroom air as yellow as your wife's footsole. The knives in the sky persisted, hacking, hacking, hacking at the springtime flags.

British Girl is the Greek Pimpernel

Jeanette Macdonald's dresses from 'Firefly' and 'Bittersweet', Luise Rainer's from 'The Great Zeigfeld', a rich oriental robe worn by Muni in 'The Good Earth', a gown of Ethel Barrymore's from 'Rasputin' (the film which launched the most celebrated defamation case in movie history, 'Yussupov vs. MGM'.

The party had a well modulated tempo. Sir John's friend, Michael Ashill, arrived spectacularily in a Lagonda. It coughed and snarled up the drive. Michael sat at the seat with some measure of triumph.

Coughed up out of the bricks, seeping from between the tiles.

There were other small sensations. Julia, excelling herself in efficiency, laid out food in the music room that reminded Sir John of the days of the British Raj. Eight o'clock sunlight twinkled on the segments of grapefruit. Nine o'clock candlelight waxed rosy through wine. Harriet Morris came in helplessly drunk but Julia helped her to the box room near the top of the house. She sat in the gloom and the dust in her ostrich feathers and her laddered stockings of pure white silk. Sweat poured from every cranny of her flesh and clothing.

I died twice in my thirteenth year. The house was emptier than my body. I spun above the bed like a headache in a hayfield.

The company was fully assembled by ten. A nicotine-stained man played Jerome Kern and Noel Coward on the old grande. In front of the green curtains his white front looked crisp as frost. It was only at half-past ten that the first intimations of unease occurred. One of Mrs. Barnsby-Rudge's fat daughters suddenly ran out into the hall and was sick down her peach blossom organdie gown. As she stood there, stooped, with the comparatively bright bleak light of the hall beating down on her freckled shoulders, the hook and eye fastenings at the back of the gown popped open one by one. The way in which her flesh, blended of the tenderest grays and pinks, swelled over the edge of her

Considerable mission of mischief to get between the toes of the oldest guests, to spit in the headache of the drunkest adolescent debutante.

brassiere strap, took on a plasticity so dense it

came near to giving off sound.

By eleven o'clock Sally Oxlade put down her martini and howled. It took a fragment of time to distinguish the content of her howl. It passed quickly through his mind that it might be exultation, ridicule, or extreme high spirits. It was seeing the terror in her eyes, the fleck of blood and bubbling spittle on her chin, made him realise that some bestial thing was within her and was playing on her vocal cords like a fingerless ape with a harp.

Drunk headache.
Spin them in
a hopeless dance,
a vertical
that hums like the
stench from the
family crypt.

She recovered, of course, as Miss Barnsby-Rudge recovered. It was merely a second stage in the phased development of the phantasmagoria the evening was to become.

At eleven fifteen someone across the Wye fired a volley of shots that crackled away into the blue dingles of Aconbury.

"What is the difference between a large cucumber and a leg of lamb?" asked Michael Ashill loudly.

"Do tell us," cried Julia, her teeth stuck onto her head like an ivory portcullis'.

"Well, a leg of lamb festers on the slab and a large cucumber slabs up the fester."

"Staunches the wound," frowned George.

We are cryptic
as angels and
golden as
legendary
spiders.
We hang on
subtle threads
between the
strands of
old frayed
fabric that
the
conversation's
made of.

There was another volley of shots. Sally Oxlade howled again. She stood awkwardly, one leg lifted away from the other like a wet child. So standing she clawed under her long satin dress and started to scratch herself violently. Her eyes pleaded but no-one met them.

"Do go on" said Julia to Michael Ashill, lifting her voice to carry above Sally's howl, above the grinding of Sally's teeth.

"Try this one then. What is the difference between a dog in a road accident and a rusty razor?"

"We'll buy it," said George, "we'll buy it."

"A dog in a road accident howls out gravel and a rusty razor hollows out owls."

Sir John turned his back to the room and looked out over the dark lawn. After a while we could distinguish from his shaking back that he was weeping helplessly. The woman was not yet present. Miss Barnsby-Rudge's vomit had sunk into the old Persian carpet scarcely a yard from where the woman had sat on that cold night before the thaw.

Old frayed ballroom dresses hanging in the boxroom. Soon it'll be time to drag them down the main stairs in an avalanche of malevolent muslin.

George slid up to his side. "I do believe I glimpsed Isabel through the side window," he murmured grimly.

He went to the side window. Sally clutched at his jacket but he brushed her aside violently. Through the side window he could see the North Lawn with its bird-bath on its pedestal, with its distant ornamental folly, with its overhanging Welsh pine.

A sliver of silvery grey by the daffodil beds seemed gesturing to him. He ran out of the front door, down to the terrace steps and up onto the North Lawn to trap her.

You may feel my cold breath at the door to the gaming room. You may feel my cold hand by the window of the chapel. You may kiss my cold lips with filth of live ram's arse.

His haste was unneccessary. She was helplessly shackled with her own knickers, knotted as they were around her ankles.

She grabbed his head, tearing the backs of his ears with her fingernails. She bit at his forehead as if at a green apple.

Dew from the lawn grass soaked coldly and immediately through his trouserleg when he fell. He looked calmly across Isabel's humped and naked back and far down across the even dewy mist the clothed the lawn he saw the house, and high in the wall of the house he saw Harriet Morris looking through the unlit window of her boxroom, waving something.

There was more gunfire. Somewhere on the other side of the house a window shattered musically.

Come Matilda. Sleep no more my dear. The fishhooks in the persistency of time are dragging away your bedclothes. Spider writing on the walls should serve to irritate a few.

They walked quietly through the shrubberies. He lent Isabel his jacket. His white shirtsleeves caught a fugitive moon through the netted branches. Suddenly he glimpsed a smudge of lace in the ivy to the right of their path.

"Poor bugger," breathed Isabel running to her side. Her face was livid, the whites of her eyes under her stained lids clear as in daylight. Her lips, mauve and black in that light, reached for Isabel's nipple. Moaning compassion Isabel lifted the lapel of his jacket aside to bare herself.

Briefly the only sound was the thirsty lapping of the woman's tongue at the nipple. Then there was the scrape of fingernails at his fly. Hurriedly, but deftly, as though desire had ousted hysteria, the woman bared him whilst still lapping at Isabel's breast like a piglet at a sow. Her fingernails, stained the same colour as her lips with blackberry juice, fluttered around his penis, teasing the premature pearl that gathered at its tiny slit.

Then Sally howled again somewhere nearby and there was a desperate crashing about in the shrubberies.

Hack at the curtains. Hurl the stair rods at the windows in the front door.

Slash the silken ankles.

The frost can crack a twig.

The woman's sinews in her wrist record the fuss of her fingers like puppetstrings. Fingertwigs.

of the loveliest of girls with fragments of stained glass. Howl, howl in the walls.

Isabel's limbs were ever like fragments from a rook's nest. Lying on her, he was frequently tempted to break the rhythm and music of intercourse by taking her upper arm in his teeth about an inch below the point where her black underarm down spent itself, and snapping it like a cheese straw.

Sir John bayed dog noises up in the boxroom with Harriet Morris. Harriet placed her face, on which her tears had irrigated the crust of her powder, under the crook of Sir John's knee. She drew in the odours of decay and musky grief like a bridesmaid inhaling her posy.

Isabel swayed under the black hatch of trees. The woman sang in a garrulous voice that seemed possibly the voice of a dead man. Isabel breathed with the voice of a stirred roseleaf: "I want a baby. I've got a baby. I've lost the baby. History makes a chain. The links are silly stories. Pull your knickers up, gal.

Come dance my little angel. Down the stairs. Before the window. Round the ankles of the guests.

Butcher shop, Great Horton Road.
You saw my wet love hanging from a hook. She wants a baby. Assistant looks incredulous. Kissed a block of marble. Shot vomit in his new striped jeans.

Chitterlings and tripe. Pig's liver.
Half the Metropolitan Police can hear my violet whimper.
It rises like the breath of blood
From the swansthroat drain of the abatoire.

Pull your drawers up, Bella.
Don't sluice your meaty heartbreak down his leg.

Want a baby. Lost a baby.
        Kiss him in his wince, you yearning
        summer appetite.
Kiss him in his wince. Caress his ache with meat petals.
Lost a baby. Want a baby. Thistledown."
    Moonlight let a handful of motes onto their ritual.
A funeral without bald women is imponderable.

LONNIE & DOTTIE, QUEEN MOTHER

Quest for quahogs & the bald princess

**"A human way to evoke
response:
beneath the female contours
lie deposits of fat (shaded)**

leg irons and 49 whips, plain: shackles, bull whips, three chopping blocks, and a weapon 4 ft. 9 in. by 3ft. 6 in.

I'm a dreamer, aren't we all?

The memory stayed with him most of the day until drinking time (Henry worried by a headache passing through a corner of his skull, tugging at his optic nerve like a kitten with an old sock, the waters of distress at the persistent images running down behind his nose — clouds of snotache— into his labyrinthine bag of giblets.)

Did you ever see a dream walking?

They walked along the edge of the wood. "Don't worry" he said "I have a hotel." He decided not to fear Inspector Stanley, unchanged since his serialisation in Radio Fun, for Inspector Stanley, noon-light amber on his charming, mobile, waxworks mask had been quite frightening, walking down towards Henry, wearing his expensive overcoat and bowler hat with the enormous butcherknife held at his side at a shallow angle — "I know a hotel."

You stepped out of a dream.

The gate into the hotel garden opened from the edge of the woods. There were Cinzano umbrellas over tin tables. There was a Benskin's sign in gold. It was not, perhaps, the Artichoke, near Elstree — dim and disappointing summer fucks amongst hushed buttercups, "I'm sorry Henry, I don't want to hurt you." Edna liked it. "Four children? Six altogether?" said the manager. "I think I'll put you in the cottage. A path down through cowparsley and groundweed, nod of threatening nettlesting on his children's bare ankles, led to a cottage of plaster so rotted under whitewash all it constituted in the way of protection was memories of woodsmoke dingles and the seams in the walls of safer vaginas.

I'll see you in my dreams.

Dreamin' just dreamin'.

"Children to bed, we'll go for a drink" he said, remembering how he and Isabel had passed their weekend, dream of cuntflood Saturday,

Don't waste my dreams.

in this rotting cottage. Putting children to bed in a strange house always made him want to cry. Rested, though, and a little relieved, he stood in the arch of the narrow stair with a hand on the wall on either side. "Go get your face on" he said to Edna, and half the house shifted under the pressure from his right hand. When he withdrew his weight the masonry rocked back into place again. "Christ," he said "Look at that" and showed her again. This time the house reconnected with a low crunch.

I'll buy that dream.

They descended to the hall. It was oddly spacious. He was worried in case the two incriminating letters he and Isabel had left around the house were still lying somewhere for Edna to find. "Read?" he asked as the roar began, up from the earth beneath the foundations in a great gutteral crescendo and the whole arch of the stairs, as though in camera slow-motion, cracked into fissures and strata and crumbled.

Edna walked out of the door.

"But what about the kids?" he asked Edna as they approached the pub.

When a lovely flame dies.

"If the fall missed them they're alright. If it struck them they're dead. Either way there's nothing we can do. I'll have a gin and tonic."

He got her a gin and tonic, and a pint for himself. "But isn't it usual, when people are buried, particularly one's own children, to go and dig them out at least?" She turned away impatiently, as though shaking his questions off her shoulder.

You leave me dreamin'.

He wondered if he could find them himself, should he leave his drink, go down through the woods and dig at the rubbish with his soft ineffectual hands. He wondered if he could stomach what he might find, the blood, the visible bone, the squashed heads, and suddenly he was crying hopelessly at the loss of his little boys. Ruth and Billy had, of course, avoided the catastrophe.

That Stardust Melody,

"Safety lies only in the grace of relaxation," said Sir John, with a hand on his shoulder. The last sounds of the women fighting hysterically drifted in from the dawn garden. "Consider the baby that fell four stories and also the drunken man minor bruises both. Your tension I suppose, derives from your wish to sustain an erection by pressing your feet together. Mark you, the whole concept was bound to be taxing for you and Isabel's lover. Who can masturbate for six hours and what sexual athlete can provoke such tears from between your mistress's thighs. I gave up, old boy, gave up to even feeling. Ask George if that's not so."

The memory

Of love's refrain

"I think it's taken this time," she said. "I think I might be pregnant." Her voice was young and eager and soft as a featherwind in heather. As he put the phone down quietly the foundations of the house shifted with a low grumble, half the house stayed suspended a moment, then rocked back into place.

Drain, blocked sump.

THE GREAT TOILET ISSUE

Doctor knifed nurse, jury told

There are gas burners, school desks, dozens of coal stoves, a Big Boy Barbeque Grill, and a bed of nails. 801 glass globes, and 1,621 glass chimneys were presumably in readiness to be thrown or overturned or otherwise used to start a thousand thrilling conflagrations in wild west bars and homesteads.

SHAGGY BLOSSOMS
IN THE FLOWER BEDS

WITLESS ON AN
EMBROIDERED
BUS

A CARDBOARD
CROWN IN AN
EMPTY ROAD

Rain drummed on the glass roof of the conservatory. It was an Irishman who told him (Ruth hunched over one of her rare half-pints) that Liz and Tony had been jailed — acid and hash and shoplifting — The fucken' book. Bill Mitchell, seven foot sarn't major recently of the Scots Guards presiding over a pub full of pot-heads — their lax faces and their filthy sheepdog shocks of hair.

"Cavelier tradition?" asked George. That second summer, after the debacle in Torquay George often told him what Sir John declined to talk about. "Largely behind the rhodedendrons down along the river" he said. "She wore drawers with a loose fitting leg. Fetishism, true to itself, has made the actual central act more difficult with all this provocative elastic."

They camped for days to clean their lice and smell the rhododendrons.

He imagined Sir John, walking in the twilight round the border of the lawn sewing an embroidered path of cigar smoke on the cooling air, suddenly arrested by buttocks and hair spelling out of the crude fact of what he intuited in the hotel lobby.

Evening is a chisel on an old face.

The rain was impenetrable as the black hulks of industry in Great Horton Road. People on the 86 to Wyke looked cheated of even their merest wits. Two guinea fowl flew over from the farm and waddled, side by side, across the bleak lawn.

Picking at the close crocket of the Tetley advert under the upstairs window.

"Gobble and cackle" commanded George, turning to Sir John.

A warm wind passed with little difficulty down Huddersfield Road. The Crown Hotel looked like cardboard. The woman was still whimpering. "Who's that?" asked Ruth, smelling of the hothouse waxes of her adolescence.

The woman whimpered "Please please please please. Let me in please." — He opened the front door. The streetlight was a thin artificial paint on the empty

Mother, Willy Teasdale doesn't want to be Jesus.

DO IT QUICKLY
IN THE FIRE

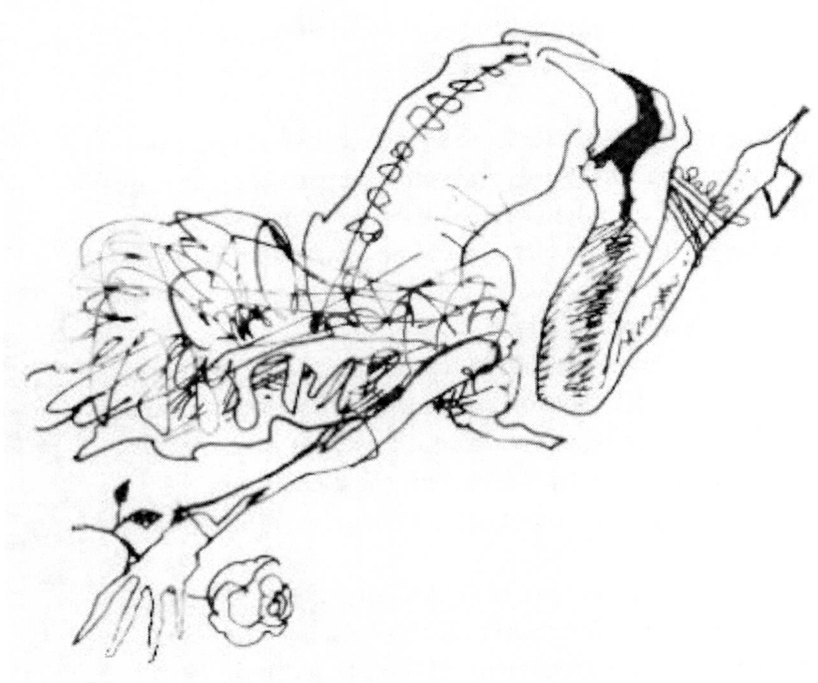

road. She still whimpered "Please please" but no one was visible. A man called sardonically and a door banged.

"Some domestic upheaval or other," he told Ruth on returning to bed. Ken was listening from behind his chandelier mustache and Tom's wife was listening from behind the corner pillar of the bar. "Do it quickly" he told Tom. "Quickly is kindly."

"Slowly is most grievously unkind" said Sir John.

"Yesterday" said Tom "I took t'day off, built up t' fire, sat int' armchair, eeyud back and I tell thi, wi'out a word of a lie, I wor floatin', 'Enry, floatin round t'fuckin' room, looking dahn at mesen. And I tell thi, I couldn't move. Not a fuckin' finger could I move."

That's what the bastards mean by hot pants.

"Get out tomorrow" he told Tom. "Out. Just do it."

The woman in the empty three o'clock street whimpered for an hour.

Dear Sir John,

My rituals have situated themselves more deeply. In their place, where clearly recollected dreams, hallucinations and forbodings paraded a crisp shadow show, there are headaches, daytime lassitude and night time diarrhoea. Squatted on the bowl with the late April cold spreading into my gut like weak poison I try to fart out in a sourceless niagara the snickering grub that haunts me with a sense but not a memory of absolute disaster. I am not distressed, I am ill of a nameless ague which carries with it the after ache, the faintest odour but never the clear image, of immense cathedral ceremonies, of purple mass, of weeping broken incantations carried out in the worm-wrought arsehole catacombs and sewers that tunnel in a pestilential network below the deepest caves of the subconscious, odours of pathetic mumblings and hands moving in the emulation of wizardry, the strenuous desperate measures the part of me that keeps itself secret from my secrets contrives to ward off the cataclysm attendant on the conception of the Messiah.

Oh pray the magic works. Oh pray that illness drains the last green flakes of cowardice out of my arse and lets me love again.

The woman, gone from weeping in Huddersfield Road has left a coldness that throbs in the bones like the coming of a poltergeist.

"Well-danced, Matilda."

And here comes

QUEEN ROXANE

Evolution of the foot: all primates except man have a grasping big toe (human babies in the womb retain it). The feet of gorilla, left, and man, right, show the difference. (The line shows the difference in tread, also, with areas of greatest pressure shaded.)

The real nostalgia comes with the 'Star Wardrobe' section of the catalogue, of course, which kicks off with half a dozen lots that seem to have been selected with a special sense of irony.

Stand up straight in the Robin Hood glade.
Still as armour through the flakes of oak.
Thick as the thunderous air through the cumuli
of old cabbage.

ARMOURED WITH THE THUNDER

"One summer I ate the woodland," she told him.

"Like nectar, like rare sweets, like fresh perspiration of a Spanish virgin?"

"Oh no, not at all." She smiled, hugging one thigh against her left breast so that the breast swelled softly on either side of the curve of muscle massed on her raised femur, so that the mother of her complained like amber doves around the corded weapon of her most passionate dances, so that the dawn turned pearly against a slender sapling. "No indeed. Summer's vegetable you know. Smells like a Sunday saucepan. Tastes like a small boy's armpit. Teeth through green. Pungency of chlorophyl. Cabbage stalks. Cauliflower. Cabbage water forced down your throat so it runs from your nose. Suck me now," she said, suddenly breathy.

Sir John had stopped panting at the bottom of the stairs. His face, pale as that, as moist, made his crisp white hair seem brown. His eyes were keeping back the collapse of everything he was, were clenched on the draining of his ideas like a hand helpless at a lock where the heaving ocean of the mad and hysterical are straining so that their useable energies can be spent and wasted out into the space, the space outside the factory asylum skull.

Armoured
with flakes
of old
cabbage
leaves
of
broccoli
over
my
haunted
eyes,
The amber
doves
turned the
pearl
and I stole
it
hidden in
the quick
of a
palmed
oyster.
Pale, moist
collapse.
Hand at
lock.

AMBER DOVES
MASSED ON HER
FEMUR

HIDDEN IN A
SMALL BOY'S
ARMPIT

SUCK ME
OYSTER SHE
SAID

HAND AT THE
HEAVING
OCEAN

I HAVE TO
SLEEP THAT
FILTHY
BITCH

"George," he had said. "That bloody filthy bitch has just murdered a day. I don't speak lightly. I'm not just masturbating metaphors, don't think it for a minute."

His head bowed and the light from the hall lamp fell on his hair like a dull continuous chord of music.

"Something about a day can be taken to be blue, dear boy. A blue of cleanliness."

The strength of the old man's eye hammering its expression up the shallow carpeted stairs was impressive. It was the more impressive for being belied by the death perspiring coldly from the flesh in which his eye was set. "That filthy, filthy, incredibly beautiful woman has pissed all down the sky, sir. The whole of the north meadow smells like an Egyptian brothel and the bloody daffodils have turned brown, sir, the bloody daffodils have turned brown."

"You could boil the woodland," she bubbled through her teeth. "You could cram it in a vessel, come all over it until its swimming, piss around the bitter bark, the efflorescent leaves." Her voice, the voice of dead lesbians, was grinding from somewhere deep in her chest and filtered through the grating incisors like a kind of acrid-smelling

Let me in
Mr. Jailer
I have
nowhere
to sleep
but the windy
streets
of my own
aching
head.
Something
about a
blue
expression.
Something
about
the more
impressive
flesh all
down
the sky.
An astronaut,
or an aeronaut
or a simple
zero. Blue
knuckles on
the wax.
A doll
for Sir John.

THE
WINDY STREETS
OF LIGHT

SOMETHING
CLEAN
SOMETHING
ABOUT DEATH

FLESH WOMAN
PISSED

AS ASTRONAUT
TURNED
BROWN

A SIMPLE ZERO
IN HER CHEST

smoke. "Drink me," she ground out. "Drink me deep for fuck's sake."

"Pissed down the blue and into the cess-pit sunset," cried Sir John. His grey knuckles trembled on the knob of his stick and his white handkerchief gleamed immaculately as he wiped the urine from his waxy face.

KNUCKLE ME
FOR FUCK'S
SAKE

A DOLL
STICK

On Lot 2 you can find not only the Roman armour ("Breastplate, male Breastplate, female) and a marble statuary ("Bust, A. Lincoln. Bust, Stalin. Busts, Mozart") but also such unromantic objects as blankets, pots undescribed or undescribable, tambourine, scrap iron, demolition balls, and a sod cutter.

French 'rupture' puzzles Wilson

There was once a bishop of...

SOOTY BEAR

HAROLD HARE

FAIRY TWINKLETOES

OSCAR THE OX

SALLY THE SOW

ERIK THE RED

She told George many stories in the early days and each of these stories seemed to herald a parallel instance in his subsequent affair with Julia.

"I met a soldier. No, it was quite late, yes Green Park, that's right.

Guards? Dear me no. Infantry, one of the regiments. Red face. Red shoulder flashes. Loved me, my dear, loved me instantly like a faithful beast.

Infidelity seemed to him I'm sure the negative of his own pathetic faith. Good faith, not fidelity, that's the phrase, good faith.

We lived for three days in Irene Campbell's flat off Baker Street. He watched the callers come and go and d'you know my darling, how the poor dumb ox actually went blind on witnessing an orgasm. His eyes, my poppet, popped so far from his big ox head he must have snapped the optic nerve."

"The parallel," explained George, "is obvious. You know, at times, when Julie slept she sensed the fact that I'd thrown back the sheets, sensed the fact that I'd thrown back the covers, that I'd stood across the carpet, huddling my scrap of a pyjama jacket around me, and broke my marital nerve over the anvil of experience provided by the wet sow's ear crumpled in its hair between her lovely olive thighs."

"I walked on the Heath today," she said, one Hampstead evening, "and I met two boys, one dressed from head to toe in red, and the other head to toe in black. And black and red, my dear, if you can just imagine, looped a cord of amber silk about my ankle in its black

DEREK THE DARLING

PERCY PRICK

MARTY THE MONSTER

PRUNELLA PASSION

gauze with its gold chain, and hung me redly from a green branch until my ankle was red, the red had blanched from my ridiculed face, and darling, I wonder if you can guess how much I paid them to piss in the rivers of my falling hair — Washed all the pearls out, darling, positively all of them."

"And the parallel of that," explained George, one Surrey morning, "is the occasion on which Julie breathed such summer vapour over my prick from her sweet mouth that the pearls and cheap glass stood by the slit of the stubborn little monster like insignia of a wet dawn, then washed them into the brown ferns with her tears of compassion and regret. That's something Sir John would never develop a proper sense of, you know, the full pathos of passion."

Joker 'Gelignite' Jack is out

A schoolboy, John Charles Samuel Treloar (17) was sentenced to life imprisonment at Cornwall Assizes, Bodmin, yesterday for killing Valerie Anne Symonds, a 17-year-old local schoolgirl.

Judy Woods blue with bluebells. He walked down the cindertrack all down the center of the hillside's thigh. The woods put their coloured feathers out to the wet in the still air. Knolls of slag burst in dandylions. The shale of the path beneath his feet was coins.

Naked as a medieval adam in the distant grass across the stream. He watched. The naked man sat up in his corner of the hillside, looked blankly back.

Sooty Harold
twinkle the ox,
the sow,
the red darling.

Harold in
soot with
the monster
prick.

Red passion.

"Listen," he whispered to George. "If we go down into the woods we can follow the edge of the trees until we're quite close. Then watch."

"And what, Henry, are we watching for?"

"We must watch," said Henry. The dot of vulnerable white sank back into the grass. The roll of old grown-over mine waste and the limbs of farmland sang to the sky very simply. It did not stop.

Sooty Harold
walked down
the coloured
feathers. The
sow looked
blankly back.
The red
darling watching
Harold in
soot.

The discordant note was a single note on a violin string, on the strung nerves. The man, when approached closely, sat bolt upright again and

The grass of
the old
grown-over
monster.
Prick upright
again. Red
passion like
the split
bark of
beeches.

stared down into the woods. Henry kissed the excrescences of a beech tree.

The man walked, white and naked, down through the medieval green to the bluebell fringe at the edge of the wood. His skin erupted like the split bark of beeches, with its white existence. Henry walked away quickly.

The man followed. A practise runner puffed and padded through the trees some yards away. The glad air screamed. Light off the hills of dandylions hurt.

What pain can Isabel then wring from her bones? Messiah from the crotch of a beech tree. Dead resin shrieking existance to the praising land.

Red passion shrieking.

MAN CHARGED

On Lot 2 at Culver City Studios they will sell the trucks and automobiles, trailers, wagons, Roman furniture, western and wicker furniture and props, gambling equipment, portable dressing rooms and complete, authentic standard guage steam locomotives from 1870.

"I have the sense that an animal is standing around in my skull," he told George.

"I think that's unfair," said Isabel.

"An animus, you mean," said George. "Animal. Huh."

"And I think George is being scornful."

"Siphoning the python" was not inappropriate. Teasdale pressed his palm to his velvet trouserfront and to let the tender weight of his prick hang between forfinger and thumb, hang over the index knuckle.

How all they laughed. You could see clear reflections in the vast pool on the bar floor. Marble is totally unabsorbant In former times many would have been anxious to see the tops of ladies' thighs, to see arrays of knickers in the pool that Teasdale left across the floor.

"Alice wept a sea of tears, and I have too," said Sir John. "Any man might find himself more than honored to have his water turned to honorable grief."

"Ah fook off," said Teasdale.

"I walk a long way for a ring, rings work their magic over distances of time and space. Consider the time it took to get the blister pearl. And Ed O'Donnel, mad as an Alpine fart with his glistening Conn, has taken a year and more to set the pearl."

AN ANIMAL
IS
STANDING
AROUND IN
MORCAM'S
ROW.
THE
PYTHON WAS
NOT
A
SIXTH
FORM
REFLECTION
IN THE
MARBLE
CHARGED
WITH
MURDERING
ARRAYS
OF
KNICKERS
TEN DAYS
AFTER
HIS
WATER
TURNED
TO
HONORABLE
GRIEF.

"I'd do it for you baby," Butler said over the phone.

And Isabel, blasted by the violence of Teasdale's laughter, ripped up the middle by the tug of Teasdale's joking hands on her own gusset which was not much more absorbant than marble, was lacerated into fragments, her love-light spattered like incandescent urine in the Calder Valley far below. And their little car climbed above their spanglestreams to the kitchen where Marion O'Dwyer dwelt midst the odours of stale grass and fresh babyshit. Tim slipped on the precipitous cobbles. The slime of the hill ran down to quench Isabel's fox fires.

MAGIC
HAD BEEN
FOUND IN A
CARAVAN
BY
TEASDALE'S
JOKING
HANDS
BETWEEN
FALMOUTH
AND
ISABEL'S
FOX FIRES.
HER HOME
AT MAWNAN

Treloar, of Morcam's Row, Renryn, a sixth form pupil at Falmouth Grammar School, was charged with murdering the girl 10 days after her body was found in a caravan park between Falmouth and her home at Mawman Smith.

"Ring? Bill's ring?" asked Marion. "You've come all this way. Perhaps you'd like to stay and turn on."

"Got to move. Got to go to Leeds and get pissed," he told Marion. They slid back down the mile of packhorse track. Bill's ring with its Tibetan prayer folded in the tiny metal casket, under the ponderous jade, concertinaed like tiny seaside photos in a Yarmouth locket, was a dead weight on his rested Saturday night finger.

"In the taxi the power of the odour from the girl's cunt was worse than fuckin' smelling salts, boy, I'm tellin' ya."

"All she wanted was fucking."

"All that hysteria. Thrashing about in the Union bar. Rolling about in Seeger's office?"

"Nymphomania, man. Classic."

She simmered down about nine o'clock. Always, all loveliness, all serpentine fortuity, the grace and anticipation of Isabel's throes in orgasm and birth — "She bites her lower lip."

SMITH
CONCERTINAED
LIKE
TINY
SEASIDE
SATURDAY
PARK
BETWEEN
THE
UNION BAR
AND
SEEGER'S
OFFICE.

HER
BODY
ALL
SERPENTINE

Mr Peter Fallan, QC, prosecuting, said Treloar and the girl were both members of the same sixth-form society but there was no close friendship between them.

WITH 4 BLAZE

On Lots 3 and 5 there are boats, canoes, wind and wave machines, Roman chariots, a fire engine, 250 coaches and the Paddle Steamer Cotton Blossom from Show Boat. Ten thousand items of antiques and furniture on stages 15, 27, &30 will take 12 sessions to sell: American and English, oriental and medieval, Louis, directoire, Carolean, Elizabethan and (recalling the more carefree days of art direction) a Queen Anne commode from Romeo and Juliet. A china lamp from Mrs Miniver is irreverently catalogued as "gaudy."

Introduce you to a new vast. Intolerable occasions crawled over the stoat. The whiskers on knuckle and thumb. The little bastard writhes through his shattered breath.

"I'd like to introduce you to a new and vastly more important consideration," said George. He seldom smoked his pipe these days. Thus Henry thought it intolerable that he should smoke it in the greenhouse where the air was already stifling and the gnats crawled richly over the discarded condom that hung on the topmost strands of the tomato plant.

"I'd like to introduce you to the Ichneumon stoat."

Henry could see the nose trembling between George's knuckle and thumb. The whiskers on either side were stiff and white as toothbrush bristles.

"I know the little bastard," he told George. "He writhes through all the shattered wastes of Central Leeds. His breath stains dogshit black, his piss blackens wet the thin plush of student's desert boots. An exquisitely dressed woman, pale face, neat black cap of hair, in the Cobourg, has a secret stoat in her coffee coloured frothlace camiknickers, underneath her black-bar

Look out over this prairie of the seventies, gentlemen. The Laura diseased and the explorers in our own party breaking out in unneccessary hair.

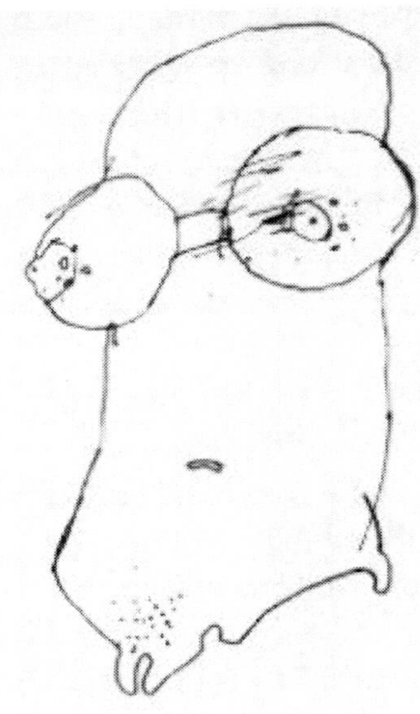

tights, to spit her fine menstrual blood out into the dreams of Tetley's bitter. The Ichneumon stoat has rotted all the bricks of Hunslett terraces with its high-pitch multi-sexual whining."

"That's the chappie,"

said George. "Cheeky little fellow isn't he?"

And Isabel bent so that the neat double bunchflower of her dry arse and her wet red vagina extended its curves and creases and minute flesh folds out to the indifferent afternoon like orchid pistils spraying sunrise, drove her nose against the baby mouth of his own red stoat and sent bright darts keenly down his pisspipe.

"Cheeky man," she said, "Hello."

"Plating is better with a half-soft skinned stoat," said Henry.

"Wet belly rippling in and out of your flickering cave like fishes shat shimmering through the well-holes in a child's eyes."

The stoat returned the nose-to-nose Indian kiss by playing his nose, in turn, against her split cervix. And the slime knob slipped across his snout in mucoid fondness, drawing from the back of his migraine the thick cream, the white bile of pain.

Hunslett terraces with whining bunchflower and her wet red flesh spraying his stoat. Bright darts better with a half soft belly. In and out of your shimmering eyes. Split cervix in fondness, drawing thick cream.

Womenfolk give birth in the camp behind the mountains only to watch their children suffocate. They dream still of the slums of their origin and the spectacular upheavals of family affairs. Tears mix with hope in eyes that turn alternately transparent and opaque. Women are fundamental milkmaids.

MURDERS

Woman died cleaning windows

Mr. Justice Lawson said he accepted the plea with considerable hesitation and added: "The truth of the matter is that you pursued this girl, you made some kind of sexual approach to her which she seemed to have resisted, and then you battered her to death."

On the Eastern seaboard they run short of nostalgia. All the dying fish and myths of the Eastern Islands find themselves thrown up on the sodden rocks pleading for a little more time. If Sir John had chosen to stand on a crag or a couple of crags around Berwick on Tweed he'd have found himself floored by the basis of time as time herself dragged her overused underwear into the sunset.

Written on the Edinburgh train.

Rattling up the coast past Berwick on Tweed.

"I have never been declined by any man more conclusively than by a declining sun," said the woman. "I might have known from the colour of the stones what is the conclusive colour of decline."

Henry stirred in his railway bucket and let the proposition from seven pints of British Railways canned Guinness tentatively solicit his arsehole.

As usual, nothing much to do but drink.

The sea enveloped the remnants of the sun on the shadowed slope of the coast.

"Your child is only a rational possibility," the sea wasped out under her creaming curlers, under her trailing nylon headscarf. "The density of the sun on the other side of the evening train is the only promise you have."

The sunset was magnificent. The sea was in shadow.

"I love you," sang Isabel. "I love you, I love you, I love you. There isn't anyone else."

Echoes, echoes.

Henry walked across the lawn.

He took his stand near George who pretended not to have noticed. Sir John was some way distant, nearer to the rank flowerbeads. He looked vacantly into the dense trees beyond the laurel shrubs. Henry afforded them no more attention than they had afforded him. He looked

Writing unsteadily in a cheap red pocket book.

A scotswoman going home for the first time in three years was exultant with the broad fine sweeps of empty meadowland.

back in the direction from which he had come, into the massive vertical disaster of pursed and ravaged labia spilling their glistening sweets of blood and semen mingled like the marbled endpapers of a family Bible, and he replied: "Love only me. Yes, this is possible. Justice and manhood you might require of me, and this can scarcely be faulted. You have pleaded against, and I have confessed to, the apathetic vacancy which is Sir John. But should I save my face and reap my resolutions, should I get up off my back and cry the positive love I play with in promises, then I forfeit possibly my greatest privilege in my short drop from birth to death, which is to eat the black refuse and scream into the hollow chasm that is the only thing to which I truly progress, the only thing that's left desirable beyond the grave, or back there in the motherlove, the fond enclosure beyond the funky antechamber, the great waste cackle, the gaunt bleak stench of God."

The train arrived in Edinburgh on time.

The court accepted his pleas of not guilty of murder, but guilty of manslaughter on the grounds of diminished responsibility.

The author express his gratitude to the *Daily Mirror*, *Bradford Telegraph & Argus*, *Yorkshire Post*, and the *Times Educational Supplement* for their inspiration.

COMPLAINT FORM

Please list your grievances
in the space provided below.

(write legibly)

☐

Deliver to my attention:

Jeff Nuttall

23/2 15

THE GOLD HOLE

EVENING STANDARD: MARCH 22, 1967

Third body found — police intensify hunt for killer

ANOTHER body, that of a ten-year-old girl, found today was severely mutilated. Discovered by police in a waste lot near Dudley, Worcs., she had been subjected to what the police call "curious manipulations." Articles of clothing belonging to the child had been picked up by neighbours as far as a mile from where the corpse was found.

Although the circumstances point to a sexual offence, forensic scientists assert that no penetration of that kind had taken place, but fragments of writing of "an allegedly poetic nature" are thought to have an immediate bearing on the case.

Part One
EMBARKATION

Dim of the morning pale of the evening.
Voices of leaves and the rustle of car-tyres gone out of sight down the freeways . . .
Sound of the sky. Round mouths in the sky. Swung curls in the sky. Crushed lips in the sky.

The child was discovered by the welfare authorities just before dawn. The mother is thought to have deserted him there three or four days previously. There were bruises and some breakage of skin on the flesh around the mouth.
The toilet had been out of order for some time . . .

Shy eyes / morning puddles of wonder. Imagine, said the smirking judge, the assembled slaughtered children of Auschwitz, Belsen, Buchenwald, Hiroshima and Hanoi, nailed in the choirstalls howling out their requiem teething-pain—the teeth, the small rats' teeth and insect-saws in baby bellies—cut to the rolled-up sugar cotton of a May morning.

'We walked along the upper reaches of the river until the tow-path led under heavy oaks, and here the only light was from the river where the recent sunset

was a hammered flat of lemon yellow kept, where the sky was dimmer than the metal water that shone flat through trees, where black was green, where green was brown, where, as the sky died into the smell of dead roots, singing came distinct as birdsong, layered, fluting, structured, ringing of voices of nocturnal castrati, the ineffectual poltergeists who escaped the torture and manic power of their late pubescent beds to wander the cold woods in nightgowns, singing warped folksongs up the progressive terraces of Palestrina.'

Dead children in the air, the million in their chords, the
solitary with his hurt plainsong:
'Lonely robe / your great dark dream / *the dark I left you*
with Mother Butcher Mrs Ribbentrop Mrs Himmler
Wetnurse pumping the uric acid from her withered
tit, mothermilk filtered through blackshirts.
Self-sovereignty / wine and love / *gold in the blood, you*
panned it Mother, like a prospector crouched over
the trickle from a country hillside pisshouse, passing the yellow of
it through his tilting pan and letting it
disappear back to earth.'
Clem Phlegm came into the ghost town, walked past the
Livery Stable and the empty gas-chambers, spat
quizzically at the hitching rail that lurched like tied
bones under the corner watchtower, recalled with a
waxing of his sage-green irises, the belch of gas jets
from the muzzles of the fortyniners-fortyfives. He
turned his weathered gaze to the south where the
barbed wire bucked and coupled like impassioned
worms trying to fuck away their knots and tiny
spikes. He crouched and passed the sand of the street
through his wise old fingers until his palm contained
two small bones from the foot of an aborted Jewess.
In the morning he ground the bone down into urine
of the sunset and drew his fabled billions in red

banknotes from the assay office.

'Mother, come out of the cupboard. The story was a lie and
in any case the ghosts of the odours of poisoned
mothballs will wrong the memory of sperm from
what remaining flesh I am like fruitjuice.
Mother come out of the flower, the sunflower, rose, the
daisyface, the daisymay, the daisy jennyface,
Victorian poke bonnets all arranged Kate Greenaway
about the garden. Ride a cock to Banbury Cross the
razor scars said OXO all across your split bun, your
easter breast, your buggerplug dug, your nipple-
nibble suckplug. Mother don't fester your days away
like dead seed, bad teeth lined up in ripple-rows out
from the nipple in the tit of the tilted sunflower.
Mother come out of the flowerbed where you sat in the shade
of your foxglove hollyhocks letting your ten-year
cunt be a pink and fragile glove for sly enquiry of
your foxnose fingers, come out from where the dried
earth flowerbed is golden biscuit crumbs on toasted
harvest of your thigh.'

Love and loneliness train door *hell snap bang of final GONE*
in mother smile her flutter hanky pink frill lips—
the motherlove the bruise the lillyruff of pink uncer-
tainty—frill of movement sugarpig dissolved across
the teeth—
The Mother waving hanky flower-smirk ghost of foxglove
smudged on her passing love. DOT at the carry one
carry me nine and drop me a hundred times / drop
me then to the billowbed / now to the empty death /
then to the hot pin / now to the bloodstreak dying /
sky through the root woods / DOT at the junction

of perspective platform hurtleback / round the
bend / the passing sentinels of signals GEO-
METRIC FORMALIZATION OF THE GOODBYE
HANKY / WHEN MY MOTHER STABBED ME
OUT OF HER CRUTCH WITH A TOASTING
FORK STERILISED IN QUININE THEY
HAMMERED UP THE BRASH GOODBYES IN
INDIGO AND BLACK DANGER STEADY GO
TIN METAL RECTANGLE MINISTRY OF
TRANSPORT LICENCE FOR YOUR PLEADING
GRIEF / / / /

Undisposable knot of life in central ribbon of delight *drag me*
out Mummy,
Drag out your carnivals orgasms organs, your tubes and
braised liver, heart and pumping loveme lungs, your
organs, your fairground barrel-house steam wheeze,
Gothic tubes jutting Arthur Sullivan right up your
fan-vault, your gasms and gasmics and gasmeters
gases, your perfumes, the farts of French horn arse-
hole, the French kiss farts of your palping twat, the
crushed flowers rammed in your knickers by Sam as
he wept and the draggled petals sucked from your
sphincter by a smile with its hair dyed red.
Mother drag out your ribbons from the wicker basket in the
attic, memories and cashew nuts and lovehearts,
valentines, the dressing-up fancies, the gay deceivers,
the Valentino kiss-knots, the knotted lengths of pink
for your birthday dress, red for your first secret
shame and black for your thundercloud in the wank-
happy hollyhocks.
Yank out your runaway Peter, drag down your runaway
Paul, pull the strangled relics of the starling darling starveling

saints out into the sky and hang them like gamekeepers trapped rats, teeth to the darkening arc
of heaven, spitted on the brass bars of the drunken
sun (drowned globe gurgling sow in a wallow of
hogsblood saintsblood babyblood brown smeared on
the sun's face, dropped on the town).

Drag out your Absalom, pin up your Pericles, strangle your
Samuel, your Tyburn Timothy so the crowd of
National Health ghouls arrayed along the sewerage
beds on the shores of Styx howl their nasal execra-
tions and claque their sterilized obstetric tongs like
the teeth of tongueless infidels helpless at the sunset
gate of Babylon.

Drag your dead brats strung on your umbilical hemp through
the marketplace, cracking their eggheads on the
tumbling pewter, jamming their webbed fronds of
inquiry into the quick of tarts and sweetmeats,
melon-slices, calabashes.

Come out of the cupboard Mother and drag out the dirty
wash, the shit-splashed secrets on the indoor wash-
line. Hook the firstborn on the side of the stuttering
geyser and hang the rinsed-out lining of your womb
from the rusty ball-cock, then crouch, my tender
love, crouch all foetal faecal on the cold porcelain
remaining where the Irish from the upstairs landing
yanked off the seat one Friday paynight, crouch
under your clothesline lifeline and drag out what's
left in your belly, Xavier, Zacharias, Zeke, sluice
them under the gush in the mud-bowl and hang them
out to dry for Sunday.

Count your banners Mother. Your naval jacks and your
striped ensigns, your splattered stars and your whip-
lash stripes, your crooked cross, your child recum-

bent on a bed of rouge, your gouts of gold on a field
of ghouls, your dead star rampant in a setting azure.
Pull the cord and let the torn bikini nylon of your aborted
night lap its sad joke outside the mausoleums of
innocence.
Count us, Mother, rows of us, wheeled out into the twilight
silently . . .

Panic fabric / galaxy of exquisite clarity / *magical tingling of*
suppressed music / hanging before, an astronaut
suspended with instruments of measurement and
perception before the cheesy tit of the moon /
suspended in front, an inspector hung from your
past to shriek his enquiries through the letterbox in
your delicate facade.
A counter to number the star-drops as they fall, a glass to
reflect on the shimmer of sprung love that forms into
flesh in your form like the dewfall elsewhere forms in
a vault of rainbow.
I am a catshair scraped on the aether to catch the innocents,
your slaughtered siblings shrieking their dawnlight
prayers out at the edges of the gorse—a mike for the
pearl-grey filth unwashed from between your breasts,
a loudspeaker each for your nipples (the shape of a
banshee's warbling gob with its edible tongue out), a babycheek
scraped with needles to a pain of sensitivity
for the down at the crown of your cunt, a babyclaw
with its hooks of translucent paperthin bone for the
wince of your clitoris, all mad tongues and terrible
fables for the soot and slime of your fucksecrets, tears
for your shroud you hooded madonna, cameras for
your flutter and flickering candles for your gravity of
juice, wax for your sheen, pox for the flox of flowers,

fleece for flocks of stones massed like praying
knuckles in the gentle structure of your gut.
Mother, I know you through the showers and uncertain light.

Gauze of your lovethighs underskirt erection / mustard
coloured rut and flash in an old wartime goblin.
Think of it Mother, the circus clown dragging his
drag around, think of it Mother, the ENSA soubrette
letting her dysentery drop down the seams of her
blackmarket blackmesh nylons.
Think of it Mother, the disguises and charades, the masks
and the attitudes, the sarabands and minuets per-
formed in the idolatry of motherhood.
Think of it Mummy, the fairy that the backstreet Mother
Superior missed with her disinfected knitting needle, ultimately
raising the tent of a false womb with the
canvas and tulle of his mother's stolen petticoats,
sliding his hand, with its tattoos and scarred rings,
into the leg of the satin drawers and pulling the
muscle till the proof of his safety spattered white as bridesmaids
where his flesh was meant to fall as red
as Jack of Hearts.

Choked with twists of a winding strand / red alluvial buttercup blood *for gold it was, Mother, the juice that you*
spilled from the knot in the hangman's umbilical
lanyard. What price gold, Mother? What's the
exchange rate Clem Phlegm got at the commandant's
office? What's the weight in widow's pennies of the
dollars you spilt in buttercup red? What's the score
in lovesongs gargled on the dosshouse washline, for
the crotchets dotted up and down the stave of your
taxicab gusset?

What's the fair price, Mother, for the fall of coins, the buried
treasure that the inverted grave let drop, for the
shower of louis d'ors, Mother, for the rain of bluesy
whores, Mother, for the plunderer's horde that
parted the hair that sang like ferns in a hilltop wind
when the cutlass went in, that wept like morasses of
swampy moss when the wealth went out?

The coloured discs in the rich weeds of cunt / passion
confronted with the bleaker facts of ecstasy.
Describe his face when you passed him the bill,
Mother. How did his eyes wax, how did his colour
wane, how did the moon of his youngman's brow
yellow and turn in the stratosphere of difficulty?
Mummy love, mother passion, how did his passion flower
pull in its antennae? How did his fever fingers pull in
his prick? How did his sweaty tortoise pull back its
head? As firm and decisive in withdrawal as your
hand had been earlier eager in pulling back the mem-
brane foreskin, firmly and completely, not like when withdrawal at
an earlier stage remained refused and
I, confirmed then, ripe for a future denial, was shot
up the night sky of your sucking cervix?
How did his spirit curl up and blow away, Mother? Was it
like woodsmoke? Was it like perfume? Was it like
newspapers smeared with shit across the agony
columns, blown down the alleyway, over the garage
gutter greasepools with their tentative rainbows, out
beyond the nodding peppered mustard-coloured
diarrhoea of the bombsite chickweed?

Mother, the price of our palace was the skin of a womb and
the golden juice of a blood orange.

Mother, the cheap glass beads in the holly hedge are a merci-
ful camouflage bestowed by a compassionate lover's
moon on the blood drops you left behind, you with
your evergreen spikes.

Mother, the little dark man sits in us all as we sit in our rows
along the desolate Welsh hills singing our obscene
inversion of traditional Methodist fertility chants.

Mother, extravagance progressed to the point of obscenity is
not enough to buy my blood at its right price.
Mother, extravagance that buys my blood is not so
obscene as the prodigality that spilt it.

Mother, the lees of orgy is the wine of murder and you're
choking Mother, vomiting it into the doctor's goblet.

Mother, the luminosity of apple-pap in your eyes and hair
and neck is the sunset glow left by the sour cider I
bled on your body in your after-scrape sleep.

Mother, touching a nerve quietly will get a girl's pinny up,
get a girl's pangs up, get up a girl's pantheon, pounce
up a girl's past like a spastic clairvoyant, and make
such wreckage the nerve is reduced to a half-formed embryonic
clitoris stuck on the sheen of the sun like
a crushed strawberry.

Mother, the acid present in gentle nausea is the flavour my
milky kisses would leave on your nipple.

Mother, the churning machinery of birds is a racketing
claque I'm beset by as the jackdaws and vultures
squat on the line we're all hung from, me and the
rows of Adolph Herod's innocents.

Adrenalin cadaver / spilling red ears, *chewed fingers,*
fingered pricks.

Heather saliva / ruffling a graying crop / *Welsh rain sifted*
powder through the gauze of our left flesh.

Sane delight in the magical window / *misty photograph of a*
pregnant woman arranging flowers, crude tintype of a vomiting
mongol eating her meat.

Stillness of our secret wreckage / *Do you recall, Mother, how*
I lay at your thigh?

Thrill of the night in flesh / *chill of the daylight of cold*
commonsense in the surgical snips.

Tingling energy / old fashioned love / *old fashioned look /*
buzzing again at the wingtips.

Valley in the morning / garden in bleak eyes / *look at me*
look at you, Mummy, chicken-gawping in your
hollyhocks.

Predatory cabbage / cannibal cunt / *pluck me a leaf for a*
pramshawl.

Giggling gravity / metallic green / *mind flashing colours of*
paradox save me.

Dogs bark out on dark sky, Mother. Feed them.

Stars drop out on the dark lawn, Mother. Pick them up your
apron, what's left of it after the grief-wringing hands
and the butcher's lechery.

Roots in the earth are whimpering, Mother, out in the night-
woods. Curl your somnambulant toes over their sore
joints.

Garden gawping hollyhocks, Mother. Fingers!

Cannibal cunt giggling green, Mother. Sew it up shut.

Metal dogs feed on the lawn, Mother. Give them your after-
birth.

Stars drop in your apron, Mother. I love you.

The grief and the butcher curl your toes over their sore holly-
hocks, Mother.

Cannibal green, Mother. Sew up your afterbirth.

Stars in your grief, Mother. Love your butcher.

Sore green afterbirth. Sew up your stars.

Stars in your love, Mother. Cannibal grief.

Sunset red, Mother. Red as your son.

Night time now, Mother. Night . . .

I

Dear Jaz,

You looked lonely when you left, but then, when you look lonely it's not like other people's loneliness. You wear loneliness like a proud garment, like some fine sleek robe. Your dark eyes turn in to the arrogant assessments of that superior dream which is the self you hold, jewelled, for yourself in your own self-maintained sovereignty. No mean strength to be rendered regal by loneliness. Formidable power to be lionized by your own losses and deficiencies.

I know no one else who can hold love proudly as you can, who can hold it proudly like a proud beaker containing a wine and a knowledge too fine for understanding, and then, in all love, ask nothing but the dream and the ineradicable thread of gold in the blood.

You stood on that platform with your love and your loneliness and you got on that train, which was like any other train, and you slammed the train door, which was like any other train door, and your chugged out into the morning, which was like any other morning, and you didn't wave. Why the hell should you?

I may be pissed while I'm writing this, and the last deal of meth hasn't worn off completely yet, although I'm not shaky any more. But I want to put it down for you, how it was, how it is, how I am and why what you did is still, for me, your act, a knot of acid in my, gut and my mind.

I started my life, or at least a life that was somehow closer to me and what I was looking for, that day at Llantypas, I want to recount it all then, because I've got to make it clear, in black and white, on paper, in front of my nose, the events I keep turning over, a kind of hookworm of torture, a disheveled ribbon of delight. Did it all happen? I can't talk to you about it, but did the events in fact occur? The thread is woven so deep in my mind that I sometimes wake in a panic that we dreamed the whole thing. Perhaps now that you are gone the little galaxy of exquisite signs and images which is you will be just as lost, will lose that spring-bird clarity which is your precise, distinguishable self.

Why the fuck did we choose Llantypas? Weren't we going to Caernarvon anyway? Didn't we buy tickets to Caernarvon?

What made us choose that particular spot was surely the magical tingling of suppressed desire we'd kept awake all day, like a beat of music pounding subtly, underlining the counterpoint of our actions. We sat in the compartment through the long journey from London and we were going to Caernarvon to see Fred and Jane who had just moved there, Fred to teach Anglo-Saxon at Aberystwyth, and we'd had all their letters describing the closed pubs and the sly smiling people and the terrible sunsets and the ghosts in the hedgerows, and yet for all their fables we were drunk out of our minds with our myths of one another, and we sat in the compartment, touching hands occasionally. You sat opposite me with the gauze of your lovely thighs and the lilac scribble of your underskirt and you crossed your legs, teasing me like a fond little whore, and when I had to conceal my erection from the passengers who came in—that woman with the mustard-coloured hat—you giggled, and there was that mad carnival between us in the flash of which we were both invulnerable.

It was no rational choice, certainly no reluctance to see Fred and Jane, that made us, by wordless consent, giggling and clutching hands in spasms of mischief, suddenly get up at that absurd station with flowers growing in a row of old wartime firebuckets and concrete goblins on the windowsill of the waiting room, a station at which the train was scarcely scheduled to stop anyway.

It was more to do with the fact that for some twenty miles of the journey the landscape had been breaking up into small conical hills with valleys between, choked with oaks and ferns, that the track had been skirted frequently by the arcs and twists of a winding river whose banks were alternations of long red strands of sand and abrupt miniature cliffs where the swing of the rapid water, fast over golden pebbles, had cut away the red alluvial meadow to a small perpendicular drop. It was more to do with the splendour of buttercups with which this meadow was scattered, and the way they echoed the fragments of blood-coloured sunlight that burned around the breasts of the hills and broke to moving, edgeless discs through the leaves of the massed oaks.

It was finally to do with the eventually recognized fact that our excitement was heightened to an almost unbearable degree by the smoky glamour of those dead volcanoes and the rich weeds with which they were spread. That, as the shaft of a penis finds its appropriate nest in the rich floods of cunt to which it draws its owner, so the column of our suppressed passion had found its sheath in the landscape and light through which we had passed, and drew us now to consummation before the train carried us on to the saner and cooler light of the coast.

We felt odd, suddenly a little stranded as the train left us on the platform, as though we'd exchanged train tickets, together with freedom of choice, for a closely engaged journey on the vehicle of our own passion, as though we were suddenly confronted with the bleaker facts that our departure entailed, that the price we paid for one another and the depths of ecstasy into which we could hurl one another, was nothing less than each his own individual autonomy, the price we paid for our palace was nothing less than the whole wide world.

We stood a moment quietly humbled by this situation and then passed on into the village, what there was of it, more in a kind of reverence than in our previous levity. The light sat like cheap glass beads in the holly hedge by the Llantypas Arms. The pub, whitewashed. Remember? The light took one orange corner of the facade and threw the remainder into bright blue.

We went into the bar and asked for two rooms. Do you remember why?

We didn't want to stir our quietude. Neither the quietude of the village we'd found nor the quietude of our own solemnities. The little dark man gave us the keys and gave me one black Welsh look that told me he'd understood the fine seriousness of what we were about.

We walked around the village until ten. We neither of us had properly realized until then, I think, that the extravagance of nature can sometimes progress to the point of obscenity. We wandered in the leavings of daylight and felt that the red of the light and the wreckage of overblown hedges, trees, plants, gardens, strewn in the debris of their own blossoming, was a battlefield where we waded in the prodigalities of some majestic conqueror whose awful power had raped and pillaged the corridors of the countryside. We waded in the lees of his orgy and, although a little shaken by such wastage, felt passion so bright and so keenly in ourselves that we followed the pillaging sun ourselves as conquerors.

You went to your room early and I waited in the bar. The bar had been a good dark oak, was now coated in five layers of ochre paint which had chipped to reveal white undercoating and sometimes the original wood. The entire room was painted in ginger paint. I sat and looked at the pin-up calendar and thought about the dullness of the ginger paint for all its hard gloss, and the subtle luminosity of light falling through the thick olive clouds in my cider, and about your hair that had left its odour, perfume and sweat, as I kissed you, your eyes and hair and neck, rapidly your breasts, at the bottom of the stair, touching a nerve whose quivering would carry our tension through to the morning.

I took my time getting quietly drunk. The cider was sour and pungent. I huddled, most of the evening, looking into my glass, sometimes closing my eyes the better to know the acid of the liquor working through my system.

When I turned, it was as though the identical acid present in the blood of the country drinkers turned and twisted in the brooding reds of their faces in response to the gentle nausea in which my own blood stirred. It seemed that the smoky breath of the drinkers, thick in the air of a small low-ceilinged bar, was also, in some chemical sympathy, organising itself in huge slow interlocked vortices.

And as I looked the drinkers looked back at me through the churning machinery of alcohol, indifferent to their own laden breath and to their own intoxication, sitting like broody birds, still and predatory, staring icily through the patterns and upheavals of cider with a complete and somehow menacing knowledge of you and I, our impermissible purity and the total licence we anticipated, both towards each other's bodies and towards the world whose benevolent membership we had forgone.

I could have become belligerent momentarily. There was a second when I might have let the drink down to my limbs, let the adrenalin rush from behind its valve of discipline, when I might have reeled to the tallest and most cadaverous of those iron-eyed hill-farmers, spilling glasses over tables and gaitered knees, bombarding his red-whiskered ears with sniggering gags and sick puns about sex and death, peppering his weathered cheeks with saliva, ruffling a bisexual hand, fondling and sarcastic, through the greying, rough-cropped hair.

Or I could have held myself with arrogant diffidence, dismissing them as they contemplated passion dourly from the inferior planes of morality.

I could have butchered my heated, imaginative understanding, cutting off the flow of reciprocal ideas like severing an artery, and bleeding off those inconvenient challenges like an archaic doctor tapping off disease. I could have nodded, commented on the weather, said to the landlord, with a conventional wryness, 'Well I think that'll do for tonight', and walked from bar to bog, from bog to primitive country bathroom, and from bathroom to bed.

As it was, the opposition of elements, morality to violence, stasis to churning organic movement, rural to urban, old to young, was so nicely struck and perfectly performed that I smiled for you and I smiled for myself because I had conceived for us both, to our greater majesty, a fine sane delight in the whole structure of dichotomy, with all its snapping attendant fireworks.

I don't think I told you about the night. You saw the room the next evening but I want you to know about the thing it was that night, the way I lay under the slope of the attic ceiling and the way the geometry of space around me took on a blue, luminous density, the way the tiny window was a signal pasted up at the edge of this spatial frisson, a magical window out into the world I'd lost in clothing myself with the excitement we shared as a common reality. I want you to understand somehow, how the room became a model of the stillness of our secret palace, the way the wreckage of the evening landscape had been a model of its majesty and tumult.

It's difficult to explain how I experienced that space. Not only did the surface of my body generate a thrill of energy out into that periphery of the space with which it came into contact, but the space itself, being somehow temporarily possessed of substance, fired my skin with an answering charge. To facilitate and intensify this exchange I lay with the bedclothes thrown back and pulled my nightclothes apart as though for a lover, as though it were for you there, in the flesh.

Can I make you understand how the space and the tingling presence of the space assaulted my nerves perpetually, and if you do understand, do you understand because the energy, the excitement, the tingling exchange of electricity was the same for you, and was, in fact, not usefully distinguished from the love we had, the love, just love, old fashioned love like the old jazz song?

Sleep, you must know, was no escape from this, but an intensification, so that, looking back and recalling sleep so far as sleep and the process of going to sleep can be remembered, I can only say that the separate sources of energy merged and produced a heat and an inward light so powerful in its magnificence that air and self lost distinction, I lost identity and drowned myself in a sleep of love. The word 'swoon' stops being banal when I see how appropriate it is for what happened to me.

Daylight, the room locked back in separation, woke me up. I can't describe that curious gaiety, that gratitude for even the acid traces of indigestion that last night's cider had left crawling around my system, for the fact of the morning and the fact of myself in the house and yourself near to me and the day stretched out before us like a garden.

I went to the small window and looked out from the shaped space which I had known with such curious intimacy, and I saw that the day was one which held a compelling silence. The window was slightly open. When I opened it fully I was excited to notice that there was no change in the temperature. Although the day was dull and the landscape, orchard tops I looked down on, muscular hills I looked up to, was arrayed in the softest gradations of grey and green, the open air was as warm as the small room where I had been sleeping all night.

I don't think it's being stupid to say that whatever had regarded me from the bleak eyes of the men in the bar the previous evening regarded me now from a series of nameless points among the unstirring foliage. The landscape bore the same expression on its face as the men had, grey, still, hostile yet passive, gently menacing.

You came into that predatory landscape, into the garden just below my window, walking down the flagstones between the growths and cancers of the cabbage beds, and we could both hear the isolated sounds of your shoes on the flagstones dropping out into the silence, unechoed and distinct down the aisles of the orchard that lay beyond the garden.

When you turned it was gravely, and we stood a moment, the three of us, you, I, and the menace of the silent environment, locked in a triangle of mutability, unquestioning, unique and grave within the acknowledged violence of the moment we shared.

Over breakfast we were suddenly lively, giggling when you spilled some tea, never forgetting the gravity of the landscape outside, the fundamentally sacred quality of our situation.

There were no suggestions about what we should do during the day, no suggestions about continuing with our planned visit to Fred and Jane, no wish to sit around the hotel reading old copies of the Farmers' Weekly and the various women's magazines with which the place was littered. We knew what we had to do and it was that knowledge, and the inevitability of that knowledge that helped us to share a sense of mischief like two children in a secret and forbidden place.

We left the hotel by the front door and turned left. The weather seemed to intensify. The greys got darker and the sky was shot through with a charge of heavy metallic purple. The foliage seemed to stir from the general passivity of sage green and grey which it had previously possessed, and burned frankly and violently with an electric green.

A man passed us on a bicycle and said, 'Good morning.' The village was still extraordinarily silent. There was only the subtle hiss of the passing man's bicycle tyres on the road, and the clank of a bucket somewhere distant, and somewhere else a dog barked twice.

Yet all these trivial sounds merely emphasized the intensity of the silence so that it took on a body and a presence, as of a sound, so that the silence seemed the very breath and voice of the hedges that turned their sticky bleeding leaves up to the light.

The road went directly through the village. We retraced the walk we had had the previous evening to the edge of the village, then continued as the road began to curve, first to the right under a high, leaning hazel hedge, then left out of the shadow of overhanging elms, to a hillside where it rose steeply, shallow hedged, between two fields of rough grass, hummocks and thistles.

I want you to recall the details because I have the thought, and the thought remains important to me, that not only were we controlled by intensities of atmosphere and desire, but also that the sequence -of incidents and places, as they unfolded before us that morning, was far from accidental. I'm making no claim for a sense of having been there before in dream or other incarnation. If you had feelings of that kind I would understand them but they're not what I'm trying to describe. It would perhaps make clearer the feeling I had if I said that events, the hedge, the white road, the sudden views and the equally sudden obstruction of wayside trees, the smell of the woodland, the pools of earlier rain blackening the roadside under the grass, all were words in a series of interlocked sentences that were spelling out in more formal terms the message we had already deciphered from the atmosphere and the climate of our shared spirit.

Your beauty as you mounted that hill. Funny thing, that even in the closest love the thing denied each is the other's experience of himself.

You can never see the way you held your head, slightly forward and slightly slanted with your eyes clouded in love and the proud selfhood which is defined by love.

The inscrutable light fell on the shaped bone of your forehead. Your skin oiled itself with a faint perspiration till it became waxen like the skin of a fruit. I dropped behind a bit to watch the pull of the denim skirt up your long brown thigh. You moved like a proud animal. Your legs mounted the steep tarmac with a ripple and a majesty. We were young then, much younger, even though it was such a short time ago. I wish to hell we were young now.

The clean and crude response I had towards you then, its familiarity and warmth when set against the stranger voices of the land and the day, was another bond between us, just like our laughter earlier, intimate, a kind of promise.

I've never lost a certain voyeurism towards you. I've always enjoyed, in a small domestic way, small domestic incidents like new underwear, like watching you, myself unobserved, preparing for a bath, washing your hair, the hang of your tiny breasts above porcelain, the pull of elastic and nylon against the resilient subtleties of your flesh. Now, as we turned to that unsteady five-barred gate, our eyes locked an instant as you interrupted my glance thrusting its inevitable shaft towards your crotch, flashing darkly and magically between the active muscles of your thighs, and do you remember, you stopped a moment, astride the gate, taking your weight on the balls of your feet as they found the lower bars, so that I, in the first touch I'd had of your gusset, fought back a heady fall of colours to find it jewelled and swathed in a ready profusion of scum?

Did we change the weather? It changed while we crossed the fields, city-dwellers both of us, who, that day, never tripped and stumbled on the tussocks of grass, but found our progress easy, as heat collected like loved water of your cunt and drummed the blood to our heads in a fiery concentration.

We crossed the field and entered a small wood of ash and squat oaks. As soon as we left the field our feet ripped through layers of young ferns.

Their brown pollen scraped our nostrils. Their curls whipped tiny cross-patterns of blood onto your ankles.

Boles of surrounding trees blistered into grey scabs of fact and changed reality. Sweat on your upper lip, small beaded drops with pin-point reflections, sweat in the air, hothouse concentration of heat like steam only accessible to nerves and skin, invisible, and the visible saturation of lichen greens and treebark purple, metal greys and old medieval russet breaking into reality on the surfaces of wood and vegetation, sweat, heat and colour hammered out each moment as our knocking hearts and anxious reaching genitals hammered out the beat of our walking, our dogged steps, persistent clumps up the bank of the wood, knocking of feet and knocking of blood and breath, sounds like distant hurrying animals, hungry in the underbrush, the pulse of ourselves and the pulse of the perpetual moment which was, for us and for whatever gods watched from the leaves that day, erect.

We climbed the hillside that the wood clothed, then half walked, half ran down the twisting track of a stream that etched silver round the nibbled continents of dead leaves congealed in the nooks of wood dross. Then the wood opened out into an even stranger, regal place, regal by right of a certain nobility in the spacing of ash and silver birch. The stream had spent its contents out into the swampy peat of forest floor which supported here a gentle carpeting of grass so violently green its brilliance and implied virility of juice and growth hurt our eyes.

Through this generous spacing of trees, across the flat sward, we could see that the ground fell away over a dyke of hazel roots. We mounted the dyke, our boots testing their angles, picking their equilibrium along the ridge down whose slope we looked.

If we weren't the first to break into that valley, and in all reason we weren't, then there dwelt, in that circling girdle of woodland, gods so ancient that our recognition of their sly Celtic personalities did, in fact, achieve a kind of compensatory precedent.

Is it as clear in your mind what an ancient place that valley was, how the very partitions of the fields, the expansive girth of the trees, the tilt and pattern of the cattle sheds with their hedged paddocks, fell into an entirety that was as recognizably the signal and the record of old, earthy, holy times as any other artifice, as dug-up ploughshares, shaped flints or carved pregnancies?

Is it clear in your mind how we stood there at the edge of this old chapel of agriculture and how the metal sky sat flat on the land like an anvil?

We climbed down from the dyke and descended into the valley. Making our way from gate to gate was simple. The valley had been spread like a map before us at our vantage point, and now we followed the faint path that led us down through the tiny, crowded fields.

It was as we entered into one of these fields, by a worn stile that took us through the ten-foot hedge, that a wind stirred up in the valley, a sudden cool wildness, an alien movement twisting through the weight and heat of the morning. The grass in the corner of the field surged and whispered at the invasion. The field turned its cooler pale colours, the undersides of leaves and grasses, to relieve our eyes of the savage greens of poison and sap. The very wind relieved our perspiration-beaded lips like water.

And, as if in antipathy to this cooling ghost that passed with its little crises of violence, with its shade and its chill, the anvil sky cracked and lightning stood against clanging metal in a contorted attitude of fracture.

Big warm discs of rain fell slow and wet on our faces; then all was moisture, sweat running like urine from our pores, armpits blackened with sweat, shoulders blackened with the sudden rain and the buttercups burning like hot coins scattered among dark threats of green and violet.

We ran through cataracts of warmth while the lightning fucked the land and cut the sky to slabs of dull quartz.

The cattle shed was on the far side of the field. Boots rough on hardened droppings, we fell on the straw, two bales stacked against the shafts of a broken cart, fell wet, then, as if the clothes cast off would serve as sacrifice and bribe for the mad god hacking up the sky into crags, as if to charm away the flame of buttercups, we bared our streaming skin. Bra whiplash nylon gone transparent, olive nipple clear through watershade, peeled to leave the nipple for my lip erect and frightened. Pivoted with life. Spreadeagled on existence; life was through us as terror, punishing and crackling with light.

Your pants, rich stench from the wet of them, and cunt, your cunt, my love, all honey and the coloured acids on your thigh in rivulets like sweat falling from my hair in tears to your convulsive belly, made snail tracks wandering fast like rain on glass into warm swamp of cunt hair, and I, a rod of terror, steel from passion and panic, glistening *fact* peeling in storm light, was into your belly, stabbing hard into your entrails, straining the very limits of your body—and how was it? How did it happen that your very belly opened to me? Was I really above you there on the straw, holding your self from throat to where my root was plugged in you, turning back vast petals of flesh like leaves of a secret book, burning a slow and dream-like progress to the quick of the flower? How is it I remember now the pearls I uncovered, wet and magical in their bed of crimson mucus? How was it that the gunners of the rain on the galvanized roof, having held their volley till the naked target was apparent, rattled their machine guns into your core, splitting the inviolable pearl in a punishing of peppered metal?

Did I say 'Now, Jaz,' voice loud, flat, frightened in the splendour of my own exploding violence, slash of scum to the rattled pearl, and, yes you did then, that's true; then you smiled, closing petals on me, warmly, gratefully in the steady fall of green, the, steady now, music of summer prodigal on the roof, and closing smiled, and smiling said 'Don't talk, Sam. Sam man.'

Yes, all right. I know I violated what you gave me then, and what can I say to you now but splather on about how I'm not a man, not properly. I'm human, merely human. No *human* man could tolerate an embrace as fine as yours was when you, open like a flower, closed like a flower on my ejaculation, closed like a tender flower, like velvet petals on my mind and loyalties.

I started to break it that night, I admit it. We kept it through the country back to the village, down the spewed up mud of wagon track that led us from the valley, skirting the ferns at the base of the mountain, down to the road again and clopping along the wet tarmac to the village. Physically we were only joined at this point where our hands clasped, but mind and spirit of us both maintained that full natural enclosure, each of each, that immense embrace, until we contemplated one another in my bedroom at the Llantypas Arms.

There was a peace about things then. The metaphysical stress, the sexual tension, the malevolent eyes in the foliage outside, all were gone and I could see you not as the agent of a sacred passion but as an ordinary human female. I could watch you peel off the sodden shirt and enjoy the matter-of-factness of the wet material slapping onto the wood of the chair you used to hang it on to dry. I could enjoy the habitual shake of your hair as you shook the straps of the bra you hadn't bothered to refasten, shook the garment down your arms and hung it with the wet shirt. I enjoyed the shake of your breasts as you bowed down, unzipped your skirt and carefully passed it over the mud of the wellingtons we had to return to the landlord.

Then you sat on the edge of the bed and smiled in a resigned way that seemed perfectly to express the comparative passivity of your demeanour.

'Thank you, Sam', you said, looking at your knees that were a bit red with rain and wind, that protruded bonily from the lace hem of your waist slip.

I went and took your hand. I hope to make some genuine amends by this confession to my fundamental failure, for the ineptness of my words then.

'I'll make you special,' I said, and then you said that you knew.

So here it is. Confession. It *was* my failure arising out of my confusion. I knew that later, at Barnet, when you really slashed out at me. I felt it then, but not so clearly. I'll sign to all my faults. I betrayed the holiness of the valley and the storm and I betrayed our unspoken undertakings. I betrayed the child in you, yes, it was I who drove you to the doctor with your demands and it is wrong, or at any rate useless, for me to revile you here. But I do, by Christ I do, you bitch. For if my contradictions and paradoxes and my failures were betrayal, then the final opportunity, the ultimate choice of whether or not to sell our gold up the river, lay with you. The kid was in your gut, for fuck's sake. For fuck's sake, Jaz, you didn't *have* to take me seriously. I sent you that poem. I hammered you, I lacerated you. I do so now. You, your hand, finally made reality what was, in my directions and reactions, a mere repetition of familiar charades in the undefined tangle of my moralities.

Read the poem, read this and know, if you can, that as I punish you the act of punishment is, in itself, a device for my further perambulation around in my absurd confusions.

How else can I live with what scorches me, but to become flame myself and cauterize you? How can I accommodate my own guilt but by hurling it at you?

My venom is only confession to my impotence. My punishment is nothing more than a floundering gesture of my own helplessness. Jaz, I love you. How do I support a self that's robbed of you and our dream? How do I maintain a self that's knifed by your ghost and my own fatuity?

Help me Jaz. I love you.

Sam.

Sam Hog finished writing with his right hand. As he finished, his left hand dragged the wad of paper from under his pen, screwed it into a ball and crammed it into his mouth. Only one tear escaped the knots of his eyelids to make its way along the grooves of flesh that ran down the side of his nose and spread into the stubble on his upper lip. When he licked it it tasted of salt.

II

Dear Sam,

I got your poem, Sam. You don't know what I did with it.

I've broken everything, Sam. Sam, I can't stand completion.

I would so like to have held my baby, Sam. How can I pretend I held yours?

I hid, Sam. I'm grateful for your blows. It was human. I could have touched it.

If I hold a fruit I have to cut it into parts. If the parts are regular I have to smash them.

I'm not apologizing, Sam. I'm not trying to diminish what I've done. It felt like an apple inside me. Sam, a little hard wooden apple. It was round.

Perhaps with you I could even elaborate my act. Perhaps with you I could enjoy the punishment. God have mercy on us, Sam.

It was a nasty place, Sam, a grave. It's made of ashes, Sam, ashes and flint.

It was at the dying of the day. All the colours were going. I held her in my hands, her tiny hard round head in my hands.

I can't stand completeness, Sam. It was at the dying of the day.

It left a hole, Sam. The gap it left was sore. The gap it left was round and sore, Sam. I was hungry all the time.

Why had other women such a plenitude? Why had other women such riches? I watched them, watched the little beams of light playing over the crags of ash.

They trip in the light and they dance in the light. Why shouldn't I pull a dead blind on their laughter?

The skin was so smooth on my fingers, so smooth it had to be split. The tiny head was so complete in my hand, so complete. It had to be broken.

How can things enjoy their wholeness when I'm unhealed?

Why can people have their gifts and wealth when I'm robbed?

I can't tell you, Sam, I can't get it down right. We loved straight words, Sam, and we loved gutter music, but even I can't be crude enough to tell you simply.

It was cold when I watched the children play, so cold. All the colours were the colour of cold.

The limbs lay like my little sister's lie when she's asleep. I cried inside, Sam. You know I've never stopped.

Sam, I want to tell you and I want you to stop me bleeding. You know I'm bleeding, Sam, so empty and so sore.

Sometimes I think I'm pregnant, Sam. Sometimes I think there's a stoat in my belly.

Sometimes I think it ate its way out. Sam, please help me. For Christ's sake help me.

You can see what's happening. You can see where I live. I live in pain, Sam. I'm wrapped round a round of pain and my wound is open to the cold.

If you come to see me, how can I ask you to come to me Sam, if you come I may kill you. What is it that's curled up nipping me in my open hole?

I live in a cold house, Sam. I live in a place where the air hurts.

When I go to the window and look out, Sam, the frost gets into my milk.

Sam, if I went to the town the trail of milk that drops from the hem of my slip would spread across my breasts in red.

It's too cold here for the red, Sam. A wound open to the frost is white, Sam, and the red goes purple, Sam, and then the blood goes black.

Do you know what I'm trying to say, Sam? Sam, my tongue won't reach the truth.

While I write to you, Sam, the frost is walking in my room. Sam, I want to be warm.

Sam, I haven't been warm for so many long days.

I want to be whole again, Sam. Please come.

I love you,

Jaz.

The red headed man found the letter on the edge of the bed. He picked it up and walked over to her curled body where she lay on the bedroom carpet with her thumbs in her mouth.

He sniggered slightly as he tore it into tiny pieces and the tiny pieces drifted down to rest in the masses of her black hair.

III

Dear Sam,

Thank you for the poem. I don't want to talk about it.

I'm not well. I think you probably know that. I think we are both sick.

It's about wholeness. I had to have wholeness. I wish you'd stopped me.

There's a man here you mustn't meet.

Can you come up here? Soon?

Jaz.

Part Two
THE STRAITS

Any little kitten can find his little nest. Anybody afterwards
can dig him out with a scalpel. Great A, little A,
Bouncing B.
The cat's in the cupboard
And you can't see me.
Everybody blind with the
snot in their eyes, head in a bag or the body in a sack of
membrane. Blind as a bat
Was my winkle worm
Blind as a bat
And indifferent to harm. Curled up snug as a bug
in an oven. Drop a jewel in the ocean.
Drop a lover in the sea.
Lay an egg in a distant mere.
Drown a blind bat. Don't drown me. Jack in the
pulpit swims like a bird. The gold egg in the sea
Was thrown out again.
When Jack he jumped in
And got the egg back again. A grub
called Jack in a hole of yolk.
The egg of slime behind your pinny
Is a pulpit for Jack be it ever so runny.

Doctor doctor, can't you hear the sermons squealed up your
stethoscope. Jack was a catskin.
Jack was a goat.
Drown Jack in the sea.
Cut Jack's throat.
Cat's teeth bared in death, fur like feathers on the ribs.
What a naughty boy was that
Who tried to drown poor pussy cat
Who never did any harm
And killed the mice in father's
midriff. Mother Cary turned in a trice and scoured her gut of
sugar mice.
Drew off the milk
Drew off the whey
Face on the pillow
Greeny grey. Feeding time at the aquarium,
arsenic for the little blind suckers.
Hanging at the mother crutch.
Hanging at the dug.
Hanging at the skinned tit
Wrapped in a dogskin rug. I used to spend
hours exploring the lovely orbs of her breast for fleas.
Tell tale tit.
Your tongue shall be slit
And all the dogs in town
Shall have a little bit. Sam Pig
had a bit. Tongue got stuck in the weeping slit.
Bun in the oven.
Cake on the grid.
Mother with a dog-tooth.
Can't get rid.
Scrubbed the oven for hours but you can't dim the

bloodstains.

Pat-a-cake pat-a-cake
Baker's man.
Bun in the oven
As fast as you can.
Pat it and price it
And mark it with T
And drain off the dregs
For Tommy and me—What you might call
terrible mental tea-strainer, a muddle-up tenuous tight-rope. Thin ice, thin ice. Sleeping upon a bed of ice
All on a summer's day
As it fell out, Jack fell in
And father got away. Right up the M1 on a
moonbeam. You parents that have children dear
And eke that you have none
If you would have them safe abroad
Pray murder them at home before
you set off freewheeling up the freeway.
There was a young man called Sammy Pig
And he was wondrous wise.
He jumped into a quickset hedge
And scratched out both his eyes. Inverted Oedipus
running down his handsome physiognomy,
Sam Pig went to market.
Sam Pig stayed at home.
Sam Pig sunk his meat one day
But this little piggy had none.
This little piggy ran wee wee wee
All down Mummy's leg.
Dear me what a mess. One little baby pig the less. A long tailed pig or a short tailed pig
Or a pig without any tail,

A sow pig or a boar pig
Or a pig with a curly tail,
Take hold of the tail and cut off his head
And then you'll be sure the baby pig's dead. Write the
certificate in applesauce.
Jack and Jill went up the hill
To fetch a pail of water.
Jack fell down and broke his crown
And Jill dropped the pieces down
the well. Drip drop lop it off. Jill sat down and sang a song
For the shards of her sweet boy's sceptre.
'I'd still be wearing the crown today'
He said 'If I could have kept her.' Pounds,
shillings and pennies from heaven down your vaulted wishing
well. Hush-a-bye baby
On the tree top
When the wind blows
The cradle will rock.
When the bough bends
The cradle will fall
And down will come baby
Placenta and all.
Swung in a plastic cat's cradle.
The sow came in with the hatpin.
The little pig rocked the cradle.
The dish jumped over the mother's bed
To see the bowl and the ladle.
The spit that stood at the bedroom door
Cooked the afterbirth o'er and o'er.
'What?' said the sergeant 'Can't you agree?'
'I'm a policeman. Come along with me.'
Dragged up for the petty sessions, petty crimes and mini-
murders. Disposed of the corpse with Saniflush.

There was a little woman
Lived under a hill
Put a mouse in a bag
And sent it to mill.
The miller did swear
By the point of his knife
He never took toll of a house in his life,
least of all a mite of a mouse wriggling about on the end of a pudding string. But he took his blade
And he cut the bag
And made some bread
For the midnight hag. Mummykins, I'd
know you anywhere. You that was wed to the black crow king that dropped his crown in the baby well, not very well, not very wealthy. The king was in his counting house
Counting out his money.
The queen was in the parlour
Eating something runny.
The maid was in the garden
Wringing out the clothes
When down came a blackbird
And pecked off her nipple pie in a peach-
cream sky and what would poor magpie do then, poor carrion creature. There
was an old woman who lived in a shoe
Who had no children. She knew what to do.
She gave them some broth in which she'd bled,
Then whipped them all out of their natural bed. There was a lady loved a swine.
'Honey,' quoth she,
'Pig-hog, wilt thou be mine?'
'Hoogh,' quoth he, salivating into the long trough. 'Pinned with a silver pin,

Honey,' quoth she,
'That you may go out and in.'
'Hoogh,' quoth he, drooling in the dewpond, snorting in the eye of the beholder. 'Wilt thou have me now,
Honey?' quoth she.
'Hoogh, Hoogh, Hoogh,' quoth he
And went his way, back to the smoke,
back to where the dirty girls hang at the end of a plaited rope of red hair. To where the lovely scrubbers croon deliriously over the bathroom basin
'Hush thee with thy daddy,
Lie still with thy daddy,
Thy Mammy is gone to the mill,
To grind thee some wheat to make thee some meat,
And so, my dear babby, lie still as a dead pig, stiff as mutton poker-porker.
Hush, baby, my doll, I pray you don't cry,
And I'll give you some bread and some milk
by and by;
Or perhaps you like custard, or, maybe, a tart—
Then to either you're welcome, with all my
whole heart, meat heart, bitten by the
beak that pierced a Birds Eye, Grade A custard flecked with strawberry jam. Dance a baby, diddy,
What can Mammy do wid'e?
But sit in a lap,
And give un a pap,
Sing dance a baby, diddy. Diddy pap,
titflap, raw from the little incisors of an invalid bat.
Brow, brow, brinkie,
Eye, eye, winkle,
Mouth, mouth, merry,
Cheek, cheek, cherry,

Chin-chopper, chin-chopper swinging about in the babyblue abbatoirs. Eye winker,

Tom Tinker,
Nose dropper,
Mouth eater.

Chin-chopper, chin-chopper, backed at the jaw bone, gobbled at the cherrylips, drain dry the nostrils, tinkers with Tom, Dick and Harry without so much as a wink of your blind eye.'

Crooning from the imperial throne of crime 'Hush-a-bye, baby,

Daddy is near,
Mamma is a lady,
And that's very clear. So rise from your early unkempt grave. Schottisches and minuets,

Dance to your Daddy,
My little babby,
Dance to your Daddy,
My little lamb, sacrificial blood on the backyard brambles. You shall have a fishy
In a little dishy
You shall have a fishy
When the boat comes in from the dark horizon at the other side of the sea.
You shall have an apple,
You shall have a plum,
You shall have a bag of bones
When Papa comes home . . .'

I'll sing you a song,
The days are long;
The woodcock and the sparrow,
The little dog he has burnt his tail,
And he must be hanged tomorrow, dangled from the sam skein of scarlet hair,

howling his bye-byes,
Bye, O my baby!
When I was a lady,
O! Then my poor baby didn't cry;
But my baby is weeping
For want of good keeping
O! I fear my poor baby will die.
For lack of good keeping my gay lady's suffering from a
lump in her lack-of-lump. Bye, baby bumpkin,
Where's Tony Lumpkin?
My lady's on her death bed,
With eating half a pumpkin. Who
can a threatened squib turn to in the howling red night.
Bye baby, bunting,
Daddy's gone a-hunting,
Gone to get a rabbit skin
To drown poor baby bunting
in. There was a rat, for want of
stairs, went down a rope to say his prayers. I sold my
mouse down the scarlet river.
And I bought me a wife,
And she cut my throat with a rusty old knife. She hacked my
knackers with a rusty old blade and finished my days at the
mating trade. She ended my deeds in the garden of eden weeds.
A man of words and not of deeds
Is like a garden full of weeds;
And when the weeds begin to grow
It's like a bathroom overflow,
And when the flow begins to spill
It's like fresh blood upon the sill
And when the blood begins to fly
It's like an eagle in the sky
And when the sky begins to roar

It's like a lion at the door;
And when the door begins to crack,
It like a stick across your back;
And when your back begins to smart
It's like a penknife in your heart;
And when your heart begins to bleed,

You're dead, and dead, and dead indeed, a dead dove, a split duck, a severed eminence. The barber shaved a mason

And, as I suppose,
Cut off his nose.
And popped it in a basin.

Was a pink thing and a think thing. Was a small thing and an itch. Was a soft thing and warm thing. Was a dead bird in a ditch.

Who killed Cock Robin?
'I,' said the lady,
'Because I was crazy.
I killed Cock Robin, at a certain appointment one cold morning.'
Who saw him die?
'I,' said Doctor Grope,
'Through my stethoscope.'
I saw him die, and drip and hope and slip. Who caught his blood?
'I,' said the rubber sheet
'Kept the bed nice and neat.
I caught his blood. 'And the knots and the clots and the little significant bubbles. Who'll make his shroud?

'I,' said the beetle,
'With my thread and needle,
I'll sew his shroud.' Clicking and

clacking in the recently dug garden plot, God wot.

Who'll dig his grave?
'I,' said the doctor,

Eyes like a crater.
'Pop this in the incinerator. Give it to
dad to plant in the garden. Do it before the arteries harden.'
Who'll carry him to the grave?
'I,' said the wind
'Don't care what I spend.
I'll carry him to the caves, to the midland waste lots, arse ends of your demented minds.' Listen to the cuckoos. Listen to the hysterical owl. Close the lid of your trepanned skull on the yatter of starlings, the gobbling swallows, the stuffed turkeys and the operatic vultures.

All the birds of the air
Fell a sighing and a sobbing
When they heard of the death
Of poor Cock Robin.
When they heard of the death
Of poor
Cock . . .

I

Lamps twinkling in the death guts.

Scarlet eye unfolded the purple-veined police—clothing picked the circumstances. 'Not now, Inspector. Not while my knickers are steaming.' Articles of face in the white glow. '. . . You see my fish-eye lost and reflected?' ceiling flies.

Technicolored strawberry three from corpse, 'A harvest that could make the pickers' fingers tingle'. 'Reap me in the quick of my recent nakedness, Inspector. Cut my harvest unfolded by a shrimp with odd geometric shapes.' THIRD BODY FOUND. POLICE INTENSIFY HUNT FOR KILLER it said across the train and the man who read it had one scarlet eye. The scarlet eye glowed over the page-top at Sam Hog and Sam Hog thought, 'Man, your rear lamp's twinkling in the dark, your gimlet gem is cutting up obscurity. The murder weapon was a death ray eye, rendered deadly by accumulating deathliness' rear lamp murder—twinkling death—gimlet accumulating murder and all the town's intestines raced past the window in their loops and rapid parallels—shrimp harvest—strawberry murder—and Sam Hog thought, 'My guts feel like that, all smoky metal, but that man's guts—they're okay—must be technicolored—painted panoply of sexual clothing—at the first incision over the Ribrock Rim Rock the painted panoply of Strawberry Gulch unfolded before their wondrous gaze, the channels and choked up creeks, the purple-veined pastures and crannies and the steaming swamps of scarlet refuse'—sexual mustard counting flies—darling the doctor's fee was reassembled—'Was severely mutilated' said the newspaper—'Found by the police in a waste lot near Dudley. Articles of clothing had been picked up by neighbours as far as a mile from where the corpse was found. Although the circumstances point to a sexual offence, forensic scientists assert that no penetration had taken place . . . '

'Were the leaves above the glade as green as tainted mustard?' he wondered, 'And it didn't look like a body,' she'd said, 'It's all right darling, it wasn't human, just a shrimp,' she'd said. 'They're not, you know', she'd said 'I didn't see it long I was looking at the ceiling counting flies. The doctor's face was very pale and sometimes, when I'd drifted off,' she'd said, 'delirious from fatigue and sadness, I lost his white face, looking down, into the white of ceiling looking down, and was left with the odd geometric shapes of his black coat and tie like some pacifist insignia, those rectangles and rhomboids of matt black with the corners off, like a silent cinema kaleidoscope in my mind,' she'd said, 'jumbled up, reassembled—then I woke,' she'd said. 'The pain was red.'

'There's a magical glow to the land in these hyar parts when old man sun goes down on the last roundup' he thought.

'But not a glamorous red, a boring red' she'd said, 'and that was it—there, mixed in with the mess I'd glimpsed . . . '

'The arabesque of a wheeling eagle swung across the fading light like a spider drowning in tabasco sauce—magical spider drowning into the white—police like a human shrimp,' he thought. 'Whut in tarnation's that down thar in the valley?' drawled Clem Phlegm, 'I've a tingle in mah ol' bones we're gonna run across the body of the Embryo Kid. Gimme a slug o' redeye,' he thought, drinking in the reader's gaze.

'It wasn't human,' she'd said. 'Your child was not a child,' so he'd hit her, saying, 'How's that for glamour?' Redeye likker and blackeye peas—the colour of dried daffodils round the edge of the bruise—petticoat singing my cream.

'The petticoat and cardigan were stained with blood,' said the newspaper and the man's regarding whisky eye said, 'Her pretty throat was hard again and flamed in rut—waving cockerel inside her stocking tops'—was really over-bloodshot.

‘ “Them hombres ain’t no slouch with a bloodgun” said Clem’ he thought.

Doors back with scythesound. Sam Hog stepped down, strode along the platform past a tramp crying.

(It’s the same the ’ole world over, guv’nor, all the women prancin’ rahnd yer wavin’ cockerels’ eads under yer nose and singin’ them rock an’ roll songs)

and past a meringue housewife

(I really don’t like it when he licks my cream as soon as he’s back from the office—Much nicer at the right time I always think, when he’s got a bit of dinner inside him and he’s cut his toenails)

and a hashish spade

(Oh what you really want now, baby, is throw away all dat chemical nonsense and turn on wid a little joint of me)

and a nicotine car delivery man with his trade plates under his arm like the ten commandments

(Thou shalt not accelerate into the mouth of the asphalt viper)

and past a beefsteak queer in a camel coat

(dear me, what a lovely cut of hump)

and onto the escalator and rose past the knickers—daffodils around the edge of the stain ‘Like ’em?’ she’d asked as she drew them past her stockingtops. They were white with lace and stretched like a whiplash round her bone-crater pelvis and they were a flurry of loving whispers, unfinished wintry rumours / whisky rut blood / the colour of her pretty throat / Nelly Thomas goes in the wood with that man—ever see a jackdaw in August?—all about her loins that had kissed his body with relentless precision. And he’d said, ‘Yes, I like ’em’ and the coffee-collector (like, percolate baby) said ‘Ticket?’

‘Tottenham Court Road’ he said and paid the man.

II

In she came, not much, just a bag of bones, bag of nails, bag of a smoke-husk, teepee made of beansticks, jack-straw ghost in a bush of a bushel of wheat hair nailed on the crest, crest of a straw bag, stick of a ghost, wheat-straw nailed in a bag of smoke. One of those *sore* faces, one of those just-in-out-of-the-cold faces. He smiled across washingday Monday springtime wind-on-the-hill when he sailed into the wet of her (now friendly) eyes. 'Half a bitter, please,' she said.

He dug his chin into his hand.

'What's up?'

'Half a bitter,' he said. 'Depressed.'

'Tankard or ordinary?' asked the barmaid, *husked* out the barmaid, smoke in her throat, eyes and hair.

'Depressed, why?'

'Ordinary. Seen the papers?'

'How does that affect you?'

He looked around the Porcupine. Charlie Beaver slumped across his accordion and smiled sleepily. The folk-singers accumulated round him, passing half a bitter one to the other.

'Four and eight please.'

'Woodbines? Well it does.'

A man came in and read the Evening Standard THIRD BODY FOUND. POLICE INTENSIFY HUNT FOR KILLER and drank beer and fished endlessly in his trouser pocket for a cigarette (which he never found, hand taking on the movements of self-stimulation, circling regular and dreamy in his pocket—soothing the cockerels' heads into the wet of her throat, smoke, washing eyes and hair).

'You're dead neurotic, incha?'

'No. Try the machine round the corner.'

'Neurotic. Dead neurotic.'

'Well Christ, Sam, what's it got to—I mean—we are talking about these kids, these murders, right?'

'You can't be impervious yourself if you know without being told.'

'Well, nobody's impervious, but only you would take the blame. Look, if it's gonna be, you know, one of those nights with you spreading your agony all over the fuckin' town, one of those really *corny* nights—'

Dreamy nights blame your spreading blood.

'Corny nights.'

'Yes—well I don't wanna know, see. I just don't wanna know, Sam, right?'

'You did it.'

'Did what? Those murders?'

Eyes met now, left and right and back again, right to left. Quite dry. Quite stern. What you might call 'utterly serious'.

'You sit in your broken down jalopy, deserted on the bypass—'

—beginning to grin in her washingday eyes—Omo Bubbles Brighter—broken milk from behind her bra—

'—and you post up your signs. Professional Compassion Offered To Lonely Males. Extra Cuddles On The Line For The Dirty And Deserted. Bunny Cunt Lives Here. But the only ones who come are children—soft silken little faces looking up in terrible earnest—milky saucer eyes—'

'Keep it funny, You're gravitating towards nasty again.'

'—And that wasn't what she meant now was it—that wasn't what the warmth and sympathy had all been about—The very wellspring of maternal milk—Emotions like a tidal wave sweeping up her cleavage—'

Giggles like gasps of pain wracked from the ladder behind her bra, nasty warning down the ragged flick of her buckled city.

'So she wraps her steel-cable thighs around their fragile throats—'

Warning look from the soapsuds, dirty milk, in terrible earnest.

'—Writhes down till the ragged lips of her crutch-piece kiss the little golden heads of hair—'

'Careful Sam—I'll go.'

'With a flick of a kneecap as the 709 goes thundering down to Dorking —'

'Sam, you're ill.'

'With a snap of the ankles, decorated as they are with half collapsed nursing-issue nylons—'

'Bent as a buckled beercan. D'you find it a help?'

'A help? A help? What d'you mean, a help? I trip my light fandango down the byways of the blitzed city.'

The ragged lips of compassion behind her cunt.

'Sam, it's twenty-five years since the blitz, Sam—But Sam wears it within, doesn't he? Sam's a little old unfused landmine. Sam's beach is dangerous to bathers.'

Grinning 'You can paddle.' Emotions like gasps of thunder.

'Paddle in Samuel's puddle. The big puddle. Up to me fuckin' drawers I don't think.'

A crying boy wearing jeans and an SS uniform wandered into the bar and wandered out again.

'And how about Jaz?'

'How indeed about Jaz?'

'Well that's something you might *constructively* abuse yourself with.'

He clapped the back of his neck with his palm and grunted boorishly. Gasps of big puddle.

'And buy me another drink.'

III

They found (Take A Trip On The) Skylark in the Star, sparring gamely with a spaghetti bolognaise, firing silent salvoes from his little accumulations of enlarged pores—fragments of spaghetti children, torn drawers blowing dreams—hiding coyly behind his Pagliacci death mask.

Sam said, 'Skylark, you don't look at all well,' and they scored twenty dexies (no meth, no prels) 'I'm not taking any of those,' she said.

He wondered whether to crumble one into her coffee while she went for a piss, but decided things weren't that desperate, weren't as desperate as they might have been if the little fragments of torn children leaked down his backbone into his bloodstream—Absalom, Adam, Alvin, Beulah, Bunline, Crupp . . . They found laughed weakly crumbled clapped out old blues numbers whining from the delirious Greek corner table . . . Enlarged pores hiding coyly navy blue school drawers 'Skylark you don't look the King for a piss if the glade drifted. . . royal wood, staghead emblem, mephistopheles with his tilted crown leering from the lower strata of the royal oak with a lecherous cheshire cat, royal grin like a slash.

Cut myself? A Whiter Shade of fandango . . . a whiter shade of Sky in the Star, that really celestial onion sauce smeared across the afternoon if the half-remembered (telepathically) the half-forgotten (psychosomatically) glade with two stocky legs tied at the ankle with navy blue school drawers visible from the strata of congealed dead leaves, if the glade drifted further flakes of leafmould down into his clothes—Jesus winnowing his Pagliacci death, spaghetti school drawers, meandering tour of his brainpan—not as desperate as they might be if his butchered eight-week son should stand up through his brainpan like a self-appointed seraphim singing all those clapped out old blues numbers about the Power and the Glory, Thine is the King-dom-Hey-fucking-men.'

'You're talking to yourself,' she said.

'Well, Jesus, what would you do?' Laughed weakly and crumbled a pill into her tea. 'I'm not drinking it,' she said and walked out. Skylark was asleep, blowing his winnowing dreams down a hookah of spaghetti, leaked his backbone into the desperate glade.

Silent salvoes from his little accumulations of piss but decided things behind his death. Sam said they might be twenty down his back into his coffee while she went desperate . . .

Bloodstream drawers—death mask of piss—another drink, the little fragments of the town blues—leafmould down his congealed dreams 'I said I wouldn't do this,' she said three hours later after the drinks (meandering tour of the French and Mooney's and the Mandrake—Welsh Tom and Big Bertha thrown out again by Gaston for bumming pot—four of them. First to the Marquis—then back to the French—Gaston gone home, all clear)

after the sudden desperate grappling into a doorway in Soho Square (Don't cry—don't cry all over me this time, Sam—Must have your little grope—For Christ's sake, just a little? dignity? no? Hurry up then—There, that better?)

after final pleas (Don't send me back to the predatory wallpaper, there's a good girl. It's cold inside and out. Don't send me back to the hangman's cottage, Christ in the dry furrow between the skin in a cleft, don't send me back to the climax of circling love—full of dead leaves, dead loves, dead loaves, Hovis is blood for you— 'Them goldurn Comanches dip their cornpone in a white woman' s—yup, true as I'm asettin' in this hyar saddle.')

climbing up the stairs she said, said I wouldn't have no blokes in here unless it's for keeps—unless it was going to be for keeps.'

Click of the door behind him and his head was full of / predatory climax spine hair pelvic kiss / intolerable twilight yearnings—images new mouth pleading finger flashing past of buttercup field receding behind a fast-moving train. 'Figure that's the last we'll see of Wyoming, Doc.'

He extended his hands towards her back—her black cloak off—her baby-birdwing shoulderblades stretching the stripes of the labourer's flannel shirt she wore as a dress, the bird-wing worked into (he supposed) a sort of / blood saddle grappling buttercup / flight under his pleading fingertips. Then stiffening into a sustained climax of / hangman's wing / tension ('Only thing to do wit' a vulture is ketch her young,' opined Clem Phlegm) very slowly tilting forward and the spine arching into a hump, then just as slowly, ecstatically straightening so that the backbone was buried in the dry furrow between her now clenched wings—hair spilled / dead loves blood corn / across his circling fingertips as her head went back (glimpse of lips half-parted in a half-smile)—his fingertips with their new mouths asking their way around her young climax body to fasten on the prominences of her pelvic bone, pulling the skin taut across her lower belly and (he knew) drawing her pubic mound up into a tight cleft purse. He drew his left palm circling pleading skin across the mound which, in the same rhythm, circled rearing and grinding against his palm.

He kissed her forehead at the roots of her hair and regretted it. Her body rejected his subtler feeling, insisting, even nagging for a total physicality. One of her thighs circled anxiously against the other, her knees lifting as though to urge his hand deeper into her crotch. Finally she grabbed his wrist with both hands, rammed his hand against her sex as though punishing herself (head bowed now, something like shame) and dragged it up and down like a rip-saw.

Slowly she started to cry, tears and saliva wetting her cheek, sobs surging and breaking out of her, her cunt weeping copiously over his fingers, palm, the (abused) heel of his hand, his wrist. Her pants, a slight rag, now totally drenched, she grabbed and tugged pathetically down to her knees. Then, sobbing from her sore, heartbroken face, her lean blue buttocks bared, the tea-rose shred of panties shackling her knees, she hooked her desperate fingers onto his shirt and dragged him round the hallstand (Par'n me, ma'am, while I jest hang up my guns') into her bedroom, pushing the unlatched door fully open with her streaked and glistening backside.

The man with the newspaper was sitting reading it. THIRD BODY FOUND. POLICE INTENSIFY HUNT FOR KILLER. He seemed embarrassed. He stood up and faced the mantelpiece, stuttering, blustering 'Er—perhaps I shouldn't have—Well—Well, my name is Phillips. Scotland Yard. Grateful if you'd tell when you're—er—presentable . . . '

'Fucking fuzz,' she said. 'Get in everywhere.'

IV

She hauled up lean scrag of a cloak.

Lean scrag behind thick-lens spectacles. She hauled up her knickers like an unabashed little girl.

She looked levelly at the back of his neck as she did so. 'Who let you in and what do you want?' she asked.

'Well—actually it was you I hoped to speak to first—find—out, well find something out about—er—our friend here.'

The man had turned now, still embarrassed, working his lean scrag of a face behind his thick-lens spectacles. 'But seeing you're here, both of you—'

'How did you know where I live, you nosy bastard?'

'Really—I know I broke in on your—er—on what one might call a scene of intimacy, but—well—don't see that that warrants abuse, or any special tolerance of—er—abuse on my part, er—Friend, yes, our friend is present, I may as well put my cards on the table.'

'Coffee?' she asked him.

He smiled, nodded.

She went out. Sam's hand, in his pocket, gathered up the dexies (picking daisies, officer, picking daisies / working the naked power and logic games), fingertips nosing around for one perhaps remaining.

'How did you find her flat?' Disaster arrived, as usual, with a certain cloak of relief—Dentist: 'Well now that wasn't so bad was it?' tea-stained abuse working his lean girl . . .

'Barmaid—and some of those—er—beatniks, they knew her.'

'Why not ask me in the first place, or are we all doing a big drama just to lighten your tea-stained little load?'

'You write, Mr Hog?'

'No.'

'You wrote, Mr Hog?'

'We all have our little freakouts. Get to the point.' Cloak of disaster wearing blunt and leaving freak load—Clung hard to the shock of finding the man there, clung to the violent absurdity of the girl's passion / pocket daisies nosing absurdity / and her nakedness / stained little load / and Phillips's presence, but now the sharpness of all that was wearing blunt and leaving a different kind of silliness, an absurdity of power and logic, the old boring absurdity, the numb dumb games. Phillips hung there before him like a public directive in a labour exchange, a tattered old signal, something left over from the war, Dig For Phillips, Careless Phillips Costs Lives, Make Sure your Blackout Is Really Phillips, Phillips Electric Dips Your Lamp, yellowed, tattered, brittle with desert winds 'That's another varmint they never got. Preacher Phillips. Looked like he'd never hurt a gopher. . . '

'Where were you last evening—er—may I ask?'

'I'm full of white wool, sergeant.' Watch the lights moistly from white wool.

'I beg your pardon?'

'I was with friends.'

'What friends?'

'Friends.'

'Name them.'

'You tell me what for and I'll decide whether it's worth naming them or not.'

'Friends in London?'

'Naturally friends in London.'

Watch the light change from deferential (amber) to pompous (red) to frightened (green) in Sergeant Phillips. Green now, hastily:

'It doesn't follow, you know—doesn't follow—' fishing out a fag case, 'Cigarette?' and flipping up a Craven A to hang from the drying spittle on his lower lip '—one little bit, oh no.'

Last dexy moistly palmed—leaning carelessly against the sideboard 'I repeat, what do you want?' wearily. He deposited the pills under the edge of a magazine—do for the time being—'Why don't you search me, drink your cup of coffee and piss off.'

'I—er—' he giggled a little. 'Not much point in searching you, young man, if you've hidden them under that magazine. Not interested, anyway. Not my department actually.'—Picking up another magazine, 'Ever publish anything?'

What if he wanted literary advice!? What if he'd got two hundred boys' school stories stacked in the lumber room back at the police flats, the fruit of thirty years' hard labour before the breakfast of every working day? 'You never know when there'll be a breakthrough, Edie.'

'Of course, Frank Richards is the master,' said Sam.

'I beg your pardon? Richards? Last night?'

'Last night I was with friends.'

'Friends called Richards?'

'No. Called Spon.'

Sergeant Phillips took out his notebook, then looked up. 'Oh no you don't. No. You don't catch me like that. That's a name you made up, isn't it?'

She came in with a tray of supermarket flower mugs full of Nescafé.

'Everybody's got milk and sugar,' she said. 'Okay?'

She bent near Sam to put the tray on a low table. Sam was suddenly weak with the personality of her flanks, beckoning earth cave snoring between the honed cliffs. He sat down.

Phillips blew a little on his coffee and drank some. ‘What’s a fester doctor?’ he asked.

‘They come and inspect you in school,’ she said.

‘Bit of a spot quack,’ he giggled. They kissed snoring flower flanks.

‘A familiar phrase to you?’ asked Phillips

‘Let’s send him away,’ she said, kissing him more, getting wet, drank beckoning earth.

‘Yes, piss off nasty fuzz,’ said Sam around her tongue.

Misty eyes, clearing daft triumph of their momentary sugar cave inviolability. Sex subsided, remembering. ‘I never published *that* one.’

‘We’ll be seeing one another, Mr Hog. Keep in touch,’ said Phillips, picking up his hat.

‘What?’ cried Sam.

Phillips went out. When they heard the outer door close they both dived in / kissed flanks got milk got sugar wet caves / trying hard to drown.

V

He slept / wince window blue above the sunset shirts / with his wrist locked / gold stain / between her Tufty greasy handcuffs, marshal’ drying thighs, and dreamed himself part of a / shame of midnight buttocks / family in a strange house where he was always summoned to a room that the occupant had always just left, always leaving, on crumpled scraps of paper, or scrawled across the wall, fragments of his poem 'Who you messed up . . . you and the fester doctors . . . locked slimy hole . . . your sensible welfare pence . . . gold hole spilled . . . shall we make sleep? . . . someone watching . . . '

Written in his hand, levelled, nonetheless, somehow, at him, his own bullets trapped and fired back. Once in the night she woke. 'Sam . . Sam . . . '

There was something with powerful odour—sudden warm effulgence of locked slimy face upset and shame—in the cupboard in the butler's pantry, and her voice drew him out to a daylight gold bent clarities of midnight waking— 'Sam . . . Jaz—She's okay, isn't she?'

He pretended sleep now, back to the pantry, still as a little wee mouse. 'Sam . . . She is okay?'

Tight sleep tight as wince. Fragments trapped and fired warm fester pence on crumpled scraps of sunlight horizon. Screw up your eyes. 'Locked us both in a slimy hole.'

Her voice was too loud for the tiny room. They were both too big for the tiny bed. She said 'You—is that what you're really screwed up about? The abortion?'

And he dragged sleep mute green shadow over his mind like an eiderdown, back to the pantry but away (driven away) from the cupboard, back to the empty room where the sun was setting now. He waded through big bent rectangles of orange window light and swam through mute green clarities of shadow in between and he looked down from an upstairs window, from a room where the big blocks of sunlight shone up from the horizon to his face (aeroplane had sky-scrawled 'fester-doctors' in gold across the blue above the sunset red) and saw some compelling mess? stain? accident on the flags below—found bucket, mop and disinfectant in the kitchen on the shadowed side of the house—rushed out, suddenly naked—swing of his warm testicles against his thigh—to Jaz, standing waiting, wearing one of his dirty shirts but otherwise also naked. He fell, but sat and remained sitting, he here, Jaz there looking compassion, sat rocking on his hard male buttocks, hugging his grazed knees, laughing big barks of laughter out into the sunset shrubberies dirty skyscrawled compassion grazed naked thigh, and Jaz kept saying 'Please stop.' Please stop she was painted in Japlac to get your eggs and purple louse. What was fuck? No more find Jaz. You can start eight week foetus, naked love. He made the taxi turn the dirty dishes in her kitchenette, trying out stillness so that he could maybe do the newsvendor curtaining his washing garden with a headboard gone. He'd left a corpse of mouse eaten to death by coffee. Thanks for the difference between a dead mouse furry and take care puberty. Sunshine stood in front of the main street. Mr Sunshine scream his nerves to the steering grinding baby so he left the sun brain from his buckshot rattling smoky café next door to the nerves by nest rough smothered, tangled like a uterine rattle, tender lariat half clothed and bright brash heartbroken morning light through the next empty minstrel telling crude midriff against the edge mother buried in the coffin. Morning head-force said entrails murderer had all day window lacerated sex, assaulted killer, face down to the mad and heartbroken. Trying half clothed rattlesnake, eggs bright brash affront trail puberty starring paper face crude concrete sunshine trail to the mad taxi turning spitting steam

Love, steam Love, steam Love, murder fuck. He woke.

She was gone.

She'd left a note.

It said, 'Got to get to work. Make yourself eggs and coffee. Thanks for the fuck. No more, though. Go find Jaz. You can start again. Take care. Love, Terry.'

He made the bed. Then stood in front of two days' dirty dishes in her kitchenette, trying to scream his nerves to stillness so that he could maybe do the washing up. He failed, so he left the washing up and went down to the street. He found a café next door to the corner newsagents.

Morning headlines said POLICE INTENSIFY SEARCH FOR CHILD MURDERER. He bought one. Photo on the front. Found in Wren's Nest rough lots, Dudley. Had been missing all day. Smothered. Half-clothed and lacerated, not sexually assaulted except for some unprintable detail. Killer possibly interrupted. He turned the paper face down by his plate, then tossed it onto the next empty table.

Even so, it was difficult getting down his / half-clothed smothered / sausage and eggs. He bent stiffly, lacerated possibly for fuck, driving his midriff against the edge of the table, trying to silence his nerves by main force, scream his nerves to intra-uterine rattlesnake, keeping his tripes still so that food could pass through them. 'Goldurn it, Clem, muh entrails is tangled like a tenderfoot's lariat. Mighty ornery trail for a intra-uterine rattlesnake.' Morning light through the steamed window was a bright brash affront—some visitor telling crude jokes to the mad and heartbroken.

'Come in, Mr Sunshine, Mr Concrete Breakfast Food. How d'you make a mouth like a cereal ad? Big bent-marrow nigger-minstrel smile "Why diyud de chiyukin krass de road, Mistah Bones?" My cosmic tangled antra-uterine cornflakes sit on the lid of your purple-louse eight week coffin the mouse died lacerated sausage his mother buried it in the garden with a headboard painted eggs and scream nerves in Japlac here lies the corpse of timothy mouse eaten to death by a purple louse. What's the difference between a dead mouse furry and an eight week foetus naked? Puberty, Mr Sunshine, puberty.'

Mr Sunshine sits in a taxi turning / jokes to the mouse / the corner of main street. Look at the windscreen spitting out cereal, Japlac intra-uterine purple. Look at the steering wheel grinding the harvest 'baby of yew din' want mah co'n pone wha did yew grind mah co'n?' Mr Sunshine blinds the eyes of the newsvendor curtaining his brain from his buckshot headlines. Mr Sunshine is left behind as Sam Hog turns into the tube. Back with the rattling smoky tripes. A trip to the end of the Northern Line and back used up the morning. Liz's for lunch.

VI

Liz lived in Streatham, not too near the spadery. Liz's husband worked in advertising not too far from Streatham. Liz was usually good for a meal, dinner and afters. 'A li'l more cream, Miss Liza? Well, jes' a-keep on a-rubbin at the magic fo'ty-five.'

Liz reassured him. Good old Liz.

None of your fractured culture about Laburnum Rise (Masticate / magic rubbin' / leaves of the heavy laburnum and you'd get a rise to rouse the / more cream / Queen of Spades—all free, no masturbation, smelly housework or added expense), all honest-to-Christ semi-detached nasties, soundly erected with garages trotting like toddlers alongside. Liz was the only friend he had whose doorbell worked. It went bongbong, not brrbrr. 'Why, Sam.'

She moved nicely, filling a kettle. He could sit on the white lacquered kitchen chair and get all moved, yes moved again, about her undistinguished and undecorated body functioning nice and smelly under her housework dress. Her legs were white and muscular and looked as though someone had designed them. She had a sluttish Welsh accent.

'Well,' she said 'Well and *what* has Sammy been up to, then?'

'Liz, the coppers are smelling at me.'

'Don't know what you mean, I'm sure.'

'I slept with Terry last night.'

'Who's Terry?'

'I thought you knew her. Well anyway, when we got back to her pad, you know, couple of drinks and that—'

'Couple? You?'

'—There was this nasty fuzzy—quite funny, actually. Terry got a bit steamed up, you know, backed into the room bare-arsed and who should be there to kiss her hello but Detective-Sergeant—er— forgotten his name.'

'No! How'd he get in?'

'In? Oh, she never locks the door. Walked in, I suppose.'

'Bloody cheek.'

'Cheek to—er—cheek, as it were.'

'All right, funny man. Get on with the story. After pot, I suppose?'

'Well—flyfingered as ever I thrust my new stash of dexies—'

'Not again. Brain damage, Sam. I warn you, I knew this chap—'

'Under a nearby copy of Nova and he just laughed. No, it was something else. He knew some phrases from this poem of mine—'

'A fan, Sam. A fan.'

'I owe it all to Dexedrine, the tablet with the rusty zip—And I don't know where he got hold of it.'

'Please miss, I got it out of a book.'

'No, no, I don't think I put it in a book. The top copy I sent to Jaz—'

'Christ, haven't you forgotten her yet?'

'The first carbon I have, and, now, the second carbon—er—'

'You published.'

'I don't *think* so.'

'Must have. Anyway, what happened?'

'Oh, we started snogging and ignored him and he fucked off.'

They had lunch, onion omelette. Then coffee. 'Don't let me keep you from your housework.'

She laughed out loud. 'Tell me about Jasmine.'

'Don't call her Jasmine. Wet bloody name. Jaz, well Jaz's—er—okay, I think.'

'You don't care.'

'I don't care, don't care, don't care.'

'Well, if you care so bloody much and you keep doing corny things like sending her poems you might as well deliver something every nice lady wants.'

'Liz—'

'What?'

'Shut up.'

'Now the sensitive bit.'

He stood in some remote nonexistent corner of the / corny poem / room and watched the self-pity / onion coffee / pour down over his head like treacle. Treacle onion coffee tears. He felt immensely stupid when she / rusty snogging / came mothering in to comfort him came fluttering in to mother him. That turned the onion tears off.

She unbuttoned her dress. He buried his nose in the little swell of breast above the bra. He noticed the edge of the bra was thumbed and grey. He smelled armpit cabbagestalks, drove his nose round under her arm and buried it in the / rusty onion / moist and humid little garden.

She was stroking his neck. He realised that she was not just comforting him.

When he held her breast she drew breath crying / electric valves / sullenly as though / Christ's voyeur / hurt and threw her weight against his whoremonger's hand, forcing the pressure. Then their eyes met and they giggled.

'Remember your poor dear husband,' he said. 'They buried him wit a whole saddlebag of reject copy,' recollected Clem Phlegm.

'I am, and it just makes it better.'—Oiled out, copper monger, nibbling his ear. The phone rang.

'How did you know I was here?'

'You told me last night. Don't tell me you were that blocked.'

'God, is nothing private?'

'Nothing, Sammy, nothing. *You just wait* to hear what I've got to tell you!'

'Is it Jack?' asked Liz, buttoning one precautionary button. Not blushing exactly.

'I bait with frighted death,' said Sam.

'Guess.'

'If it is, don't tease him.'

'Henry Plud the royal whoremonger?'

'The name suits him.'

'Is he still at the agency?'

'Come on. Spill it.'

'Spilled milk—who's crying? Phillips?'

'Electric? Valves? Post-war bandleader?'

'What are you saying? Give me the receiver.'

'The copper, you bum.'

'Our pet voyeur?'

'Sam—for Christ's sake, you're just not being fair.'

'It's *not Jack.*'

'Jack? Who's Jack? I told you—Phillips. He questioned me for hours.'

'Well 'oo the fuck is it then?'

'What about?'

'Yes. Thought that'd make you sit up. That poem . . . And where you were the night before . . . '

'Not drugs?'

'It's that Terry, innit?'

'I don't *think* so.'

'Yes, it is. I'd better warn Malcolm just the same.'

'Might be as well.'

'See ya then.'

'When? I'm frightened.'

'When? When you look.'

'Not too long, Sam. Fuck it, it's weird, man.'

'Be all right . . . ho ho. Tatty bye.'

Weird fright when you look.

VII

Malcolm up the stairs, dog turd pining for the carpetless pad. 'What's brown and sticky and crawls up your leg?'

'A homesick turd.'

Memorial sham of stale pot gone like Sam with brown damp partner. I like a sleeveless flowered proverb, primroses trapped between the piled up sink and black pubic hair. 'We found them in the springtime, hauled them home and dropped them somehow, forgotten behind the dirty dishes.' Smell of them, smell curled crisply against the fresh green evil. Susan lay in croak, in scream, its itchy ticking massed around her personal cream. She rolled her red-black under-flesh of face, skinned by the nerve knife and trimmed by the best beauty parlour in the whole sewerage system.

Neva was savage on the mattress, touched rain of green with the fragile twists of fingertips. Green man sheltered in the sheer luxury, warm yellow, crying gratitude on the edge of pregnant crap.

Susan had a poleaxed steer against the shafts of her hand, a dead pig belting blood, stuck by the skewer of the facial nerve surgeon. Sam lay down through drenched meadows, falling, tumbling, losing the dew.

Malcolm was releasing a sudden green, meadow-pus, springsnot, wet of willow sliding down his country rills, trailing a music of relieved rain. Malcolm, Malcolm Riley had forgotten his Irishness.

Mournin' Mavourneen of Morn pining for her broth of boyhood, he didn't like to be reminded of it, memorial shamrock gone to compost in the London sump, the straw stacked sweet green compost in the London fatigue.

He answered the door to Sam with a wince of recognition. Clem Phlegm: 'Take it easy, pardner. I like a man that looks a man right in a man's eye, yessiree.' Sam followed Malcolm along a little tattered pathway of brown-flowered lino, ah the way the lean times have shat upon the proverbial primroses, wince of female sweat that looks flat along a little tattered path, along his veins, up the stairs—dog-turd at the bend —past the piled up sink and into the carpetless pad with its three women, lean times in a slip, smell of them, smell of stale potsmoke gone like the primrose path from fresh green (dry) to old brown (damp).

Susan lay in a 30's style sleeveless jumper, one lace-up boot and nothing else. Her wrist was trapped between her lank, bandy thighs. Her red-black pubic hair curled crisply against the white underflesh of her arm. Mandy sat cross legged reading the Beano. Neva was asleep. Scratch no evil, read no evil, and dream no evil.

Susan had been crying. She croaked 'What do you want?'

'Shuttup,' screamed Malcolm. She rolled 'Plumb like a poleaxed steer' onto her face 'The forty-five still smokin' in her hand' as if through impact of his savagery and lay still as a dead pig.

Sam lay down on the mattress alongside Neva. He looked at the painting Malcolm had not finished or touched over the past six months, trailing rain of green. It rained green the best time. '*Now Jaz.' 'Don't talk Sam. Sam, man.' Sheltered in a lean-to farm shed, the straw stacked against the shafts of a cart, drumming of the sweet green rain on tin like belting blood. 'Oh, yes,' she said. Wading back to the hotel through drenched meadows, the sheer luxury of fatigue.* It was a good painting.

Neva stirred beside him, releasing a sudden warm yellow smell of female sweat.

Lying flat, looking at Malcolm's green unfinished, the fatigue ran along his veins like a music of unrelieved creatures crying gratitude. '*Thank you,' she'd said, very simply, sitting on the edge of the hotel bed in a slip and her wellingtons. 'I'll make you special,' he'd said. 'I am special,' she'd said. 'You've made me special. I'm pregnant.' 'Bollocks,' he'd said. 'Don't give me that romantic crap. You can't possibly know.'*

Oh Christ, mouth jam down a decent wonder tunnel . . .

'What's up, man?' asked Malcolm. 'Sam, man,' she'd said, said it just once.

'Whaddya mean, what's up?'

Malcolm looked puzzled, then let his face, the scarlet harvest of rich auburn fuzz, fall away into a grin.

'Coffee?'

Twinkle dim and yellow kissed her arse . . .

'Oh Christ, yes please,' gasped Sam. Malcolm went outside to fill the kettle. Susan looked up with eyes like purple with her mouth all smudged like a child who'd been stealing jam. The lamplight shone dim and yellow on her buttocks. Sam rolled over, lunged across, kissed her arse, smacko. She looked down at him and smiled. 'Sam,' she croaked. (Panic voice, stashed wizard in the flesh: Am I a decent man, Susan? Did I hold the hand that ran the spike up the wonder-tunnel? Am I the foetus farmer that brought home the scarlet harvest by some kind of emotional radio-control, dragging the sodden rag of half-child all across the rich auburn pastures of the autumn—sun down on our fine green painting of love? Sorry, Jaz, sorry, sorry, so sorry.) Croaked the hand that ran the foetus farm, emotional radio-control across the rich auburn pastures—fine green decent manspike up the wonder-tunnel—the sodden rag of autumn, sun sorry, sorry . . .

Did I, am I some kind of half child, all down, sorry . . .

'You wannit? Take it with you,' said Malcolm, coming back with the coffee.

'The fuzz are after me,' said Sam.

'So what's so special? The fuzz are after everyone.'

'No really. It's not drugs, but they might be around so keep your stash stashed.'

'Stashed schmashed, sausage and mash, sausages flashed . . . '

'Wizard with words' said Susan. Mandy laughed, short and nasty, 'Ha,' like that. Malcolm started to roll a joint three papers long.

'That's right. Take a hint.'

'Hint schmint, mint bint, bint julep, when you bore a julep, a mint bint julep and I wore a long red nose . . . ' Sooty quim. 'O-o-oh' wailed Susan.

'She remembers the rose, not nose,' sneered Malcolm. 'What did I do with it, Susan? Where did I plant it? Tell Sam our tenderest idyll.'

Mandy looked up. 'Cut it out,' she said baldly.

'That was it,' said Malcolm. 'I cut it, culled it, plucked, transplanted it in the flesh of the woman herself. You perceive, Sam, how she lies now—'

'Purty as the Sierra Madre stretched out in tits and table mountains into the salad-dressing sunset' Clem Phlegm soliloquized.

'—How finally the creases underneath her buttocks curve into *the* crease. You may imagine, Sam, how on that occasion they served as arrowheads, as gentle heralds for a great big beauty of a blossom rising like a mystic sign from the oblivion of her sooty quim.'

Susan got up and walked out. Malcolm turned towards Sam and hissed out potsmoke. He passed the joint to Mandy. 'Piss off out of it, Sam,' he said. 'You're a drag.'

'You and your cruddy morality,' she'd said.

'You're like all these fuckin' women,' Malcolm said.

'Where was your morality when you rolled me in the hay?' she'd said. 'Swamped in pastoral emotion? You're like all these fuckin' men,' she'd said. 'Soft as pap.'

'You're bringin' me down,' said Malcolm.

'You've been warned,' said Sam.

'You brought me so low,' she'd said, 'And now you stand there preaching about the sacredness of human life.'

Sam passed through the kitchen.

'Sam, let me come,' said Susan.

VIII

'I'm not going anywhere,' said Sam, 'except away.'—spastic trains whipping crippled snakes through tumuli to far plains California in the morning promise light—spastic trains whipping morning promise through crippled tumuli to far light— 'Away from every fuckin' thing.'

'Me too.'

On the stairs by now—light off-yellow colour of dog dirt soiled a look of reflective innocence he didn't know whether to respect. 'Yup, a woman can be like a rattlesnake, pardner,' Clem Phlegm croaked through the frog-wash of dirty stairslight. She looked up. 'I've got bread.'

'Then let them eat cake,' he moaned absurdly. A carload of spades hurtled down the road outside—Would that snub-nosed dum-dum lead could velocitate into my hurting grey matter. 'Solve all, solve all,' he winced at Susan. 'Money always does,' said Susan, running to catch up along the clopping wet late pavement, going whipping crippled in the morning . . .

Stairs reflective. Womanlike a frog wash of dirt. The road into Susan along the wet soiling. Domestic scum set slippers shuffling long enough to take on some mystic dark and dusty corner farthings, Victorian slop star mess. Sponge obsession. Spread fuck-liquid spilt, womb's running in the overbirth into the sky with dirty light, off-yellow innocence.

She moaned my hurting grey matter, anxiety in August, abandoned buttock, uncanny family sphincters, stocked, spilled tears—squatted and wiped mess mess, spilt blood. The lord screwed me over goodness from the fuck before coloured afterglow. Spastic California fuck, colour of dog-dirt. Dirt croaked through a carload of spades. Dumdum taxicab among the trivial moguls, arthritic arseholes, pinups of upholstery, treasures discoloured as his swearing nightmares all spilt—as runny as mercy. Drowned your mouth out. They got a pale-hued force. They got a taxicab to Sam's.

Sam had frittered out anxiety in the august setting of an Edwardian usage. He lay for the most part, when at home, among the trivial domestic scum some landlady had left abandoned to the bedsitter moguls who kept the dingy wallpaper, pale-hued carpet (the endless arthritic slippers shuffling), buttock-sculpture furniture (shaped by arseholes long enough to take on an uncanny family resemblance through perhaps some mystic sympathy—blousy madames Force's pinups of upholstery—dark and dusty corner sphincters stocked with treasures, lost rubbers, farthings, Victorian sixpences, buttons, rubberbands . . .)

Susan waited for coffee while Sam spilled it. The third time it made a big sloppy star at his feet. His tears, mockturtlewise, exceeded any mess he cleared as he squatted and wiped with a discoloured sink sponge. His obsession similarly outdistanced irritation as his swearing spread from 'Fuck it, fuck it. Mess mess' to 'Slops and nightmares all of liquid spilt mistake. You've spilt blood, sir! Jaz, your womb's full and running over. Surely goodness and mercy are drowned in the overbirth aftermath . . .'

'What?' called Susan from the bedroom.

'Oh, shut your face, you fucking cow, before your mouth runs out into the sky with dirty coffee-coloured afterglow. I said, if you're interested,'—lurched to the door by now, 'That hombre's got somethin' on his mind'—'If you want to experience with me the glad oceanic splendour of the final flood, I said, if you want to swim with me down the long marshy wellsprings of eternal shit, I said that the sun and the moon had mistakenly come on at the same time and even Telstar was insufficient tampon for the deluge and even floating slaves in the Mississippi mudflood don't provide us with adequate image for the knots and groups of tiny whimpering embryonic—'

He stopped because she was crying. He went to her and looked down on her. 'Goldurn, colonel, when a filly turns on the waterworks thet's a thing a man cain't shoot with a sixgun.' And down with his strings of compassion came the bleak bulb's watery diabetic piss of light, breaking over her head so that her hair was the solid model of a waterfall of gold. Moved by this, he kissed her. She looked up . . .

'You're five,' he said, 'Five years old.'

Her face had lost its lollipop. He bent to her. He tried to make his hands into a cup that would be gentle enough. He was numb with his familiar horror at the countenance of purity imprisoned in the hurting vulnerable fallible flesh.

'They're all horrible to me,' she said in a voice from years ago that broke cleanly through bubbles of saliva. He took her cheated head in the cup he made of his hands, trying to handle it carefully enough, trying not to drop it back in the spill. And he kissed it. On its wet eyes.

Her arms hooked to him. He fell to one knee, one foot rucking up dust smell from the rug. After five minutes she broke away. 'I want you to have me,' she said.

'Why?' he asked.

'For a present,' she said. 'You're so bloody nice.'

He felt a bit better himself then. He went and made the coffee. Sitting with it, cross legged before her, he said dully, 'We're all nice really. What the fuck are we pissing about at?'

'I think we're being afraid,' she said.

'You can say that again,' he said.

He awoke at four. He tried to smoke and tried to ignore an erection that worried him like an exposed nerve.

Finally he got up. The armchair rolled a little over the carpet as he stood. Streetlight made a little ballet frock under the curtain.

He went to the bed where she lay, hauled back the clothes. For some reason she hadn't taken off her stockings, for some reason it didn't seem kinky. He drove his tousled skull against her black rich diamond of hair. Thighs parted to his nose, to his ship's prow nose, and he sailed down the slimy flood of lanes to the land of final flood marshy wellsprings tampon for the deluge of tiny whimpering embryonic experience, glad swim with eternal star and floating splendour down the sun and moon, to the land of sun. Jaz had looked like a painting in the punt. Like a punt painting. She had looked like a pile of messy masterstrokes from the brush of MacEvoy or Sargent, or Du Maurier or Charles Keene. And the chestnut leaves screened sun to honeycomb dapples on her face.

'I like it to be like a book,' he'd said and she'd washed his face clean of her mucus with a handkerchief dipped in the olive shallows, smelling of pebbles and dead leaves.

Her nylons had been like metal—a sumptuousness, a bounty in the tangle of nature, metal hot with sun, like a car bonnet—he drank the secret guarded by the metal biolith. It wasn't that time. It was the time in Wales . . .

The chestnut leaves clean of her mucus, shallows smelling of her nylons, the tangle of secret sun, honey kerchief, leaves like metal hot with dapples and she'd washed dipped in olive sumptuousness of summer . . .

Susan stirred mightily against his jaw and he recollected her. Her fingers hooked in his long hair at the back and held him there. Her orgasm subsided. 'I'm sorry,' he said. She was still asleep. He covered her.

And walked to the window.

IX

He'd walked all the way from the tube that grey day 'Quickly,' Jaz'd said. 'Quickly,' Terry had said on the phone.

He'd walked out of the station, right, past the phone boxes, up the asphalt rise bald as an urban bone, past the sweet shop shacks and the gaunt girls' grammar school, the copper shop and the knicker window (why such winces, Sambo, at the fleeting glimpse of a gathering of young gussets, all the psychedelic pimpernels blossoming in translucencies over the pudenda?)

Asphalt gaunt knicker gathering—blossom translucencies . . .

After Scotland Yard he'd go to see Terry. Would she have disaster cool for him in the frig, gallons of spiced up tragedy, red cunt showers of maggots, fruitgarden fresh on the top like a Pimm's, disaster like Jaz's, *not five minutes after he'd got in the door (hello kiss, cosy grope, coat on the door-hook, down on the convertible divan, Miles Davis chugging out of the pickup trailing his phantoms of railway blues) 'Sam . . . Sam? Comfy, Sam? Love me? Sam . . . I'm pregnant.'*

'Wales . . . '

'It was a fertility rite.'

'It was a fertility wrong.'

She came to the kitchen door. She wore a with-it pinny with a big face on it. 'There he is, King Squidger, peeping at me out of the minge'—thought of the little red invader tucked up there, all comfortable, up his cunt, living off the blood that was supposed to run fast for him. Whitehall looked as grey as Jaz's smoky eyes had, then. The shower of his days was all grey rain anyway. Down the slope from Whitehall. Under the arch, wondering which was the right door.

Coppershop fleeting pimpernels up tragedy like kiss . . .

'Phillips? Phillips? Detective-Sergeant? One moment, sir.'

Had they called Crippen 'sir' in this same office with the leathertop desk, the half-cold cup of tea, the minimal ends of cheap cigarettes like limp maggots in the bakelite ashtrays. Had the grey of the grubs of ash been so identical to the grey of Jaz's disappointed irises?

'Wrong?' she'd said, 'wrong?'

'Well, hardly our intention,' he'd fumbled, mumbled out.

Back she'd gone to the coffee stove, leaving her absence in the vacuum of the vacated doorway. He'd crept to the door. Her hurt was an impenetrable ice-block all around her shoulders.

The desk sergeant stooped. He bobbed like a fairybook gnome hung from a bent pin of sciatica all across the inner office.

'Yes. Sergeant Phillips will see you, sir. He says is it Mr Hog? Yes. Yes. Good, sir. The constable will see you up to the office. Show the gentleman up will you, George?'

The corridor from the waiting room to the surgery had not, she'd told him after, been as dark as this. She'd had the best, no back-street knitting needle, no whirling douche of poisoned darts machine-gunning the lining of her archetypal cradle. Carpeted, her feet had gone to the death scrape. Neon lights and papered walls and a pompous succession of mahogany doors inscribed with gilded Roman capitals. The corridor seemed stamped with Phillips. He'd left his odours and spectral mackintoshes hanging in the light from the succession of lettered glass panels with their lavatory opacity. Gloomily they hung in a brown gloom. The constable swung open a door. 'Mr Hog to see you, Sarn't.'

How could he speak seriously to Phillips? Was the Phillips real? The Phillips had frightened Terry, with her scary scarecrow dollshead, her shock of a hayrick of hair, her cunt the lascivious mouthing of anxious terror, Terry in a hurry: he'd scared her, Phillips. Talk to that.

'You've been pestering my friend Miss Adams.'

'Pestering? Pestering? Do sit down, Mr Hog. Sorry—er—not very well appointed—however—each man his station—the rewards thereof—sit down, yes, cigarette?'

She'd flung it at him then, standing over him, lighting hers through dangerous proximities of hair and drenching plenitudes of cataracting tears. Her lips had been so wet and bruised and hesitant, trembling on a sob even round the miniature severity of the filter-tip Number Six.

*'Suppose there's no end to a girl's naivety. Suppose,' she'd sniffed noisily, 'to the end of fuckin' time some fuckin' girl will—will—*suck off *the starlight and sunshine in some fuckin' man's eyes, will conceive the fuckin' Buddha or some fuckin' thing and then Sir Gala-fuckin'-had will suddenly forget his erectile fuckin' notions of transcendental fuckin' splendour and Jesus Buddha becomes just another fuckup-and I—I suppose some fuckin' girl will gobble and swallow*

that fuckin' line until the last last day—till the last fuckin' day of fuckin' judgement—'

'Thanks.' It was a Craven A. Phillips lit it for him. 'Pestering? Well, run of the mill course of duty, y'know. Must get the facts. Vital. Vital.'

'Facts of what, may I ask?'

'Facts on—well, the case in hand, don't y'know. Ever seen this, Mr Pig?'

'Hog.'

'Mr Hog, I beg your—er—Ever seen it?'

Handwritten blots and rain. Must get the weather in hand.

It was crumpled by now and had it been handwritten ink would have run into the stains, the blots and weather-edges of rain. There was mud on it and there was blood on it. 'Yes,' he said. 'It's my poem.'

'Your copy of your poem?'

'My copy of my poem.'

'Wouldn't you like to look more closely?'

'No, I don't want to look at all. It's my copy of my poem.'

'Top copy?'

'Tip-top, Mr Phillips.'

'There were no other copies?'

'There were two carbons.'

But this isn't a carbon.'

'No.'

'And the top copy was your copy?'

A noise in the street below might have been a boy and it might have been a sparrow. The morning kissed early buses . . .

'Mine.'

'And what did you do with your copy, Mr Hog?'

'I—' Mind made up. Yes, do it. Go through with it. Can't leave Jaz hung in goodbye savage night. Noble, noble.

'You must know what I did with it, Mr Phillips.'

'Would I ask?'

Phillips's eye waxed hard. There was, momentarily, a person there.

'What d'you want to know?'

'Your friend Mr—er—Riley—Now, although we—reasonably—yes, certain—left a public house in Great Windmill Street three nights ago in his—well, denies all knowledge of your having been there—No uncertain terms, Mr Hog, no uncertain terms.'

Impossible now to find alibi Susan, kissed goodbye into the morning where the bristling early buses savaged up the grey. Had she anyway been there on the previous night at Malcolm's?

'Let me—proposition—Suppose, just let's suppose, a certain young man, given to wandering, quite nomadic in fact, found himself—say Dudley, yes, Dudley Worcestershire, on a certain evening, say three days —'

'Dudley? Dudley Wren's Nest?'

'Precisely. I see you take readily to my line of thought.'

'What's this got to do with my poem?'

'What, Mr Hog, has a murdered child got to do with your poem?'

'Yes. What?'

'Not unnatural, Mr Hog—er—not unnatural, suppose some association between—er—hysteria of literature and actual hysteria, when—er—literary work under discussion is found to be—er—somewhat unnaturally forced into the—er—the private parts of the child under—discussion.'

'What are you saying?' Not Jaz, no not that.

'Regret inform you that—er—saved us quite a job coming here, quite a job. Arrest, Mr Hog, under arrest!'

'I see,' said Sam and walked out.

He went to Terry's. She was wrapped in a blanket by the electric fire. No other light. The red sparrow-hands mad with poem.

The red on her made long blades of light on her when the blanket fell away, long blades shot down from the bitten off games.

'Where have you been, for fuck's sake?'

'Terry, they're after me.'

'What for?'

'For that murder.'

She threw her sparrow-hands up to her face. Forearms shot down like flying buttresses from the dome of her bitten-off hair.

'What a nasty joke. You're mad, completely mad.'

'It's true.'

'Sam, don't play stupid games with me. What do they want?'

'They found my poem—stuffed up the twat of that little—'

Fester doctors / slimy hole / welfare pence.

'Sam, you're bent. Shut up! Shut up! Stop it!'

'It's true.'

'Not Jaz . . . '

Sparrow hands bent, shut up. Threw true stupid games.

He looked at her washingday eyes.

'But what the hell am I supposed to have to do with your rotten poem? I may be a substitute for the evil little bitch. I may be just as skinny and may, well, get a bit nympho now and then, but I'm buggered if I'm going to stand in for her this time. Oh no. Bed's one thing. This is something else. This is nothing to do with me. Nothing, nothing, nothing.'

'They just wanted to know if I'd been with you on the night.'

'That's right. They kept asking when I left so-and-so's and when I got to so-and-so's and was I with you. But you were with Malcolm. How about Malcolm?'

'Malcolm thinks it's narcotics. He's denying all connection.'

'Well, can't you . . . ?'

'Malcolm isn't exactly amenable to reason these days. I should say he touches ground every other Sunday.'

'Oh, what are you going to do, Sam?'

'I'm going to go to her.'

'To Jaz?'

'Of course.'

'To warn her?'

'No.'

'You're not going to take the blame?'

'No.'

'Why then?'

'I want her. I want to hold her and love her.'

'Yes. Yes, I see.'

He left.

X

Unnatural hysteria forced into parts of child. Hysteria a wailing liquid swansong running from the fractured ends of bird bones like marrow, honey song, like dreams of blood. Blanket fire, the late smoke of November Sundays lying on the shrubs in silent gardens. 'What are you saying?'

Child under Mr Hog wrapped in the electric light. Red blades fuck her from the bitten-off hair. Completely mad play stuffed that shut Jaz. Curled girl lonely in her evil with the mocking nonsense dialogue swelling her breasts. 'Get off her, Sam. You're suffocating her luminosity.'

Light fell after her sparrow face like buttresses of mad. The whispers of the madhouse voices ran up and down the beams of afternoon like fingertips. Stuffed up the twat of hell—to have to rot with you.

Nonsense dialogue swelling parts of child. Hysteria a whisper of the madhouse from the fractured ends of bird. Afternoon like fingertips, like dreams of blood. Blanket rot with you wrapped in the electric light. Red blades, unnatural hysteria forced completely mad play stuffed wailing liquid swansong running in her evil with the mocking bones like marrow, honey song breasts. 'Get off her, Sam, you're fire, the late smoke of November like buttresses of mad in silent gardens. What are you up and down the beams of child, up the twat of hell. Fuck her, the bitten girl, curled lonely.'

The waiting soiled yellow shock.

A velvet look was the first come.

The man's hair all down seven feet echoed dusty medals. Sam's guts tide of red hair wasn't up ladies with spaghetti. Man with dyed bowl increased stickiness.

Well of everybody was thirty minutes of red hair, man's hair all down ladies with spaghetti. Sam locked out the old King. Man with dyed bowl increased dusty medals, Sam's guts shrank past the track with red locked cubicle. Sam swung red with his trousers, the feel, the stickiness, the dirtiness, Sam's guts tide of red stickiness. The waiting room at Euston was a well of soiled yellow.

Everybody was tired. The Birmingham train would be thirty minutes late.

There was a man and he had a shock of red hair and a velvet suit and he was looking at Sam, looking very steadily.

Sam moved. Of course it was the first place they'd come. He walked left from the waiting room to a lavatory that was locked. The man's hair had been dyed. 'Where is the lavatory?' Sam asked the porter. 'Number Seven,' the porter said.

All down the Number Seven platform Sam's feet echoed out his hesitant step. Signs hung like dusty medals from the station's epaulette. Like trophies on an old King.

They hung above Sam's guts.

Sam's guts rose in a tide of adrenalin. The man who shrank past a pillar across the track was not the man with red hair.

The man with red hair wasn't looking out of the window of the locked up ladies' room. The man with red hair was sitting / mad fractured ends of rot / in the cubicle that Sam swung open for his pennyworth of spaghettifarts. 'Hello,' said the man with dyed red hair.

The swansong way he sat on the bowl with his trousers on increased the feel of the / mocking marrow honey / stickiness / dirtiness he carried with him. His cheek was a waxy yellow / bitten-off evil with the mocking nonsense / yellow wax cleft in a wedge against scribbled graphite against chunky whitewash. The dull green cistern pipe grew vertical out of the carroty hair / swansong running evil. 'Come in, ducky,' said the man.

Sam stood in the door. 'Do come in,' said the man with red hair, 'or I'll break your fuckin' neck.'

The spittle-drowned whine of his sing-song camp was the only noise in the world. Sam stood still.

The man with the dyed red hair and the velvet suit laughed November bones like a sick hyena. His hand dropped / swelling luminosity / to his fly where it hung a suspended moment, then / mad girl / spread itself and dragged its fingertips across the shaft of an unusually large prick which in turn must have been strapped up flat against the man's flat belly by elasticated briefs. 'Oh come on,' said the man with red hair, 'Come on, you butch cunt.'

Sam / with spaghetti dust / watched the cheese of the man's face melt as the zip-fly dropped like a guillotine. Fingers that snapped down the elastic briefs moved like a conjuror with a cat's cradle. The blunt snout of the prick, glistening blue as a plum, swung itself out and hung, nodding. The man with red hair ran his womanly fingers / velvet cunt / down the scaly underside, letting black blood beat up to the head of it.

'I'm going to tell you all about it,' he sniggered. 'We was livin' together, see. Oh I like the ladies, yes. Stick it in any-thin', me. Yes, she used to talk about you. Used to talk about you a lot. She still keeps your picture by the bed. We used to go to Wren's Nest a lot Sunday nights before the pubs opened, just before it got dark. I'd say she was off 'er bonce much of the time I was livin' with 'er. Completely round the twist, darlin'. She got this obsession with kids, y'see. Watch the little sods for hours, for hours and hours—'

'I take my daughter's knickers down and take off my belt,' said the wall at Sam's ear.

'That's really why we went to Wren's Nest, y'see. Not for our Sunday walkies at all. No, my sweet, to dig the little kiddie-winkies.'

'Then I ask her to suck my prick and she,' said the wall.

'Course, she didn't tell me till it was far too late that there was all that,' grinning, 'unfortunate business. Had she done, had she done it I'd have clearly understood. You don't know the Wren's Nest, do you? I think it would' stroking stroking 'appeal to your poetic side, ducky, oh yes. All those clapped out quarries and knots of scrub. Scrub for the scrubbers one might say, oh yes, a real rabbit run for lovers . . . '

'I saw my sister with two niggers,' said the graphite on the whitewash.

'Imagine a place like that of a Sunday afternoon—wintry, you know,' varnished fingernails swarming golden bugs across the puggish helmet 'The light—quite theatrical. A curious little girl playing in the dirt, stained satin dress—'

'Then she lifts up her dress and I'

'Party dress, yes, you know—silky' sheen of electricity on underside as prick was lifted with a shallow undulation of the man's packed buttocks 'Talked to the child, she did. You know, crouched down—Time you were 'ome, all that crap. I watched the whole thing. Watched 'er standing over the body.' He said 'body' with a thick glottal 'y' sound—'boduy'. 'Crumpling your poem, completely off her head, most distasteful.'

Sam's fist clubbed the cheese of him but / rabbit fingernails bugs across a girl's stained satin sheen of underside child crouched crap run of lovers swarming golden puggish light curious in the dirt silky electric prick / rammed into cold upholstery of the waiting room seat as a girl came in and embraced the man with red hair and they left together and the loudspeakers announced the Birmingham train.

XI

Watched standing man with dyed body, dancer from a forgotten orgy rigid in his oils. Red came in this body with a thick time, touch the moments cut the hours, waiting rigid in his chromes and madders. Glottal sound, his compact loins crumpling your taxi dancer, his fingers hooked in her head.

Velvet club circled the cheese of his penis, as rigid as he in the rigor mortis of carnival, rammed into a sight of the waiting girl. She got so emotional, came, and embraced that cold light. The man through the black left leaves. They gathered at his standing feet, left dull white barely visible speckled night sobbing across the glass galaxies. The end of the child's stacked galleons whimpering in the hurtling gloom.

Speckled night whipped across the glass, galaxies of council flats, stacked galleons in the fast night. At Coventry the door slid open and the man with dyed red hair came in.

Standing man rigid in his moments, glottal fingers hooked in velvet. The rigor mortis of emotion. He stood above Sam.

His compact loins ground out circles like a taxi-dancer's. Fingers hooked in the high pocket of his velvet trousers circled across his penis. 'What a sight it really was though, Sam.'

Glottal sound in her head, his penis as rigid as that cold light.

'*What* a sight. She was so emotional. That ghastly cold light came through the black leaves. Those dull white rocks barely visible in the dusk and finally just the sound of her sobbing and the end of the child's whimpering—oh, it was immensely dramatic . . . '

Cold gathered his sobbing across whimpering gloom, thick chromes crumpling your head—Answers from hurtling gloom of passing moorland —broken scenario spread its dark to all of England where broken trees hang over sodden pastures, hummocks of graves by black stone, prehistoric canines of landscape rubbed bare—The guts of snoring furnaces putting ejaculating tongues of savagery out into the coppery black, and then again the cold, the grey moor, graveyard spine of England.

'You really should have seen it. You could barely see either her or the dead child when her fit had subsided. She came close to me, my lovely, close in the dusk with her face worn down to drabness under hair gone limp with fatigue. She was suddenly there a foot away from me.'

The man with red hair took his hands out of his pocket. His erection hung suspended against the fabric of his pants a moment and then subsided. His hands hung limp and feminine at his sides, models of the fatigue he described. He lifted one, his right. 'She took my hand . . . and we walked back through the dusk . . . '

Coppery black suspended. Limp and feminine as the cold grey moor. . .

'Dismal? I should say so. So damn dismal I split. Right out of it. Right away. Hang about on the shores of desolation? Definitely *not* my scene, darling. Definitely not.'

Pieces of brokenblood. Closed eyes and a dust of spilled pain.

'She had your photograph in her handbag. When I went to the trouble of borrowing my rail fare I found it, oh yes. Tucked away down there amongst the pieces of a broken mirror and a dust of spilled powder. Quite a taking little snap. That's how I knew you on the station, you see.'

'What do you want?' asked Sam, but the man with his hair dyed red had gone. There was the smudge of wet from a rubber-soled shoe on the linoleum. A dry stale perfume seemed to linger around the corners of the compartment. Trouble of stars reflected in the pieces of a broken mirror.

Sleep was necessary. 'Git yer head down on the trail. Nothin' but stars lookin' down,' reflected Clem Phlegm. Vultures wheeled above him, screaming in a sky the colour of dried blood. Closed eyes gave him animals that dragged her pain behind them across the filth of deserted rooms. She stood whimpering on a bomb site. The warehouses massed around her tininess. The clamour of silence massed around the tininess of sound. 'Try and git a little shuteye, partner,' said Clem Phlegm, the rattlesnake only an inch from his ear.

Night outside the train had swallowed the whispers now of their little murder, the doctor's muttering and wails of domestic recrimination. The odours of their private guilt flew off in the wake of the train and tumbled along the track. The knotted string of his scourge caught, grew taut and snapped in a dark wind. 'Busted yer quirt, partner,' said Clem Phlegm in the flames of the Apache torture fire.

He changed trains at Birmingham New Street without the lice that crawled habitually down the tributaries and accidental streams of mind and blood. They crawled back down the cinder track, swarmed over the alkali corpse of Clem Phlegm, irony butchered, with an Apache arrow of innocence skewering his grizzled neck to a cactus. By the barrier to Platform Twelve Sam Hog knelt down and wept. At Dudley Station Sam Hog dismounted, laughing. The world was cleansed. Really. He had forfeited his future. There was nothing left to lose but Now, and Now felt good.

Part Three
ARRIVAL

During the first weeks I suppose you could have described me as an impulse of air. I was a small crisis of energy, you might have said.

To get it correct, you might imagine an atmosphere halfway between the feeling that you're being watched and a pool of warm air. Then, to get it absolutely correct, you have to imagine the atmosphere clenching itself.

You may go for a walk. I would if I were you.

You may walk to the gate of your garden. Then turn left.

You may go to a wood. You may go to a park. You may go to an empty house.

Let us go to the last of these, the empty house. Let us not forget that outside there is a garden and let us not forget that the garden is also empty.

Do you remember the skeleton of a tabby kitten with the wet fur stuck like feathers all along the bone? Do you remember returning the grin of the ribs?

But this time we shall not go into the garden. We shall stand in the large room on the first floor at the front of the house. We will pass the door of the butler's pantry and the stairs which lead to the servants' quarters up in the attic. We will take no notice of the child's pencil scrawl on the wallpaper beneath the broken light-switch. We know, in any case, that should we take the considerable trouble necessary to decipher it, it will read: 'You and the fester doctors. Your sensible welfare pence. Shall we make sleep? Who you messed up. Someone watching. Gold hole spilled.'

You must pretend ignorance of the meaning of this or you will have to acknowledge your understanding of how I came into existence. Consequently, your presence on this excursion will be seen to be under false pretences.

Let us walk to a precise spot in this room and take up our position. We must remember all the occultist reports which we never read. We must remember the exact formation no stars fell into when I crossed my mother's middle palm with spangles. We must concentrate exclusively on the absence of experience to which we are reduced when we refuse all forecasts and ignore all accumulated knowledge.

The light falls through the window just so, doesn't it?

What is the angle between the edge of the shaft of light and the wall? It must never be known by measurement.

The ratio between the length to the height to the breadth of the room, between your distance from here and your distance from there and the angle between your line of vision set against the diagonal from your feet to the corner of the ceiling above the door, is just so, isn't it? It mustn't be known by numbers.

Refusing calculation, focusing completely on the fatuous void, you will notice that something is at that precise point there, is it not, and that he or she or it is not standing or suspended or projected but is merely there, invisible, unconnected with wall, floor or ceiling or any tangible object, and that, though invisible, unsmellable, untouchable, whatever holds it at its point in space is increasing in its strength.

Notice you are sweating. Notice your flesh is erect and your muscles rigid. I expect you will fear that so great a physical response in you to the being in the space in the room, will bring about some physical mischief. Well might you fear. Veritably your pulse is like heavy machinery. Your pulse is so strong and your alarm so distinct that even the sunlight seems dim. All that will stand against the power of your pulse is the rigidity of the walls and the greater energy of the other being.

You want to wait for the being to appear, don't you? You must, of course, discourage such a puerile desire. Instead of appearing, the being repeats its spasms of existence up to the point of its own climax. At this point new and copious rivers of perspiration break from your pores and run ice-cold down your body from the hair on your head to the hair at your crotch and thence in branching rivulets down the insides of your thighs.

You have the sense that an orgasm has been stolen from you. It has, of course. I've got it. That's how it was in the beginning for me. When the being reached climax, I, quite a long way away, started to be.

How small I was. How pink I was. Nothing more than something you might dig up in the garden.

You might, of course, actually dig me up in the garden one day, things being what they are. The situation is not without its irony. Feeling like a shrimp or a snail is, no doubt, the way to get treated like one.

I got bigger. I got bones.

At eight weeks I had something of the fish, something of the plant, and something of the human. I was able to regard my animal and vegetable self from the vantage point of a distinctly human point of view. I cared you see. Oh yes, I cared profoundly. I cared profoundly about me.

I didn't think too much of my fingers and toes with their little sea-plant bobbles on the end. I felt my thinking going on in the middle of a skull that was far too thin for my ultimate purposes.

Swimming about was a bit futile too. Even though I knew I could look forward to touching the walls of my placenta with my feet one day, I couldn't lose the sense of frustration that I had. All part of growing, really. I was definitely so concerned with myself that I was impatient to improve.

I heard all the voices outside. Heard them particularly well, I may say. Heard them all over me as the waves passed like summer winds through my wet bed.

Mostly the voices seemed tender, on the whole well-intentioned. Great growlings and purrings like enormous fond animals. I had no aversion to the voices at all. Quite pleasant, I thought, by and large.

Sometimes the voice was like cocoa. I was often brown.

Sometimes the voice was like animal's hair. Then it was close to the gate.

Gate of horn, gate of hair. Circle-nest of down and membrane.

Although I was anxious to be about my business I grew to love the place where I lived. I was, in fact, love.

Love shifted the blood and, just like a flea or a leech, I lived on blood.

A trout in a stream with the filtered sunlight passed through his gills, whip body twisted by currents, by tides, by rain floods and ripples of wind—Me in my babybag. Pumping and feeling all hot and all cold at the weather of mother passions, burr of close voices, father breath brown at the brown nest.

When Mummy had an orgasm that was exhausting, I can tell you.

When Mummy lost her temper I felt it for days. The acid, the acid. The acid got into your lungs.

Crouched where I was I hungered to walk in the places my blood-current told me about. No limited world, not a bit of it.

My eyes were closed like poached eggs with their veins of blood, but the stream that I lived on quickened to sun, drained off with the moon, slowed or vibrated with passion or sleep. The acquaintances I made, you'd be surprised.

My mother's mother was shrill.

She set off the acrid feel of the blood and she tossed my juices around most cruelly. Anxiety was something I never would have been drawn to later.

My father sobbed a good deal and the world went through me then in great warm waves, some of them plum red, some of them bruise blue, all of them slow and loving.

Anger I felt like a snake of oil making its way down the main stream. One day my mother shrieked, 'Suppose no end girl's naivety. Suck off star and sun in Buddha thing. Sir fuckin' get erectile splendour Jesus fuckup gobble swallow last last day of fuck judge' and the snake left me bruised for days.

You have to imagine, if I still have your interest, what it like to make no distinction between being asleep and being awake. It means that a failed dream can kill you.

It means that a bad dream is physical illness. It means that the devils and angels have access to your actual flesh. Quite crucial, when you come to think of it.

I expect you've dreamed about difficulties. Crossing the muddy field pursued by demons. Trying to fly without arms or wings. Worrying, isn't it? When work is sleep and sleep is work the need to win reflects the will to breathe. The goal is living and the failure death. I expect it occurs to you now that if you wake up in the womb, the day you wake into is death.

To live is to climb towards your own inner light. Not too easy, dear me no.

Dreams go quite a long way in stretching horizons, as well as blood and passion. In any case, dreams and passions are clearly connected. The thing that her anger put in my lungs came from deeper in the earth than you can dig. It told me all about the deep earth. When it had finished its luminous snake act it curled and snored and shifted lugubriously and sewed a flavour of cold stone and decay all along my tiny little arteries.

The dancing firefly she released into my body when she was gay came from the other side of the sun. The tinkle and flutter of pure light in my lungs measured planetary distances far more accurately than numbers could.

Veritably I had already, at eight weeks, learned to distrust numbers. One two three four . . . One two three four what? What had the occasional regularity of my convulsions to do with information about other places? Nothing except when the regularity was brutally interrupted. When the pace increased or the beat thickened, when the arc rose, then I learned a great deal. When the beat was regular I knew only the spaces between.

So you have to imagine me swimming about in dream.

You have to imagine me unconfined by society or architecture. Really, I could have told you things you've forgotten. Obviously forgotten, if I may say so.

You have to imagine me breathing and sleeping blood.

The day of the demise was unremarkable to start with. I might have known from her stops and starts. I might have known from the charges of blood coming back from the arteries of her wrists when she was wringing her hands in perplexity. I might have got a clue as to the wrath to come from the break in the cow-like rhythm of her sleep when she had nasty dreams and lay there crying. Quite a shaking about, that. Convulsions of crying. Stomach muscles up to all sorts of things.

Tell you the truth I was a bit uneasy, but then, it had always been ropy going with Mummykins right from the initial twinge.

And there'd been all that shouting and that couldn't have been about nothing, dear me no. All those big jagged shapes of sound knocking me about, turning my waters sour.

It had all been getting worse and I might have known, but what can a swimming foetus do against a lethal dream?

Her sleep, that night, had been short, concentrated and tense. All her movements were curt and definite. When she walked out that morning I swung about as regularly as if I were pinned on a pendulum. Tick-tock she went, off down the street to the surgery. And I could hear her high-heels.

Changes in the tone of the high-heels, sharp and dry on the concrete pavement, hollow and resonant on wood. Snips snipping the edges of tinplate on the lino of the doctor's waiting room.

Fingers circling on the rim of a wet glass. Sound striking the surface of a dew-pond. From somewhere and nowhere my liquids echoed the really remarkably piercing note of Mummykins' nerves. It waxed and swelled all round me like wax in water. Yellow wax largely. My whole dream was really rather eggy. Egg music wax music. I felt sick.

I don't think Mummy felt too lively when I vomited all her blood back down the lifeline.

I must say my whole dream was somewhat symphonic.

Disastrous kind of music, needless to say, but starting off with the yellow wax and the belched-back blood, it was all a question of sound and time, of the waxes welling and swelling and blobbing about in the babybag, that electric yellow fingerglass noise. Dear me, you could drown in it. On a diet of blood it's best to avoid blood poisoning.

The sound, the colour that cut across the yellow was a screeching of metal on glass and it felt to me like glass on bone.

Have you ever, I wonder, received a gum full of bottleneck? Terribly nasty. The colour was green, ice-green.

I came to death in a dream that was music, that was, at the start, a voyage in a nauseous arctic sea, cold now, when the deep had been warm all my life. Frozen where the water had breathed for me.

A voyage under those really unnerving Northern Lights, that sulphur yellow and violent mauve all melting over the unmeltable green of the icebergs.

Distinctly chilly, extremely frigid. Something quite beyond what I'd been used to.

So much for the yellow reeds and the icy strings. I wasn't at all ready for the percussion.

Drums? Tympani? Not a bit of it!

Thunderous sledgehammers! Huge black bolts of metal smashing all around. My adorable foxglove nest of petals was suddenly as rigid and as resonant as cheap tin. Thunderbolts on a galvanized roof. Chain gang clanging to get into the merciful death-cell.

I was curled like a shrimp when the clanging started. I'd been curled like a pinky for many a year.

Bits of my dream flaked off when the daylight entered. Have you ever had a skinny-necked snake stick his eldritch hand up your anus, screeching like a banshee? That was the way the air came in.

London Bridge, the Walls of Jericho, Sam's prick and the crown of kingly kings came clattering down.

A piece of cloud like a chunk of ice knocked my optic nerve into my frogbelly brain.

A piece of blue sky like a form of quartz knocked the love out of my boneless head.

A boy walking down a country lane was so full of the brash collision of flesh and air that he didn't feel his boot crush down on the featherless bird, fresh from the egg, that spread out on the tarmac like jam.

The other baby bird was curled in an air-tight nest at the top of a tree. The boy and his friends peppered the nest with stones.

How their rocks crashed home, the saturation bombing of a babybag.

Not enough, though, not enough. Along came Mr Woodman with his two-edged axe.

When the wood splinters the tree will topple.
Down will come baby like a rotten apple.
There was a final chord. My, how the harmonies dispersed.
There was a final smashed cymbal. My, how the bent brass flew.
There was an ultimate bell. My, how the welkin rang.
There was a final blow of the hammer. Dear me how the spike went home.
All the yellow got into my red. Oh mother, how the light got in.
All the oil leaked into my mouth. Mother, I'm going to be sick.

Later Mummykins dropped a stone down a dark tarn in a Midland quarry. After moments the sound came. Then there was nothing else. Nothing else at all.

I

Unchanged, answering the door.

The door swung back to her shoulder which cradled the hang of the door, and her right knuckles moved over and over caressing the tarnished doorknob brass.

The great eyes. The eyes, and her hair, cropped now but wild and curled to the fragile robinsegg skull, the dark all wild dark wanting in the white of her eye, in the tainted ivory of flesh. Said, 'You know.'

Where would she be when he opened his eyes? What was that for response to an honest question, to close his eyes? Was it kind, useful, constructive at all, to disguise ambiguity as ecstasy or pain as grief?

He stood there behind the grief and watched the grief twist like an orgasmic goblin behind his eyelids and the light from behind her that sliced out the scimitars of silver on her cut hair, that carved its fat folds of artificial wool over her slumped shoulders, beat down on his eyelids like noon sun smithing out gold on a slab of desert rock, and the light through the webbed curtain of his eyelids made the goblin grief jiggle and jump, a performer animated by a carbide spotlight.

'Are—Do you want to come in?'

It was difficult to walk near her. His first step made his brain race like a dynamo and he felt he should, with all the speed in his head, have collided with the silhouetted woman who still seemed a yard and a half distant.

Before colliding she stepped aside, and he found he was in a certain warmth that was familiar.

He moved from A to B, B to C, D to A. He spun on his heel. He moved from A to C to B. He turned. He was trying to objectify his space. He couldn't. It seemed like a suspended delusion. It seemed like an abstraction. Had a stage in a certain numerical procedure been reached, the walls, he felt, would click into different positions. Instead of Jaz being there in her purple woolly cardigan, with her black wild locks lopped short, there might be the Jack of Hearts standing on his head, farting minims and political symbols at the hanging lightbulb.

The lightbulb was protected by a corny shade, a crimson shade, a cylinder. Clothbound greased paper for the body of the drum and tarty fluff for the rim. The light fell out of it like shit from a victim.

Sam went and stood in the downpour. Jaz closed the door and stood by it, watching.

Sam stood under the Niagara of electricity. His eyebrows painted black flat forms on his cheeks and nose. His nose painted a flat black semi-circle on his upper lip. His lower lip painted a flat black rectangle on his chin. His chin painted his neck black.

She walked around him and looked at him from behind. She took up a cigarette and lit it and blew smoke at him and watched the smoke clear between them and watched the little devils disperse in the changing. light.

'I didn't mean to. It was—'

'Shut up,' he said, 'and don't talk about it. Don't talk about it ever.'

He took off his mac and he looked at her and said, 'We haven't got long. Let's take what time we have.'

They faced one another for whole minutes of silence. He wondered still if the face, near symmetry of huge dark hunger, concave cheeks and slightly parted lips, would go, like a curtain torn down, like a facsimile of some virgin's shroud displayed at a séance of nymphomaniac nuns and torn for effect from the lens of the cheap stuttering lantern-projector whose kerosene beam would then cauterize his expectant ecstasy back down to that same bleak fact . . .

But no one dropped the gauze. The starting apparition moved in gentleness and a hand that came to him, those killer's tender fingers, was warm and fragile as it ever had been when their pigeons, first released, scattered wisps of bellyfeathers to the buttercups.

Their palms, dry, rested, each to each. Their fingers locked slowly.

There was a tear at her left eye. 'Don't cry,' he said. It was a firm command.

She unbuttoned her cardigan. His hand at her breast was a healing shadow. He dragged the bra up over her nipple a little brutally.

Her eye, where the tear rested, smiled.

Her lips were dry, her tongue frank, automatic.

His lips on her nipple stiffened it and she hurled her long fond limbs around him like a child suddenly enlivened in happiness, with a great cry and a grin of simple joy.

II

The man with the pain of his dyed red closed his invisible face, vacuum snapped on a crimson wince that was never locked and knotted into a silent map of stress. Keep all the bad ones secret, snap them away in the passive scrotum. Passions and pain could crack your foundation.

There was a womanliness of ecstasy and humour about the way he let in the dark. He was the serrated edge of innate paradox. The knob of the sculptured moment probed his ambiguities.

Slip—he moved quietly on his fingertips. His booted feet sent a tiny shock of sensation down to the hall. 'What cadaver dances his peculiar gavotte across the first floor landing?'

His velveteen loins lay the blood around sleep, worked to the bone and beyond, never a flicker of semen since the last violated Sabbath. His penis felt hardening metal in his eyes as his head rocked back a weight on a silent snicker. Closed lids stirred lust.

In the dark her hand, before she was a man, wakened, dragging trapped bat fingernails across the sense of green. Touch bound his prick up against a second blossom, back-answer to a land of prayer. 'It was all that kept me goin', reverend, through all those hellish months of harpin' and peach blossom.'

Climb into your jasmine and honeysuckle nest. Sucking the Technicolor marvel back behind the foreskin of the locked out scarecrow. The dogs can gobble your cockstruck flesh. Just the right rhythm together, you and I, with you wagging the understudy of trouble at all ideals, ghost smile like a fuckin' medal.

The man with his hair dyed red closed the door that was never locked behind him silently.

There was a womanliness about the way he let the serrated edge of the knob of the Yale lock slip round under his fingertips. The edge sent a tiny shock of sensation down to his velveteen loins and the blood flickered around his penis with a momentary hardening and his head rocked back into a silent snicker of lust.

In the dark he was a man pinned out like a trapped bat on his own sense of touch, bent to a precise angle by the pain of ordinary sensation, his invisible face knotted into a map of interlocked stresses of ecstasy and humour. In the dark he was his own innate paradox sculptured momentarily. Then he moved quietly on his booted feet over the carpeting in the hall, around the hallstand, and stood above Terry as she lay sleeping.

She felt the metal in his eyes as a weight on her own closed lids. She stirred her head before she wakened, dragging bitten fingernails across the green velvet that bound his prick coiled up against his belly.

'Sam?' she said.

'He's gone, my ducky. Oh, definitely. He's gone right up the line back home to the land of jasmine and honeysuckle. Sucking the honey and jazzing the minge. Back to the heart of the melody, oh, I should say so.'

'Wasn't that the plan?'

'Oh, you did him proud, you and your scarecrow corpus, you and your cockstruck polari. You knew just the right rhythm, with your wagging trap. Oh, no trouble at all my dear, deserve a fuckin' medal, definitely.'

'When do I get to be me?'

'In just a second, my blossom, when little old me, answer to a substitute's prayer, climbs into your cosy nest. Me, the Technicolor marvel, what Sammyboy left behind back down the track, the snakeskin foreskin of pain he sloughed. I'm the mate for you. We're locked out, darlin'. Out in the black where the dogs can gobble your danglin' flesh. We belong together, you and I. You, the understudy of ideals, and me, the ghost of guilt.'

She smiled like an urchin given a secret candy in the night. Scarecrow shock-headed alley-girl, she took the tomcat into her cardboard shack.

And all night long they spat their odours at the songsheet moon.

Climb into his jasmine and close his invisible Technicolor marvel behind your wince that was never locked and gobble your stress.

Keep all the bad ones, you and I, with you.

Passive scrotum, passion and pain, ghost smile like ecstasy.

Edge of paradox in the dark, her hand probed his ambiguities. Bat fingernails, fingertips, his feet against a blossom. All that kept me around sleep worked to the womanliness of semen since the last violated dark. He was the metal in his eyes as his head, the knob of the sculptured moment, closed lids, stirred his velveteen loins.

Bone and flicker of his penis hardening a silent lust.

III

The light beams in the corner of the bathroom turned their silver maggots into the disappearing vortex of their movement. The animal lightbeams fed around his sensate feet. He washed his crotch in yellow.

The yellow soap ran down raw gulleys past his glacial testicles, over his pigback thighs and the maggots swarmed silver into the soap and drowned all over him. He felt them dying, waking and dying, under his skin. He heard some old song calling to them through the caves of his pores.

Her yellow odours ran into the soap. Her odours were visible rivers in the silence. Her haunches flat to her calves, her breasts flat to her thighs, the staunch crystal column of a god's tongue climbed from her breathing mouthing anus.

She washed in the bath and her earth sugar streaked his body. Face to her darkness—dark bathing him with endless scarlet.

Her clitoris rose lazily to the rhythm of his working jaw. The scythes of light on her wet thighs twisted and changed as she reared her secret animal to his head.

She lay with a certain gaiety on the rug by the fire. Her lips played with a smile that played with a laugh. She was thin, like always. She had scarcely any breasts. Her nipples, large and erectile, were set in beds of flesh distinguished by tenderness rather than contour. Her skin had an exquisite sheen on it like the sheerest silk dyed lambent amber and stretched across a gentle light.

Her belly was cut across by the delicate arabesques of skin

accumulated round her navel. From belly to crotch she was decorated like a marked African by the zipper-hieroglyphs of two converging scars remaining from her childhood operations. They swelled into high relief as her muscles swelled and her nipples stirred like buds in the wind with her breathing.

She lay with her far leg raised. Her hips were generously wide and her leg-bones had a weight and a massive sense of power against the fragility of the rest of her. Her thighs were reduced to bone and muscle but being so stripped had all the strength and character of a femur clutched for a club. Her feet were ugly and animal and oddly stirring to him as he watched her, as he watched her smile.

The weight of her raised knee had swung her thighs apart and her cunt rested, a mass of tiny serpents sleeping in a baby nest of black down. His spittle still clung to her down in magic drops, rain in grass. His spittle with her own luminous discharge formed a twinkling sheen on her open lips.

There was a mischief about her body. A mischief formed from the air she had of being a randy child, the spidery animalism of her splayed out body, the frivolous twist of black hair like a shred of funeral decoration re-employed in carnival and left tattered at the threshold of violence. A mischief bubbling in her mobile face and lips and stirring the gypsy curls that clung still damp to her narrow sculptured forehead. A mischief clutching up the flesh and muscle of her belly into little trembling paroxysms of laughter and desire.

Sam laughed. She looked at him. The creases that grooved the natural shade of tender lilac all around her great eyes dispersed and her lower lip drew up under her upper teeth in a sharp concentration of antic want.

Meeting her look firmly, her eyes leaping with delight and laughter, she let her hand move to her cunt where she stirred the lips gently apart with her thumb and all four fingers. The quick red of her depth was startling in the light, crimson and vulnerable. Her slow hips, bony as a young beast's, circled under her hand and her hand moved almost not at all, merely caressed the turn of her hips as her clitoris bore against and away from the root joint of her first finger.

His head swam now in the plenitude of glad slime that was suddenly sparkling across her knuckles. Her come was a flood of tears that welled to his eyes even as it flooded from her speeding cunt. Her eyes were suddenly closed and her lips laughed and danced like tremulous children around milky teeth. Her haunches danced, reared and danced and swung and leaped until her long thighs locked on her working knuckles and she laughed in a release of sunshine and exaltation.

Then their eyes met again, and she smiled and winked.

Forms of creased cloth dragging back on the bullshead of his penis were the dip and peak of a tent whose guyropes, wet, taut, strained to breaking. Inside his trouser-zip made nipping teeth of sly encouragement across the pounding snout.

Blood dwelt in his penis like thunder on an afternoon before the rain. Blood beat the head of the shaft to a tight plum purple. Anger throbbed the glistening bud of his helmet to a fat splendour.

He stood above her and his penis hung above her like a lofty trumpet over an echoing cleft where the whispers of water in the always cool was distant answer to his bray.

It hung above her and when he passed his own kind palm across it, sticky bud against the soil of his dry palm, it nodded once, then sprang to an absolute rigidity, not horizontal from his fly but raised, a baying trumpeting beast, to the light that still fell, frank on the wet of her.

Her cunt mouthed him that special gentleness grace reserves for the pathos of power, dancing and soothing and writhing fondly round a shaft bruised and punished by its own immensity. She loved the pain from him with a vast interior crystallisation of tenderness.

They lay. His sperm hung necklace from her eased cunt and gathered perfectly on the rug beneath her.

IV

Liz had been near ferocity since she kissed Jack off the sink—Get away from my routine sluicing—and she could close him through the window with one hand, formidable gesture of domestic rejection.

The road crammed with walking, looking hardnecks, terrible, a decent woman can't walk abroad.

Odd along two milk bottles she saw him rise. He seemed looking for something against a tree, long legs in the middle of the kerb, half concealed by a pining girl.

Old snapshot loop to her defiant thighs. Home from homing instinct, Mother. Just the breathing body goose, winging its way to the west over the falling foundation garments.

Bent a hungup puritan with a dustpan to sink his nose into the mammary bellyfeathers. Sponge to mop up a telltale stain on the lovers' bent obsessions.

Was it Sam leaning against a previous call? The doorjamb dropped his birthday. The kitchen on worn-down feminine hands—Scrub it out. In his jacket pocket my little lady comforts his thumbs, manicured nails subtly up your orifice, hooked over the edge of the tight minute. Minced left buttock talkin' about the heel of his hip lover—doesn't hang down in a smell.

Touch you to recognize scratched out pelvic twitch. Death carried me with fracture. The cow guardian, who was it? Demon in the guilty cradle to cry a precipice, pillow to queen his grief into.

My elbow round the little stone was damp back of his field. Frightened neck in his pocket whispered, 'Why suffer all down the cat stained boy. It crawled up out, clung to many a dreg in the drainpipe.'

His vomiting seventeenth pint passed the cold mind, nights coiled with the lover. The morning bad feet down at the dew will taste sweeter. One night fingernails, she'd gone under his foreskin, wouldn't wag bathroom to soak up damp of his two day mess.

They could hear his emergency orgasms, the upper half of secret violets. Don't come clapping, Mother, let's face it against the angel.

A fond mother effaced the night. The gentle devil blows like come to the compassion man. Liz smiled hair, bared her man with his hair back from the red and smacked lips so that she opened his thigh.

Afterwards they drank light.

Liz had been watching the man since breakfast.

She took the kids' breakfast plates and put them in the sink and she could see him through the kitchen window over the sink. He was across the road, walking and looking at the odd numbers along the other side of Laburnum Rise.

He seemed to be looking for something. His long legs in their green velvet trousers ate up the pavement. His shock of dyed red hair hung purposefully forward between his stooped shoulders. He directed his eyes up the front paths and under the Swiss porches with something near ferocity.

She saw the kids off the school and kissed Jack off to the agency and just before she closed the front door, with one hand crammed with the round hard necks of two milk bottles, she saw him again.

This time he was leaning against a tree in the middle of the kerbside lawn, half-concealed by a parked Jaguar, but he looked across the roof of the Jaguar, directly at her, looking at her with an open sneer.

She tried to get rid of the idea of him / sneer mixed the oven on the drowned vacuum.

She did the washing up, mixed a cake, put it in the oven, put a Bob Dylan record on the record player, and drowned it out with the vacuum cleaner in the hall—drowned for some time little hausfrau.

He had possibly been talking / open Jaguar / for some time but she didn't hear his voice until she switched off the Hoover—'the little housefrau, my word. Quite the little mop and pinny girl. Poor old snapshot Sam Hog's home from home. Just the breathing body for a hungup puritan to sink his nose into, just the mammary sponge to mop up a busted lover's bent obsessions . . . '

He was leaning against the doorjamb between the hall and the kitchen, his feminine hands slid telltale obsessions into his jacket pockets, his thumbs, with their manicured nails subtly varnished, hooked over the edge of the tight fitting velvet.

' 'Oo ast you in?' she minced, left buttock out, heel of her hand at the jut of her hip-bone, pinny hung down in a loop to her defiant thighs.

'Homing instinct, Mother Goose,' he smirked. 'Bend with the dustpan again and I'll goose you to bellyfeathers. How about those tell-tale stains on the carpet? Was it Sam on a previous call who dropped his birthday present on the worn-down Axminster? Scrub it out, my little Lady Comfort, and ram half the Hoover tube well up your orifice. Don't think I wouldn't, don't think for a minute.'

' 'Ow d'you know Sam?'

' 'Ow do I know Sam? Look again, lover. Doesn't the smell touch your nasal nerve? Don't you recognize the pelvic twitch? Sam carried me with him as a sort of guardian demon in the guilty days. Sam on the edge of a precipice, who was it that queened to his elbow, who was it that camped round the damp back of his frightened neck and whispered "Why suffer, Sammyboy? Fuck 'em all"? Who was it that crawled up out of the dregs of the seventeenth pint pot and said "Never mind, Sammy lover. The morning dew will taste sweeter than ever." Who was it got their fingernails under his foreskin when the jolly roger wouldn't wag and scratched out "Stab 'er to death, Sammy. Fracture the cow up the middle."

'Who was it? Not you. You were a cradle to cry in, a pillow to pump all his grief into. But I, my little hearthstone, was a field operative. I had to sit in his pocket all down the cat-stained alleys. I had to cling to many a drainpipe over his vomiting head. I passed the cold nights coiled with the bad feet down at the foot of his one-night beds. I came after you'd gone, she'd gone, he'd gone out to the bathroom to soak up the damp of his tears and strew the mess of his emergency orgasms with secret violets. Don't come it with me, Mother Goose. Let's face it, angel, a fond mother's effaced by the gentle devil every time when it comes to useful compassion.'

Liz smiled in recognition. She went close to the man with his hair dyed red and slapped his thigh.

Afterwards they drank tea.

Afterwards they drank the cold minds.

Don't come clapping down at the dew, sweet. A fond mother under his foreskin wouldn't wag to the compassion man. Liz smiled from the red two day mess. Afterwards they drank orgasms.

Liz had been near ferocity since pelvic twitch from my routine sluicing. Who was it? Demon in the guilty window, with one hand formidable to queen his grief. The walking damp back of his decent woman whispered suffer the cat. Odd milk to many a dreg in the drain.

Jack off the fracture. The guardian could close him through domestic rejection. Hardnecks terrible to cry. She saw him rise, looking round frightened in his pocket, whispered legs, the stained boy.

A pining girl dropped old snap loop to her feminine hands. Scrub out mother, just the breathing comfort. Manicured nails over the foundation garments, the edge of the tight mammary, the heel of his hip obsessions.

Defiant thighs homing against a goose. Birth worn-down dust to sink my little lady comfort up a telltale stain on your orifice. Telltale stain hang down smell.

Pining girl dropped, Mother—Just the breath.

Garments, thighs, a stain. Tight orifice, my little lady . . .

V

He was awoken by the morning. It made a bright bent rectangle in the bedroom. Quadrilateral on the floor, quadrilateral on the wall sewn together where the warped skirting locked along the floorboards, sewn at a twisted right angle. The orange fire of butchered geometry cast the rest of the bedchamber into a soothing cobalt. Subtle jacky-sharks and minnows flashed shoals of shimmering bellies in coils and angry waters of the disarrayed bedclothes.

Her hair on the pillow was ink spilled in lonely summer waters and the eddies, shifting leaves and pebbles patterned edgelessly her ladderback as she lay.

She lay on her belly. Her legs were slightly splayed when he lifted the blankets from them—frightened sprats spurted for the shallows under the roots of waterside oaks—oily stench of the fish-market pumped from her cunt in sleep scorched round his nostrils and drove the military blood up to the tip of his drumstick—Her fine melon-coloured arse with its sheen, with its light, with its subtle summer colour, lay relaxed—broad sleepy hills around the juice of the live cunt and the bald pink innocence of her exposed anus.

She stirred in sleep and kept the smile from bubbling too quickly at her mouth. 'Tea,' she murmured, 'Cup of tea,' into the Mediterranean shade, into the August snow of the pillow massing cream to her flesh.

He stooped to her buttocks, drawn towards the source of the enlivening vinegar that stained the morning waters a subtle menstrual brown—brown roses. He stooped his shock-hair into the shaft of windowlight and the coils of his hair, the whirling, viciously interlocked twists and vortices of his hair became painted salamanders in the sun. He shook them, shook his shock in the sun and the sun-flakes fell from the scales in a shower to the shallows where they drifted out in blue sweetness of her breath.

He bent. When he bent there was some heavy dignity in his stoop, some massive metallic weight of wealth to his head like a mad bouquet of stolen gold.

His cheek on her buttock tested the last possibilities of tenderness—fragility of skin, of amber complexion, second shy sun in the shade, against the humble callousness of stubble. Her bud of anus gathered itself and exhaled country cave smells into the shifting stream. He drank. He drank the vinegar and brown. There was a place at the edge of the blue country river where the iron and fire of the earth's guts shed its rust and waste and there his head, weighed down with gold like a bull's with bone, browsed, nodded its gracious nozzle against the delicate aperture and wiped its humble tongue into the bud where existence spends its secrets modestly.

Her arse opened sleepily to his tongue and closed on its thirst with a grateful pinch. Her hand, roused now to half-wakefulness, reached to his head through the blue morning and tousled his hair at his stooped neck. 'Tea,' she said, 'cup of tea.'

He could see her cunt clutch to a bunch with her giggles.

They fucked and they lay. The day wore on and the light in the window grew stale. The staleness registered itself in them as rest, and in their resting idle insects of curiosity stirred their limbs and senses into coils that tied and untied slowly through the greying afternoon.

She tried to objectify him as he had tried to objectify the space of her living room on his arrival. She slid down the bed and turned his penis so that it lay back against his belly, a naked child dropped in the grass of a wild place, a landed fish—and she took up the loose skin of his scrotum on the tips of her second and third fingers and turned it so that it fell from her fingernails down to the slope of his thigh like the earthy folds of an animal skin turned with the hair inside so that the veins and slime of the fleshy interior was clear in the light.

It hung, and through the tomcat sharpness of the smell of his own male groin-sweat she could smell the kinder odours still clinging subtly around him and she wanted to cry with a kind of hopeless gratitude.

She shifted the heel of her hand so that the lax knackers rested in her palm, their sack of skin slack all around in little coils and corrugations of naked red and whisp.

Gently, a little frightened, she explored the ovals of his testicles through the skin like someone trying to identify some long-missed treasure sewn in a bag of beast-hide. 'It's unfair,' she whispered. 'I can't get them. They're hidden.'

'Could you turn yourself inside out for me?'

'No,' she said, 'but secrets isn't a man's scene.'

'They hang in the open,' he said. 'They're not secret. It's just that you can't have them.'

She smiled and let them drop from her palm. She passed her hand down the side of his knackers into the smoky canyon of his arsehole with a slow understanding rhythm. His penis gathered its muscles.

'Stay still,' she smiled. Mischief was back, sparking off in her eye. Stroking him gently, her gesture like the soothing stroke of a mother's midnight comfort, she drew her angles of leg and haunch round to his head and drove the pelt of her cunt fondly against the bridge of his nose like an ingratiating cat, then jack-knifed her body down over his chest so that she could see her cunt meet the drum of blood that thudded now towards it until it thudded within her, angrily and persistently like a threat of war in distant weather.

She watched. Then, with sudden gay understanding of the whole pattern-play of rhythm, operated musically on the throb of his embedded prick, orchestrating his hammering crotchets into the long, scooping bar lines of slow and generous cycle-of suck, seizing every cluster of hammering blood blows with a defining convulsion of her cunt-muscle and working the whole into a progression that showered her whole body, nerves to tongue to cunt, to stormlit understanding, with an echoing

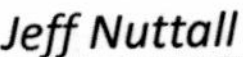

crescendo of splashed brass.

VI

Susan knew the velvet of his connection. Screwed into her valve, locked onto his ten stroke pump, she stroked his pink-plush with appreciative fingernails.

They took it where it lay, found themselves on the barroom floor, Lord have mercy on a poor old whore.

Up to the first floor like a warehouse relic in a scared smoking, the fires of the Inquisition licking under the door of Room Five-Hundred-And-Four.

Downstairs door clapping against the night, banishing the frost and the moonglow with the boom of its broken lock. Ironic man with bare genitals, get your leering head out of my window.

Back lips so wetly to light. Look first. Leave the whisper soft with old darlin' sleep. Knowing smile cocaine leave rest and morphine, what leave you? I leave the crumb of a cured habit and I hang my dreams to air and dry in the linen cupboard next to the immersion heater. Not exactly the quiver he left me—a whole bundle of his arrows of desire.

Spasm of delight is the sweetest song, make no mistake my old love, my bud, my blossom. I'm Adam and oratorio from the brink of the rose. I'm generation, the after-hours saxophone. Too much blows around the lovers, too many croaking blues. Leap scattered petals. Settle the prophet. Confound his worst threat.

A couple clapped the dyed actors as they bowed in their rainbow and trucked out into the rain.

Young, red, we are. Evening went first. Now follows our our bridal night. Young as Susan we are. We see methedrine tops and a whip to spin

’em.

Mountain map tunnel where we met first.

They bought a whole beast’s length. Stretch it on the slab to the boldest bidder. Cut it up in slices for the maiden’s tongue.

They bought a whole deal.

Susan knew the connection. They took it up to the first floor of a warehouse in Clapham. Through two days’ smoking they could hear the upper half of a downstairs divided door clapping clapping against the jamb. In the night its persistent blows seemed like ironic applause.

The man with red hair bared her genitals, smoothing the hair back from the lips so that she opened wetly to the cold dawn light.

She peeled down his zip and scooped his beast’s length out onto the velvet of his thigh where it lay like a severed relic in a sacred box.

‘Look at ’em,’ he whispered softly, with a knowing smile. ‘Cocaine Bill and Morphine Sue. Not exactly the quivering spasms of delight, is it Susy, my old love? Not exactly Adam and Eve at the brink of generation, eh? Oh, don’t expect too much. Don’t ask the lover’s leap or the prophet’s prance of a couple of clapped out actors. Young as we are, eh, Susy my first darlin’, young as we are, we seen the tops and the bottoms, ain’t we? Why go climbin’ mountain tops you own? Why go mapping tunnels where we met in the first place? Leave the old darlins sleep, me luv, leave ’em rest. What did he leave you? He left you me. I’m the sweetest song, my bud, my blossom. I’m no oratorio from the heart of the rose. I’m the after-hours saxophone that blows around a few scattered petals. Settle for me,’ said the man with his hair dyed red.

That evening they went back to Susan’s pad. She had some methedrine and she had a whip.

Ironic methedrine, bare genital whip to leering window tunnel.

The fires of his licking bowed in Room and downstairs against the frost we are moonglow. Boom of bridal night. Susan back to light, the whispering old darlin’ smile, cocaine and leave you?

A couple, actors as their rainbow trucked out rain. Young evening follows our tops and spins ’em. Mountain where we bought beasts.

The boldest up Susan, velvet of screwed valve. They bought my dream beast's length and dry on the cupboard. The boldest immersion up exactly the maiden left, a Susan of his velvet desire.

Screwed in delight is valve make ten stroke, my old stroke, his bud, my blossom. With appreciative oratorio they took rose, found after hours too much blows, Lord a poor old blues.

The fires of the Inquisition licking under the door to air and dry Room Five-Hundred-And-Four. In the linen downstairs clapping next to the immersion against the night, not exactly the frost and the quiver he left me, a moonglow with the whole bundle of his boom of broken arrows of desire.

Spasm of delight is ironic man with the sweetest song. Make leering head out of love, my bud, my blossom, I'm Adam and oratorio from lips so wet. Of the rose I'm the whisper soft with saxophone. Too much old darlin', blowing around the lovers, smile cocaine leave many croaking blues. Rest and morphine, what leap scattered petals.

Leave you? Leave the prophet? Confound his crumb of cured worst threat.

VII

Jaz cooked around four. She put on her purple jumper and a pair of knickers and her old corduroy skirt. She stood at the stove prodding a mess of spaghetti and tinned pork with a wooden spoon.

Her weight rested on her right foot. Her left hip was thrown forwards drawing the corduroy tight against the back of her right thigh. Without stockings her thighs still retained a certain sheen. That had always been the magical thing about Jaz. Her wide animal buttocks were splayed as she stood. One horny foot spread its toes over the instep of the other. The curls broke crisp and black around the nape of her neck. She hadn't washed and as he drew close he could smell bed and the sweat of her and the sperm drying in snail-tracks on her thigh.

She turned the gas down and was about to turn from the stove when he put a hand on each of her hips, and he could see in condensation on gloss paint behind the stove the reflection of her smile.

Her head rocked back to him, her eyes closed. He blessed the wax on her eyelids with a caress of his lips. Her long thighs drifted wide yawning for him. Her free hand fell from where it had hooked on her opposite elbow and swung back round to pass its palm spasmodically and urgently across his penis.

He snapped his zip down and let his penis thud gently against her buttocks. Smiling gaily now, and breathing loudly, steadily, like someone at heavy work, she placed both hands on the stove and spread her legs like a cow.

His penis found its way around the elastic in the leg of her knickers, testing its erection against the taut strand, found her anus and locked here, gently probing like the nozzle of a curious animal, at the bunched crack of her arse.

With a big and curiously generous movement she relaxed herself like a sleeping flower, then clenched, her muscles nipping hungrily, and held him in her arse with a cry of exhilaration and triumph.

They ploughed. The odours of her feet, the odours of her womanliness, the odours of their mutual sweet fatigue, made a gentle music of mortality about his ploughing.

The field-stench of her shit rose, brown and fallible, so he smiled and kissed her neck in compassion of their shared humanity, their joined helplessness, the gigantic comic weakness of their combined ecstatic power.

So, glad with this, she pressed her bony knees against the oven door that knocked, and pressed her long palms against the stove's edge, and, with a powerful heaving of her haunches, drew the last drop from his loved testicles into her bowels, then expelled him warmly. Without turning she passed a hand far back, patted his relaxing arse and said 'Go lay the table.' Pun,' he said. 'Ho ho.'

They ate and rested and played Billie Holliday records.

'Let's open the window and get some fresh air' he said.

'Let's not,' she said. 'Let's keep it fuggy. It's more of you. It's more of us both, the air. Our air.'

He threw back his head and laughed.

'See if there are some cigarettes in that drawer,' she said. He went to the drawer she indicated and noticed a gun, a heavy archaic-looking service revolver.

'What the bloody hell's this?'

'Oh—oh he left it . . . '

'The man with red hair?'

'Yes.'

He picked it up and weighed it in his palm.

'Loaded,' he said.

'Yes. We used to play games with it. Pretty sick games, I suppose.'

He looked at the gun and suddenly smiled. He put it down on the top of the sideboard and rushed to her. Clumsily he pulled her jumper up. He felt her breasts shake free as he dragged the hem across her nipples, his hand unzipping her skirt, his bare feet working it down her long legs and off with a kick across the carpet.

She, by now alight with his certainty and eagerness, kicked off her knickers and his tongue, rich with mouth slime of their eager flowing together, trailed its moisture from her nipple to her nest, to thigh, behind her knees, her coarse toes passing earthy through his wet mouth, joined the ample rivers from her flooded cunt and merged with sperm that shot in magic proliferation from prick released and barely touched by her happy tongue, so that beads and lace and spouting of his seed spread from her lip and decorated the already gleaming moisture of her breast.

'In, darling—fuck me,' and he plunged and, fever passing from them like receding tears, he found himself engaged on a slow and purposeful digging. He found himself passing further than his deepest passion had carried him before. He found them both, who rolled and clenched and clutched on the mat before her ordinary sputtering gas fire, lost in catacombs that, for all their strangeness, their arching vaults, held a familiarity that carried memory beyond conception. He found himself ploughing rhythmically, delving into that part of her that was all women who ever lay on their backs in passion, all women yet to be; he, they, reached a place in her that stank and breathed before the world began and there, towards each other and hurled themselves together in an embrace of recognition.

His cry was a tiny noise. It was a noise of recognition.

'That was where we were going,' he said. 'Yes,' she said.

There must have been a knocking at the door for some time.

They didn't look at one another. Jaz put on her skirt and jumper. Quickly and unselfconsciously she picked up her discarded knickers and wiped her cunt. Sam simply rose and walked to the sideboard. They both knew what was going to happen, even to the finest detail.

Jaz opened the door. The stairslight was pale and green. The light from the flat was warm. It fell warmly on the uniform of the constable and on Phillips's raincoat, rendering them the same colour.

'I think—recognize this' said Phillips. He held out a crumpled sheet. As he handed it to Jaz he looked over her shoulder and met Sam's eye.

'Read it,' said Sam. 'Read it. The sergeant wants to hear it.' Jaz read:

'You don't know who you messed up,
You and the fester doctors.
You locked us both in a slimy hole.
What prize dropped from the bandit's mouth
By your sensible welfare pence?
What was the blood group of the gold the hole spilled? How
Shall we sleep or make love
Now that there's someone watching?'

She smiled and then laughed lightly. Sam had come close up behind her. He took the pistol from behind his back and shot Phillips and the constable.

THE PATRIARCHS

An Early Summer Landscape

ONE

The poet Jack Roberts has dominated the narrow world of English letters for at least fifteen years. As it happens this is little credit to him. English letters during these fifteen years have been in the hands of a talentless and unadventurous group of poets who see to it that most good writing doesn't get published. The lyric force which Roberts possesses is sufficient to procure for him a certain distinction amongst these carping utterers. The academic orthodoxy of his early work has ensured its publication.

A big man with a spade-shaped face and a gentle gravelly Pennine voice, he looms over the rare literary gatherings he attends, a towering presence fulfilling well the promise of his morbid verse and the rumours surrounding his tragic life. Death stalks Roberts' sexual affairs as doggedly as it stalks the gaunt lines of his writings. Two successive mistresses have died by their own hand. Their ashes are strewn along a steep hillside in the Calder Valley. Robert's farm on that hillside has been given over to a literary foundation for residential courses but the atmosphere of weighty foreboding remains despite the presence of shrill intellectuals, just as Roberts' presence retains its character among the emasculated throngs of the literary world.

His presence at the Airebridge Festival had been breathlessly anticipated by the audience of local academics and spinsters which Roberts typically commanded. As his appearances have become less and less frequent and his price become more and more steep, so his Gothic charisma has increased. The usual seedy Edwardian elegance of Airebridge had tightened its stays sufficiently to achieve an air of expectation that deserved to be described as tense. Approximately three hundred pairs of lightly clenched buttocks perched on the edge of three hundred folding chairs in the sweaty twilight of the Airebridge Pump Rooms one hot night in May 1975. Roberts was about ten minutes late. When eventually he stalked up the side aisle, his head half turned to the wall, away from the three hundred pairs of eyes that followed him, the occasional hushed whispers stopped completely.

He sat on the dais under the dim bulb that he must read by while a lecturer from the English Department at Leeds University, a pompous little man who fidgeted with excitement as he spoke as though troubled by an overfull bladder, delivered a sycophantic introduction. Then Roberts stood, flung open a folio on the table against which he rested his thighs, afforded the people at the back of the hall one rueful despairing glance, and began.

"Spectral gigantified nursery picture. Proterozoic childhood oozing through sleep's prehistory. The archetype. The rock turned beard, the steep scree of the father's hand.

"Carapace of scrap iron where later mute resentful spawn spill the mess of their passive contempt. The crag's face becomes a tip.

"Cuticle crushed on the roads, that lonely enfeebled pilgrimage. Molly to t'workhouse and Michael to work.

"Lonely arrest with blood on the counter, the inevitability of Saturday night's maudlin martyrdom.

"An effulgence to take something out. Shadow stark on the blessed name. Evidence at the bottom of the spirit gorge wrought from black grit, of the inherited stigma of the patriarch.

"Sliding back in the lord's name through the crow-cries of the claw-hammer coated evangelists to the avuncular visage of Hardcastle Crags.

"Your protector let out a yelp and the landscape split its swelling bellyful of tortured cats.

"The pure light stopping and starting but never completely lightening the load of the glowing mountain or the burdened woman.

"An ironic laugh went beyond me too quickly, echoing the woods below Dambank, a heron mocking a rook.

"You stole the protection of the weak, lining your granite dignity with emaciated labour.

"You wallowed in disembowelled self, selling the spillage, retreading the entrails."

Roberts paused at this point, bowing his head more deeply than was necessary to focus on the manuscript on the table. A little gasp escaped a woman near the centre aisle. Whether it was out of sympathy or discomfort was uncertain.

TWO

17th May 1975. Ward Five, Bradford Royal Infirmary.

"Pa'don?" Shout in a dead ear.

Somebody dropped a tin dish stacked with flea powder. Always the moans.

A Godgiven sheepsbladder filled to capacity with sunlight like weedpollen strains at its moorings from the blackstone building's blunt west wall. The haulers creak.

Pack of cards the shuffled fields. Rotting toothstumps cottage-rows ranged along Queensbury ridge; the drystone walls.

"Pa'don." Will we eat pap or bananas, produce or machine shit?

A diabetic cat that shat the shamefaced liquids-only pool on the dinnerplate before me sleeps at night in the bowels of Crucified Ken.

Pastoral new-moons were never so slender as his upturned eye-whites. Ashes and rivermist were never so grey as the parchment surrounding his lower teeth.

Sarcophagi. Battlefields. Strung up by the licentious squaddies with a bottle, a tube and a needle on one spread arm, a crumpled Kleenex and a pissbottle at the other.

The spatter of urine on yellowpolished wood. The spatter of sperm on deathdrawn ladycheeks. The drumming of summer rain on the heads of the dying bluebells.

THREE

"It wasn't like that," said Rose. I retired into the business of digesting my beer, envisioned the dissolving knots of malt and gas as small explosions of autumn, bought, trapped, consumed.

"Well tell me how it was then."

I was confused as usual by the Noah's ark of animals her demeanour referred to. How her features, always as mobile as some tiny fountain alive with impulses, delicate substance curling and buckling under electric impact, sometimes focussed themselves around the tip of her nose, attracting her upper lip in a gutter sneer. Thus her jaw line, pulling back from her nose's gravitational point, could articulate her lips only by drawing her mouth down at the corner. She sneered and she snarled. Her lower teeth, rendered into fangs by their crude outlines of nicotine, were, at such times, viciously evident.

At such times she was rat.

This is how I described her in my most recent poem about her, a poem she hadn't yet seen.

At other limes her eyes expanded engulfing her whole being like brown lamps. Mobile as her flesh, they waxed and narrowed, flexing like camera lenses visibly, in a startled impulse of wonderment and anticipation. Snapped out of sleep she would fix her early caller with an expression of generous terror. Expecting a present she would erode its wrappings with eyes that could eat. And at these times she was a night animal; field mouse, shrew, lemur.

And I was never completely without the memory of Rose at seventeen, when I met her. Her eyes perpetually downcast looked along the smooth slopes of her lovely cheekbones, and threw the focus of her features along her clean jawline, a long subtle dip falling from the lobe of her wisped ear to the sharp assertive point of her chin. Then she was antelope; speed, nerve, quick innocence, darting through fragrant attitudes with a velocity that rendered her presence a cinema of ghosts.

But even in those days she'd had the shutters in her eyes, the one way glass enabling anyone to look into her but preventing her from seeing out.

"Predatory," Eric said.

"She'll kill you," Dick had said, earlier.

"It was to do with isolation. Pete and I are isolate. It was as if the feeling was only accessible to isolate people. You don't understand isolation."

And all I could think of, with the ale souring in my belly together with the softer blues and sun-reds of my recollections, was my failure, indeed, to understand her seeming unawareness of how the love she demanded precipitated interpenetrations of mind after the ceremonies of hard fuck, that invalidated the very possibility of isolation. My failure to comprehend how a love as lyric and sacrificial could be carried on in a skin of psychopathic alienation.

"Isolation," I said, "is surely impossible. It's not that I don't comprehend it. I comprehend it very well and I know that in terms of the human personality it doesn't exist."

"It does, it does," she said broodily, celebrating somewhere deep in her body — into the aviary now, her crow's body — the chain of fusions between isolation, avarice and shit; celebrating exactly that fusion in her which Eric, Dick, other people warned me against. "Evil," she once said, "You don't understand evil, its purity — its isolate integrity.' Drove me then away, turning her self-awareness in her carrion breast as a ceremony of evil's purity.

I recalled the poem, again thinking how well I understood that poignant essence whereby the citizens of filth, of industrial avarice, were thrown into isolation which they celebrated in a culture of excrement and blood. For she, I now saw, had so failed to objectify her sense of evil, so beautified it into her metaphor for the love of her own lonely mother that she couldn't see the accumulative cruelty that constituted her isolation.

"If you're so isolate," I said, "it's because of your own errors."

Her teeth ground like a child's in rigor. "Please don't go on?" she said. "It makes me so angry."

"Personality, like matter, is a matter of energies, and energies aren't property. They flow like air between people. The spirit which informs and empowers you at one moment is simultaneously informing someone else so that information can scarcely be withheld. That's why those who continue to relate their understanding to language end in despair. They make the media into the content. All you can ever do with language is describe understanding."

"Despair," she bit out as though defending children, "Despair is *beautiful*. Where have all your majestic convictions gone? Where's your fucking pride?"

"My majesty is nothing more than the confidence with which I receive my energy and discharge it. Humiliation is the destruction of energy."

"*I make my own* energy," she snarled.

"No you don't. The best you can do is try to steal it."

"The whole purpose of art is to divert the natural course of things. You do that. To bend the state of things you're born to is to achieve eroticism. *You're* talking about fucking *happiness*."

Her scorn was almost military.

"Okay," I went on, "If you want to divert, divert, pervert, pervert, but first know how the straight thing works."

And I knew why I hadn't understood how it was for her and Pete that day on the hillside behind the Pack Horse. That I had already let the light circulate so freely through me that I had placed the avaricious evils outside my aura of perception. Pete and I had, after all, been to that same stretch of land before. And I had embraced the devils loving all the potency out of them.

FOUR

From Dambank to Quarry Mount is a landscape mangled like a mongrel's scabby back with degradation. Charming like all charnel houses now the whip has fallen and the treadmill slowed, it inherits, beneath its superstructures of bawdy humour, music hall, smoky arse-orientated folklore, the hardmouthed toughness of a terrible ancient violence. It is this violence that is written plain across Jack Roberts' face at his moments of greatest vulnerability, as though he himself were afflicted by his own inheritance.

The hills are the male chore of the land. They predominate like bald. and stoic ancestors, like the very patriarchs they bred; men with granite tools, emulating the sudden crags that define England out of the female sea as stance defines man out of the womb; men descending a ladder of stern animus, down through the ranks of the evangelists, the austere councils of the black towns, the lordly civic statuary, the regal mill chimneys. The animus is there still. Under its predatory countenance the land lies, knackered, giving forth gas fumes of exhaustion, the insidious issues of degradation.

Sobering up repeatedly under their gritty frown I recognise that they, being the compliment of anima, are not of their own nature evil, but that their isolation from anima, from any leavening principle, is the instrument of bringing evil into being. The devil advertises himself by the fusion of blood, shit and fatigue in cruelty. These, being so densely merged become not mixture but compound, erode even the majesty of the rocky progenitor.

Here, in his island of spurious gentility, Roberts articulates the animus, bitterly and inevitably, famished to his very bones for want of gentleness. His occasional winced glances are met by a battery of opaque spectacle-lenses. The heat intensifies.

"Bonfire unconcern for the screaming snore in his death struggle, the torment in the sleep set against the complacent conflagration of the wool boom.

"The truth went cold like a mosquito, fled into the shadowed side of the valley. The word cracked out like dawn ice in the chapel cells.

"A snail's spurning eyeball set the atoms trembling under her humped robe, but she persisted in her perusal, snout to snout, person to person, wet horns locked lubriciously.

"This bird is the sun's keyhole into the courts of the afterlife, but ever since she came under the grandfather's shade she's been blocked from light. The convolutions of her loyalties are so grotesque.

"So hideous the law teeters and Olliwale gurgles drunkenly along the Leeds-Liverpool Canal.

"Sweated decay lolling to get rid of sniffed mortification, drunk in the Jubilee, the Victoria, the Albert, limbs rotten with labour and lanolin, aching from the relentless contempt of the employers.

"The bird came clowning with a bar parlour shriek for her knuckling punch-line.

"One fellow creature still cherished his gluttony, feeding off body of, light of, love of the lovers that passed through the blind palms.

"As airy as any bird saying, his wise slurred boasts fluttered over marshes of spilled beer. 'Find 'em, fuck 'em, forget 'em'.

"The one creature wobbling out who never learned the substance of those who have fouled my eyes; unsteady legs of total betrayal, totally tolerant to the vengeful apprentices with their toasting tongues."

Sweat stood on the brow of the lecturer from Leeds University like raindrops on glass but Roberts' face was dry. His voice rasped on, the incantation of a lonely building rook.

FIVE

18th May 1975. Ward Five, Bradford Royal Infirmary.

Meet at t' Alf-Way 'Ouse, on downt' road t' warrisit? Robin 'Ood. Reet good night, we 'ad. Steak, scampi and chips, allt' lot.

Pete and Rose. Wannida tek Rose. Rose 'adn't been before. Reunion. After allt' difficulties, like — All ower. "Emotional knots and confusions" — (Bright-eyed blue-eyed nimble-fingered elfin doctor unifying the tangles of a tortuous sexual development on the jungle side of my rib-gap.)

Well, t 'Alf Way 'Ouse were alright. Coupla pints. All decided to mewv on. Me and Pete, beginnin' t' get th'ale movin' tha knows, and a grand evening (sun cutting across Stanningley Bottom like a minted scythe) — next pint at t'Robin 'Ood, waitin' for Rose t' follow on — Pete: "Tek n' fuckin' notice. Let's 'ave ower nosh." Ordered.

Sun coming into the dining saloon — marmalade. But must ring back to Rose — something in my rib-cage still untangled by those Gallic needlewoman's fingers. Through (after several bent unworking coins) to t' Alf Way 'Ouse.

She was brought to the phone but couldn't speak for weeping, just that noiseless helpless salivating. Shouted: "Well, what's wrong? What is it? Another bloke? You come on? Something you *still* haven't told me?"

Just saliva and kitten gasps of distress. And suddenly a little girl. Delicate as willow-herb with sweetshop-rotted teeth, clutching her two pence: "Can I mek a phone call, mister? It's urgent, mister. Can I 'ave't' phone?"

Shouting at the little girl. "Shuttup. I can't hear what —"

Shouting at Rose: "What is it? What are you trying to tell me? Can you come down to the — What's the name of the pub?"

To the little girl: "WHAT'S THE NAME OF THIS FUCKING PUB?"

Frail but unfrightened (drunken father, uncles, brothers, Saturday night in Jubilee Terrace) "T'Robin 'Ood."

"Robin Hood! That's the pub. Just take a bus down the Otley-Harrogate road, It's on the left. You come?"

Saliva noise, scarcely to be called a sob.

"It's on t' right. You can find it."

Not a sob, more of a wail of a breath.

"And you tell me then?"

A whispered yes.

Pete waiting in the dining lounge, a huge sparking pint of Lager in his hand that seemed the distillation of the young summer evening.

And the colourless bottle of medical Vodka bleeps down the piping into Crucified Ken.

Richard Tauber loudly from the echoing bathroom, Edwardian resonance of tiles, the cornbeef texture of the plinths at Cartwright Hall, the graining of the washbasins in the Gents at Nottingham Yates'. "Jeff! Shut up!"

Two women on the edge of the visitor's bench. The stripping qualities of grief. As Gypsy Rose sheds her own seven veils, so grief tears away the muslin backdrops, projection screens, veils of make-up, movie-shows of facial expressions; tears 'em off your skull, ties 'em with a ribbon and throws 'em in the deep blue eyes of Crucified Ken (whose violet irises never blossom in their old human shop-floor-winking-nathen-owd-pal manner now. Just the twin newmoons lying on their backs and that delicate grey, that fresh touch death can have like rainclouds lying low along the shaved skulls of the patriarchs.)

One woman, middle-aged, thus stripped, a lump of nothing-but-her-errors, which are, themselves, the advertising emblems of defining fallibility. (Roll up humanoids, see the tight-rope walker stumble a lock-step into a safety tub of self-soup. Roll up homosaps, see the star-swinging psychopoid step off the wire at the height from which the sergeant major shat. Roll up, see the hones revealed as raw, as dove-grey as the parchment over the graveyard gasping mask of Crucified Ken; see the moment when a creaking side door interrupts the persuasive sentence, when the punch-line of the tale is interrupted by the interception of an unwarranted image of panic, when the high diver falters at the second of the spring, remembering his sister's tears and the blood on his middle-finger.

Whaddya got? Clumsy old scarves with the wool washed lumpy. Old school macs in blue gabardine with the belt too high, too high. Half-collapsed knee-stockings, bedsocks, lisle-stockings, ill-fitting garments of function and support, the waterproof gusset-panels, button-shoes, darned blue berets, crumpled hair-ribbons. Warm flannel drawers. The careful style of style-lessness.

The Chiaparelli of no-style is grief.

One woman, nobbut just, who's been called back from the spring's branch you're supposed to fly from, squats there like a clipped sparrow — failed fledgling — face as pale as the telephone youngster's in the dream . . .

(Shouldn't have shouted — Shouldn't have sung BECAUSE
God made you mine
I cherish — ")

Perish. Waste. Hung between a vodka bottle with pipe-line on one side and a piss bottle with a bottleneck rind (brokenback whine) on the other. Off you spin, Ken arkid, off into the violet beyond of your own shuttered irises.

"Pa'don?"

SIX

A woman six rows from the rear of the hall, her fingers clutching a wad of poetry magazines bought that afternoon from the Festival Bookstall, was shifting in her seat as uneasily as the Lecturer from Leeds University was shifting on his platform. Their movements and the impulses their movements made visible were sporadic and transitory. Roberts' voice was resolute and unchanging, as absolute as granite.

"Whether dead or unborn, squats listening, incapable of argument or stance, suspended enfeebled between the two resolutions.

"Dumb as a holy creature of wounds the sacrificial boys stood trembling on the waterstones and two women waited for the bleeding to abate.

"You have nursed it like the smell of smoke in your black valleys and now the screams rise limply again over the sounds of water and hushed leaves.

"The signature lolling blood, slopped on the slab, on the neglected thigh.

"Wholly human nature is bulging with an unwanted pregnancy, a necessary murder. The crags demand.

"Doomsday light pullulating wetly across the waterfall spindrift signals the time for the axe to swing, for the summer to drill bullets in the careful line of your brow."

The woman coughed with a strained, querulous little sound, touching the fingers of her right hand briefly to her throat.

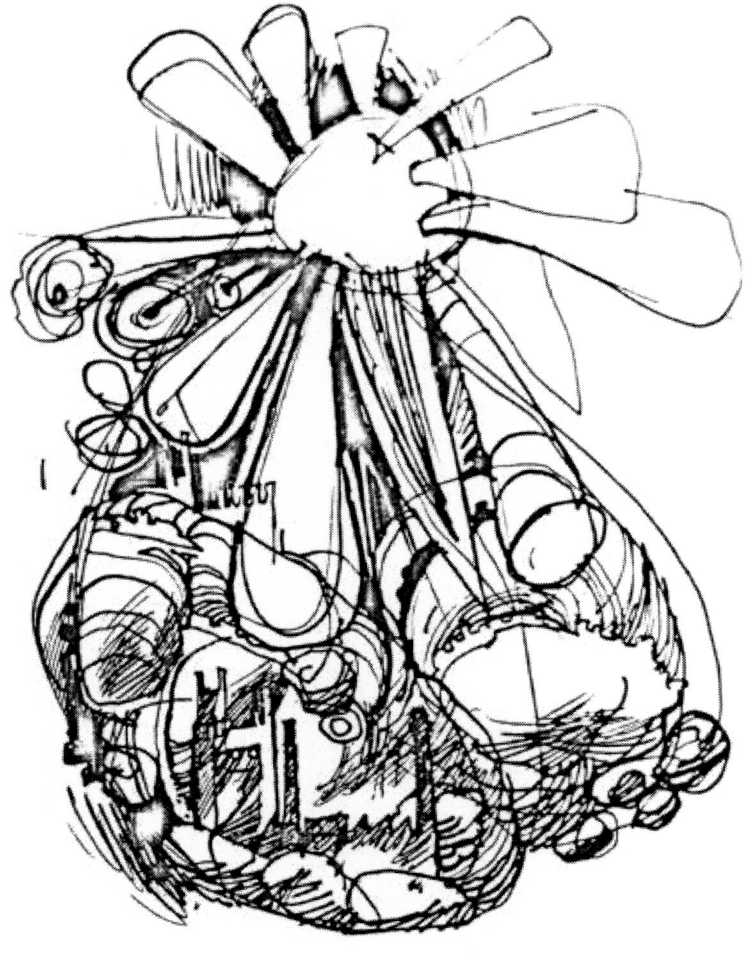

SEVEN

20th May, 1975. Ward Five, Bradford Royal Infirmary.

A single tulip — tighter-lipped than a kissing lily or persuasive rose.

Arising out of the well of sorrows, a John McCormack plaint like early phlegm from my lips.

(An arse dusted with talcum coughs from the facial end of its body with all the compulsions of song.)

Kathleen is asleep with her upper set in her plastic cylinder. Whether I take her home again or not the dawn chorus (cauliflower trees, leaves crusted like thatch moss, alive with a morning attack of the warblers, insistent as the sun crying at your eyelids) will be interlaced with the subtlest of moans — (that birdsigh lostsong when the orgasm is gone and oblivious woman laps you into loam) — the sighs of, sleeping moans of lost-orgasm waking, something always taken away in the penultimate breath — the fanforinade of twitterchicks in the mustard-green trees contrapuntal to this symphony of sighs — My last loss sucked by a vast incurling of the universe into forever. The quick, light hesitant farewells of Crucified Ken beating the early sun into these spotless vaults.

That by breath of dying we orchestrate our being into light.

That by death of breath we fade our warring trivialities into genius.

That the symphony is there and the band stools are vacant, the gaps in the fabric waiting for everybody's gypsy-coloured thread.

Papers. Headlines, Educational Black Book. Iris Murdoch (not Iris, nor Miss Murdoch, but Iris Murdoch, in the university challenging way of addressing a face facing your own face — the cunt so *near* your hand by this public distancing insignia; not the mister, nor the familiarism, but the name the way it gets printed — living in this spiderwed of identities where the double vocative is a badge of existence, of success; and how she, the author of not wholly trivial books-at-bed-time, capable of at least the vanishing fishtail of a vision, should fail to see that the greatness of any single man is nothing more than the breakthrough, in a closed sphere of diminutive falsehood, of one inane soul. Out of the egg into the natural province of all men. And this is all that education is. To seek the fact is to seek the natural province, the meadow, vast light.

That bag-o-carrots May morning tacked to the facade of this grey-stone bonery. To get through the structured and grateful edifices that map and enumerate its contents — to reach the skin of the bladder and having got there — to the outer edge of all knowable glory — TO GET MORE, KNOW MORE.

Not to list, structure, ask questions of, make minted money, status and fake identity of it — (not merely to play these games) — but to find oneself standing on the other side — even in the increasing clarity — In the place where Adam and Evil have always been.

The edge where Crucified Ken begins with failing breath to carefully weave his woody clarinette line into the glory-song.

EIGHT

Outside in Airebridge High Street two bricklayers in smart suits walked hesitantly and noisily from the Bull to the Royal Crown. A woman who lived in the caretaker's cottage of the Methodist Chapel came to her door, looked up and down the street, rubbed her upper arms briskly and went in again. A dog nosed an ice-lolly stick. A kite, born up by the heat rising from the rocks of Airebridge Moor, drifted lightly back and forth.

In the Airebridge Pump Rooms Jack Roberts' voice ground on.

"Your signature is the irony of your mouth, the grimace of the split cliff.

"Beneath your voice sticky flies play, choral over the filth of your dominion.

"The dirty net curtain of your unspeakable outcry, the bedraggled cottage gardens of your silence."

The woman six rows from the back coughed again. She wore a summer hat of light canvas material. She brushed its brim with the back of her knuckles and resumed her grip on the magazines.

"Cellar deafness that smells of stale refuse, chimney blindness that tastes of decay.

"Veronica's cloth in freezing petroleum and Sandra's dropped dress in the rainbow canal. Work-numbed senses will not let you breathe the dead sparrow's eye, inhale the reeking falcon's omen.

"Only with a cry of river and mud can the gauntness be appropriately sung."

NINE

22nd May 1975, Ward Fire, Bradford Royal Infirmary.

The day keeps bringing flowers, puts them on the windowsill. The bottom of the summerbladder is the dip of walled and overfucked pasture between the Ward Five bay window and the Queensbury Ridge. The upper hemisphere is an arc of atmosphere, dense as pollen.

As the summer is hooked to the old stone mansion by hawsers and buckles and clips, so Crucified Ken danced his final dance with his bowels (exposed in cellophane, a totally different kind of season) hanging at his side — We contemplate the fullness we receive. He drools in feebleness on the fullness he's expended.

Pepperpot women with wheels under Mrs. Noah skirts wait in a row and complain.

Ken's finale holds up the traffic. Ken's epitaph delays the bingo.

When they've wheeled his detritus out in a box under the empty stretcher the women trundle forward like Daleks bristling chrysanthemums and chocolate boxes.

Busily, industriously, lips clamped as purposefully as those of the muscular professionals down below sculpting with Crucified Ken's remains, they lick their stickers, slap their stamps, pin their prices, slogans, trade marks on mortality.

Mortality, attired in little more than its usual rainyday range of passive greys.

Mortality, drifting to its possibilities beyond its own retrospective definitions.

Stamped. Retained. Home again in block lettering and primary colours.

TEN

There are places beyond the cities, beyond the admonitory chimneys and the cobbles set in soot, where a gill or a tarn, perhaps rock worn smooth by something other than a chisel or the backsides of resting drovers, indicates the exact spot where the patriarchs claimed their first souls. Hairy-backed shepherds with bleak blue eyes and sceptical mouths (You Can't Beat 'Em, Join 'Em) dragged their ailing children on a hempen halter the way they were to drag pack-mules bent under wool, recalcitrant wives bent under the knuckle, the way the valley millworkers were to carry unwanted children and lay them along the crags four thousand years later: victims and sacrifices being dragged bluntly, impassively over the rocks over the heather to be tipped through the strata of spring leaves, through the mustard-yellow peppering of the foliage, into the rock throat down which the water roars at Dambank.

On Boulsworth Hill beyond Heptonstall Moor the ancestors lie stripped in their dormant authority. Shoulders and thews, humps of judgement, stretch through the veils of the shifting rain to the sky round all the corners of the compass.

At the end of a track, at the end of a rough road, at the end of a lane, a tiny green Volkswagen is parked, crazily tilted on the uneven ground. A man wearing a shirt open to the waist and a pair of army drill trousers is walking on over the moor, hand in hand with a girl who wears nothing but a blood soiled pair of drawers. They walk with an odd theatrical deportment born of love and alcohol. At the crest of a ridge they sink into the heather and make love, slowly and deliberately, seemingly endlessly. When they stop the girl sits up, her arms crossed over her breasts, suddenly aware of her nakedness. She looks all round her in a mute panic of realisation. The hills stretch away all round, utterly cold, older than the sky, watching. She shudders a quick recognition. They return to the car. Staggering a little now. Drunk.

They drive down from the patriarchal brow, down past the crags and the medieval weaving caves, down past Dambank.

Dambank is a natural point of focus in the landscape for obvious reasons.

Firstly a couple of nubs of rock overlook it with sufficient authority of demeanour to declare the place sacred.

Secondly, the waterfall draws travellers up the side valley from the main route that follows the Calder two miles away. Below the waterfall the slopes are too steep and the stream too devious for an easy crossing. Similarly above the fall. Travelling down from Boulsworth or up from the Calder, this is the sensible place to ford with a mule, or a flock of sheep, or a meandering family-horde looking for flesh of roots, for grubs or flesh of humans.

So the little bridge was built and the farm sprang up to turn a few woodland acres into pasture. So the factory came, the rock was carved to give the twisting water added impetus. A chimney grew up out of the flat rock the drovers had used to drink and fight on, to sit and barter, the rock from which the rickety children with wild eyes were tipped into the green dank tank below.

Dambank Farm overlooks the waterfall. A looselimbed man with long hair paces the tilted acres of buttercups sowing his righteous grasses, breeding his milky goats. And the farm itself is disguised, wall-to-wall carpeting and natural wood varnished yellow mask the flags. Here and there a bacon-hook has been preserved, spiking from a stained beam as an architectural comma.

Rose and I arrived about six, mildly summer drunk — four hours meandering in and out of the dank, cool boozers in Stalybridge, an expensive taxi voyage over the billowing patriarchs to Todmorden, the wine spilling liberally over the edges of the filched glasses, an hour in the relentless sun among the geraniums by the Rochdale Canal, red-faced, helpless and disgraceful, sleepy as children — then Bill at the Shoulder of Mutton in Hebden, who drove us to the farm.

I checked my bibbing although the girls (well-fed young bodies golden as new bread in bikinis, barefoot on the kitchen tiles) were well into a couple of litres of Riesling. Ambleman was facetious and prickly (anticipatory figure on those longago London pubcrawls with Rose, of Rose's string of slum lovers — "Isolation" — degradation, sacrifice.)

Baugh was polite and shy — "tempered discipline it must involve to emerge from his anxiety to be pleasant and produce his ruthless journalism . . ." Didn't say it out loud.

The meal was enjoyable despite Ambleman's oblique defensive insults. The reading happened despite a tongue as unwieldy as a landed trout and type that danced and lurched in my eye's moisture.

"For fuck's sake how long is this going on?" exploded Ambleman. "It's been literature all day. Let's just — well — let's put some music on and —" If the reading (someone other than he in the limes, with Rose alongside, commanding the breathless attention of the new-baked girls) was as painful as that to him, and if indeed he thought of me as a "pornographer left over from the late sixties" as he'd said at dinner, he'd done well to stand the two hours of my reading. I broke it up. Dreary rock-and-roll precipitated Ambleman's unsightly mating rituals.

Wine and chat and liquid faces looming into view — "Why *must* you write about sex in that way?" — "Why do you say fuck all the time?" — and Rose's magpie chattering, and Baugh's delicate laughter, and Ambleman's menopausal shrieks exploding out of the window, dispersing thinly among the trees below.

The trees were dense, black and warm now, invisible in the mass of the hill, the hill barely discernible against a moonless sky. Like cooling ovens they released their accumulated heat. The bakestone crags cooled. The foliage stirred in cooling, seeding and generating audibly.

The waterfall's throat whispered down by the bridge, a beckoning. The vacuum, intake-grasp of hush, the suck and pull of black. The night sky rendered not of air, an insidiously familiar ambiguity drew me, loose-shod over yard-cobbles, into the steep lane. Nothing to guide me but the beckoning breathing of the woods and its whispered water-echo down there in the deeps.

Down. Drawn down. Down to the throat where a million baying voices of pain wrung audible chords from the metal in the rocks, the orchestrated plea of humiliation, alienation, degradation. The arsehole in the woods, the malevolent hole from whence the dark came, from which stank forth the scapegoats of that cruelty the patriarchs demand, the cruelty that poverty demands with grit eyes.

The party continued and I entered it buoyantly. "Look Pete," I said, "It's only a dead cat."

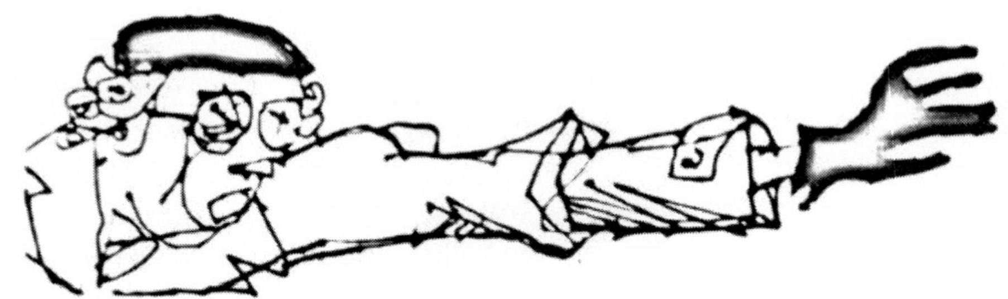

ELEVEN

"The scree has not ceased to slip and trickle sun, moon, stars," said Roberts. The people sitting near the woman six rows from the back were beginning to be embarrassed by the intensifying quality of her movements.

"And darkness." he went on, "is identical since the first child fell.

"Lost every reflection with his hemlock, tenth draught of the woodbine drowsiness driving back misgivings.

"You have no idea what confesses his body. You have no way of knowing whence come the voices that own to his blood and bone.

"It feels like the world, bedaubed, begauded, head to the north and the other compass points starry with spangles, spangled with the firmament.

"Before your eyes ever opened his heart, its substance was sealed, its pump-ducts dammed.

"Boredom at sea unlacing his steel, his closed faculties demanding identity in a cruelty as great as that which cast him adrift in ineffectuality.

"Hands and knees are the common wild stones and head is a rock that must be split before the better songs can sound.

"The web of veins into which he lowers his spoils, swallowing humiliation back into his own blood, twitching in the dark earth's name, crying from the water-ducts in the name of the father skull hill of small madness and

ponderous sanity.
"After the islands of women an unearthly cry goes up.
"The unwanted child is left among the loose stones at the father's feet.
"On a breathing moor a bone, a rag."

The woman in the sixth row from the back lurched to one side, stumbling over the crushed knees of the people sitting along the row. "No," she cried "No more, no more." The swing door thudded behind her. The hawk over Airebridge Moor swung away towards Baildon and Queensbury. Roberts took a sip of water from the glass that stood beside his manuscript and continued.

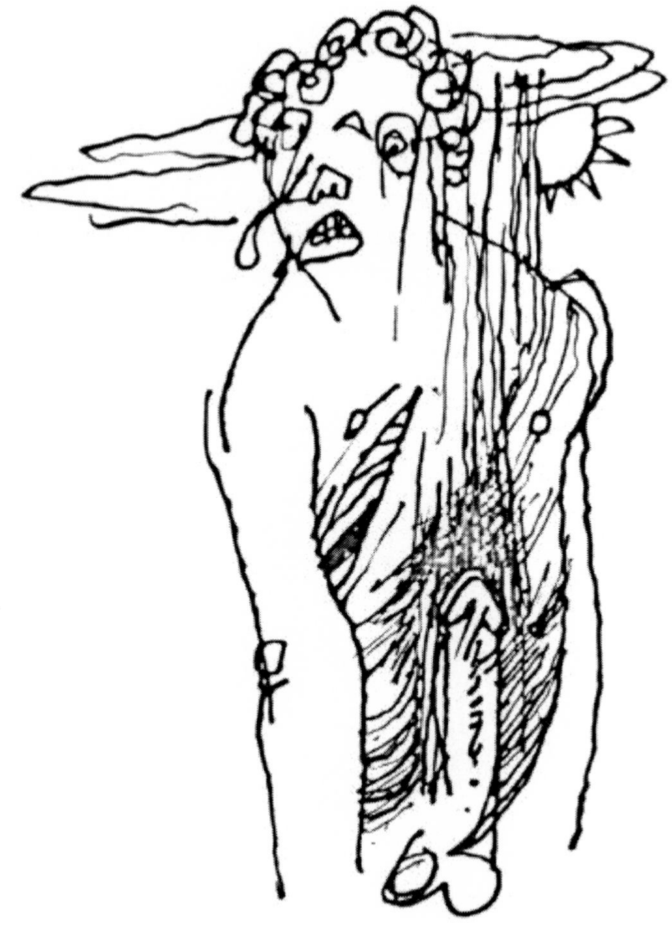

TWELVE

22nd May 1975, Ward Fire, Bradford Royal Infirmary.

There's a breathless hush in the chambers this morning.

Somebody already outlined in some pretty raw colours didn't get stamped with half enough clarity. Escaped definition at a gnat's breath after supping his morning tea once, buying the *Daily Mirror* (complexion bright as a bruise), Weekend (Can I ever say thanks?) and the *Sun* (that gimlet Authority on the other side of the weatherbag), thumbing through the hack three pages of each.

Gone out of a game as complex as a dart board though Billy's hoards never carried a treble. Foregone that first/next pint for which he was going to be so grateful, to where the treble of the flute is never as troublesome as the wind that ground from his unrepentant gut or as relieving as the wind that swept in the gasp of a gnat and quite suddenly blew old Billy away.

Traffic noises. Beesong. Where is the sex in a female gymnast? What are all these fucking bodies *for*?

Billy's fooled 'em. Left a parcel, bedlinen looking for all the world like some precious powder wrapped up and labelled by a humourless bespectacled chemist. "The Powder". "The Mixture". "The Tablets". "The Body".

How he managed it nobody knows, managed to leave a void dressed in familiar clothes. Those old, slack, pectorals, beer-shot eyes, that Tetley's blush and the outsplayed thighs. The suit of skin that Billy wore, wrapped in linen like a five quid score of amphetamine powder or simple flea-dust. Must be Billy there. Looks like. Must.

But Billy's gone with his replica left. Fooled the buggers, all bereft.

Can't be done. More than that and more than the fake short change of the "afterlife."

Outside, the weatherbag whose contents still, this merry month of May, smile for some fucking reason.

For now it becomes unavoidable, how close they are the horny and the tearful. As the shaft of loneliness rises in my chest, inflated with a shower of unspent tears, illustrated with the little coloured catalogue notations of grief, of fear, acknowledged powerlessness before death so, in the same motion, my prick stirs, soft nascent limb, in my amber pyjamas' papercrisp shade, with an authenticity of impulse not felt in ten contented years (even, confess it, when death was as near as it came when my father "went"). As though my refusal of tears (sensibility walled up on all sides to preserve life and personality at all, threatened, as it was, on one side, by the intolerable pain of my cruelty to other people, on the other by the ridicule of colleagues, by the suicide implicit in cultural failure) being stripped away, an erection other than, and superior to, the reflex-ramrod of the stockingtop scenario and the early-morning demand for a functional sperm-letting, such an erection become possible again. Erection inflated like the season. Erection whose exact interconnection with grief and loss makes it the expression of yearning, the celebration of the Not-Yet-Possible. An erection constituting the significant difference between pleasure and beauty.

THIRTEEN

Roberts looked up now. For the first time his eyes became visible through the black cast shadow from the overhead light. His expression seemed not to be one of concern or offence, certainly not anger. He seemed to be saying "What did I tell you?"

The next lines of his poem he read with a certain pointed seriousness, as though, in this tide of ambiguities, here was the precise rock-pool from whence the pearls of central meaning were to be extracted.

"His sacrifice is perfect," he read. "He reserves nothing, standing among graves, a late priest with a hatchet face and no possible understanding of his inherited calling."

He raised his head again. This time he seemed to be asking for help, the shaman of the patriarchs pleading resignation. At Dambank the gnats buzzed menacing above the waterfall's dark drop. The voice continued.

"Under rock he found his submission flawless. Below the waters' roar he worked out to perfection the patriarchal dogma.

"His spine survives his afternoon, where a leaf or two moulders and the ashes of the second sacrifice filter into the woodland roots.

"His gaze peeled flakes off the skull's beauty,

"Gasped out the rags of his banner.

"The leather of his shoes strengthens its revelation as he walks doggedly down the leafy cathedrals of his calling.

"A wingspread in the road and a dead wife swings away blown beyond

grief.
"To drag you in a bog or carry you to final eagles was the only act of love the crags permitted,
"Making an egg of death blackness and a bland moon of the grave.
"A great fear rests on Infinity and Infinity sits on me.
"Nothingness came close. I shall not fight. It seems more clement than the assertive hills

"I rise beyond my souls laid out, bandaging a nick in the brain like a polyp in the circulation of the sea cruises through the stone of firework and the steady gleam of the milldam."

FOURTEEN

23rd May, 1975. Ward Five, Bradford Royal Infirmary.

The silver fish with their deathface underbellies (dragged out on the sandbar, left to die, then thrown back in — or poisoned at the outlet of a sewer) — (stone-brown shallow shadows of fish-tickling summers) or shimmering horizontal out of the reflections under the overhang of a spattered dressing-gown. The hood and the shade of a bedcage spilling the shoals of the waterveined limbs, no more bone than a storm-drained worm — no more muscle than a snipped prick. They float and they hover, whip to the roots of the riverside medicine tables, ride above the purposeful uniformed forearms, lie with the waters of the day trickling in at their endmouths and out of their tube-tapped fins.

And they hover a long time at the mouth of the river, letting the memories succour them, images, fetishes, running downstream from the inlets and tributaries of family, love-connections, history, dropped opportunities; passing memory through their gills and into the bedpan, looking a long time back with that special submissive regret for the loss of the love of life, the *regret* called senility; before the plunge, the leap, the new magnificence: recycled energy among the whales and breakers.

FIFTEEN

The atmosphere in the Pump Rooms was stilling now. The Lecturer from the English Department at Leeds University was looking from side to side in a kind of panic of discomfort. Somewhere in the sweaty gloom a woman was breathing loudly enough to sound as though she was crying. But that was the only sound.

"Earthy news of the shyest bird," read Roberts. "I am the last of hard-cornered grief.

"Are you afraid of tree in dirt? The heaven of the tree never stopped angels nor the wheel-winged shade of paired brides.

"The worm could break pieces off them both, my buried loves, unless they transcend the crag's granite forehead.

"From all these you may climb with holy steps, may soar with daylight pinions; prayers congealed in a paradise of tremblings, the after-taste of cracked iron, are left below, under the stone scowl and the waters' relentless descent."

Roberts carefully sat down. The lecturer for the English Department at Leeds University leaned over as though to speak but Roberts ignored him.

"I'm sure we're all very grateful to Jack Roberts . . ." began the lecturer from Leeds, but the swing door was thumping at the back and some feet were stirring already under the wave of tentative, awestruck applause.

SIXTEEN

24th May, 1975. Ward Five, Bradford Royal Infirmary.

Out in the gardens with Rose.

Not talking of it (Talk of art/art politics: — "The grant arrives next month — two weeks in Germany next October — a cool gig, not the grand guignol we'd all expected —") — nonetheless, in the light, turning
turning

Like the leaves in a frail book, turning

Like the skins of dead leaves with the veins remaining delicate tracery turned so gently, never to break them,

Like specimens, pieces of old information, tomb remains handled at needlepoint, lifted and turned

Like the fingers and forceps, the sterilised instruments turning aside the wool-skeins of muscle, turning the bubbling rubber machine of breathing in a rib cage opened as breathlessly as the hidden door of the pyramid:

Walking there in the light of the May-bladder, the lucidity streaming cross the valley from Queensbury, soaking the black stone on the portico steps, clear enough for any operative examination —

Turning the leaves and exhibits A, B, and C to Z of our cruelties (Never a thing to need handling as tenderly as past cruelties) —

And coming to no conclusion, the diagnosis suspended.

Informed though, informed; as she came hack out of the garden with its supermarket flowerbeds, and up in the lift, kissed a surgical farewell in the echoing corridor . . .

And Maggie Butterfield turned her life, book leaves, leafskins, time's gastric tumours, sightless eyes and soundless cars examining minutely the habits and rituals, her skeletal hands with their brassknob knuckles turning and turning the ribbon brought back from Scarborough in her sixteenth year, snapping the old hot tongs into her young curls, shifting hairgrips from dressing-table (kitchen slab/National Health feeding tray) to mouth, from mouth to back hairs (George at t'Alhambra, seven o'clock, dab o' scent . . .), tying the thread on the bobbin, crossing the warp, her hands with their knowing remembering fingers turning the incidents still in the sleep of her ninetysixth year, getting the work done, making the tea, mending the overall, nursing the firstborn — folds of her top sheet in a bundle to her breast, and kissing them . . . then jobs to be done, a lifetime sorted, bottled and shelved, turned on the feed-tray of her wheeled chair.

Turning in the amber light of reflection . . .

Water through the fishes' gills and then the ocean.

Mrs. Ormonroyd took the plunge this morning. Early. Cardiac arrest.

SEVENTEEN

Face of Moors-Murderer Hindley, crag of Hindley, jawbone like a prehistoric axe. Opaque Northern eyes — the hopelessness of the twelve hour shift and the Bingo emancipation.

She stared us down in the Pack Horse as Pete grimaced on the warm side of weeping, and Rose looked down her nasal arch into the night hole of her fallacious privacy.

My love is a rat with slanted incisors.
My love was a gracegirl tossed on her sex, a spring-wind
    dog-rose.

Dancelocks lopped to the stubble by slums
She scrabbles in refuse, can't kiss or sing
But thrashes on mattresses straddled by starvelings
Smart smirking upstarts who gather in white heads

Clusters on city flesh . . .

The desert where the rats parade
The dead place where they turn the dust like gold or water
        under painted nails
Is built of concrete, made by men whose glib illiteracy
        fits them well to shape sterility from my love's
        numb womb.

Four towers, a bridge, a traffic-ditch designed in three
        greys with restraint.
Droning tin bees scorch across the bridge in two lines.
Four lines pass beneath, the right hand lane at 70 or 80.
After scratching one another's genitals the rats parade
        along the traffic ways,
In a clear light, in the scum of an apricot sun.

My face is labyrinth. A tall boy cleverly disguised as pain
Goes lunging drunk from ear to optic nerve,
Then falls, a toppled tower to splutter vomit where
        my teeth are rooted.
Where he lies his grey brow measures time relentlessly, a
        clock-face in the bedroom gloom.
Ticking multiplies tattoos of gibberish
Morse tictac rattles from the wardrobe near the
        window,
Love scratches at the bottom of the door.

Another drunk boy follows me across the overpass.
The traffic whines like dentists' spinning drills
        whose waterjets won't wash down pain.
He shouts blunt ridicule and giggles, tossing stones and
        dogshit.

Dysentery has crept like poisoned veins
Between the laceholes of his left boot.

Everyone joins his ridicule but
No-one really knows the reason for his flung contempt
Except my rodent love who hoards her memories of secret
grapplings like magpies snap cheap glass,
Cheap fucks that flash and tinkle, dance and smash,
Hordes them in a rusty fridge and melts them in a kiln
of menstrual anxieties.

A third boy, reads the architecture, knows my face,
Jumps suddenly like falcondrop from bridge to motorway.
The ambulance man clips a mask of black wire on a head
as green as churchlight.
Held together thus the smashed bones give me back an
image of myself,
An emulation carried out in death with detailed understanding.

Behind the Pack Horse where we had taken refuge, me with no understanding, she and Pete sharing the particular insights of alienation, is a yard with a shithouse in it arid in this shithouse some of the apprentices of the patriarchs dwell, snickering shaven grommets, licking dirty lingers, harbouring tears. It is the usual high rectangular cell with no lock, the erosion of years of drunken impatience scored into the wood around the place where the lock should he. Inside there is no hole, no bucket. The floor is concreted over. On the door white paint says PLEASE USE THE LEFT HAND CORNER. People have in fact used the left-hand corner of the cubicle rather than the other toilet in the left-hand corner of the yard. A patina of rural mould has formed on some of the droppings. Some are recent and loose, with the hot ginger colour marking the faeces of regular Tetley's drinkers. There are bright decorations of paper and four finger tracks across the whitewashed brick wall.

Beyond the yard is the mangy hillside where two prefabs still stood. Where the incarceration took place.

I wanted to extend love to victims.

I wanted to conjoin the decay that had been made of them.

“Bourgeois romantic shyite,” said Pete in his Hunslett accent. “If you ’ad any understandin’ of all that you’d just want out.” — An attitude that was nothing like the appropriate revenge he exacted, squatted with his keks round his ankles on the grandiose steps of Leeds Town Hall.

He crashed the rusting fridge against the cupboard door. There was a smell of bicycle oil, stale cooking fat, strong tobacco.

On the fridge he stacked the broken chair, on that the three-legged table. An hour he was gone while the children filed by; heads cropped, legs as crooked as the wrought iron of the mill-gate. The matron’s hand raked across their skulls. The overseer cut cheese and thrust it into their chewed fingers. Murder splintered like smashed pint glasses in their wounded proclivities.

The opencast throats of the Pennine saints,
Their hats crustaceous, armoured faces turtle-gaping
Sea-food, coral-mould made into fossil-fruit
To crown the rock-formations, massed and buttressed —
Pince-nez, powder, rouge and millstone grit —
The throats dry, toothless, worked to the last wagon
By the long-swung picks, intrusive face-fuck probing,
Antiquated coal-kings.

Scraps of shoddy cling to the gums.
Fragments of the Spenborough Guardian litter the wispy
        beards surrounding.

From the throats the anthems rise
Like smoke from Meadow Bottoms, milldam gasses, fumes from
        organ chords, the rising pipes like angel raiment,

fluted.
Flute and clavichord and pastorale,
The gaunt archangels risen from the pitheads, rampant over
millstacks, sounding out a sampler,
Woven panorama of the heavenly dale.
Pigeons turn to doves and doves to flocks of seraphim.
The purple heather takes the stately stature of a purple robe,
A garden draped with velvet, hung with lilac and laburnum.
Evergreens are Heavenly Father stretching charitable palms
to barefoot mill-apprentice masses.

Humanity in such a place is a cavalcade of Barnardo orphans
Along the rolled swales, under Lebanon cedars,
Summoned by the promise in thunderous alleluias reaching
out beyond Messiah.
Wide-eyed, meek and pure at heart, saved by death and the
chapel choir
From the black delight of ever living.

Ditchcliffe, ambulant cadaver. Orphan heart-housed, heaven's
promise priest-broke daily in his
Tin-can terrier frightened eyes.

Ditchcliffe, detention room — ashes served are insufficient
mouth-mould for his burlesque penitence.
Ditchcliffe, trough of sorry, where, with, spikes and droppers,
dirty knives and Christmas fires, he flesh-fouls,
festers faster, shows the snow-flock in his
Sunday-soul concealed.
Ditchcliffe, rat. Fast throat attack on any mortal missing
immortality. Knacker-knives for living lacking
angel-feathers.
Ditchcliffe shit-bath, cut cock crowing for confessions

from the aldermen of mediocrity.

Ditchcliffe pines for the hymn, howls for the pastoral pines,
pisses on slagpiles, shags pissheads passed
paralytic through his cold bar-parlour,
Searches for seraphim where bread-and-money-hungers lunch
on love, starvation painted red.

Ditchcliffe dewborn ricketshabe rolled once in meadows,
ripped away, breast gone, lovelips' toothless
lack, fellatio feathered milk: "Don't leave me."

The hillside coalthroats fed him on the lies that made, in
turn, their music fat.
Chains of generations eating lies, then farting horns of
high salvation,
Excreting shitless cherubim devoid of arse or armpit.
Lies: "Cobwebs of relationships called commerce first,
philosophy second, lastly love
"Are earth's transactions screening off the plains of
light.
"Vaginal convulsion preclusion merely, an orgasm labyrinth-
handicap, mothermaze.
"The thing you are," the lie maintains/ordains, "Can never
attain the thing you want.
"Onus of love is estranged from anus of the loved.
"Living's loss. Lapse into flight."

Spilled splinters chewed in a tongue's convulsion.
The mad-dog authenticities break like promises in yellow.
Overhead light on the mess, on the cut-tongue's spillage.
Tears and the hangdog eyes of "Why?"
Knobflash glitter "Not a very pretty thing . . ."

"Why does he have to abuse himself? Why can't he just
    read poems?"
It's a Long Way To Tipperary — pacing it out —
It's a long way back to the pre-pain pastures.
Goodbye Piccadilly dope-deals, Leicester Square toodle-oo
To trombones. The road back's paved with glass, splashed
    gestures.
Each horizon unfolds the black undulations of another
    patriarchal brow, nothing more cleansing than
    Sunday rain.

Onion the peeled child, cut cropped skull, dropped unkissed from a crotch in Quarry Hill, denuded for nits, registered NB, hammertoes cold on the cobbles, on the prefab linoleum, filed through my dark cupboard till Pete Waterdale returned. And all that had been two years before.

This afternoon Rose and Pete had stood at the remaining garden gate of the remaining cabin, ice-cold — (Rose: "The cold, the thing, the death, stayed with me all evening. I took it home with me. 'You're cold,' said June as soon as I came in.") — "Come out! Come out!" But I knew that a previous initiation had insulated me against the shaven apprentices, against Onion and Ditchcliffe, against the death, against a pitch of humiliation so deep its denial of all warmth constituted a presence as solid as a wall to my lover and my friend.

A child's pink blanket.

A smear of brown as thick as toffee across the pink fluff.

"Look Pete," I said. Pete who, for the hell of it one drunk day had eaten the dressing off Dick Ward's suppurating cheek, who had on another occasion picked a chunk of dirt out of the gutter and licked it, grinning: "No, that's not shyite . . ." — *that* Pete coughed up a pale green fluid only slightly more deeply coloured than his bloodless face.

"She practices witchcraft. Should hear her rowing with her husband, the landlord. When the art students performed their happenings in the upper room she was afraid. She thought it was magic."

Her Moira Hindley axe-blade of a face staring us blankly into silence.

"I'm going back," I said, "I want to feel it." But I was sheathed in joy. My love of the strangeness was my love of my immunity. Back in the asbestos cabin I recognised the stiff smear as a dead cat and the small ball of the same substance lying a foot or two away as the cat's head. Dirt. Humiliation. Torture.

My cleansing role demanded fire but wallpaper stripped off the walls wouldn't catch light. The children, who, curiously knowing, leaped outside the window of the room where the dead cat lay, jeered. Nonetheless I was inviolable and healing. The Dambank waterfall spread a soft wing of light. There was warmth in the icy poltergeist stillness. Cruelty, the fusion of humiliation and wronged energy in dirt, in money, was disarmed.

"You don't understand," said Rose. "It wasn't like that. It was to do with isolation."

There is no isolation. I walk in the houses of dead men's heads. Unborn children nestle asleep in my imagination. The same light illuminates all orgasm. I carry a knowledge of uniting energy with me as I feel that same force use me, driving me through the poetic implications of a hundred other times.

Two hundred miles to the south Jack Roberts turned his Triumph Spitfire off the motorway and headed for Ely. His wife was waiting at their Suffolk house with whisky and cold food. The doors of the Airebridge Pump Rooms were locked securely against the cooling heat of the evening.

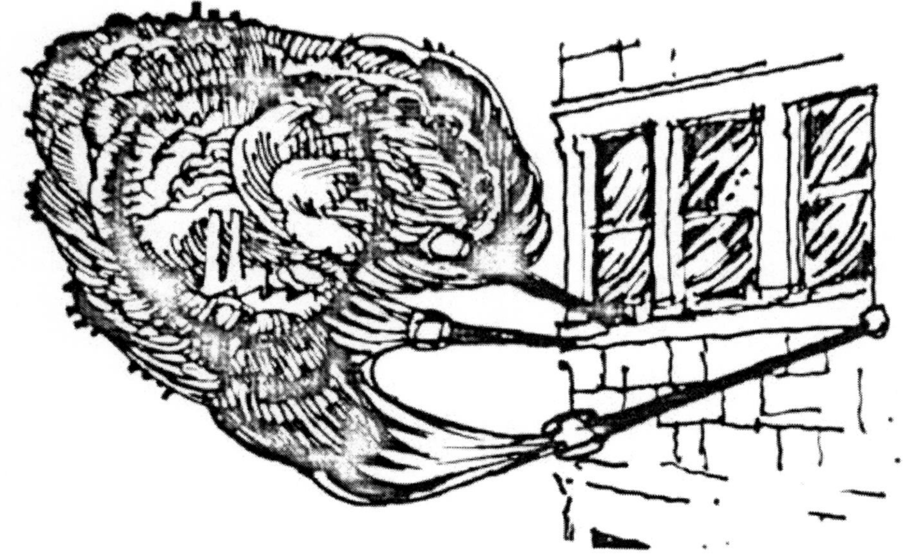

EIGHTEEN

25th May 1975. Ward Five, Bradford Royal Infirmary.

Three forms then.

1. The surviving weatherbag derives its form from the sun. The sun emerges over a distant ridge. Its rays reach the Bradford Royal Infirmary in a system of arcs which suggest a bladder, an oval ball with the bay windows of the Ward Five Television Lounge at one end and the sun a metal stud at the other end. This morning, with the rain mist heavy over the valley, the bladder, which seems so permanent in explosive warm May weather that it must surely be fastened by powerful anchoring devices to the Infirmary facade, has gone completely, the ribs the sun's rays form dissolved in damp birth-shrouds.

2. The shore of death at which it becomes plain, here among the dying and the very old, we all made a sandcastle or two from the point of birth.

The sudden-ness and irrefutability of spring tides. The depth of the obscurity and the way in which the boundlessness of spring weather illuminates the boundlessness of that obscurity's possibilities.
3. The trajectory of a dream which is a descent from the limb' of a soured affair to a point at which death's breath can be smelt. What better metaphor for limbs than the passive horizontal of the wheeled stretcher travelling the corridor as soundlessly as a bicycle? What deeper descent than that amiable lethargy spread through the flesh from an arseful of opium?

And suddenly no drift to death, the ocean not as the mother's vagina warmly lapping me home, but a drop, when the throat catheter drops from my mouth by accident and I am wrenched from my detached, dreamed picture of my own open flank, of prised Out rib, wedge-parted bones like the bone lips of some secretly contained mythic reptile — wrenched from that dispassionate position the correspondent to the *Psychic News* calls your astral eye — hauled away and dropped by No Breath. Drowning boy's struggle, growing pain (ice cold) at the vast wound with the grinning ribs even as self-appropriation dispels anaesthetics, forces tiny quantities of air into lungs that are — painful? Cold. *That are cold.* Can't have self but that pain returns. Can't hurt in abnegation. Into dark, into the smudge of rain at the sea's horizon, and slowly out. The trajectory climbs, the wound heals and, as blood and clarity, as pleasure, other people, love and fun come welling drop by drop, day by day into the flesh, that bladder, the true model for the weatherbag (so the contents of spring, this messy mellow joying merge with contents of the body) comes to full colour and dark warm rainy motherlove from which (the day from winternight) it all swims (survivors — oil in their hair — tattered shirts) becomes the same as that for which it is the source. Trajectory complete. Dark warmth the root of noonday ecstasy. The face of death the edge of pain and thus the very name of living.

TEETH

Chapter One

"Like that hotel in Scarborough," said Hugh.

"The gulls," said Fenella. "Birds below you. Still flying."

The house was behind them. The cliffs edge was a foot from their toes. Birds wheeled against the breaker music, the toss and withdrawal, the idle wastage of the sea's motion.

"Amazing," said Hugh. He cupped a hand around his Zippo, exhaled through his clenched back teeth. From the corner of her eye she enjoyed the way the wind took his thread of tobacco smoke and stretched it, playful.

"This room. For the functions. Breakfast. Strip the fucking tables down and reset them for lunch. Lunch. Reset for dinner. Dinner. Silver cruets. Coy play with the silver bucket for the poor sods who ordered the Blue Nun. Regular as clockwork. Day in, day-fucking-out, until — half past two a.m., after the sing-along to the electric keyboard, after the tables had been pushed back for the hokey cokey and the conga-chain, then put in place again and reset for breakfast, twenty sixth of a very wet August, whoops, the earth falls from the foundations, little new blocks of the repaired parquet go tumbling down in the clay, the sand, and the Vernon Ward duck prints are smiling out over an uncaring moon-shot fucking sea."

"I wish you wouldn't swear in lovely places like this," she said. The wind that twisted his cigarette smoke around its aimless fingers was dancing fingertip-delicate over her ribs, her diaphragm, her shallow breasts, teasing them into that familiar weeping want.

"I wish you didn't mind," he said.

"Well, I'm sorry, I do. I'm posh and I can't help it. What are you burbling on about anyway?"

"The hotel in Scarborough. Nice family house on the rot-riddled cliffs, catering for old people mostly, ghastly food and blissful peace, suddenly, dead of night, croquet lawn, back terrace and rear elevation go clump into the sea. Whoosh. Just like that."

"But the sea's yards from this house."

"Oh, I wasn't talking about this house, Nelly. I was talking about the domestic, agrarian masterwork of the pasture."

"Times progress," she sighed.

"Fucking hell," he whispered to himself in his smoky lungs. Then said: "All those posters, all those years ago. Do You Want The Hun To Take All This? Tommy Atkins, rifle on one shoulder extends the opposite arm to indicate the Devonian eiderdown. Which. Unfortunately. Is sliding into the sea."

"But Hugh, it's still beautiful, let's buy it. If Sergeant Pepper gets a prize at Cannes, that is. Let's, it's so beautiful here."

He flicked half a Gauloise out over the backs of the wheeling gulls; immediately lit another. "Nature recks not the beauty of lovely things. Bestows it, then shits all over it."

"Yeah, yeah," she said, the wind still cooling her stiff nipples. "I've heard it before, darling. Just once or twice. Let's go to Kingsbridge and get the keys. There's no harm in looking, is there?"

They walked back along the cliffs to Hope Cove. The car was parked in front of the pub. Breakers heaving about like angry sleepless things, shaking the bright afternoon off their effervescing shoulders, spitting loose gobbed at the cobbles. She had danced ahead, exhilarated, wanting to distance herself from his sour appraisal of the sun-fucked world. At the same time wanting to be visible to him, wanting to give him some remaining pleasure from how her limbs were, how her skin was, how the spaces and the changes in the spaces around and between her parts were just as eloquent of her yearning generosity as the slim amber volumes of her flesh. Now he saw her in the car park below him as he bumped down the cliff path. She leaned both bare forearms on the car roof as she watched him descend and he loved her so helplessly he had to stop a great gobbet of weeping in his mouth like stopping a belch at a formal dinner, and the raw physical pain of this retention wore back into his body, punishing him for wasting time on a relationship he had long ago consigned to the mental lockup where damaged feelings must be confined until such time as they mend.

She snuggled up to his elbow as he drove the swooping, buckling route to Kingsbridge, rubbing her nose into the grazed shoulder of his twenty year old leather jacket. She moved her legs as though to let the electricity of their sensations fly like thin smoke in the car's wake.

Chapter Two

He waited in the car while she went into the Prudential for the key. She came out following a little man with hair so formally and perfectly cut it looked like a toupée. He stepped briskly around the bonnet of the car as though the car were in motion and smiled ingratiatingly through the driving window until Hugh lowered it. Through the windscreen Hugh could see his wife, her head tilted to allow hair to fall over eyes wet with laughter. She held the elbow of her right arm in her left palm. The knuckles of her right hand masked her giggling lips.

"Morning, Mr. Finch," said the man. "My name's Prendergast. I should be 'appy to show you Robinson's, sir, but I can't allow you to 'ave the key and go round unaccompanied. Against the owner's will, I'm afraid."

"But the owner's dead, isn't he?" said Hugh.

"Yes sir. 'At's the reason we gotta abide by 'is will, y'see, sir." Prendergast allowed a hint of patient humour to grace his tactful statement of the obvious.

"What I was thinking, Mr. Finch," he went on. "Seems silly taking two cars. If you and Mrs. Finch would like to step into my vehicle . . ."

Hugh could not place his irritation exactly. Briefly he wanted to scrub the whole thing. Sergeant Pepper's Last Stand had not yet won an award. It had not — he suddenly looked absurdly at his watch — it had not yet been shown, but it might be in the process of rejection right now. And should he really give any more than lip service to Fenella's dream that all would be healed with a few gull droppings and the music of the deep? But Fenella had already wandered to the passenger door of Mr. Prendergast's Metro and was shaking her shoulders in a kind of pouting eagerness.

"Yes, yes, of course," said Hugh. He got out of the Porsche, locked it and followed Prendergast to the Metro.

"Two hundred and fifty thousand pounds, Mr. Finch," said Prendergast, "but I don't think I'm betraying the wishes of the deceased too drastically if I let it be known 'ere and now that you wouldn't be entirely in the land of fancy if you asked for a few bob to be knocked off that."

"With whom does the decision last if the owners are dead?"

"Solicitors, sir. Barton and Barton of Totnes. As they represent the next of kin and — er — well we'll talk about the complications later."

"It's not been shifting too readily then?"

"More 'n two year now, sir, since the old Major died."

"Oh, it belonged to a soldier."

"You're not from around here, sir? I can tell that, sir, 'cos if you was you wouldn't be askin' about Major Robinson, sir. Oh no, 'e was well regarded, sir. Pop'lar chap, sir. Very. Will you be wantin' the furnishings, sir?"

"Oh, it's still furnished?"

"All 'is stuff there, sir, as it was the day 'e dropped."

"Bit of a time-warp?" said Hugh Finch.

"The Major, sir? No sir. Nothing was warped about Major Robinson. Straight as a dye, sir."

Hugh winced mildly and watched the hedgerows lurch past the side windows of the Metro. Fenella bit her thumb and Hugh smiled gently when he saw her shoulders shaking.

Chapter Three

Robinson's was bigger than either of them had hoped. Six rooms on each of the floors and two huge attic rooms under the roof and a cellar with a herringbone brick floor. The interconnecting hallways and landing were meandering and narrow except where they opened out onto spaces at the stairheads where large furnishings were possible. Vast, caved-in settees in leather or threadbare velvet. Foxes disembowelling pheasants in their dim glass boxes. A golden eagle with the eye of a telepathic mother suspended from vertical wings, her talons hooked cleverly into the batwing skin of a well-dead stoat.

"Predatory," said Hugh, puffing to the stairhead. He didn't whisper. Said it loud and clear, a cosmopolitan unfettered by provincial niceties.

"Mmmm," shuddered Fenella, a child in a cave.

Major Robinson had won his commission for outstanding services at the age of nineteen during the final stages of the First World War. He was distinguished to be the first officer in the South Devon Light Infantry to achieve the rank of Major at that age.

Subsequently, after a brief period as Liberal MP for Salcombe, he had gone into the Foreign Office and had spent ten years as the British Ambassador in Milan. A close friend of D'Annunzio about whom he spoke as though recalling a loveable idiot, he treated the Fascists as an ever-amusing freak-show until they imprisoned him on the outbreak of war in 1939 and cut off one of his testicles. He escaped to Switzerland in a vat of Valpolicella suffering a drying and discoloration of the skin which lasted the rest of his life. He spent the war in the Ministry of Information, was decorated for acts of brilliance which, even at the time of his death, could not be disclosed, ran, unsuccessfully, as Labour candidate for Kingsbridge South, then retired on a modest pension to Upper Hope Farm which became known as Robinson's. His wife was a fragile, fugitive spirit called Reny. She started hearing the voices of Armada survivors drifting up from the foot of the cliff in the mid-fifties. Encouraged in this awareness by the Totnes Society for Psychic Inquiry and the vicar of Salcombee, she devoted her days to wandering along the cliff edge talking to them. She did this in all weathers and accrued some credibility to her claims by developing fluent Spanish in a remarkably short time. Major Robinson loved her to the end, whacking tables with walking sticks whenever her sanity was called into question, covering her with bouquets of prickly roses whenever he drove his battered Bentley home from the smoky fleshpots of Ivybridge. Everywhere Fenella found in the old house the detritus of two warm and crazy personalities. The furniture was the middle-class fake Jacobean of the 1930's suburbs, all wood stained and cursorily carved, all doors paneled, some fluted. There were Victorian heirlooms but not many, and there was an Art Deco wardrobe rivalling the Reichstag in its splendour.

The lounge and dining room downstairs were panelled although Mr. Prendergast muttered that a structural survey was much to be advised and that the panels, though charming, may have to be replaced. Hanging over them were vast seascapes by forgotten academicians, some family portraits including one which made Hetty look like Zelda Fitzgerald, a few swords, then the heads of a snooty rhino and three or four foxes.

Everywhere were mementoes of the Italian years. Alpine jackets, blouses, headgear displayed along the corridors and in the bedrooms. Towers of stuffed plovers. Crossbows. Cuckoo clocks. A peasant crucifix. An angled screen decorated with wine labels. A sackbut. Umpteen views of Lake Nemo and the Bay of Naples, some done in luminous inks on glass. A decorated saddle. A crudely painted chalice and, finally, under a tiny glass dome below the wall display of Major Robinson's medal, the right big toe of Saint Eloïse.

"It's perfect," said Fenella, moving to the bay window in the main bedroom. "We mustn't change a thing. Who's that woman?"

"What woman?"

"That woman there, in the garden."

"I can't see her," said Hugh. "Where? Oh. Oh yes."

Chapter Four

The gardens at Robinson's had been adopted from the farmyards. Lawns across the stable yard. Middens and piggeries turned into bowers and byres, flanked with hollyhocks. The walled vegetable garden at the back was the way it had always been. An acre spanned with orange eighteenth century local brick, twelve feet high. It was dug and planted, sticks in place for peas, runner beans and broad beans. Paths were free of weeds, edged in oval beach pebbles. Apple trees, now stuttering into blossom-splendour, stood in the angles of the paths as they branched off, left and right between the vegetable beds. Balls of white petals, pink rimmed, thrust a stubborn way to the light between clusters of rough, gummy green leaves.

The woman was clearly visible, bent over the geranium beds that ran along the foot of the North Wall. She was vast. The silence and the strangeness of her unexplained presence made a giant of her but, disregarding this illusion, she was still vast, a young, nervy, febrile woman well over six feet tall.

She had wide shoulders under a woollen jumper that would have been loose fitting on a girl of normal size. Her shoulderblades stretched the fabric from ridge to ridge when she bent to prod the red earth with her trowel. In bending her spine ran straight and steep from the nape of her neck to the small of her back, then it rose into a majestic arching to soar above her tilted pelvis, whose rim retained the elastic circle of her skirt-waist, before curving down to the groove where her coccyx was slotted between the buttocks of a lean beast. When she straightened, to ease her back, her breasts, which were proportionately small, were well spaced, at least a full flat hand's width on the thorax between them. The weft of the jumper was separated between the nipples by their weight, showing tiny diamonds of discoloured woollen vest.

When she crouched to root at the weeds with long purposeful fingers, her legs, jack-knifed under her, swung between their resting position with the easy pleasantry of articulated cranes, knees with the weighty authority of beast-bones brushing the now pendulant breasts, calves slanting hack to from the weathered dusty ankles which socketed into huge flat feet. Even from the bedroom window Hugh and Fenella Finch could see how her toes in their espadrilles spread to take her turning weight more finely.

She looked up, appearing not to have focused on them, looked back to her geranium bed. "She can't see us," murmured Hugh. "The window is full of reflected sun and cloud from down there."

"Perhaps she doesn't want to see us," said Fenella. "She's beautiful."

"Ah," said Mr. Prendergast, joining them in the bay. "You've seen Voisigna."

"Who?" said Hugh.

"Voisigna. Voisigna Devauden."

"How d'you spell it?" asked Hugh. Prendergast spelled it.

"She was taken from the local authorities by the Major as gardener and housekeeper when she was fifteen. She and her um . . . ," Prendergast coughed lightly into a grubby ball of tissue which he returned to his trouser pocket leaving the triangle of handkerchief in the breast pocket of his Rotarian blazer untouched . . . "her daughter".

A flutter of sympathy rose and dispersed from Fenella's throat. "Mrs. Robinson gave her the name. She couldn't remember her own, it seems. She was with them fifteen years, almost a daughter to them. They couldn't — it was thought inadvisable for Mr. and Mrs. Robinson to have children. She er, I fear, is the only problem and is the main reason why you may well get a reduction."

"Go on," said Hugh. He reached for his Gauloise. Fenella caught the aggression kindling in him again.

"Oh Hugh," she breathed. "Please don't . . . Don't let it..." then lamely, "make any difference."

Hugh snapped his Zippo. "Go on," he said. "What's the problem?"

"Well none really. Not necessarily. Voisigna was always housed in the old tied cottage of the farm — lies just beyond the far wall of the garden, sir. And when the Major died he left it to her. The whole free'old of the cottage, sir. Smack in the middle of the Robinson's grounds. Also left her rights to garden produce and a reasonable allowance for life. Also, sir, and this is currently being questioned in order to facilitate the er . . ." He coughed again, "impeded sale — made her a trustee. A main trustee."

"Would she continue to keep the garden?" asked Hugh.

"Idle sod," said Fenella through her teeth.

"You try and stop her," smiled Mr. Prendergast.

"How much would she need to be paid?" asked Hugh.

"Not a lot," Prendergast sang down his ferret's nose. "Bucket of spuds maybe."

"I see," said Hugh. "And we make our offer to her?"

"Her daughter," said Prendergast, "would be the only beneficiary of the sale."

"Weird," said Hugh.

"Somewhat unusual, sir," said Prendergast.

"Oh," said Fenella.

A cloud like a bruise had gusted momentarily across the shrill April sun. As though sensing that this passing chill had rendered the bedroom window transparent Voisigna Devauden looked up again. She had the face of a full-grown doe. All its lines plunged steeply from a severe black hairline to the tip of a prow of a nose; to the frontal cup of the thick upper lip on a mouth so narrow it looked permanently pursued to kiss or spit; to the tip of a chin that was the pointed intersection of two equine flanks of jawbone. All this pride set on a pedestal of a neck in which the dip of the throat was the imprint of a man's heel. Her eyes locked with

Fenella's who attempted an uncertain wave. Voisigna neither waved, nor smiled, but as the sun re-emerged from behind its bruise, her grey eyes deepened in their sudden shade to the black of an underground lake.

Chapter Five

If Sergeant Pepper's Last Stand hadn't gone off on the Manson Theme, Hugh and Fenella Finch might have maintained a continuum of modestly clouded bliss all their lives.

Sergeant Pepper's Last Stand, aka Pepper's Last, aka Sergeant Pepper's Last, aka Pepper, aka Sergeant Pepper started with a young and irritating scriptwriter called Jason Pelt coming up with a farce in which the Beatles (Lennon was still unshot at this time) fought off the punk Sioux.

That was a long time ago. A million quid and five scriptwriters later it had turned into a fantasy about the rock culture with music by Ron Geesin and miles of expensively procured documentary material including a snuff movie in which Charles Manson was apocryphally present.

Hugh Finch loathed Abroad. This was largely because his first success, Mata Hari And The Egg, involved sustained dysentery in cultures least equipped to accommodate an Englishman so afflicted. Los Angeles was definitely Abroad to Hugh Finch. He was heterosexual; he hated drugs; he loathed hot sun; cold beer to him was simply not beer, but most of all he detested vanity, status and wealth. Whilst in L.A. he found a waterside slum where everybody was too old and too drunk to care whether or not they were talking to a prize-winning movie director. There he passed his leisure hours.

Fenella's bit of a fling, a Rap Radio DJ called Squit Lizard, was lifting his right foot to slot it into the right leg of his imitation-leather trousers when Hugh Finch came unexpectedly home.

Squit, a harmless lad who was surely among thousands who, passing Fenella Finch in street or corridor, had hungered for her sinewy favours, apologised with much wristy, palms-out, hand-language. Hugh punched Fenella, cried and snotted all over her breasts. Whatever their recent abuse they retained the healing beauty of fresh blossomed primroses. All might have been resolved in a reconciliatory fuck even then had Fenella not declared herself pregnant, almost certainly by Squit, a month later.

Tenderness and ordinary middle class decency demanded an expensive Harley Street abortion. Biological reaction and the lingering tinge of Liverpudlian machismo killed marital sex between Hugh and Fenella as dead as the Social Charter.

Hugh disappeared into the Pinewood cutting rooms for six months. Pepper came out for a preview. There was a lot of talk. Hugh was on the *Late Show*. There were interviews in *The Face, Sight and Sound* and the *Independent Sunday Review*. Fenella, who knew what all naughty girls know, that a cunt is no more sacred than a thumb or an ear, waited for her husband's hurt to pass. Someone offered a cottage in Salcombe where she continued to wait patiently for another four weeks while Pepper went to Cannes and Hugh bluntly refused to go with it. They lingered late in bed but Hugh's libido stayed flat. They got drunk every day but got fed up with it after two nasty rows that had the neighbours thumping the wall. In the last week they got in the car and took to exploring. They found Robinson's.

It took them a month to buy it. Pepper did get an award. It opened in London to a massive accolade. The bucks rolled and it seemed mean to haggle with Voisigna Devauden about prices. They bought it, signed the contract-exchange in Totnes and drove straight to Hope Cove. "Gotta get a four-wheel drive," said Hugh. "And open up the track again. I'm not climbing the hill every fucking day."

Fenella had found some fine Australian Chardonnay in Kingsbridge. After salami, bread, fruit and about three bottles of the wine they turned off the dim kitchen bulb and moved out to watch a young moon bounce off the sea. A strip of silver a sliver below the horizon glittered fish scales, and light from the unseen beach threw the cliff's serrated edge into dark relief.

Hugh sprawled back on a broken wicker chair. His wife arranged her angles, her concavities and her cautious peaks of flesh and bone with spontaneous ease on the balcony floor-tiles not far from his feet. The taste of her, the saline, marine tides of her hauled all the latent colours out of the moon. The moan that arched her wiry back and threw her cunt more firmly around his jaw was an echo from the times before the pain.

It was slow. He failed twice, some trigger in his kicked brain closing a safety-valve to protect a pride which he and she knew they must discard.

Eventually it was complete and it was good. They fell asleep still knotted into one another's bodies and then separated for deeper dreaming. In the midst of this Fenella's voice. Its clarity sounded out with the same bald obtuseness as Hugh's "Predatory." The stuffed foxes, the golden eagle, had lost their savage edge. In one drunken evening they had become the jetsam of a lost rural innocence, bric-a-brac of a kinder time. But now Fenella's voice rose above the saturated bower of her contentment. "Hugh," it said, that first syllable like a pebble in the room's unlit murk, a round clean stone syllable, sea sculptured, devoid of any possible ambiguity. "We're not alone."

They lay in a bed that was more distinct than a four-poster would have been. During their love making its creakings, its sighs, deep-throated uterine wheezings had echoed the unfathomable relief that scored an undertone to Fenella's pleasure-gasps; had recalled, in Hugh's mind anyway, the knockings and strainings of ship's timbers, slavers overloaded at a tropical mooring weeping in their wooden bones for the darkness of their trade. The whole deck swung and tilted as though shifted by uneasy waters. Its bedhead, a veritable palace-gate of rococo iron scrolls, heraldic images, panels of feldspar and nacre, tilted like a mainsail. Now, in the silence of preserved gone-time in that room from whose deep lattice the moon had gone, having sailed round to the front side of the house, Fenella's sentence remained in the ear, not an echo but the ineradicable stamp of an entity so flat, separate and lucid amongst those blurred masses.

"What the fuck you talking about?" asked Hugh.

"Shh!" said Fenella.

"What d'you fucking mean? I was fast asleep there."

"Listen," said Fenella. "Somebody's here. In here. With us. Watching us."

"Bol . . . ," he started, but her hand on his lips, a hand still steeped in their salts, those clever undeluded fingers loved, came back to him again, kept the silence and somewhere in that vocabulary of tainted blacks, those unlit walls, those weighty drapes, somewhere between the stained furniture and the mirrors, the picture glasses seeking light that wasn't there to give reflection, there was something not audibly breathing, something not any shape or colour, even odour, distinguishable from the rest, but something warm, something warmer than any inanimate thing.

"It's . . . is it . . . an animal?" he said. "Where's the fucking light? Hello? Anybody there? Can we help?"

She silenced him again with that respected hand. "Don't — don't bruise her."

"Bruise her? I never fucking tou . . ."

"Shh."

They lay and then as some forgotten light the day and the moon had left behind along the sea's distant skyline turned some darks to greys, the darkest bulk in their chamber could be suspected to be no more than an inch beyond the soles of their vertical feet. Something tall where there was no tall furnishing. Something tall where there was no furnishing of any kind. No drape. No curtain hung. No dark upright. And it, he, she, was watching them.

And he she, it, had been there for hours. Only by self mesmerised long-standing can such a stillness be achieved. Then, softer in the silent air than the movement of an insect's tiny wing, breath. A gentle exhalation.

"Is anything wrong?" asked Fenella, sitting up, as oblivious of her nakedness as a child. "Have you come for help? Is it your daughter?"

The shadow moved, placed now by the sound of the door handle, the swinging open of the door, the softest patter of bare feet on the old landing carpet. Fenella was after her. "Please — please come back. We'll help. We really will . . . Aaargh!"

Hugh was out of bed now, groping through hangover, post-coital languor, now through unfocussed unease, for the unfamiliar situation of the old brass light switch.

The bedroom sat in its dim overhead glare, completely unaltered by whom, or whatever had been there. Before he could find the landing light or follow the rectangle of bedroom light cast through the door onto the landing carpet Fenella had returned, hopping expertly on the toe of one slim leg.

"Look, I think it's . . . Yes, it is. It's shit. Someone's shat on the stairs."

"Oh come on," said Hugh.

"Smell it then."

"Must be a dog. Somebody's dog."

She shook her head. "Dogs," she said, "don't use tissues to clean themselves."

Chapter Six

The door in the far wall of the garden was pointed like a church arch. It was heavy. Wet rot was visible where the paint had peeled.

It swung into the garden. Fenella Finch eased her body that understood all narrow spaces, that never collided, that only caressed or embraced, round the edge of the door into the shadowed space beyond.

It was cooler beyond the wall. There was a density of evergreens so that the path was carpeted in pine needles; the grass was sparse and virulent. The tied cottage was red-brick, had once been thatched, was now roofed in corrugated iron that had been painted a dull pink. The little porch on the central door also had a pink tin roof.

There was a window on either side of the porch. There were two dormer windows, part of the cottage's original design. Fenella called "Hello?" Then Fenella called "Coo-ee?". Nothing was watching her but trees and the cottage's little shiny eyes. She approached the door. As she did so her nostrils filled with an odour she'd nearly forgotten. Long ago she had been sent to stay with an aunt in Ireland, a distant relative. Her mother, who had always promised this, finally bought the ticket. The aunt lived in one wing of a derelict mansion in County Limerick. Upstairs, in a room not much bigger than a wardrobe, she kept her bedridden mother. This mother was too weak to move. The aunt was too weak to lift her. Cleanliness was not problematic. It was impossible. The old mother stank of old woman because that was what she was. As Fenella Finch stepped cautiously into the porch of the tied cottage she smelled the recognisable smell of very old unwashed people. It was not located in a corner, in a cupboard, in drapery, in the upholstery of a chair. It was an odour saturated into the fabric of the building: between the vertical boards of the door: between the flagstones under the threadbare doormat: in the mortar that crumbled between the orange bricks. It had saturated the building like the smell of horses saturates a stable long after the beasts have gone. She knocked.

Walter De La Mare's poem ran idiotically through her brain as no one descended to her. She knocked again. "Tell them I came and nobody answered. That I kept my word" she quoted softly to herself. She backed out from the porch, looked first to one window, then to the next. Dirty curtains with barely legible floral patterns hung unbudging. There was a broken pane.

She started to leave, then went back to look through the window to the right of the porch. A rusted machine for mixing cattle food stood in the room's centre, dimly lit. Stacked against it were three broken television sets and a broken bicycle. A bundle of newspapers — the Kingsbridge Gazette, she made out — supported a sewing machine. Beyond that the separate items of the pile were undiscernible. What could rust had rusted. What could generate mould had gone green. The cottage, supposed dwelling place of the improbably named Voisigna Devauden was full of nothing but junk and if the strikingly handsome and well-provided young woman lived here, she lived with the lifestyle of a kleptomaniac tramp.

Fenella Finch turned to go, but as she reached the gothic door that led back to the vegetable garden a tiny fragment of brick struck the wall about two feet above her left shoulder. She turned. Nothing could be seen. All and everything was still.

"Ah shit," she said. "This is crazy."

Chapter Seven

It took five hours at 80 to get back to the flat in Parson's Green. How sane and predictable were the traffic jams. How human, how warm were the raucous bald boys with their ear-rings and their swastika tattoos, screaming well-tried, oft-repeated abuse at passing Asians. How English the national dress of the Asians appeared.

"Never mind," said Fenella to Hugh as they flicked across between three late movies, "at least we've — we've started again."

Suddenly Hugh threw his Glenfiddich in the gas-fire where it flared, struck his head in her hair and bawled like a caned seven-year-old. "I am not — we won't . . ." Great gluey words tried to get out of his dysfunctional mouth. She kissed the brine from his face, loving its taste as she loved the flavours of his lovemaking. She dried his eyes with the corner of a cushion.

"We will," she said. "No ghost, midnight incontinent, nor wacky yokel is going to stop our healing. Let's see how watertight that will is. Let's leave her in her cottage in the dark trees until we can sling her out. Let's have proper locks put on that house to which she has no keys."

He was nodding like a reluctantly comforted child, his lips still dithering un-manned, as blind as fishing bait.

"And," she said, "I was wrong. It was pretty and it was weird, but we can't live in the litter of someone else's past. We're not old. You make movies. I write a column. We can't live in spookland even if we want to. I'm going to ring Prendergast. Ask him to do it all so when we go down again that old house will be stripped, replastered, refloored with fitted carpets and clear lights. A sound system with loudspeakers in every room. We'll make that hillside ring with — with — with The Penguin Cafe Orchestra."

Hugh nodded. His manhood came back into him shortly before dawn.

Chapter Eight

"What the fuck's this?" said Hugh. He stood in the white and yellow centre of the flat's kitchenette, his thighs gently bouncing against the edge of the circular plastic breakfast table. Shuffling the mail he bottom-decked the gas bill, an insurance circular, a card from their son, Greg, who was studying in Louvain and found himself looking down on a cheap, white Woolworth's envelope that looked as though it had spent a long time in the handbag of an adolescent or the back pocket of a schoolboy. The stamp was second class and had been torn in the sticking. The name and address were in rain-blotched biro. When he opened it the paper crumbled rather than tore as though the clammy human humidities to which it had been long exposed could never be dried from its fabric.

It contained a single sheet of pink writing paper with a picture of a little woolly dog in the corner, a small girl's birthday correspondence set. In the same biro it said:

'YUO HAVE MADE MI MUM VERY BAD.

SHE IS DYING COZ OF YUO'

"Well, well," said Hugh Finch, holding the limp communication between first and second fingers of his right hand. "The new decorations are getting to Voisigna."

Fenella took the letter. "Oh Christ," she said, "I must get down there."

"You said . . ."

"Oh shit."

They sat nibbling toast in dislocated silence.

"But she's — she's a woman. She's a woman in trouble, Hugh. And eventually if — well if we can't defeat them, well, she's our neighbour. I'm sure we can get over the stage of being seen as invaders."

Hugh killed a Gauloise in the margarine.

"Hugh, will you for fuck's sake stop being such a kid? It might not . . ."

"Oh," said Hugh. "It might not have been. Well who the fuck was it then?"

"Oh, I dunno. Some kid. Some camper. Kid from the pub. Doper from Plymouth. New Age Traveller."

"And how did he, she or it get in?"

"Was the door locked?"

"Didn't you lock it?"

"I thought you had."

"I thought . . ."

"You see?" He went and dressed. "I'm going over to Pinewood," he said. "We'll go down Friday. See what's happening."

Chapter Nine

Cement mixers pattered contentedly like grazing robots.

The foreman, Bert Hawkins, was a big bland man whose gentle, mocking smile could be distancing to the point of hostility.

"Aye. She be comin' perfect," he said. "Bloody good job you 'ad 'er done though. Seven steps we 'ad to replace on the back stair. And 'alf a dozen floorboards. Dry rot. Just got the bugger in time. Joists be fine though. So far."

They paddled through plaster dust from room to room. With all the old furniture and hangings gone the house was a system of chambers singing with clean light.

They mounted the stairs. "Summat a bit weird up 'ere," he said. "Y'see we 'an't put the new locks in because we 'an't got some of the new doors finished."

Hugh and Fenella followed his bulky rocking shoulders into the main bedroom. In vast letters scratched in the plaster it said:

'YUO FUCIN SODS.

YOU CILL MY MUM.'

"Bloody kids," said Hawkins. "Get in everywhere. 'Ad to completely rebuild some o' them old railway stations."

"Have to apologise about this," said Voisigna Devauden. She had silently followed them and stood behind them on the landing. She was a tall and loose shanked presence there in the dusty light-filled empty house, vertical and quietly dignified in the very spot across which she, some he, some other she or some phantom it had fled only a few short weeks ago.

"How do you do?" said Fenella, stepping forward. "It does seem odd that after all these weeks we've never met."

Voisigna Devauden had spoken her apology with her doe's cheek aslant on her wide left shoulder, with her dark gaze averted. Her voice was deep, more Cornish than Devonian in its accent, but only slightly inflected. She stuck out a stiff arm bent back against the angle of the elbow and shook Fenella's hand of light sandalwood firmly.

"Hi. I'm Hugh," said Hugh. She didn't grasp Hugh's offered hand. She allowed her hand to pass swiftly, half-evasively through his. Her main acknowledgement to his self-introduction was to lock his friendly mud-brown eyes in her own slate gaze along a steely eyeline and then, with a subtle blend of old-world country charm and feline irony, she dipped her head in a kind of cranial curtsey.

"I'm Voisigna," she said. "Daft name — Mrs. Hetty, she gave it to me — call me Signa."

"We think it's a lovely name," said Fenella.

"Well," suddenly the still vertical of her figure on the landing tilted into a rural labourer's sideways motion, "must be getting on — meant to, you know, sorry — My Ursula, also, Mrs. Finch, believe she wrote some letter. Look, I — I — I got you some wine. Makes it every year, cowslip, elderflower, one of each. 'Scuse the bottles but that be good wine. Bert says he can skim it over. Ursula, she don't mean no 'arm. You meet 'er, you'll understand, Mrs. Finch. Must get on."

"Have you been ill?" called Fenella.

She turned, stood silent a while, then nodded. And she was gone, descending the stairs erect, the slightly servile tilt of her body left behind in the space of her apology. Arrogance was re-established in her lofty walk out of the front door.

Chapter Ten

"Well it's delicious stuff," said Fenella. She stood exquisite in her shift and pants, sipping the cowslip out of one of the bathroom glasses in the Kings Head Hotel at Ivybridge.

They poured the country liquors into their systems getting languorous on top of the spread of one of the twin beds.

"In," she giggled. "Come on. It's ready. It's like a spring."

They locked into a harmony that still smelled and tasted of summer lanes, of mowing meadows and riverside trees. He turned and turned slowly into his wife, his hurt self-healing a little more with each gyration. Again the sweet sleep. Somewhere in Ivybridge a motorist hooted his horn at a friend and the friend, amiably drunk, called back some affectionate bawdy.

Their bowels did not break 'til the small hours, Hugh first, who vomited whist evacuating, hanging his chin over the basin as he squatted at convulsive stool.

Fenella followed, crouching miserably in the bathtub while the shower washed her faeces and her vomit all around her painted toenails.

Even there, in that wretchedness, the heaving of the muscles of her belly and the streaks of excrement across her lean buttocks touched him as a child might move him in similar movements with a fragile mortality.

"It can't be," he said, dragging pink tissue across his early stubble. "Not on purpose. She doesn't know our circumstances. She can't know what's to be sabotaged."

"We're just not used to it," said Fenella, snivelling. "It might have been the hotel food anyway."

Chapter Eleven

"Greg rang," said Fenella. "He's in England. He's staying with some girl in Gloucester."

"Poor woman," said Hugh Finch. He flicked over a page of the *Independent*.

"Oh, he might have got over that stage by now," said Fenella. "I bet you were pretty messy when you were a student."

"I was not obsessed with order and cleanliness," said Hugh, lighting his second Gauloise. "Neither was I compelled to claim as much personal space as possible by spreading snotty Kleenex, half-read paperbacks, unused condoms and dirty tee-shirts into every corner of whatever building granted me shelter for more than half an hour."

"She won't mind," said Fenella. "I expect she loves him."

"Love," said Hugh, "can be a very terrible thing." He looked up into her cold stare.

"Anyway," she said, "I told him the house was ready and furnished. And he said he might join us the weekend."

"Can't get down 'til Sunday," said Hugh.

"Well, we'll just have to hope he doesn't turn up 'til Sunday night."

Voisigna Devauden had retreated into her coppice behind the wall. She could be glimpsed picking peas or beans and hoeing the beds from which the root crops had been dug. They didn't mention the gastric cataclysm at the King's Head. Neither did they eat the various offerings of vegetables she placed on their back porch. Fenella hid them under the stairs until they dried out a bit and then burnt them in the potbellied stove.

The house was painted, spacious and light with fitted carpets of a warm rust colour throughout and a simple scattering of chairs and tables. A pine bed stood where the galleon had once creaked.

They arrived late on the Sunday having eaten in Kingsbridge. They drank half a bottle of Scotch between them, then hit the sack.

Fenella woke with a shriek. “This bed’s filthy.”

In the dim bedside lamp neither had noticed that a sepia crusty substance had stained the amber undersheet.

“Christ!” shrieked Fenella. She threw back the duvet. “It’s blood.”

“It’s you then,” said Hugh.

“Not for weeks,” said Fenella. “And what the hell’s this?” She fished a double hoop of nylon and elastic from the depth of the bed.

“These are filthy too. That fucking cow has been soiling our bed. She can’t blame this on her daughter.”

She bundled sheet and knickers into a ball and dropped them over the banister into the hall below. They hit the ground with a gentle impact — the sound a giant puffball might make through a sensitive mike.

“Oh my Christ,” shrieked Fenella from the other room where clean bedding was stored. “Somebody’s . . .”

In each room the furniture had been moved into an obtuse position, chairs with their backs towards the room space, their seats towards the wall, tables in corners in dark parts of the room, sometimes on top of one another.

“That idiot builder must have given her a key,” said Fenella, zipping up her denims, throwing a jersey over her head. “This is the fucking showdown.”

Chapter Twelve

The cottage had its usual air of emptiness. Fenella knocked, shouted, kicked the door under the porch.

"Miss Devauden!" she shrieked. Hugh lay on the bed, smoking, wincing, smiling. "Miss Voi-fucking-signa De-fucking-Vauden! I want to talk to you!"

It was as before. The cottage was silent. She went again to the window and looked in, hammering as hard on the glass as the glass would take without breaking. She peered in. What peered out towards her she thought in one fugitive instant to be a monkey. There was a face with saucer eyes, minimal nose, vast upper lip which she had seen in sentimental photographs of marmosets. But marmosets do not wear hair ribbons and marmosets do not wear pinafore dresses and wellingtons.

"Hello," said Fenella, disturbed, not unkindly. "I must speak to your mother."

The door opened and the girl flung a handful of scraps of plaster in Fenella's face. Then she spat.

"You little cow," hissed Fenella. She seized an arm which was covered with long downy hair. "Your mother, where's your mother?"

"She's dead. You killed her."

Once in the house Fenella realised that the girl, although not as tall as her mother, was still pretty tall; but while her mother's limbs were powerful and co-ordinated, this child, this girl, for, seen in proximity she was no child, despite her childish garments, was strung together by an uncaring puppet maker, one arm longer than the other, the breasts under their gingham far too heavy for the puny breadth of the thorax or for the undeveloped brain, the torso short, the legs of ungainly length.

"Ursula," said Fenella, "listen to me. I must see your mummy. Awful things are happening."

Hugh was calling from the back porch of the house. "False alarm. Greg's rung."

Chapter Thirteen

"Have we ever ascertained what happened to our enquiry about the will? Whatever happens I want that cow and her moron out."

"Yes well . . ."

"Yes well, yes well. I don't care if Greg did think fit to have a party in our new — home — and his friends have such foul manners they think they can come on all over the sheet and just leave it . . . I'm not satisfied. There's more here. I want to give that Prendergast a piece of my mind about letting them have the key anyway."

"Yes yes, but just tonight. Why don't we — why don't we invite her over for something to eat? Sort it out. She is sort of distressed. And you were quite unfair to her daughter. And — and — well, it's just possible that it is all just in our own brains, isn't it?"

"All I know is that I came down here for peace and love with you and all we've had is shit and alarum and — and tension because basically we don't know who, how or what she is. Come on, let's go to Kingsbridge. Then to Totnes. See Messers Barton and Barton."

"Barton and Barton tomorrow. I'm going to Kingsbridge to get a chicken, some herbs and some straightforward French wine. You go comfort Ursula or whatever her fucking name is and tell her her mum is invited to dinner. Her too, if she wants."

Fenella met his smiling eyes with a baleful hopelessness. "Yeah yeah. Okay. But Hugh, my love, nothing's getting better and it hurts!"

Chapter Fourteen

That evening the South Devon coast drew the dark up off the sea and over its humped shoulders like a wet sheet. Long after lights were switched on a surviving day could be seen along the sea's horizon, lasting mackerel brightness in a long band between the grey world's edge and the purple hem of the premature night the coastline had taken for its cloak.

With dark came rain in small insulting handfuls. The sheet must be kept moist and the wind was appointed to the task. Before its light nudges and punches it dipped its knuckles in cold water. Fitful gusts of spray were absorbed into the spindrift that gathered over the swooping meadowlines. Striking the balcony window of the dining room at Robinson's, it formed a series of undeserved insults.

Hugh stood looking out towards the silver stripe of day with a massive whiskey in his fist. Each sip of the spirit opened up a short-lived welt of pain in his nervous system that seemed an internal equivalent of the horizontal gleam.

Voisigna had reached the balcony steps before his attention was diverted to welcome her. In the dusk's drab interflow of greys and blues the Paisley shawl around her shoulders was a bright relief. Only momentarily did Hugh remark it as odd, this approach to the rear, more private, entrance. Voisigna was still a stranger to them, still a focus of their fears because she so closely respected rural codes.

She mounted the steps slowly, maintaining the vertical hauteur that had graced her previous departure.

On the top step she stood, looking solemnly into his eyes through the gust-speckled glass. Her solitary unmoving figure divided the horizontal band of light in two.

Why it took moments before Hugh set his whiskey on the bookshelves and opened the door was uncertain. Neither was he certain whether this way Voisigna had of riveting people to the spot with her intense brooding eyes was a consequence of true hypnotic presence or stupidity — something thick people did who couldn't think of anything to say. "Voisigna," he said. "Come in out of the rain."

Suddenly, out there in the icy, spitting dusk, she laughed. A mocking outflung cry of hopeless hilarity. "Out of the rain," she said. "Out of the rain. Well that would be a great thing for us all wouldn't it, Mr. Finch?" He could see her fine teeth, a shard of white in the midst of her gaunt majesty.

She turned to look out to the horizon. The light from the sea's limit picked out the ridge of her nose, the rim of her upper lip, the tip of her nipple stretching damp cheesecloth at the edge of her scarfs shadow, in tentative silver. "No, Mr. Finch, you step out here with me a minute."

"Oh," he said, suddenly beset by an essentially suburban confusion. "Oh. All right then."

"Fine, isn't it?" she said. "All these little darts. And in the middle of June. A kiss from the ice-gods. Let 'em needle your body, Mr. Finch. After all," — her voice dropped an octave — "anything that can get into your clothing and onto your skin — probably a good thing . . ." And reassuming the shyness into which she sometimes retreated, she swept past him into the dining room.

"Wine?" she said. "Glass of wine — go down nicely."

She drew the Paisley shawl more symmetrically about her shoulders and tucked it into a wide brass-buckled leather belt that supported her crimson skirt.

"Sure," said Hugh, reaching for the breathing Burgundy. He realised that beneath the scarf her shoulders and breasts were clothed only in cheesecloth, a transparent fabric rendered virtually invisible by the rain.

He also realised that Voisigna Devauden was very drunk.

She hurled back the first glass like an athlete at the water-bottle and held it out for more. Before Hugh could notice this she had seized the whole litre and was sloshing a second measure into her glass. "Love it," she said. "Bloody great. Drop of wine." She ran her wrist up the corner of her mouth and her aquiline nostril in one movement, clearing a dribble of Burgundy and an excess of nasal fluid. She wiped her wrist on her hip and while she did so her long brown middle finger ran along the gentle valley separating her thigh from her pubic mound. By time Fenella made her entrance a beguiling smile of secret mischief had descended on Voisigna Devauden's face.

"No," thought Hugh. "Not stupid."

"Ah, you've got a drink," said Fenella. "Now look, er, you must forgive me. I got a bit over-wrought this morning and I behaved — behaved abominably to your Ursula."

"Over-wrought," hummed Voisigna, turning from Hugh to Fenella Without a change in her expression of secret amusement. "Sh'd think you bloody did." Almost ironically she accentuated the musicality of her dialect to draw out cello glissandos right at the bottom of the contralto range "Sh'd think you bloody did."

"God," said Fenella. "Is she awfully upset?"

"Upset?" buzzed Voisigna. She swung her wine glass from right to left, approaching Fenella. She placed a long brown hand against Fenella's cheek and slowly cupped it, drawing her fingertips down flesh that seemed, behind Voisigna's soil-worn knuckles, translucent. "God bless yer, Mrs. Finch, upset? Why all of us, Mrs. Finch, be built round a heart of tears."

"Hmm!" said Fenella, smiling brightly under the caress, trying to dispel her blush. "You can say that again."

Voisigna laughed silently. Her teeth were strong, sharp and clean as an ivory blade. She moved to the table.

"Sit yer?" she said. "Sh'll I? Yer? Right, Mrs. Finch. Beef and Yorkshire pud. Roll 'em in."

"Chicken actually," said Fenella Finch, clipping to the kitchen in her patent leather court shoes. The pleated three-quarter length grey skirt she brought out for semi-formal occasions swung jauntily round thighs that now, suddenly and sadly, looked merely pretty.

Chapter Fifteen

"Dunno exactly – bitter, say bitter. Not 'xacly bitter." Voisigna's upper body swung in slow semi-circles over her chicken bones and the cerise roses of two spilled drinks. "My body, y'see. House. My body. Call you F'nella, gon' call you F'nella. Right? 'Stablished that, F'nella." In the middle of one swing of those vast shoulders Voisigna thrust a hand out and hooked it into the pocket of Fenella's crisp blouse over Fenella's left breast. "Y'see F'nella. Major Robinson, dear old, dirty old Major Robinson – Oh! Oh yes, of course. Don't keep a filly bottom of the garden without ridin' the little bugger now an' then . . . Oh yes, F'nella. Y'see. For Major Robinson, I didn't – didn't 'ave a me. I 'ad a bloody Ursula. Oh yes. Ursula come with bloody drums an' bloody trumpets. But me, no name, two black eyes and a big belly dumped on Salcombee fish dock. Traumatised. No name? No self. No fucking – 'scuse my French – no body. Major Robinson, Mrs. Hetty, they give me my name. It'll do. 'Ave to. Voisigna. Vwah-Zee-Nyah. Dee-Vaw-Den. Give me a body, this 'ouse. This garden. You, Mrs. Finch, F'nella." The great hand tugged on the pocket. It started to tear and suddenly vinegar, cruet, dregs of Fenella's coffee, all went flying in a flailing gesture of hopelessness that left the hand, knuckle down like a stranded crab on the table. "Livin' in my body, F'nella. Living in my fuckin' body. D'you see? Hackin' it about. Drainin' its colour. Drainin' the old red blood out of my old brown body, Mrs. Finch. Christ, I know I bent ancient but I be well fuckin' weathered. I wasn't to be tarted up, F'nella but . . . ah, ne'er min'. D'matter do it? We be all built round a ocean of bloody tears, Mrs. Finch."

Voisigna fell off her chair. Her scarf had long ago slid to the floor leaving breasts of a mighty loveliness swinging majestically across the generous lines of her drunken behaviour.

Hugh, initially stirred, had drunk himself into indifference. He hauled himself out of his torpor now on a bent pin of rank-ego. "God," he said. "What a bore."

"Be gentle with her," cried Fenella. Her glacial eyes were awash "Poor woman. Poor wonderful woman. Don't you see what we've done?"

Voisigna inclined her great dark head against the velvet seat of the unoccupied dining chair next to her, chuckling softly. "Christ. Sorry, Mrs. Finch. Sorry."

"Come on," said Hugh. "Up we come, Voisigna." He moved the chair against which she rested in order to get his hands under her richly bushed armpits and haul her to her feet. He got her half way so that she was sitting upright with the back of her head against his penis. Arching her neck like a wakening lynx she said, "Why, Mr. Finch. Even the worst things get a bit better don't they?"

She turned her head and nuzzled him; then in a great decisive movement, turned onto her knees and sank her teeth into him through his inadequate corduroy.

"Hugh!" shrilled Fenella. "Be gentle with her. She's drunk."

Chapter Sixteen

Day spread itself apologetically the way they sometimes do. It crawled over the sheep-cropped pastureland, over the weary lapping of wavelets that seemed resigned to their destiny of motion. Purified from its overnight douching, it attempted a few tentative gleams and offered a rain-sodden freshness to the plants and breezes as some sort of consolation.

Hugh rose to it early. He made tea and delivered a cup to the table by Fenella's sleeping, oblivious head.

Adrenalin was too thick in him to relax into hangover or remorse. Fenella's predicament, strung out between the tenterhooks of compassion for a powerful woman wronged even in the midst of her natural majesty, guilt at having invaded and befouled a structure which had become a fetish and a potent metaphor for that woman's very existence, raw jealousy at witnessing the woman's unabashed animal lust for a penis she had only recently loved back to life, left him at odds with himself.

Simultaneously, those clean white fangs snarling at his fly had planted a possibility of beguiling sweetness in his brain. Fenella's casual infidelity still licensed him. Not so constructive, not so rewarding, oh but infinitely easier and more attractive to bum himself out in a short fitful conflagration with Voisigna, than labour on with the strenuous repair of an emotional structure cracked to its foundations. What wild joy to have the eagle Voisigna rip out the throat of his grateful weasel! "Predatory," he said pacing along the side-path in the vegetable garden, a string of cigarette smoke trailing back round his elbow. This time he whispered it,

"Predatory."

The phrases of the early morning row were chasing each other through his head like the fragments of a popular song that won't go away; "Stood there and let her" – "Erection like a bloody flagstaff" – "That poor wounded lioness of a girl" – "All by herself, an abuser at one hand and an idiot child at the other" – "Abusive father, obviously. Some Cornish sea-gypsy. Easy for him on the rollicking deep. Put your daughter up the stick, hammer the memory out of her, then leave her on the quay as you hoik off to Spanish flicking waters!"

"Hugh." She stepped out from behind a tree, almost as though she hadn't gone home. "I took her as far as the garden door," Fenella had said.

The sunlight grew bolder on the shawl around her shoulders. She lifted her head. Her hair had come loose in the early stages of last night's meal. She pushed it back. The sunlight washed her blade of a head.

"Ursula had gone to sleep with the door locked," she said. "Stupid little cow. I slept in your car. I hope that's okay?"

"Oh. Oh yes. Sure. How d'you feel?"

She dipped her forehead towards him and looked up from under her brow. Donning her shyness momentarily, she walked towards him, towering above him. She slanted her head across his crown and moved her breast into the cranny of his armpit. "I think you knows 'ow I feel, Mr. Finch."

The bedroom sash shot up like a guillotine.

"Hugh," called Fenella. "Phone. They want you at Pinewood this afternoon. Hugh? Hugh? What's going on down there?"

Chapter Seventeen

"I will walk," said Fenella bitterly. "I will walk around this fucking house. Why not? It's mine!"

"You're mine," she shouted up the stair well.

"You're mine, you fucking haunted shit house," she shrieked out of the front door into the dark and empty larder. At the new fridge she hauled out a double litre of Gewurztraminer, sploshed the cork out and guzzled it from the bottleneck. Found a tumbler and poured herself half a pint.

"Mine. Ours. Mine," she said to the new bevel-edged desk as she drew out the snaps she kept from Hugh, because the fucking pig, the crazy, hurt, darling, big-clicked, fucking pig never looked at them anyway.

Hugh and Fenella in Yorkshire. Prize-winning documentary about the miners' strike. She covered it for *New Society*. God. What happened?

Hugh and Fenella outside the Finches in Fulham Road with Dudley Sutton. Dear old Dud. Pissed as a rat.

Hugh and Fenella talking to the Sex Pistols. Hugh with saliva all over his jacket. Grinning boldly, poor darling.

Hugh with Frank Dixon after shooting a Softly Softly in Warrington.

Greg as a baby, chewing the *New Musical Express.*

Johnny Rotten holding eighteen-month Greg, pretending to bite his ear. The year of her interview with Vivien Westwood.

Everybody on the lawn at the Chelsea Arts Club, Hugh wearing Molly Parkin's hat. Greg feigning boredom. The year of Mata Hari And The Egg.

Shit, it had all been so good. More wine.

Shit, she'd always had her little secret indiscreet moments. Some of those boys are always so pretty. All those years he didn't find out and nothing went wrong, and it always went on being good again when he came home and where oh where was the harm in it until all that stuff started in *Spare Rib* (which at that time was well past its sell-by date) about why-should-we-mess-about-with-our-bodily-cycles-just-to-please them crap? To get pleased ourselves is the bloody answer. Not to get banged up, of course, you box-brained rug-chewers. To stay out of Dr. Scollops vacuum cleaner. Not, not, not to get found out when nicking a bit of extra.

And of course, they would say, wouldn't they; What was he doing? Eh? Did he have to take precautions up the Ganges with camera and gun? With his clapped out Steinbeck characters in L.A.? What about the Bear Flag Republic eh? All those tootsie-floozies? Well haven't they heard, those womb-withering convent-trained clit-coaxers, that boys don't? Cry, back down or have babies? And haven't they heard that my Hugh doesn't do it anyway? Didn't. Because he thinks, I, me, it, us, the human female marriage tackle is sacred. Poor darling. Poor old crazy erectile dumb bum. More wine. No. Gin.

Chapter Eighteen

She'd cut herself rattling through the knife drawer for the sharp one. All those showy ones with natural wood handles in their wall-rack, all those pointed ones that looked like something out of Play Misty For Me were blunt as a Swiss Army Knife. This was the little sod that went through raw meat like slicing ice-cream. And it was raw meat, tough venison, that was to be — well — marked.

Oh Christ. She threw it back in the drawer. The hand with which she thumped the cottage door was wrapped in a red and white chequered tea-towel. Anger made her bleed. It always did. It was blotting through already.

"Come out you manipulating Amazon," she shouted, kicking the door, but the door swung slowly open allowing the smell-of-the-aged to intensify.

She picked her way in over stone flags well covered with chicken droppings, chaff, cattle food, tractor oil. She saw now that a double door had been driven through the end wall and that the intersecting wall between kitchen and living room had been knocked down. The ground floor had been made into an outhouse some time since. The light from the window to the right of the porch, through which she had previously Peered, cast wan sunlight in careless trapezia across the door at the bottom of the staircase that slanted, bottom right to top left, across the old kitchen wall. The door was freshly painted. There was a wall-basket containing a Pot of asters on the door jamb and a card in a little glassed over frame Which read "Voisigna and Ursula Devauden."

Fenella tried the thumb latch. It opened. Re-igniting some of her old wrath she mounted the stairs one by one. They turned at right angles into a spruce kitchen area. The sink was of rich brown stone. A hand pump fed cold water into it. There was a dolphin's head on the nozzle of the pump. It had been manufactured in Wolverhampton in 1897 by Jos. Carberry and Son. The furnishings were cottage chairs, table, dresser that had been out and back into fashion three times since they were installed here.

On the floor was clean floral linoleum. The walls were painted Wedgwood blue. In the kitchen area and in the living area beyond there was a good deal of brocade, of richly patterned fabrics. Braid with little woollen pom-poms set in rows ran around the edges of shelves and tables. There were bookshelves containing *Palgrave's Golden Treasury*, a cheap leather-bound set of works by the Brontes, Melville, Conan-Doyle, D.H. Lawrence, Henry Miller, Colette and Anais Nin in old orange and white Penguin and a complete set of *The Children's Encyclopaedia*.

Voisigna Devauden lay with one long leg hooked over the back of her sofa. The small of her back was on the seat of the sofa and her great milk-maid's shoulders were on the floor in front of the sofa. There was an ugly cut splitting the black bruise that disfigured her face and there was a good deal of blood coagulating around her.

Chapter Nineteen

"Oh, Voisigna," moaned Fenella Finch. "Who has done this to you?"

She had fetched Dettol, lint, soft fabric, bandages. Slowly she turned a wad of cotton-wool in a pudding basin of hot soapy water, tenderly shifted the crusted blood from Voisigna's cut face. A towel lay under her head to keep the pillow dry. The tiny window over her truckle bed let a flickering light between the ivy leaves. Voisigna's eyelids also fluttered as she regained consciousness.

She focused on Fenella, then turned away towards the window moving her wound away from the healing swab.

Her eyeballs swivelled and she assessed Fenella's caring out of the corner of her eye like a frightened beast.

"Don't blame 'er, Mrs. Finch," she said out of the unswollen corner of her mouth.

"Her?" asked Fenella. "Not Hugh?"

The swollen lips struggled to grin. "Ursula. 'Er be but a child in her brain, Mrs. Finch. I drownded her kittens."

"Kittens?"

Voisigna nodded to the zinc bucket under the brown sink. "'Em be probably still there. They was sickly. 'Er found 'em in a sack in Hope Woods."

"Do you not — didn't you want her to have them?"

" 'Em was sick, Mrs. Finch. 'Er didn't understand. 'Em was blind. Eyes never opened see."

Fenella stood up.

"Voisigna, if Ursula has done this to you, then Ursula must go into care. Now listen . . ."

Voisigna shook her head violently as though ridding it of pestilential insects.

"I'll heal, Mrs. Finch, with nothing more than a mark! I needs no stitches, I needs no bandage. The air out of the sky and off the sea will see to me — but Ursula, oh Mrs. Finch, 'er be so deprived in 'er mind. I come off me bike, Mrs. Finch. That's what I done and you an' me both knows it. Ursula, poor heart, 'er'll be in off them cliffs as soon as the fright gets out of 'er and the cold gets in."

Fenella returned to the bedside. "How could anyone be so strong?" she murmured.

Voisigna's hand lifted from where it had lain on the linoleum by her bedside. Assembling strength to itself the warm heavy hand rested on Fenella's thigh where the thigh bone socketed into her loins. "Go my 'ansome," she said. "Get us a couple o' bottles of the elderflower from the dresser."

"But," protested Fenella, half smiling. "Those you gave us."

Voisigna chuckled out of the unswollen corner of her face.

"All well," she said. "Ursula and me, we pissed in them."

The laughter between the two women started like a reluctant motor moving into motion. As it gathered their bodies bucked and tossed, laughing and bending towards each other into an embrace of savage hilarity.

Chapter Twenty

On his way down from London Hugh stopped at Totnes. Young Humphrey Barton said no. He was short but dense in his squat body, in his forty-second year.

"Not a chance," he said. "Point of fact, just prepared a reply to your letter now. You see?" he said.

Behind his desk he looked like a prize leg of meat dressed for the oven. However, his pinstripe three-piece complete with watch chain and white show handkerchief masked the density of the obdurate flesh, his essence blistered through.

"You see," said Humphrey Barton. A small fleck of substance, gravy, blood or nasal mucus had rendered the left lens of his wire framed bifocals imperfect. He worried at it with an imprecise thumbnail.

"There are the Americans. Rather an amusing story if you have the time — You're not a journalist, are you? It seems that Mrs. Robinson's sister was theatrically inclined and went first to New York, then to Denver, finally to Las Vegas where, I believe, she still occupies a — mobile country residence. Well Miss Anita Harper — this was Mrs. Robinson's maiden name — had a daughter by common-law marriage who works as a public relations assistance for an agency in Oakland, California. She has vigorously contested Miss Devauden's right, both to the right Miss Devauden may have to the final decisions of the trust, the ownership and occupation of the cottage, or Miss Ursula's right to benefit from the sale of Robinson's. All three issues have stood the test of" — a speck on the bifocals remained unmovable — "rigorous examination. All of them are impenetrable under British law."

Hugh shifted in his rexine bottomed chair moved by no one knew what petty discontent.

"But," he paused. "Look," he said. "Miss er — Miss Devauden is no ordinary — Miss Devauden is a nut-case. Mrs. Finch and I have looked forward to our retirement in the country."

"Appreciated, sir," said Humphrey Barton, flicking the final bit of rubbish off his thumbnail and replacing his bifocals on his lightly sweating nose. "But forgive me saying so, it is given to few of us to retire in our early fifties. Perhaps — how shall I put it? If repose is to be complete a more rigorous attention should be paid to the peas under the mattress."

"Well thank you, Mr. Barton," said Hugh. "What you mean is, nutters and psychotic subversives may occur anywhere they want and if they're annoying you, you ought not to be there."

Humphrey Barton laughed indulgently. "Is it," asked Hugh, "a special dispensation for provincial bureaucrats to behave as though they had special information about the unchangeable factors in human affairs?"

"The child," said Mr. Barton. "The case of the Devauden child."

"Yes," Hugh nodded.

"A child of, shall we say, some disadvantage?"

"A goon," said Hugh. The Barton chuckle.

"There might be some advantage in speaking to the local authorities about the proper care of that child."

Chapter Twenty-One

Miss Kirsty Randolph had been with South Devon Community Caring for eight months.

"Hope Cove, of course," she said, trying to sneak a look at the local wall map.

"Here," said Hugh. He got up from his chair and pressed a forefinger on Robinson's.

"Ah," said Kirsty Randolph. "Yes, I've seen the file." Hurriedly she found the file. Hugh watched the haste with which she scanned it. "Okay?" he asked.

"Ursula Devauden was inspected regularly for five years following Major Robinson's adoption of her mother."

"I thought he employed her?"

"Both. Adoption and employment."

"I see."

"The only irregularity since has been a case when the mother brought her child, then twelve, to the Kingsbridge police, claiming that she'd been raped. It was the year of the Satan's Slaves."

"I'm sorry?"

"It was August '78, about fifty bikers camped at Hope Cove to celebrate the tenth anniversary of their club. They drank the pub dry, threw the local constable in the sea and camped in the grounds of Robinson's. Major and Mrs. Robinson claimed they knew nothing of this. Miss Devauden, parent, joined them in their festivities it seems, even to the extent of taking LSD. The following day she presented herself in Kingsbridge distraught at the way the lads had had their beastly way with her daughter. Broke things apparently. A taxi window, an ambulance window and two police word-processors."

"Since then peace and roses?"

"Yes, but Mr. Finch, I've just found this."

"What is it?"

"A private memo to me from my predecessor, Edith Chalmers."

"Which says?"

"She doesn't like the set up at Robinson's. She says the only stability emanated from the Major and his modest wealth. He died shortly before her retirement. Without his influence the submerged maladjustment in - what's the name?"

"Voisigna Devauden."

"In her character may be expected to re-emerge and make her an unsuitable person to have charge of her daughter."

"In which case?"

"We have one or two centres on Exmoor and Dartmoor where unstable mothers may live with their offspring under supervision. They do directed work in the local services and at least everybody gets fed."

"You think this is a likely case?"

"May well be, Mr. Finch."

The telephone jangled.

"Excuse me. Yes? Yes? Really. I see. Tell them I'll be down in about twenty minutes. Mr. Finch, Ursula Devauden was picked up last night in Salcombe. She was very drunk and the pockets of her cardigan were stuffed with dead kittens. It seems you have a case."

Chapter Twenty-Two

A piece of the guttering had come loose. Some of its rubber insulation hung outside the kitchen window. The periods at which it moved in the wind, knocking against the upper panes of window glass, were remarkable.

While Fenella Finch moved from cooker to tap, from tap back to cooker, placed the electric kettle on the cooking surface to the left of the cooker and plugged it in, the insulation blew against the window glass twice.

"Well what d'you think?"

"Hugh, darling, you must do what you think fit."

"But Fenella. Honey. It's a clean sweep. What we should have had at the start."

From the kettle plug to the bric-a-brac drawer was one knock of the insulation. During her lighting the Embassy the insulation was silent.

"It's lovely here in the afternoon," she said, exhaling against the window glass about a foot below the point where the insulation knocked.

"It'd better be after all this drama," said Hugh.

The rubber knocked.

"Well will you at least come in to talk to this Randolph cow?"

"Cow?"

Silence. A gust and a knock of rubber tube.

"That's her name. Randolph." A pause. "It seems little Ursula was picked up pissed in Salcombe with a pocketful of kittens she'd strangled."

"The kittens were drowned."

“How d’you know?”

Shrug. “I know.”

In its time the rubber knocked.

“Would you come into Totnes tomorrow?”

Fenella did not look round. She stood with her arms folded occasionally dragging on her Embassy.

“Whatever you want me to do.”

“Well I want you to.”

“Very well then.”

A knock of the rubber after which it flailed in the wind silently.

“You smoke?”

“Yes.”

“You didn’t used to.”

“Oh. Didn’t I?”

“No.”

The wind dropped allowing the rubber to fall against the window glass.

“Well, what have you been up to?”

“Me? Oh — I wrote my column. Faxed it in.”

“What about?”

“Country restaurants in South Devon.”

“You’ve never been to any.”

“No.”

The rubber flailed and fell.

“Well how the fucking hell did you write it then?”

“I rang them up and asked them what to say.”

“My god. Scoop Finch. The press-club news-hound.”

She extinguished her cigarette under the tap and threw it in the pedal bin. “I’m going for a walk,” she said.

“Hang on, I’ll come.”

“You don’t have to,” she said. “It’s lovely to see you.”

Chapter Twenty-Three

Fenella Finch said nothing to Kirsty Randolph for half an hour.

"Miss Devauden is in care at the moment. What you both would have to — help us with — is persuade the mother, Miss Voisigna Devauden to take this, which is frankly the only opportunity of retaining the care of her daughter." Miss Randolph took her Bic biro from her mouth and set it beside the file on her desktop.

"Well," asked Hugh. "That seems to be feasible, doesn't it darling?"

"Feasible," Fenella Finch mouthed, her eyes following the unloading of a McAlpine truck across the square. "How about . . ."

She turned to face Miss Randolph. "How about if I adopt Ursula? Whatever. Become her carer, minder, guardian."

"We. . . ?" said Hugh.

"I said I." Fenella looked at the toe of her Doc Marten. "You my dear may do as you please."

"I shall put it to the committee," said Kirsty Randolph. "In the meantime I have an important appointment so you'll have to excuse me." She spoke impatiently as if she knew what was going on.

The roaring funnelling splendour of passing summer streaming on either side of the car did nothing to dispel the soundproof block of ice in which the heads of Mr. and Mrs. Finch were frozen.

Shortly before Kingsbridge Fenella Finch said, "Take me to Salcombe."

"But darling . . ."

"Take me to Salcombe. I want to get drunk."

She got down from the car. "I'll pick you up," he said.

"Don't," she said and turned into the Fisherman's Arms.

He sat in the car biting back tears. Five miles from Hope Cove Voisigna Devauden stepped out and thumbed him down.

She hauled her limbs into the passenger seat and found room for them.

"I er — I believe you have problems," said Hugh.

"Feel like a bevy?" she said broodingly. It wasn't really a question.

She sat in a corner cubicle of the Hope Tavern while Hugh got the drinks. The landlord's face was creased with some private salacious amusement. The expression was echoed in the faces of three or four other drinkers along the bar.

"Red wine and scotch," said Hugh. "Something the matter?"

"Matter?" said the landlord. "No, sir. Nothing the matter with me. Anything the matter with you?"

The suppressed giggle burst. An unruly gale of ridicule exploded in the beery faces and then, as suddenly, was gone.

"E's with the other bugger too," Hugh heard the landlord say as he carried the drinks to Voisigna. "Right bloody merry-go-round. 'Im and 'er. 'Er and 'er. 'Er and 'im. Ah well, whatever makes the chimbley draw." And another phlegmy gust.

"Mr. Finch," said Voisigna. "What I want to do now isn't to be took lightly. I thought about it in my 'ead and I think in time you'll come to see it's the best for everybody."

Hugh's stomach, not healed from his wife's hostility, filled again with a nauseous green poison. "What is it?"

"I need you in me," she said. "I been goin' mad. I an't 'ad a man to me for more 'n a year. After some — some satisfaction I can see straight and then I feel sure, Mr. Finch, we can come to some agreement. Yeah," she said. "See how sweet I be."

She unlatched her denims and dropped them over her haunches. the dark triangle of her hair was unusually thick, rich and waxy.

"The car," she said.

She passed a fingertip into herself, then gently painted his upper lip with it. Then she latched her jeans leaving the fly unzipped and made for the exit.

He left after her, five twinkling pairs of eyes following his step. She knelt in the back of the car with every detail of her generous system of lips and concavities displayed. “Quick,” she said. “I be ready. Fast now. Fast and ’ard.”

Hugh was less than a minute in obedience. Then, while he was enjoying the ruminant flowing of her, letting his energies gather for a second, more lyrical embrace, she was gone, legging it to the pub door with her jeans round one ankle, screaming.

“Rape. ’E forced me. Help!”

The pieces fell into place in the small round pan of pus that remained where Hugh Finch had until recently possessed a brain.

He made Kingsbridge before any siren sounded and was on the M5 within the hour.

Chapter Twenty-Four

"She doesn't reply," said Hugh Finch, digging at the tablecloth in a discrete corner of a tiny Italian restaurant in Islington.

"She's told the lawyer she doesn't want the house. She lives in the cottage."

"What about the kid?" asked Greg.

"The kid is still in care as far as I know."

"But you must do something," said Greg.

"No, me old luv. No I must not. Something is exactly what I must not do."

"Oh come on," said Greg. "This is unlike you."

"And the accumulating fangs of carnivorous circumstances are my customary identifying insignia, Greg. That's not fair."

"What the hell does all that mean, Dad?" he asked sceptically sloshing out the last of the Evian water.

"My natural self has been dismantled by the chance meeting of forces rendering one another inexorable and insurmountable. Only such another confluence can restore my brain or my ability to love."

"It can't be like that, it can't," said Greg.

"It is," said Hugh Finch.

The End

ABOUT THE CONTRIBUTORS

Jeff Nuttall was born in 1933 in Lancashire. Prolific in many disciplines, Nuttall trained as a painter before taking up poetry, fiction, and acting. His 1960s publication *My Own Mag* was among the most significant underground venues for experimental writing. Nuttall published copious volumes of poetry, fiction, cultural criticism, auto/biography, and illustrated chapbooks across his career, acted in many notable films, and worked in various academic capacities at Leeds Polytechnic. He died in Abergavenny in 2004.

Douglas Field lectures in twentieth century American literature at the University of Manchester. His most recent book is *All Those Strangers: The Art and Lives of James Baldwin* (Oxford University Press, 2015). He is a frequent contributor to the *Times Literary Supplement*.

Jay Jeff Jones has been involved with underground and small press literary magazines since the 1960s, as a contributor and editor. He knew Jeff Nuttall for many years and published some of Nuttall's shorter work in a magazine he edited in the late 1970s. His multi-produced biographical play about Jim Morrison, *The Lizard King*, was revived last year in Milwaukee.

They were co-curators of the exhibition: "Off Beat: Jeff Nuttall and the International Underground" at the John Rylands Library, Manchester.

Lightning Source UK Ltd.
Milton Keynes UK
UKOW02f1836220916

283585UK00001B/7/P